GALENA PUBLIC LIBRARY DISTRICT
3 8512 00163 4427

P9-DDB-517

Saving Grace

ALSO BY JANE GREEN

Tempting Fate

Family Pictures

Another Piece of My Heart

Promises to Keep

Dune Road

Straight Talking

Jemima J

Mr. Maybe

Bookends

Babyville

Spellbound

The Other Woman

Swapping Lives

Second Chance

The Beach House

Saving Grace

JANE GREEN

St. Martin's Press
New York

This is a work of fiction. All of the characters, organizations, and events portrayed in this novel are either products of the author's imagination or are used fictitiously.

www.stmartins.com

Library of Congress Cataloging-in-Publication Data

Green, Jane.
Saving Grace / Jane Green.
p. cm.
ISBN 978-1-250-04733-5 (hardcover)
ISBN 978-1-4668-4773-6 (ebook)
I. Title.
PR6057.R3443S28 2007b
823'.914–dc23
2014032274

St. Martin's Press books may be purchased for educational, business, or promotional use. For information on bulk purchases, please contact the Macmillan Corporate and Premium Sales Department at 1-800-221-7945, extension 5442, or write to specialmarkets@macmillan.com.

First Edition: January 2015

10 9 8 7 6 5 4 3 2 1

Saving Grace

One

There are only so many hours Grace can stay away from home.

Her husband's car is still in the driveway when she pulls in, her heart sinking at the sight. As if she should be surprised. Where did she think he'd be going at six o'clock in the evening? It was the triumph of hope over experience, she thought to herself.

Luck is not on her side today. It wasn't on her side this morning when she woke up to hear a door slamming downstairs and her husband bellowing her name, and it isn't on her side now.

Although perhaps it is, she thinks, gingerly pulling up alongside his car and steeling herself for whatever might meet her inside. Perhaps his mood will have changed. Perhaps he will be the loving attentive husband the rest of the world sees, as long as they don't get too close.

After almost twenty-five years of marriage the only thing that Grace is ever able to predict is the unpredictability of her husband's moods. He can throw his keys at the wall in a rage, then reappear twenty minutes later with a sunny smile, as if nothing had happened, as if Grace hadn't spent the prior twenty minutes quaking with nerves.

He can throw his keys at the wall, followed by a vase, followed by rageful venting that *this*, whatever *this* might be, is all Grace's fault. That Grace has somehow screwed up.

This morning Grace heard the doors slamming downstairs before she had even opened her eyes. She was woken up by the noise, sat bolt upright, heart pounding, realizing that Ted was in one of his moods. Terror flooded her body for a second. Sometimes, when this happens at night, she locks herself in the bathroom and runs a bubble bath, flooding out his anger with the water from the faucet. She has learned that if she removes herself, he will frequently take his rage elsewhere, distance allowing it to simmer before disappearing. But if Grace is there, if he sees her, she becomes an unwilling victim of a predator who will not leave her alone until he is sure she is completely destroyed.

He doesn't mean it, she thinks, when he is back to being kind, loving, appreciative. He has terrible mood swings, which is part of what makes him a creative genius. I should be grateful, she tells herself. If Ted weren't allowed to be this kind of person, he wouldn't be able to write the books he does, wouldn't be the success he is.

I mustn't take it personally, she tells herself all the time, even as she feels her ears ringing with stress.

Her ears were ringing this morning, in bed, as she heard him downstairs. They always ring when she is frightened. She read somewhere this is a symptom of anxiety, and one she has had as far back as she can remember. She has a theory that it helps drown out the noise of whoever is raging at her—her mother, her husband—but isn't sure that's why it happens.

This morning, moving quickly, she pulled on yesterday's jeans, a clean T-shirt and vest, and slipped down the back stairs, carrying her clogs in her hand so as not to make a sound before softly walking out the back door.

Ted heard her car start, as she knew he would, and she wound her window down as he came tearing out of the house.

"Sorry!" she called as she reversed, pretending she hadn't noticed his face contorted with rage. "Early start. I'm hugely late. See you later!" She waved a cheery hand out the window and zipped up the driveway, her body flooding with relief.

Her cell phone buzzed. She turned her head, the ringing in her ears starting back up, an automatic response to her husband's name flashing on her screen. She wouldn't answer, never answered when he was in this kind of mood, but nor would she divert, for then he would know she was diverting him, which would infuriate him still further.

She pressed the top button to turn off the volume, waited until the call went to voicemail, then turned the entire phone off, knowing she wouldn't turn it back on until Ted was back to normal.

Please let things be back to normal now, she thinks, hoisting the grocery bags into the house and onto the kitchen table. She has been out all day. First to work, then filling the rest of her afternoon with errands to keep her out of the eye of the storm.

The house is quiet. Ted must still be in the barn, which is a good thing, as it means he is writing. Work helps him to focus his mind elsewhere, and hopefully, *please God*, enable him to gather his equilibrium.

Grace puts the tomatoes in a bowl on the counter, the milk in the fridge, sliding the kettle onto the range to make tea. She once loved this house so much, this rambling antique on the banks of the Hudson River. That very first time they saw it, she knew she had found a place to call home.

Sprawling, peaceful, filled with nooks, crannies, and charm, the house has low ceilings and French doors that open onto lawns that lead gracefully down to the water.

She loved this house, before Ted's moods had the ability to discombobulate her in the way they now do. Back in the early days, Grace would laugh at him, would wander off, letting his insults roll off her back, happy to play with their daughter and wait for things to pass.

But the years have taken their toll, his rages lasting longer, gradually grinding her into the woman she is now—the same Grace she has always been, with a ringing in her ears, a quickening of her heart, an overwhelming urge to run far, far away.

She used to fight back. She doesn't anymore. She withdraws into a well of pain and resentment, removing herself as she did today, or hiding in her bathroom, the one room that feels safe.

Now, so often, the rest of the house she loved feels like a prison.

She jumps as she sees the barn door open, Ted emerging, his glasses in his hand as he runs his fingers through his hair. She squints through the window, reading his face, his mood, bracing herself not for fight or flight, for neither is an option right now, but for the third option: freeze.

Ted sees her through the window, his expression changing, as Grace holds her breath, to a smile. Relief floods her body as he waves a jaunty hand, slowly making his way up the path. She is close to tears as she raises a tentative hand back at him.

Thank God! she thinks. *Thank you, God!* She goes to the fridge to pour him a glass of wine, the ringing fading in her ears, wondering how on earth life ever got so hard.

Two

In the beginning, when she first met Ted, it felt as if she had fallen into the kind of life that only happened to other people, and usually only in movies. It was a life she determined to enjoy while it lasted, convinced it wouldn't last long, for Ted could have had his pick. There were always women more exciting, more glamorous, more beautiful than she.

Ted Chapman. One of the rising stars of the literary scene, the thinking man's Grisham; a writer of clever political thrillers that straddled both the literary and the commercial. When Grace met him, he had only published three books, three books that had been huge, and the publishers were doing everything they could to keep him happy, knowing they hadn't paid him enough, aware that every other publisher was circling now that he had come to the end of his book deal, concerned they could no longer afford to pay him what he would doubtlessly demand of his next contract.

He was speaking at the annual sales conference, joining the publishing team's table for dinner. Grace, only twenty-two and an assistant cookbook editor, was stunned she had been asked to join the table, more so when she discovered she was seated to the right of Ted Chapman.

Assistant cookbook editor was not nearly as glamorous a job as it sounded, and it was unusual for a lowly assistant to go to the sales conference, but her boss had demanded, and when her boss made demands, she had no choice. Perhaps he understood these were the perks that made the job worthwhile: going to publishing dinners, meeting famous chefs—Jacques Pépin and Julia Child! She met them! And they talked to her as if she were an equal!—the perks made it all worthwhile.

Ted Chapman was not often seen in the office, and when he was, he seemed frightening. Dark and brooding, he had the kind of aura that made you want to stare, made you want to please him.

Grace had arrived early to the dinner, had allayed her fears during the cocktail hour with two glasses of cheap white wine, and by the time they took their seats in the banquet hall next door, her fear of Ted Chapman was tinged with intrigue. She sat, shaking, at the table, wondering why she had been given such an onerous and terrifying seat.

"Gracie will charm him." Grace looked up to see Bill Knight, the publisher, toasting her across the table with a wink. "Right, Gracie?"

Of course, thought Grace. "How could he even think of leaving when we have such talented and delightful people working for us."

Grace forced a smile, feeling sick. She was here as bait. And there was no way to leave. She would have to do her job, charm Ted Chapman, and then perhaps, *certainly*, look for another job.

Ted was the only empty chair at the table. He was too nervous before public speaking to sit at a table with other people, explained his editor. He needed quiet, but would join afterwards.

Oh God, thought Grace, her heart sinking. How pretentious. The excitement of meeting him was beginning to pall, the whole evening starting to feel like a huge mistake. How ironic, she thought, that this morning she flew around her apartment, trying on dresses, tipping her makeup into her purse so she could get ready for this event, exhilarated at meeting someone whose work she adored. Now she would have given anything to get out of there.

Grace had no appetite, unusual for her. She was a cookbook editor because she loved food. Coming to New York, she was amazed at how few girls her age knew how to cook. She learned to cook at university, going home to her roommate Catherine's house where her roommate's mother, Lydia, was so thrilled to have an eager student, she sat her at the kitchen table for hours and taught her everything she knew.

She loved creating, loved cooking, and loved writing. What better place to put all those skills together than working for a publisher in the cookbooks division, and where more glamorous than New York.

She hosted impromptu dinner parties all the time. Two folding card tables—one she had, one she found on a street corner one afternoon—served as the dining table, with long wooden benches that had been made out of planks of oak by a handy ex-boyfriend.

Grace would throw burlap over the tables, fill mason jars with flowers and line them down the center. The food was inexpensive, and back then, in those early days in New York, frequently had an English bent.

Her coworkers delightedly cooed over toad in the hole and treacle tart, as Grace dreamed of one day writing a cookbook of her own.

At the event dinner, the waiters started to hand out the plated food. Wilted salad followed by dry chicken breast in a mushroom sauce. Grace took a few bites before pushing the food aside, bored with the empty seat to her left, the man on her right—another author—too busy talking to other people at the table to pay any attention to her.

A tinkling of spoon on glass, and the CEO of their company stood up to introduce their keynote speaker. To a whirl of applause, Ted Chapman appeared through a side door, tall, much taller than Grace had imagined, as he strode up to the podium, notes in hand, shaking the CEO's hand and murmuring "thanks," before turning to face the audience, clearing his throat, and pausing to take a sip of water.

He looked at his notes, then shook his head and grinned. "Sorry," he said. "I'm much better off without the damned notes." And then he spoke.

Grace didn't hear the beginning. She was so stunned by his smile, by the transformation of his face, she couldn't concentrate on anything other than how she could have possibly missed, in all those photographs, all those book jackets, how attractive he was.

When she tuned back in to his speech, her disorientation grew. She had heard that he was difficult, moody, high-maintenance. The editorial assistants at work had developed a Pavlovian response of fear to the phone ringing, scared it would be a furious Ted Chapman, in a rage because he'd just flown to Cincinnati for an event and—shocker!—there wasn't a single book of his in the airport bookstore. Or he might have been complaining about the marketing department, or that he'd just been sent the large-print version, and what the hell were they thinking, putting this godawful cover on it?

This man standing up on the podium, telling witty, dry stories, punctuated with sardonic eye rolls that made everyone laugh, had everyone in the room in the palm of his hand. This was not the man she had heard about, this couldn't possibly be the same man of the terrible reputation.

Had she imagined it, or had he somehow transformed?

By the time he finished his speech and came to sit next to her, she was no longer nervous, but intrigued. Who was this humble, humorous, brilliant man, and if it was true that he could be difficult, impatient, short-tempered, which one was the real Ted Chapman? Which was the personality he tapped into in order to write?

She never had a chance to ask him, not that night, for Ted, smitten as soon as he laid eyes on Grace, did not stop peppering her with questions. He sat down at the table, allowed the perfunctory introductions to be made, and turned to shake hands with Grace, pausing for a second to take in her prettiness.

"Well, this is a lovely surprise," he said. "You're not the usual publishing type."

"There's a type?" Grace said, deciding to be flattered.

"You're English too? Goodness. This gets better and better. What brings you to these shores, Grace?"

The questions continued all night. Where did she grow up; what were the things she needed in life to be happy; what were the things she missed the most about England; what books had most influenced her life and how?

Grace had never been asked questions with such intensity, had never been fixed with such a forceful gaze, had never had so much fun, nor felt so . . . special. There was a chemistry between them that was obvious to everyone sitting at the table, and yet, at the end of the night, Ted merely bowed his head as he kissed her hand, and told her what a delight she had been.

The next day, at her desk, a bouquet of russet and flaming orange roses arrived with a note. "These made me think of my delightful companion of last night. Drinks tonight? I will pick you up at work at 5. TC."

There was no question of Grace saying no, or having made other plans. She had, in fact, made other plans, but only a movie with a girlfriend, which she swiftly postponed, berating herself for not having made more of an effort with her outfit at work today, wishing she were wearing something more glamorous.

At lunchtime she ran to Bloomingdale's and got a free makeover at the beauty counter, excitement and anticipation giving her a radiant glow.

Drinks at the Carlyle led to dinner, led to Ted insisting he bring her to a party the next night, led to Grace moving in with him three weeks later. His apartment was so much bigger, he said; she could save money living with him, he said; why would they ever want to be apart when being together made both of them so happy, he said.

Those days were a whirlwind of romance, passion, excitement. Grace swiftly became a fixture in his life, adoring the glamor and thrill of mixing with the great and good, for Ted was in great demand, and Grace the perfect partner.

When Ted signed a second three-book contract with the same publisher, Grace was promoted to cookbook editor, their way of saying thank you to the woman who now went everywhere with Ted Chapman, who was surely instrumental in ensuring he stayed true to his roots.

It is presumed by many that Grace learned to cook at her mother's knee, but her mother could barely boil an egg. Grace was entirely self-taught until the age of eighteen. She had to learn to cook in order for her family to eat, her mother far too unreliable in her mood swings to ever be relied upon to serve them dinner, not, at least, with any consistency.

Grace's rudimentary skills were honed and crafted as her roommate's mother, Lydia, gave her cookbooks that Grace read like novels and taught Grace everything she knew.

Back when she first moved to New York it all seemed so sophisticated. Grace brought Delia Smith's cookbooks with her to New York, and wowed her colleagues by staying loyal to her English roots: buttery kedgeree and cottage pie topped with mashed potato, sliced leeks, and melted gruyere.

Years later, when Clemmie entered middle school, Grace decided to indulge her passion further by doing a cooking course. Not just any cooking course, she wanted to do the Cordon Bleu, but there wasn't anything in her area, which left the Culinary Institute of America, the Institute of Culinary Education, or the French Culinary Institute.

She chose the French Culinary Institute, seduced by the promise of learning to cook the true French way, as espoused by the great chefs, Escoffier, et al.

The first day she turned up, she stood in line waiting to be handed her uniform and knife set, aware she was so much older than the other students, but thrilled to be back in the human race again.

Motherhood had isolated her. She loved Clemmie, loved being her mother, but she missed being out in the world; missed being defined by something other than wife and mother.

It was a year-long course. A year during which Grace wasn't special, wasn't valued because of who she was married to, wasn't anyone other than another student in the class.

She loved it. She loved standing at the train station with the other commuters, her bag full of knives over one shoulder, her bag holding her chef's uniform over the other.

She loved getting into Grand Central at rush hour and moving through the station with swarms of commuters, climbing onto the subway and taking the 6 train downtown to Soho.

She wore flip-flops and cargo pants, T-shirts and no makeup, and felt twenty again, a lightness in her step, a glow on her face, a light in her eyes. She felt alive again, part of the world in a way she hadn't done since marrying Ted and settling into married life with an older man.

Her classmates ranged mostly from Clemmie's age to late twenties, with a few fortysomethings like her, looking for a new career for the second act of their lives, although this wasn't going to be a career for her, she just wanted to learn how to do the one thing she had always loved.

Grace was not used to doing things wrong, nor used to criticism. She thought she was an accomplished cook until she got to cooking school, when Chef Z would shout at her on a daily basis because her sauce was too thin, or too cold; her beef too well done, her pastry too thick.

"Sorry, Chef," she would say, ashamed, humbled, as she slunk back to her station vowing to do it better next time.

And yet, he was her favorite teacher. He may have shouted at her, but there was always a twinkle in his eye, and every time he said something in his thick French accent, she couldn't help thinking of a TV show from her childhood, and it made her laugh.

It also taught her. She kept a notebook with her, scribbling down all the tips offered, everything they said that wasn't in the manual: the tricks of the trade that would truly transform the food she made, the skills and the science of cooking. She went from being a very good cook to one who could be described as serious. *A serious cook*.

Now she cooks as a professional. Over the years she has had her own catering company, gaining an excellent reputation for cooking easy food that can be thrown together quickly, that nevertheless looks and tastes as if she had been cooking carefully and diligently for hours.

More recently, she had become the chef at Harmont House, a home founded ten years ago in Nyack, for families escaping abuse and addiction, helping them get back on their feet.

Ten years ago, Grace's friend Sybil came to her and asked her if she would be interested in joining the board. Only, Grace said, if she could actually do something there. Clemmie was in middle school, Grace counting the hours until she got home, desperate for something to relieve the boredom of having nothing to do.

She became the chef. Not just cooking for the residents of the home, but teaching them how to cook, just as, all those years ago, she herself was taught. This was now her passion, and her job, and the one place she truly considered her sanctuary.

Grace teaches them the way Lydia once taught her, and throws in the lessons she learned at culinary school: how to organize a kitchen, how to shop for food, what makes the basis of a great sauce.

Five days a week sees Grace, feet slipped into clogs, an apron wrapped around her, hair scraped back into a bun, cooking first in her own kitchen, then showing up to Harmont House with the ingredients for one last dish for her lesson.

She introduced the English classics Lydia had taught her to cook and that she had learned to love: toad in the hole, bubble and squeak. The cooking humbles her, but more than the cooking, more than the service she is providing, it is the relationships she has with the women, the friendships she has made, that bind her. She has the ability to make a difference in these women's lives and they, equally importantly, are open to her help.

Her passion, her job, and a way to heal the wounds of the past.

Ted will tell people he loves Harmont House, has to tell people he is supportive of the work Grace does, but in private he is jealous of the amount of time it takes up in Grace's life. He has learned to keep this to himself, but it comes out in bitter sideways swipes.

Still. This does not change Grace's commitment. She loves cooking for these women just as much as she loves cooking for friends. Her dinner parties, particularly since her success as a chef, are legendary, desserts more so. Anyone coming to the house to write a profile about Ted knows in advance that part of the profile will include long and loving descriptions of the delicious food that Grace provides.

Whatever her passions, whatever her work, still, she has time for Ted. She must make time for Ted, ensure he is the number one priority in her life. Whatever is going on in Grace's life, and it is by no means as easy as it sounds, from the outside, Grace's life looks perfect.

"You look as if you have never had a hard day in your life," someone once said at a dinner party. Grace smiled, for she had learned to hide her secrets and shame well. She had learned to never discuss what she came from, the hell of growing up as she did, having the mother she had.

The more perfect the illusion, the more her secrets will recede. Or so she thinks.

If she just keeps running and running, keeps being the perfect wife, mother, cook, the past will surely just disappear.

BUTTERY KEDGEREE

(Serves 4)

Adapted from Delia Smith

INGREDIENTS

1½ cups smoked salmon trout filets

1 stick butter

1 onion, chopped

1 teaspoon curry powder

1 teaspoon fish sauce
1 cup uncooked rice
3 hard-boiled eggs, chopped
3 heaped Tablespoons fresh parsley, chopped
1 Tablespoon lemon juice
Salt and pepper

Melt half a stick of butter in skillet. Soften onion in it for 5 minutes.

Stir curry powder into onion, stir in rice, and add 2 cups water and fish sauce.

Stir well, bring to boil, cover, and turn down to a gentle simmer for 15 minutes, or until rice is cooked.

Remove salmon trout flesh from skin. Flake. Add to cooked rice with eggs, parsley, lemon juice, and remaining ½ stick of butter.

Cover pan and replace on gentle heat for 5 minutes before serving.

Three

There is nothing Grace loves more than being alone in her kitchen, surrounded by food, inspirational recipes scattered on the counter in front of her as she tries out new dishes. When she is working on a book, she will use assistants, but it is during these moments, when it is just Grace, alone in her kitchen experimenting, that make her happiest of all.

The process is almost meditative. The vegetables are gathered, washed, placed carefully in a stainless-steel prep bowl to the left of her chopping board, an empty bowl at the top for the scraps to go on the compost heap, a tray with small empty bowls to the right, waiting for Grace to chop the onions, the celery, the carrots, her bay leaf, peppercorns, parsley stalks, and thyme already tied up in cheesecloth for the aromatics to bring her braised short ribs with marmalade glaze to the next level.

The oven is preheated, all the knives, peelers, paring knives she will need by her board. Her apron is on, a bar towel tucked into the tie around her waist, another in a bowl of soapy water ready to clean down her board.

Cooking was always something she loved, but pre-cooking school it inevitably meant chaos. The sink would gradually pile up with dirty bowls and spoons, as Grace raced around the kitchen grabbing things out of the fridge, chopping and sautéing as she went, stopping to pull the canned tomatoes from the pantry or the chicken from the fridge.

Cooking school taught her how to organize. It taught her how to prepare her *mise-en-place*. It taught her that if she prepares everything first, the very act of preparation becomes a joy, the cooking is made easier and more enjoyable.

Now, as she lines up her knives, starts to peel the carrots, her cell phone rings. With a sigh she wipes her hands on the bar cloth and picks up the phone, squinting to see the name on the screen before deciding to pick up. Ellen.

"Is everything okay?"

"It's fine," says the voice on the end of the phone. "I just wanted to let you know the driver will pick you up tonight at five thirty, and Ted's tuxedo is being delivered back from the dry cleaners this afternoon." Ted's recently ex-assistant is as efficient and organized as ever, even though she no longer works here.

"You don't have to do this," says Grace. "I'm handling all of it. Really, Ellen. You need to concentrate on looking after your mother, not on organizing us."

"Until we find someone to take my place, you know I'm going to keep doing it. If I left it up to you, you'd be hitchhiking."

Grace laughs, for it is true. Organization has never been one of her strong points—hence her need for cooking school—and she had meant to organize a driver for tonight, but, as Ellen well knows, it had slipped her mind, and had it not been for their former assistant, Ted would probably have ended up having to drive himself, which would have upset him, because when he is a keynote speaker, he uses that valuable time in the back of a town car to fully memorize the words.

"How are you, though?" asks Grace. "Really?"

"I'm fine," Ellen reassures, although Grace knows this cannot be true. Ellen's mother is now struggling with Alzheimer's. Ellen is moving to Florida to take care of her. The strain is enormous, even though Ellen is loathe to let it show.

Ellen has been part of their lives for fifteen years. She is the kind of assistant you dream about: efficient, kind, thoughtful, discreet, and loyal beyond anything Grace had ever known.

Ellen can handle Ted. However bad his mood, Ellen has a way of calming him down, of making him feel that everything would be fine, and it is the loss of this, more than anything else, that has been so difficult since she has stopped working for them.

She worked in the small office at one end of the barn, Ted in his large, book-filled library at the other end. All he had to do was bellow her name—no time, no patience for emails, or texts—and Ellen would appear, framed in the doorway, notebook and pen always in hand, ready to do whatever Ted wanted: research a lobbyist, fix the damned screen in the library, get rid of the yapping dogs outside before I kill them.

She headed off his moods before he had a chance to take them out on anyone else; on Grace. She masked how temperamental he had become.

Their author friends in New York all had assistants, but none of them were like Ellen. Everyone wanted to find an Ellen, but instead found themselves drawn to young, glamorous women, fresh out of grad school, who were starstruck and eager, unable to believe they would now be working for someone famous.

Out here, in Sneden's Landing—it may have been renamed Palisades, but Grace and Ted have been here too long, and it will always be Sneden's to them—the pool was smaller.

The glamorous literary chicks didn't want to cross the bridge and work in a quiet hamlet in Rockland County, and truth be told, Grace wasn't sure she particularly would have wanted them anyway.

The other authors they knew went through a revolving door of young, pretty assistants. However good they were, it was only a matter of time before they left to work for someone bigger, or because they were getting married, or had decided to move to Paris. All of them had landed in New York City, and that was where they were going to stay unless somewhere even more exciting presented itself.

When Grace and Ted first saw the house in Sneden's Landing, twenty-two years ago, with Clemmie toddling around, they fell instantly in love. For eighteen months, Clemmie had been the only thing Grace could think about. From the moment the squawling newborn was placed in her arms, Grace came undone. She fell head over heels, didn't care about anything other than being with her daughter. Even now, years later, they are bonded together, as much like best friends as mother and daughter.

Back then, when Grace was interested in nothing other than Clemmie, stumbling upon the house at Sneden's Landing was like something out of a dream, giving Grace a focus outside of her daughter, a focus that grounded her and made her feel safe.

All Grace had ever wanted was seclusion, and water. They wanted to be close enough to get into the city for meetings with publishers, for events they were expected to attend, but far enough that they had, at least, the *feeling* of country, even if wasn't the deepest, darkest depths of Vermont, as she would have liked.

They came up for lunch with Katie and Richard Walbert, a couple they had developed a couple crush on. The friendship burned brightly and with great intensity for a year, before sputtering and dying. This was at the height of their mutual affection for one another, and the fact that Katie and Richard had a weekend house in Piermont but wanted to live in Sneden's Landing was enough for Ted and Grace to want to be there too.

As the four of them toured the small hamlet, Grace fantasized about waking up every morning with these stunning views of the Hudson, the vibrancy of neighboring Nyack, the quiet and privacy of Sneden's Landing.

Katie vaguely knew the people who owned a house in Sneden's, knew they had been talking about putting it up for sale. In a haze of excitement the four of them all showed up on the doorstep—which you could do in those days—and asked whether it might be possible to have a look around.

Grace didn't need to look around. Even as they rounded the curve of the driveway she caught sight of the old rambling farmhouse, lawns leading down to the water's edge. There was a dilapidated barn, an old cow shed, various other outbuildings that had been left to rot; all she saw was magic. The interior of the house was terrible. Grace and Ted didn't even have to look at each other to know this was it.

By the end of the day a deal had been made, sealed with a handshake. A month later they moved in, terrified that Clemmie, racing around in excitement, would topple into the water.

Six years later, when Ted was no longer seen as a hugely talented newcomer but had become a fixture at the pinnacle of the literary world, Grace was in Nyack, getting groceries, when she stopped by a noticeboard, seeing a sign for a Mrs. Fixit looking for work. "Experienced house manager," it said. "Great with animals, kids. Will clean, organize, drive, cook. Ask and it shall be done."

Grace had scribbled down the name and number, liking the way the ad had been written, the cartoon that accompanied it, of a woman juggling children, animals, groceries, tools, all with a big smile on her face.

That afternoon Ellen walked in, sturdy, solid, smiling. She had an air of calm that allowed Grace, unwilling to admit she was utterly overwhelmed by all she had taken on, to finally exhale.

Ellen was the same age as Grace, and her husband, Glenn, ran the local garage and took care of their cars, turning out to be an excellent handyman on the side. Ellen took care of everything, and over the years, as Ted's star had continued to rise, it had become more and more about taking care of Ted.

Ellen updated his Facebook, Twitter, the calendar on his blog. You may think Ted Chapman is the one responding to your generous tweet, thanking you for your kind words, but in fact it was Ellen. Always.

She wrote his newsletters, responded to his fan mail, coordinated meetings with his agents, and was on first-name terms with the assistants of the biggest and most powerful agents and actors in Hollywood, not phased should Harrison Ford or Bradley Cooper phone the house.

She was able to decipher his scribbles, type up his notes, spend hours online, or on the phone, researching anything he needed, last minute, for his latest book.

She accompanied him to literary events—unless of course the invitation was for husband and wife, in which case Grace would attend—and television shows, ensuring he was comfortable in the greenroom, the cars arrived on time, he had everything he needed.

Ellen organized his book tours, arranged his travel, ensured the hotels he stayed in had the correct suite, a basket of fresh fruit, and a bottle of pinot noir, and Perrier, on arrival.

But more than that, more than any of that, Ellen was a friend. Ted talked to her, had been known to hang out in Glenn's garage, delighting in the local gossip Glenn shared with him, in the glimpse into another world he was afforded just by knowing Ellen and Glenn.

As the years have rolled by they have come to know each other intimately. Ellen understands him as well as she understands her husband, is far better, in fact, at anticipating Ted's needs than those Glenn has.

Grace adores Ellen. She refers to her as Ted's other wife, the *good* wife, the one that knows where everything is. When Ted was away, Grace delighted in stealing Ellen away from her office in the barn and planting her at the kitchen table with a cup of tea.

Ellen leaving was unthinkable. There was no question that Ellen had to leave, that her family took precedence, but none of them could bear the thought of it. Grace kept thinking the problem might go away. Perhaps her mother wouldn't be as bad as Ellen thought. Perhaps she would be very much worse. Perhaps the end wasn't far away and Ellen could come home, back to work as normal. Surely Grace could pick up the slack for a few months.

Grace has been trying to pick up the slack for weeks and it had been disastrous. Her memory, never wonderful, had in the last couple of years appeared to have gone to pot.

She decided to write everything down. It seemed like a brilliant idea, except everything was written on little yellow Post-its that would end up crumpled in a pocket or at the bottom of a handbag, never to be seen again.

Grace thinks about something Ellen had said yesterday on the phone. "I put an ad on Craigslist. For my replacement. Apparently this is where you're supposed to advertise these days. Don't worry. I used the anonymous email address and of course I didn't say who it was for."

"Craigslist?" Grace scowls. "I'm not sure how safe that is."

"Darren found his wife on Craigslist," says Ellen.

Grace laughs. "Not exactly. She answered an ad to be a roommate. That isn't quite the same thing."

"Point being, Sarah's lovely. And he found her on Craigslist. I spoke to one of my friends who works for a domestic staffing agency and she says these days lots of the domestic agencies find their staff there too, there or *The New York Times*. It isn't like before when you paid all that money to an agency knowing they'd do all the background checks so you'd know what you'd be getting. They're advertising in the same places, and it's up to us to do all the due diligence. Anyway, I haven't had any responses yet, so I'm putting an ad in the *Times* next week. If I get anything that sounds interesting, I'll forward them to you. How does that sound?"

“Worrisome,” says Grace.

“Only because you and I are so old we don’t understand all this technology. Trust me. It’s what everyone’s doing. I did advertise on the noticeboard at the library, but I haven’t heard anything, and I’ve passed the word around. Didn’t John Foster say his old assistant was looking for something?”

“Yes. We met her.”

“And?”

“She was twelve.”

“Oh dear.”

“I know I sound completely ageist, but I don’t want a young college graduate with stars in her eyes. I want someone like you. Mature. Efficient. Someone who has common sense and initiative.”

“Young people can have that too,” Ellen says.

“This one didn’t. She was an hour and a half late because she got lost and had no service on her cell phone to check the GPS.”

“She couldn’t have stopped and asked?”

“Exactly!” Grace says. “Maybe Craigslist is the way to go . . . if you’re sure.”

“I’m sure.”

Four

"Ted? Are you ready?" Grace slips the second diamond earring in as she calls up the stairs. "The car's here. We have to go."

"Coming!" The sound of footsteps as Ted clambers down the stairs, pausing as he catches sight of Grace. A smile spreads on his face as he looks at Grace, Grace mentally exhaling a sigh of relief.

"Have I ever told you how lovely you are? How lucky I am to have such a beautiful wife?" In the mirror, Grace looks at herself approvingly, aware of how they look together, he so debonair, so elegant in his tux, she in a white silk shirt and long black velvet skirt. It could so easily have looked frumpy, but the skirt is an inch tighter than it needs to be, the shirt a centimeter lower, the heels a smidgen higher. Her auburn waves are glossy and loose, and the only jewelry she wears besides the earrings is a chunky, modern gold cuff.

"I scrub up well, don't I," she says. "Although I may have to concede that you scrub up even better. Do you have any idea how well you look in a tux?"

"Hmmm." He raises an eyebrow before gesturing upstairs. "Do we by any chance have time . . . ?"

"No!" She pushes him away with a laugh. "But ask me again later and I'll see what I can do."

Thank God, she thinks. Thank God my husband is in a good mood. These flashes of Ted at his most charming, no traces of anger or irritation or disdain, are what Grace lives for. So often, of late, he has been at his worst, and Grace is beginning to feel more and more like she is walking on eggshells.

And yet, in moments like these, it is easy to remember why she married him in the first place, easier still to imagine this may be the turning point, that this good mood may last for days.

Even though it never does.

Hand-in-hand, they go out to the car.

Tonight is the thirtieth anniversary of the magazine *Country Flair.* A glittering occasion, the magazine has taken over the ballroom of the Mandarin Oriental, their guests an assortment of luminaries featured in the magazine over the years.

Grace and Ted have been inside the pages many times; snapped at society or literary events, Ted interviewed for his new book, or, as in the thirtieth anniversary issue, on the cover as the personification of what every country dweller should aspire to.

It is true, the house at Sneden's is a beautiful example of a restored antique farmhouse, the barn, lined floor to ceiling with books, sliding ladders running along the length of the shelves, regularly featured in articles about dream offices, and one of the most frequently repinned photographs on Pinterest.

But it is more than the rambling house, the pretty gardens, the solid barn. It is Ted and Grace themselves, Grace unwittingly having become something of a style icon, however reluctant she may be to appear in public.

Her casual style—jeans and Bean boots, teamed with sloppy oversized sweaters and one of her husband's ubiquitous Barbours, some fabulous huge ring or a pair of abstract gold earrings—was never something she thought much about, and she is constantly surprised at how people compliment her on her style. She wears what is easy, comfortable, without much thought as to what other people think.

On the cover of the thirtieth anniversary special issue, a bumper issue, it is Grace and Ted smiling out at you, sitting on their bench overlooking the water, a chicken perched on Grace's shoulder as she tips her head back with laughter, Ted turned to gaze at her. His long legs, in old jeans, are stretched out in front of him, one dachshund on his lap, the other two at his feet. Behind them are the apple trees in full bloom, for this issue was planned months in advance, and the photographs taken during the glory days of summer, when the house and garden are at their most beautiful.

Grace's phone rings, her face lighting up as she looks at the screen.

"Clemmie!" she says, lifting the phone to her ear. "Darling daughter who we never hear from anymore. How much money do you need this time?"

Her daughter's laughter rolls down the phone. "Can I name my price?"

"Only with your father," says Grace. "I'm a harder sell, as you well know. Where are you?"

"In my apartment getting ready for a hot date, and guess where he's taking me?"

"Dinner? A movie? A walk in the park?"

"Much more glamorous. To the thirtieth anniversary gala for *Country Flair* magazine."

"No!" Grace can't hide her delight. "We're on our way too! They're honoring us!"

"I *know*! But my date doesn't, and now I have to tell him who I am. Unless I ignore you all night, but what if this is 'the one' and he ends up proposing before diving into a fury that I withheld the terrible truth from him."

Grace starts laughing. "You like him, then?"

"He's kind of deliciously sexy in a sexily delicious way." Grace can picture her daughter's swooning smile as she speaks.

"Name? Age? Prospects?"

"You'll find out for yourself in about forty-five minutes," says Clemmie. "But briefly, he's Luke, he's a musician who teaches guitar to kids on the side, and this is our first grown-up date."

"Forgive me for asking the obvious, but what on earth is he doing coming to the *Country Flair* gala? That doesn't quite compute."

"That's what I said! Turns out his mom is an editor there, and she invited him, with a date. She even, apparently, rented a tux for him. See what a good mother does?" she says.

"I give you all my old clothes!" says Grace.

"And I'm grateful. I'm wearing one of your favorites tonight."

"The silk skirt and bustier top that I gave you last year? The Yves Saint Laurent one?"

"The very same."

"And you're complaining? That was always my most favorite outfit in the world. The only reason I'm not wearing it tonight is, thanks to the delightful side effect of aging, my waistline appears to have gone AWOL."

"Your waistline is fine. You're beautiful."

"You have to say that. I'm your mother."

"I'll say it to your face soon. I have to go. My hair still looks terrible."

"Wait! This is important."

Clemmie's voice is again loud and clear. "Yes?"

"Hair. Up or down?"

"Surprise," Clemmie says, putting down the phone.

There is nothing Grace loves more than spending time with her daughter, particularly when it is unexpected. Those times when Clemmie calls and their schedules align to enable them to have a quick lunch, or a rush round Bendel's as a treat.

When she was pregnant with Clemmie, Grace worried terrifically about what kind of a mother she would be. Her own mother was terrifying, nothing like the loving, present, warm mothers she read about in books. Grace had been so frightened she would follow in her mother's footsteps, had determined to be the sort of mother she had always wanted, but she hadn't counted on Ted; on having a husband who had so many demands of his own.

Would she really be able to shower love and attention on both Ted and a child? Would Ted simmer with resentment because Grace had to give the baby a bath, or walk them through the fields, take them to Mommy and Me groups, at which all men, even the great Ted Chapman, would be excluded?

She had nothing to worry about. From the minute Clemmie gazed up at her father with her big blue eyes, she had him wrapped around her little finger. She was fiery and funny and stubborn, and instead of finding her distraction a problem, Ted welcomed it.

Clemency. *Noun: mercy; lenience*. There was a reason for her name.

Grace taught Clemmie to cook, the two of them side by side at the kitchen counter, baking pavlova, Clemmie delighting in watching the egg whites transform into pale, puffy clouds as she whisked. Grace wanted her to love cooking, just as she had loved learning from Lydia, but Clemmie wasn't a cook, couldn't be a cook, not when writing called to her as soon as she learned how to put pen to paper.

Of course Ted had bought Clemmie her own notebook and set her up on his old vintage Corona typewriter. She would punch down the keys while biting her lip, telling endless stories, before gathering up sheaths of paper and sitting at her own little desk in the corner, with a box of crayons to illustrate.

"She's rather good," Ted would say in delight, bringing her finished books in later that day, showing them off to Grace. "I think we may have another writer in the family."

She *is* a good writer, thinks Grace. Better than that, she is a wonderful writer. Every door could be, would be, open to her if she announced herself as Ted Chapman's daughter, but she had always refused to use her family's name or influence to help her work get published, which Grace cannot understand.

Clemmie could be, should be, pushing out novels. Instead she works at a local paper in Brooklyn, writing features every day, which is—as her father always says—the greatest training a writer could hope for: when an editor is standing over you every day requesting a thousand words in an hour, you aren't able to say you're not inspired, or ask that they try again when you feel a little more motivated. At home, in Clemmie's nightstand, is three quarters of a novel that no one has read, other than Grace, who was sworn to secrecy.

Grace is not a fan of nepotism, but she saw instantly that Clemmie's work stood up for itself. Clemmie's refusal to jump on what she calls the "celebrity offspring bandwagon" makes no sense to Grace, who wants her daughter to do what she loves, who knows that she is merely treading water at the newspaper while her manuscript sits, doing nothing, at the back of her nightstand drawer.

Grace suggested Clemmie use a pseudonym if she felt that strongly about not being connected to her father, but Clemmie said no, that people always know when a pseudonym is being used, and as a child she featured in enough articles about her parents that everyone in publishing would know who she is: word would quickly get out.

In the world of newspapers, no one cares. Clemmie Chapman is just another journalist on the job, trying to make her way in the world. No amount of pushing, pleading, suggesting from her mother will make her step out of her comfort zone and follow her dreams.

The car pulls onto the Palisades Interstate Parkway and Ted reaches into his bag for his speech. He rustles back and forth, sighing as he pulls the bag onto his lap and pulls out all the contents.

"Where's my speech?" Ted's voice is dangerously cold as he flicks through the papers, his jaw set in a familiar way.

Grace's heart starts to pound, the familiar thumping in her ears as anxiety forms. "I haven't seen it," she says calmly. "It must be in there somewhere."

"It's not here!" he says quietly, dangerously calm, even as he hits the seat with the sheath of papers, the loud bang making Grace jump.

"Why didn't you put my speech in my bag?" he says slowly, looking at Grace with an expression that turns her blood to ice. Grace deliberately keeps her voice calm and soothing, in an effort to regulate Ted's mood. She read somewhere this was a tried and tested method of calming down the angry, but it has never worked. It doesn't stop her from trying.

"Ted, I'm sorry I don't know where your speech is. I didn't know anything about it."

"Of course you don't," says Ted, his voice dismissive, dripping with disdain. "Of course you didn't think to do this." He shakes his head before practically sneering. "Ellen would not have let this happen."

I'm not Ellen, thinks Grace, who says nothing, dizzy with fear. There's nothing she can say to calm him down when he gets like this. She cannot say it's not true that she does nothing, that every moment when she's not at Harmont House she runs around making sure her husband is happy. She cannot say that his speech and the placing of it in his bag was not her responsibility. Whatever she says will fuel his rage, so she sits, her heart pumping, praying this will quickly pass.

She recognizes her terror has less to do with Ted and more to do with her childhood. Anger instantly sees her regressing to a small child, cowering in fear, helpless and hopeless in the face of a fury that has nothing to do with her.

By the time they pull up outside the hotel, where a host of photographers await, Ted is calm and Grace is, as she always is, determined to keep her pain and fear to herself. Thank God Clemmie will be here, she thinks. Clemmie always puts him in a good mood.

They exit the car, Grace putting her arm through Ted's for the photographers, the picture of a loving couple, no one guessing that she is terrified of the man she stands beside, that right now, in this moment, she is about as unhappy as it is possible to be.

Grace glides into the foyer alongside Ted, she air-kisses and smiles, air-kisses and smiles, all the while her eyes scanning the room for Clemmie, relief flooding her body as Ted turns to her and kisses her on the cheek. His mood has passed. All is well with the world.

For now.

PAVLOVA

(Serves 6–8)

INGREDIENTS

4 egg whites, room temperature

1 cup confectioners' sugar

1 teaspoon white vinegar

½ Tablespoon cornstarch

1 teaspoon vanilla extract

½ cup heavy cream

Fresh fruit and/or berries, e.g., strawberries—cut up; raspberries, kiwi fruit

1 Tablespoon lemon juice

Preheat oven to 275 degrees.

Whisk the egg whites in a squeaky clean bowl until soft peaks form. Add the sugar while whisking, a spoonful at a time, and keep whisking until the peaks are glossy and stiff.

Sprinkle cornstarch, ½ teaspoon vanilla, and vinegar and fold in.

Spread the meringue on an oiled baking sheet or a Silpat, in a circular shape. Make a slight well in the middle.

Bake the meringue for around 1 hour and 15 minutes, until a pale eggshell color.

Turn oven off, but DO NOT REMOVE MERINGUE! Crack the oven door to allow the meringue to cool in the oven. Expect cracks.

Plate the meringue before serving.

Whip cream with remaining ½ teaspoon of vanilla until peaks form.

Spread cream over cool meringue, cover with fresh fruit.

Five

I told him," Clemmie whispers in her mother's ear as she reaches up to kiss her cheek. "Mom? This is Luke."

Grace steps back to greet Luke with an extended hand and an approving smile. He is handsome and sweet, bearded, with the bloom of youth that instantly makes Grace feel old. Too old. She shakes her head to dislodge the thought, pleased that her daughter has such good taste.

"It's lovely to meet you, Luke."

"It's lovely to meet *you*, Mrs. Chapman. Are you having a good time?"

Grace laughs. "We just got here, but I'm sure it will be a wonderful evening."

"Not for Dad," Clemmie says, turning to Luke. "He detests small talk, but he'll be fine if everyone is pandering to his every whim." The three of them turn their heads to see Ted, surrounded by acolytes, playing up to them, enjoying the adulation.

"See?" Clemmie says. "He's fine. Give him a drink and he'll be even happier." As they watch, someone comes over and places a glass of scotch in Ted's hand. The three of them burst out laughing.

"How's Ellen?" Clemmie says, her face suddenly serious. "I feel horrible that I haven't phoned her."

"She's refusing to stop working for us," Grace says. "She has so much on her plate with her poor mother and trying to organize the move, but, bless her heart, she's still helping us manage the chaos of our lives. Our assistant." She turns to Luke, explaining. "She just moved to Florida to look after her mother and we haven't found a replacement yet."

Clemmie frowns. "Have you advertised on Craigslist?"

Grace nods. "I think we just haven't been on top of it. I'm going to have to try and find someone soon, though. Your father goes nuts when I forget anything."

"I still love you, Mom," Clemmie says, putting an arm around her mother and squeezing, the two of them tilting their heads together, mutual love and affection flowing between the two, making Luke smile.

"Oh, dear." Grace looks up. "Your father needs me. Make sure you come over and talk to us after dinner." Blowing them a kiss, she glides over to where Ted is furiously beckoning her, taking a deep breath as she slips into the persona of Grace Chapman, wife of Ted, mother, occasional celebrity-by-association, and friend.

The dinner is long and arduous. Not that you would ever be able to tell by looking at Grace. Her face is animated and interested. Her eyes sparkle as she makes sure she has conversations with each and every person at the table, excluding no one. This is who you become, she thinks, married to a difficult man. Ted's moods, his manners are so unpredictable, she has become her name personified, Grace. Gracious. Graceful.

Grace.

She has trained herself to consciously compose her features in order to appear happy, whatever her state of mind. She is charming, asking questions, staring deeply into people's eyes, making them feel as if they are the most important person in the room. It isn't that she *isn't* interested, but that she recognized, long ago, how awful it was to be talking to someone, particularly someone you admire, to see their eyes constantly moving, searching for what else is going on, who else they would prefer to be talking to. It may not have been that Ted particularly wanted to be talking to anyone else, but that's the impression he gives. Grace knows how that feels, remembers it well, how it made her insignificant, irrelevant. She vowed never to give anyone that same feeling.

Ted has been known to turn and walk off, in midconversation, leaving Grace to apologize without words, by linking her arm through that of a stranger and asking a thousand questions about their lives, making them feel important, making them forget they were just dismissed by Ted Chapman, or, if they remembered, making it immaterial.

Much of her life, she realizes, is spent cleaning up after Ted. Apologizing for him, or charming those who have been snubbed. It has become a reflex, an automatic response to his rudeness. She recognizes dismay, or shock, and sweeps in to make it all better.

Grace is known for her smile; a wide, luminous smile; a smile that looks like her world is perfect. It is this smile she is wearing as Ted takes the stage, ruffles his papers, adjusts the microphone, pats his pockets for his reading glasses, then stares over at Grace, who is holding them up above her head, this time with a genuine smile on her face as the room laughs.

"My beautiful wife." Ted leans into the microphone. "Where would I be without her? As blind as a bat, for starters." The audience is delighted at this impromptu repartee as a young waiter scurries through the tables to retrieve the glasses and deliver them to Ted.

Ted accepts the glasses, extending a hand to Grace as the audience cheers and applauds. "My muse," he says, as Grace tilts her head in acceptance, placing a hand on her heart. She is the very picture of the perfect wife, gazing adoringly at her husband and blowing him a kiss.

No one would know that much of the time Grace wonders why she is so unhappy; no one would guess that when Ted shouts at his wife, belittles her, bullies her, it is as if her mother has risen from the dead, determined to ruin the rest of her life too.

Mom?" Clemmie bends down next to Grace's chair as all around them people are getting up to leave. "I need you to meet someone."

Grace turns to see a young woman standing just behind Clemmie. She is probably in her early thirties, with an open face. Little makeup, natural dark blonde hair, she is confident and self-possessed, meets Grace's eye with an assured smile. Sweet. Compelling. And possibly perfect.

"This is Beth. She was at our table, and I was talking about Dad looking for a personal assistant, and guess what! She's an assistant, and she just left her last job so she's been looking for something new!" Clemmie's voice is quick, excited. "Isn't that an amazing coincidence? I told her I had to introduce you. Don't you think that's weird? It must be fate, surely."

Grace smiles indulgently, but yes, she thinks, how odd. What on earth would a personal assistant be doing here? And what are the chances? Could this be, as Clemmie has said, a sign?

"Beth?" She gestures to the young woman to sit. "What a wonderful stroke of luck indeed. Perhaps we ought to talk."

"We don't have to talk now," Beth says. "I know how busy you must be at these events and I'm so sorry to disturb your evening. Clemmie insisted on bringing me over, but I know this isn't a good time."

"Sit," says Grace, pulling a now-empty chair closer. "There's never a good time. Tell me, where do you live? Tell me about yourself and what you're looking for."

Grace watches as Beth sits down. "I live in Connecticut but I'm looking to move," Beth says, her voice soft, but with a surprising confidence that belies her youth. "I just looked at a small house in New Jersey that

I fell in love with, but I know I can't sign the rental agreement until I have a job lined up."

"Where in New Jersey?"

"Northvale?" Her voice tilts up in a question, as if Grace wouldn't know it.

"Northvale!" Grace's eyes open in delight. "That's right by us! I know, we're in Rockland County and Northvale is, as you pointed out, in New Jersey, but it's ten minutes away!" The excitement dances in her face. "So close!" She refocuses. "And for work? You really are a personal assistant? What kind of work have you been doing?"

Beth smiles, her face lighting up, imposing a mask of beauty onto features that seemed so plain.

"I've done a bit of everything," she says. "Jack of all trades . . . I started nannying for a family in Brooklyn a few years ago, and I guess they just ended up giving me more and more to do, and it really became a household manager-assistant job. It wasn't what I was looking for, but the kids didn't need me so much, and I really loved the organizing of the house. I worked in Connecticut for a while, doing much the same thing."

Grace tries to quickly process this in her head as she looks in the young woman's eyes. Nanny. Loves children. Trustworthy. Household manager. Good with responsibility. Personal assistant dealing with sometimes egomaniacal famous author? Unclear.

"What kinds of things did you do as a household manager-assistant?"

"Anything and everything that needed to be done," Beth says. "For the Brooklyn family I booked all the travel for the husband. He runs a big hedge fund so even though he had an assistant at work, he had an office at home, and I just ended up taking on a lot of his work."

"You must be good."

Beth shrugged, unwilling to divulge her obvious talents. "I kept on top of the household, which I did for the family in Connecticut too. I had a schedule of who was supposed to come when. I'd make sure the windows were cleaned when they were supposed to be, the pool was opened, the floors were waxed. They had rental properties too, so I was the point of contact with the tenants, fixing anything that needed to be fixed, making sure everything ran smoothly.

"I was in charge of making sure nothing ran out, that there were always household supplies. I'm kind of a control freak, so that wasn't difficult. I'd walk their dogs and take them to the vet, arrange all the children's activities, drive them to airports. I'd go grocery shopping, and I got into the habit of cooking for them."

"You cook?" Grace's interested delight is apparent.

Beth looks bashful. "Not very well, but I love it, and the wife didn't cook at all, so my chicken with pasta and rosemary seemed like a gourmet extravaganza. I've read a few articles about you and your cooking," she says. "I even have a few of your recipes I cut out from a magazine. I love how passionate you are about cooking, and how accessible you make it."

Grace cannot hide her delight. "Flattery, as I'm sure you know, will get you everywhere!" They both laugh. "Is there anything you don't do?"

Beth thinks for a minute. "I don't sew," she says finally, which makes Grace laugh.

Shrugging her shoulders apologetically, Beth continues. "What really makes me feel good is making people's lives easier. If I've got nothing to do, I'll go in and organize a pantry, or a closet. Something. Anything. I kind of think that when you're working in someone's home, you have to be willing to do whatever needs to be done. I'm happiest when I'm busy."

This girl might be perfect, she thinks, studying her. She is hard to read—plain in appearance, there is a confidence to her voice that is in contrast to her looks; it is confusing, and unexpected, yet confidence is undoubtedly a good thing.

All of which is irrelevant if Ted doesn't like her. Given her skills, Grace would like to offer her the job anyway. If Ted doesn't like her, she could come and work for Grace.

"Darling?" Ted is bearing down on them, barely noticing Beth. "Are you ready?" He often does this, speaks at large events, is able to be gregarious and charming and warm, but as soon as the window of opportunity to escape opens, he is out of there. His limit for socializing is finite. He can do it, and at times enjoys it, but when he decides he is ready to leave, he must leave, regardless of what anyone else wants.

"Almost. I was just having a lovely chat with Beth. She's a personal assistant, looking for her next job." Grace surreptitiously raises an eyebrow as Beth turns to Ted, standing to introduce herself properly.

"It's an honor to meet you," she says, the disarmingly lovely smile now on her face again as Ted pauses, noticing her properly for the first time. "I've been a reader of your work for years."

Interesting, notes Grace. She didn't say "fan." *Everyone* says "fan." What does it mean that she said "reader"? It feels as if it was a word chosen deliberately, as if she wanted to praise him and elevate herself at the same time.

She is clever, Grace realizes, and cool. The combination is ever-so-slightly unsettling, that quiet confidence in one so young. But *is* she so young? Grace watches as Beth chats to Ted, who is clearly delighted, wondering just how old she is.

She moves to watch Ted, seeing he is charmed. He has always loved young women, as long as they are not foisted upon him as his editor, and is busy telling her a story that has her laughing, pulling herself quickly together as if embarrassed to reveal so much of herself.

"Make sure you give Grace your details," he says, now ready to go. Beth scribbles her number on a paper napkin, apologizing for not having cards, looking Grace in the eyes and smiling as Grace relaxes, wondering what on earth she was concerned about.

• • •

I enjoyed myself," Ted says in the car, going home. "I always dread these evenings, but this was fun."

Of course this was fun for you, thinks Grace. It is always fun for Ted when he is surrounded by people who feign adoration, particularly when his star is so very faded from what it once was.

In Ted's mind, he is still one of the greatest writers in America. It is a throne he refuses to relinquish, even though he has been overtaken by many, his book sales are suffering, he is no longer talked about in *The New Yorker* as one of the greats, is usually not mentioned at all.

No one dares to tell Ted about his dwindling numbers, his changing rank on the ladder of literary success. His agent blames the smaller advances on the state of publishing in general, the poor reviews on the youth, inexperience, and stupidity of the reviewers.

Ted's fragile ego could never handle the truth, that his books have become long-winded, dull, and mostly irrelevant. He still gets awards, like tonight, but that is largely a nod to his past, to who he has been, rather than because of who he is now.

"You were wonderful," Grace says, relieved at his good mood for the rest of the evening, hoping to keep it that way.

"Thank you. And what a lovely surprise that Clemmie was there! Not sure about the fellow she was with. Looked a little frightening to me."

Grace shakes her head. "He was delightful! You just have a thing about bearded men. You always think they're suspicious, but I thought he was rather delicious. He had fantastically soulful brown eyes. I quite wanted to be thirty years younger and single."

Ted looks at her, aghast. "Do not turn into one of those dreadful, middle-aged women competing for their daughter's boyfriend's attention."

"I wouldn't. But I can see how it happens."

"You think twenty-five-year-old boys are attractive?" Ted is amused.

"I'm sure he was around thirty. And yes, I did think he was attractive. In a nostalgic, yearning, never-going-to-happen kind of way. Speaking of finding younger people attractive, how about that Beth? The potential assistant? What did you think of her?"

"Ah, Beth. She of the utterly plain face but strangely compelling and confident smile."

"Yes!" Grace sits up. "That's exactly it! She seemed so mousy, but then she smiled, and it was like looking at a completely different person. It made me want to just stare and stare at her. I couldn't figure her out. I couldn't decide if she was this quiet librarian type or someone far more confident. So hard to read. Do you think we ought to try her out? She does sound perfect for the job. My God, Ted, she even cooks! Not to mention all the other things."

Ted shrugs, picking up the paper with the article he hadn't finished reading on the way in. "Why not start by calling her references. If she is as good as you seem to think, we can always try her out for a month."

Grace turns to look out the window. Of course this is the sensible thing to do, yet letting anyone new into their life is frightening. Ellen had been with them for years, and they trusted her implicitly. They never had to worry that they would suddenly open the *New York Post* to find some snippet of information, of gossip, that could only have come from someone on the inside.

They have had their fair share of mistakes: the gardening company whose price tripled as soon as they discovered the Mrs. Chapman who had spoken to them, had asked them to quote, was married to Ted Chapman.

Grace wouldn't be looking for anyone new unless it was absolutely necessary. It does rather seem that the gods have been looking out for them; that in Beth they have placed the perfect candidate right in their laps.

She has all the right experience and is looking to live ten minutes away. Could anything be more perfect? More right?

She will phone the references tomorrow, and if everything works out, she will offer her the job.

There is a part of Grace that feels instant relief at the prospect, as if she is finally able to exhale. The stress of trying to cope with everything herself has been more than she has been able to admit. What a relief, what a joy to be able to hand it off to someone as capable and confident as Beth.

What a relief not to have to mother her husband; for her husband needs not just a wife, but someone to hold his hand, soothe his soul, keep him calm, and there is only so much Grace is able to do.

Six

Their lovemaking was never filled with huge passion. Tried and tested, less passionate than well worn, it had been satisfying; comfortable. Often it was quick, routine. Often, they didn't kiss. It felt perfunctory, Grace acquiescing to fulfill her marital obligation, Ted initiating, more because, it seemed to Grace, it was what he knew he was supposed to do rather than because there existed a great passion between them.

There had been desire in the beginning, but age, exhaustion, their busy lives made that seem a very long time ago. For years it had been more duty than fun. For years Grace had prayed for the sound of Ted's snoring long before she reached the final page.

How different it was from what she expected as a young woman, convinced marriage was the beginning of a fairy tale. All those years ago she walked across a country field to an arbor strewn with flowers, her eyes sparkling with hope and love and daydreams. She had visions of a perfect life, of endless romance, of finally being able to breathe now that she had found her life partner.

There was nothing that had prepared her for real life, for real marriage, for the ups and downs; the times when you look at your spouse with something that feels very much like hatred, only for it to pass into numbness, then circle back around into deep connection and love.

This morning, Grace looks into Ted's eyes and realizes she has once again come full circle. There are times when his ego, his demands, his moodiness, his temper are exhausting. There are times when it's all too much, when she feels herself retreat to lick her wounds, leaving him in the care of Ellen, leaving him to his own devices, unable to deal with his criticism, the way he blames her.

There are times when she finds him exhausting, exasperating. When her feelings for him run much closer to hate than to love. But it doesn't occur to her to leave. She made a vow, and the only thing of which she is absolutely certain is this too shall pass. It always does. The good, the bad, the ugly, the beautiful . . . it all passes.

When she looks at him with disdain, finds fault with everything he does, she has learned to take deep breaths, to keep herself busy, to be more careful with how she spends her time—to do things that make her happy, bring her joy. She will ring Clemmie and take her out in the city or go see a movie with her friend Sybil. Things she can do on her own, things that remind her of the good in life.

She will keep the focus on herself rather than look for someone to blame and wait for it to pass.

It has passed. This morning, as they make love, slowly, mindfully, she looks into her husband's eyes and feels a thread of connection so strong she can almost see it. She loves him. She loves him. She has only ever loved him. These are the times when that is easy to believe.

Afterwards she gets up, goes into the bathroom as Ted watches her from the bed, manuscript in hand, peering over the top of his reading glasses, laying the manuscript down for a few moments to admire his wife.

"You are still the most beautiful woman I have ever seen," he says, admiration and gratitude both apparent in his gaze.

Grace pauses, smiling at the unexpected compliment, glad they have circled back to finding love and appreciation for each other. She blows him a kiss before going into the bathroom, a newfound lilt to her step.

"How's the manuscript?" she calls, hearing Ted's foosteps on the stairs. "Is it still the one you were reading? The writer being hailed as the next Ted Chapman?" Ellen is the one who usually sifts through the manuscripts and advance reading copies that arrive, but these last few weeks it has been Grace, and she is interested in what he thought.

"It's good," Ted says. "But not great. A compelling story and moving characters, but overwritten. A little too much. Still. I'm blurbing it. It's from my editor and I think it's good blurb karma. Will you send it back to the publisher today?"

"Which publisher? Did you keep the cover letter?" Grace's heart sinks, knowing how Ted always loses the letter of introduction, the letter that names the editor.

"No. No idea where it went. You'll track it down. It's someone at Penguin."

Grace will track it down, by first going through the ever-growing piles of papers in Ted's office, then, when that fails, by ringing Penguin and speaking to editorial assistant after editorial assistant until someone discovers the editor. It will take at least an hour, and it is an hour that needs to be spent testing new recipes for Harmont House and preparing the grocery lists for next week.

"Of course," she says, staring past the mirror on the makeup table and looking out the window.

The garden is starting to bloom and nothing was cut back last year. She could employ teams of landscapers, but nothing gives her more pleasure than getting out there herself. Even when the work is backbreaking, it grounds her, in the truest sense of the word. She isn't a style icon, or a writer's muse, or the wife of an important man when she's on her knees in the garden, hair scraped back under an old hat, clippers in hand: she just *is*.

She doesn't think, doesn't worry, has no anxiety. She feels no pressure when she is in her garden. She can weed for hours, losing all sense of time until her back starts to hurt and she remembers all the other things she has to do.

Today was the day she planned to do the garden before a market run for ingredients for the week's cooking at Harmont House.

Perhaps, she thinks with a sigh, she will postpone the gardening. The only thing she won't skip is Harmont House.

TOAD IN THE HOLE

(Serves 4 to 6)

INGREDIENTS

1½ cups all-purpose flour
1 teaspoon kosher salt
Black pepper for seasoning
3 eggs, beaten
1½ cups milk
2 Tablespoons melted butter
1 Tablespoon vegetable oil
8 sausages, preferably pork

Preheat oven to 425 degrees.

In a bowl whisk flour, salt, and pepper.

Make a well in center of flour, pour in eggs, milk, and melted butter. Whisk in with flour until smooth. Cover and let stand for 1 hour.

Add oil to skillet, add sausages, and brown on all sides.

Coat bottom and sides of a heavy dish with oil—never extra virgin, which has an extremely low flash point and should not be used in frying/hot cooking.

The oil in the dish has to be sizzling before adding the sausages and batter. You can put the dish in a hot oven and wait for the oil to heat, but I use a heavy Le Creuset pan, and heat the oil on the stovetop. As soon as the oil sizzles, add the sausages, then pour the batter over.

Bake in the oven for about 25-30 minutes, or until the batter is golden and puffy.

Seven

Jennifer grins at her from the other side of the room, watching as Grace pulls the knife honer out of the drawer and starts to sharpen the knives.

"What?" Grace looks up, surprised to see Jennifer still in the doorway.

Jennifer shakes her head. "You and I go back years, and to me you're always just Grace, but every now and then I'll open a magazine, or watch a TV show, and there you are, wife of the famous Ted Chapman! I just can't ever compute the glamorous woman in the magazine with the woman who shows up here and cooks her ass off five times a week."

"You mean, the woman who shows up here looking like crap?"

"You could never look like crap, sweetie," Jennifer says. "Your beauty shines through, whatever the exterior. I mean it, though. I constantly forget who you are."

Grace straightens up. "I'm no one, Jennifer." Her voice is soft. "I'm no one. Just a gal who loves to cook. The only reason anyone has ever taken notice of me is because of what my husband does. And even that doesn't make him better than anyone else. He just happens to be incredibly talented. We're shockingly ordinary." Even as she says it, she knows it's not true. In many ways she is still unchanged, but how could Ted not have been affected by all the years of everyone telling him he was wonderful.

How could Ted think he is no better than anyone else when all he has heard, for years and years, is that he is superior in every way.

She still loves him, of course. But she loves him partly because she sees beyond the veneer, because although his persona is firmly in place, she sees the insecure little boy hiding behind that, and it is him that she loves.

She loves him even when he drives her mad and she tolerates his ego that has, despite what she has just said, grown exponentially over the years.

Harmont House has been her refuge, the place where she finds a sense of peace; she honestly doesn't know how she would have survived without it.

When Grace was twenty-three, her mother died. The last time Grace saw her, six months earlier, her mother had been living in a facility behind Oxford Street, a facility Grace thinks of every time she steps over the threshold of Harmont House.

They took in homeless women, provided them with a roof over their heads, fed them, cleaned them before attempting to put them on the path to rehabilitation. Unlike Harmont House, however, it was a state-run facility; Harmont House without the love.

Which is what brings Grace to Harmont House five days a week. Why she bonds so closely with the women who live there, with Jennifer, who runs the home. This isn't about Grace doing a good deed for those less fortunate than herself; this is about Grace assuaging the guilt of not being able to do anything for her mother; this is Grace having the ability to love these women, these women being able to receive her love, in a way her mother never could.

Ted's refuge may be his barn. Grace's? Surrounded by women who have come to feel like her family; there's no question that hers is Harmont House.

Jennifer is the house mother and the driving force behind the organization. It was her brainchild, fresh out of recovery all those years ago, wanting to give something back. It was Jennifer who raised the funds to buy the big, old Queen Anne-style house in Nyack and reworked it so there were five small studios, each with a small kitchenette. There was a large playroom and kitchen, the dining room table seating twenty at a push. There was a communal living room, and a smaller room set aside for twelve-step meetings, for many of the women arriving had their own issues with alcohol and drugs.

Jennifer is strict and tough as old boots, with a heart as big as the ocean. As head of Harmont House, she takes in families broken down by fear and abuse, gives them jobs in the house to build their self-worth before helping them get jobs of their own in the real world.

Her mission in life is to rehabilitate these women enough for them to have their own lives, away from the men who have abused them. They need to show they are clean and sober before going on to support their families, before they can think about moving out of the house.

Families come and go, but the one constant, who stays in touch with all her "girls," is Jennifer. Grace, full-time chef and current chair of the board, is at the forefront of all decision making, but it is her kitchen prep work there five days a week that is the most fulfilling.

She isn't the great Grace Chapman when she's there, isn't a style icon in her jeans and clogs, her hair scraped back in a bun, not a scrap of makeup or jewelry.

She shows up for shifts, either six or eight hours, giving Jennifer a break. She is there as the fill-in house mother, assigning jobs, organizing the house, leading meetings, giving out many hugs, and teaching the women how to cook as she cooks for them herself.

The children in the house at any given time all fall in love with her, as do many of the women. The hardest part of the work is the turnover. After all these years, despite knowing she must not attach, it is impossible not to, particularly when you see the women come in scared, beaten, tight, then watch them unfurl over the months, watch their faces fill with pride as they get jobs, find self-worth, become peaceful in a way they never dreamed possible before now.

" 'Ordinary' is not a word I would ever use to describe you," Jennifer says. "It's your kindness, Grace. And your cooking. We'd be living on boxed mac 'n' cheese if it weren't for you, and I'd probably manage to mess that up. So what's on the menu today?"

Grace grins. "Your favorite. Cottage pie and apple crumble." She turns to the bag, rooting through the ingredients.

Jennifer swoons. "I'm going to put on even more weight!" she grumbles, delighted. "Your mother must have been an amazing cook. I wish someone had taught me to cook like this."

Grace pauses. "Oh, damn. I can't believe this. I forgot to buy the beef. How could I have forgotten that? It was first on the list."

"I can go and get it," says Jennifer. "I'll run out."

"I'm so sorry. I seem to be forgetting everything these days."

Jennifer pats her reassuringly on the back as Grace leans her head briefly on her shoulder. Jennifer is the sort of woman you confide in.

If there were anyone she could tell the true story of her mother, anyone she could trust, Jennifer would be the likeliest candidate.

The only people in the world who know are Lydia and Patrick. Ted knows only that her mother died young, that Grace and she hadn't been close, that Grace longed for a secure family because her own was so fragile. He doesn't know the true story, only Lydia and Patrick know the true story. She hasn't spoken to Patrick in years, and although she phones Lydia at least once a month, it is hard to jump right in to the big stuff when you are so far away.

Sometimes she thinks about sharing her story with someone here, wondering if it would release some of the shame she still carries today, some of the fear.

But the words won't come. Even when she knows she is safe, even when she wants to not feel quite so alone, the words are never there.

When Grace's father, Albert, met her mother, Sally, Sally seemed like the most glamorous, exciting woman in the world. She had more energy than anyone he had ever met, met every day with a new adventure, was filled with ideas that made him feel alive in a way he never had before.

Their courtship was a whirlwind. Sally brought up marriage after three weeks; instead of thinking it was a terrible idea, Albert, who had never fallen so hard nor so fast, immediately proposed.

They eloped, took the train to Gretna Green, and were married. Everyone presumed Sally was pregnant, but she didn't become pregnant until six months later, and everything changed once Grace was born.

The doctors said it was postpartum depression. Sally stayed in bed for the best part of a year. She would barely speak, cried every day, and Albert, desperate for his wife to come back, took care of her, and the baby, as best he could, terrified this depression wouldn't pass.

One day, Sally bounced out of bed, fully made up, bright, shining. *Back.* There was a buzzing edge to her as she left the house that morning, returning later that night with armfuls of bags stuffed with baby clothes and toys.

There was nothing that the baby Grace needed, but Albert understood Sally would want to buy her things, given she had lost the best part of the last year. The shopping would pass, he thought, along with other behavior he hadn't noticed before. She would drink every day, often staggering up to bed, entirely drunk. When sober, she was distracted to the point where she could barely focus.

It didn't seem to pass.

Out of nowhere, a temper appeared. If he did something "wrong," not as she wanted, or if the baby cried, Sally would whirl into the room, screaming in fury. After a while, she would go back to some semblance of normal, but normal never lasted long. At any point she could either go back to being wired or go back to bed. Flat. Tired. Teary.

In those days, in England, people didn't believe in doctors unless you were truly at death's door, and certainly not in *psychiatrists*. If something didn't seem quite right, you would generally try to sweep it under the table, pretending that nothing was wrong until it passed.

Manic depression was something that happened to other people. No one knew much about it; certainly no one talked about it in anything other than a shocked whisper.

Grace grew up with the knowledge that her father was the only one on whom she could rely. There were times when her mother was normal, but it could change at any time. She learned to walk on eggshells in her house, to relinquish her childhood, to try and take care of herself, and her parents, as best she could.

She tried to cook by watching *The Galloping Gourmet* on television, and Delia Smith on *Swap Shop*. For Christmas her father bought her cookbooks, which were quickly decorated with grease and gravy as Grace attempted to re-create Smith's recipes, many of which—including the cottage pie and apple crumble—she still uses today. Cooking was all a bit hit or miss until she met Lydia, her university roommate's mother, who really taught her how to cook.

Lydia became Grace's substitute mother, her roommate, Catherine, her sister, and the two noisy twin brothers, Patrick and Robert, not so much her brothers as the most important male figures in her life.

Robert was her secret love and Patrick her confidant. They provided her with a stability and a consistency that had been entirely missing from her own family.

At Lydia's house, Grace was not only allowed to be a child, she was celebrated, even when she did something wrong. Not that Grace was a child who often misbehaved, but Patrick, two years older than her, led her into all kinds of trouble. When Patrick "borrowed" his father's car without permission to take Grace to Sherborne for the day, then drove into the back of a truck, no one screamed at Grace or told her they wished she had never been born.

Grace cooked all the time with Lydia, not because she had to, but because she wanted to. It was a world away from her own home, where cooking, cleaning, self-parenting were expected from Grace because there was no one else to do it; where she shouldered the entire responsibility of running a household she wasn't old enough to run.

Today, her mother would, should, *could* be given medications to stabilize her, manage her condition, enable her to live a normal life. Had Grace's mother been alive today, it is entirely possible her life would be manageable. It is entirely possible she and Grace would have discovered how to love each other.

As it is, shortly after Grace left home to go to university, her parents divorced. Her father, by then a shadow of the man he once was, left the house and cut off contact with everyone.

Grace would come home on weekends, attempt to look after her mother, but half the time her mother had disappeared, the house would be filthy, and chaos awaited her in every room.

Grace learned more about manic depression and alcoholism than she would ever have dreamed possible. Back then, however much Grace recognized that it was the disease talking, her mother never lost the ability to hurt, to poison, to wound.

The last time she saw her had been six months before she died. Grace was staying at Lydia's when she got a phone call. It was a cousin she hadn't spoken to in years, who had somehow tracked her down. He had seen her mother, knew where she was, and thought Grace ought to know.

Lydia had offered to drive her in to London the next day, but in the end it was Patrick who drove her. Patrick to whom she told the whole, sorry story, sharing the hell of her childhood, her fear of anger and volatility, her sense of never having a safe place to call home.

"You do now," he had said quietly, expertly steering the car along the M4, then through the winding London streets, saying little, glancing over at Grace from time to time to check that she was okay.

They had the radio on, Grace grateful that today, Patrick wasn't his irreverent, amusing self, but in a nod to the seriousness of the situation was quiet, reflective; a wonderful listener.

"Are you sure you want to go in on your own?" He pulled up outside a dark brick building, bars on the window, weeds sprouting from the base of the walls. It was depressing, even from the outside, and Grace suppressed a flutter of fear.

"I have to," she said, grateful he took her hand and squeezed it before she opened the car door. "Will you stay here in the car, though? In case I need to . . . I don't know. In case."

"Of course. Good luck!" he called as she walked to the front door and rang the bell.

A woman appeared at the door. Middle-aged, although it was hard to determine. She had long, white hair pulled tightly back from her face in a bun, a face that was lived-in; sad.

"Hello," said Grace. "I'm looking for Sally Patterson."

"Yes," said the woman whose name tag announced her as "Margaret," appraising Grace coolly. "We were wondering if we'd see you."

"I'm Grace. Her daughter."

"I know." Margaret stepped aside, finally, to let her in. "Your mother has been wondering where you've been." She started walking into a large hallway, Grace presuming she was expected to follow.

"I've been trying to find her," Grace said, flustered, not expecting to have to explain herself here. "Much of what my mum says is . . . fabricated."

Margaret seemed to consider this for a while, then nodded. "I'm sorry. I shouldn't have judged. It's just that it's so hard on these women when their families desert them."

"I didn't desert her!" Frustration took the form of a hot lump in Grace's throat. "I've been looking for her for months."

"She'll be glad you're here," Margaret says in a tone conciliatory enough that Grace, correctly, takes it for an apology.

"How is she? How long has she been here? Is she taking her medications?"

"Come in here and sit down," said Margaret, leading her into a small, dark, windowless room lined with institutional green chairs. "I can give you her recent history, at least what I know, then we can go to see her."

COTTAGE PIE

(Serves 8)

INGREDIENTS

2 cups ground beef
1 Tablespoon oil
1 large onion, chopped
½ cup carrots, finely chopped
¼ cup celery, finely chopped
½ teaspoon cinnamon
2 sprigs fresh thyme, finely chopped
1 Tablespoon fresh parsley, chopped
1 Tablespoon all-purpose flour
1¼ cups chicken stock
1 Tablespoon tomato puree
Salt and pepper
2 pounds potatoes
¼ cup grated cheddar cheese
¼ cup butter
Seasoning

Preheat oven to 400 degrees.

Heat oil in skillet, add onions, sauté for around 5 minutes, until slightly brown. Add carrot and celery. Cook 5 minutes, then remove from pan and set aside.

Turn up heat, add more oil, season beef well before adding, then cook, breaking up with spatula, until brown. Add onions back into pan with rest of vegetables, cinnamon, thyme, and parsley.

Stir in flour, then stock and tomato puree, mixing well. Turn heat down to low, cover, and cook gently for around half an hour.

While meat is cooking, peel potatoes, dice into even-sized rough cubes, and add to pan of cold water. Do not add salt as it breaks down the starch in the potatoes. Bring water to boil, and simmer for around 25 minutes, or until potatoes are cooked.

Push potatoes through a ricer, or mash with a hand masher, but do not use a blender or the potatoes will turn into a sticky mess. Add butter and salt and pepper.

Transfer meat to casserole dish, cover with potatoes, sprinkle cheese over the top. Bake for around half an hour, or until top is golden.

Eight

Sally, it seemed, had recently been in a housing and treatment program. She was calm, not drinking, neither agitated nor unhappy. If you didn't know better, you might even think her entirely normal.

The hostel was very familiar with Sally, said Margaret. When Sally was in a program, or in a psychiatric hospital, as had happened before, they didn't see her for months. But her pattern was always the same—she would seem to be normal, before mania would strike, and everything would go wrong.

Lithium was the accepted medication for people like Sally. She had taken it sporadically, but complained of feeling "flat," the drug making her lethargic, tired, lazy.

"People don't understand medication for manic depression," said Margaret. "They think that people start to feel so good they think they must be better, and that's why they stop taking the lithium, but it isn't that. It's the opposite. Generally these medications make people with this kind of depression feel completely flat, and these are people who are used to the highs of mania, so to them, it's tantamount to being dead."

She stopped suddenly, peering at Grace. "This may all be stuff you know," she said tentatively. "I know how difficult it can be for families of those who suffer."

"I know a little," Grace said. "She has tried taking lithium for years, but it never seems to last long."

"She definitely hasn't taken anything recently. We got her back here two weeks ago. She's in one of her more manic phases, although she did seem a little calmer yesterday. We've put her back on the lithium and we try and monitor to make sure our residents are taking their pills, but it's impossible to keep track of all of them."

"So she's . . . manic? Still?"

"It may just be that they haven't got the dosage right. Or she's hiding the pills."

"And there's nothing you can do?"

"We do the best we can. Are you ready? We can go and see her now."

Grace said nothing when she walked in the room. She should not have been shocked at what her mother looked like, but nothing could have prepared her to face this woman who gave birth to her, who was now almost unrecognizable.

Sally was sitting in the front row of chairs facing a television, holding the remote control, zapping quickly through television channels, never settling on one for more than a few seconds, much to the frustration of the four other women in the room.

Grace stood off to the left, devastated at the toll living on the streets has taken on her mother. She had remembered her as young, pretty, normal looking if not always normal acting, but this version of her mother was years older than Grace would have expected, and so much bigger than when she had last seen her, almost a year ago.

Her pretty features were masked by doughy cheeks, a double chin.

If Grace hadn't known it was her mother, she would have walked straight past her.

Unexpectedly, Sally laughed. Grace saw her teeth, one missing on each side. She looked exactly as she was: a toothless, homeless woman with a glitter in her eye and a force field of energy around her that had a buzz that was almost palpable.

Grace remembered this buzz, this energy, from her childhood. This is when her mother would go on huge shopping binges, or drive Grace miles from home on a quest for some sort of treasure. It was exhilarating being in her company, and exhausting. And completely unsafe. Grace never felt she was in the company of a responsible adult during those times, would pray that nothing would go wrong.

"Mum?" Grace ventured after Sally paused to look at Grace, her eyes sweeping over her dismissively before going back to the television. "It's me. It's Grace."

"I know who it is," said Sally. "Are you coming in? What are you doing standing in the doorway? You look like I used to look, years ago. I may not have seen you for a while but I'd know you anywhere. I thought you were too busy in America to bother with me. I know you're living it up in New York. What are you doing here? Nice of you to come and see me. I'm surprised you're not off with your other mother." She gave a gap-toothed grin before handing the remote to a woman sitting next to her and standing up. "Don't just stand there," Sally said, walking toward Grace. "You can give your old mum a hug."

What had I expected? she thought. A Waltons-esque reunion? The two of them flying into each other's arms, tears of gratitude and joy rolling down each of their cheeks.

Well, yes. She had expected something like that. Had hoped her mother would be pleased to see her after so, so many years, but perhaps this is her mother being pleased to see her. Perhaps this is to be as good as it gets.

She felt her mother's small body against hers, incredulous that she came out of this woman, that this was the woman present for the first eighteen years of her life. She expected to feel this huge bond, the invisible umbilical cord still stretching between them after all this time, but holding her mother, feeling the boniness of her spine, her soft, distended stomach, noting her wiry grey hair, Grace was astonished to feel little other than tremendous sadness.

"Come and see my room!" Sally disengaged, tugging on Grace's arm. "I have a picture of you on my wall."

"You do?" Grace was momentarily thrilled, reaching the room to find an old photograph of Grace as a child with Sally, one she didn't even know her mother still had, Blu-Tacked to the faded yellow walls of a room that contained three iron single beds and three lockers, each carefully locked.

"See?" Sally said, proudly pointing out her room. "There you are. And there I am." She moved closer to the picture. "Not aging so well, but I'm not running around America without a care in the world, am I."

"You look well," said Grace. "I have spent a long time hoping to find you. I didn't know about this hostel. I'm glad I now know where you are."

"Here for the time being," said her mother brightly, spinning around and pulling a small key from a string tied around her neck. "With all my worldly possessions. Want to see?"

"No, it's fine," said Grace, but Sally was already on her knees, pulling things wildly out of the locker and flinging them on the bed. There was nothing of value in there. A tennis ball, mismatched socks, an oversized, filthy sweater with holes all over it, a plastic doll with a missing leg, a green plastic bowl, a child's plastic tiara with one remaining red gemstone stuck in the middle, a lipstick, a scarf, sneakers that looked to be at least three sizes bigger than Sally would wear, and an empty plastic bottle that once contained Coke.

"That's quite a collection you have there," said Grace, sitting down on the bed.

"I know!" Sally was proud. "These are my favorites." She pulled the lipstick out and inexpertly applied it over the lines of her lips as Grace felt a twinge of pain. Everything she had always dreaded was right there in front of her—her mother with lipstick all over her face, glittering eyes, appearing to be the craziest of crazy old ladies.

When she wasn't even old.

"And this!" Her mother perched the tiara on her head and laughed, dropping into a curtsey.

"Very pretty," Grace said. "Mum, I know it's been a long time since we saw each other, and I'm only here for two weeks, but I'd really like to help you in some way. I have a job now, in publishing, and things are going well. How can I help? What can I do for you?"

Sally seemed not to hear. "I loved it when you were young," she said suddenly, her eyes whirling around the room, settling on Grace every few seconds before darting off somewhere else. "Didn't we have fun, Gracie? Remember when you and I would climb in the car and go off and have adventures? Wasn't that the best? Just you and me?"

"It was," lied Grace, astounded her mother had such fond memories of a childhood that was so completely disappointing to Grace, so completely unsafe.

"Mum? Margaret tells me you're not taking your medication. She says you were doing really well until that point. I was wondering whether you might be willing to go back into a treatment center, just to get you back on the straight and narrow again."

It was like watching a cloud descend over Sally, a veil drop over her face, and instantly Grace knew she had said the wrong thing. Instantly she regressed to a little girl, knowing that she had set a foot wrong, that her mother was about to embark on one of her terrifying rages. There was no place to hide.

"Why?" barked Sally, her voice loud and aggressive. "You think there's something wrong with me? You all think there's something wrong with me! All of you lot who want to drug me up with pills that make me feel like I'm half-dead, who tell me there's something wrong with being who I am. Look at you, all fine and fancy in your fancy American clothes. Who do you think you are, coming here to sneer at me? You don't know anything about my life. You don't know what makes me happy and what I need to get by. You don't care. No one cares." Her voice dropped as her mood changed from rage to self-pity. "I don't need some busybody do-gooder swanning in and telling me what I need to make me better. I'm fine. Better than fine, and I don't need anyone's help."

"I'm sorry, Mum. I didn't mean to offend you. I just wanted to . . . help."

"Everyone wants to help," she spat. "I don't need help. I don't need you, do I? Can't you see? I've managed perfectly well all these years without you and I certainly don't need you now."

"I'm your family, Mum. I'm your daughter. Daughters are supposed to take care of their mothers when they get older. It has nothing to do with me thinking I know what's best for you, it's just . . . biology."

"*Hmph*." Sally turned away, busying herself sorting through the pile on her bed. "Like my bottle?" she said, brandishing the Coke bottle with sudden delight. "It's my water bottle. I fill it whenever I find a tap. Or a half-empty beer bottle. Beer. You don't have any beer, do you?" She looked at Grace hopefully, who shook her head wearily. "Vodka's my favorite," she said, almost to herself. "But not much chance of getting hold of vodka these days. That's my treat. That's the thing I really look forward to."

Grace desperately tried to distract her, even knowing what a futile exercise that had always been when her mother was . . . like this. What is it they say about the definition of insanity? she remembered thinking. Ah, yes. The definition of insanity is doing what you've always done and expecting different results. "What about food?" she offered. "Can I at least buy you something to eat for lunch?"

"They feed me here," said Sally. "Are you staying for lunch? Soup. It's good. You should stay for lunch. Dinner's usually leftovers, or something pretending to be different to lunch, but it all tastes much the same to me."

"Would you like to go out for lunch?" Grace ventured. "We could go to a restaurant. You always used to like fish and chips. Maybe we could find fish and chips nearby?"

But her mother wasn't listening, was busy pulling things frantically out of the pile, organizing them, messing them up again, then starting all over again, all the while muttering to herself.

"Mum?" Grace said, leaning forward. "Mum? Do you want me to stay?"

"No!" Sally said. "I didn't want you here in the first place. Why are you here? What do you want from me? Do you want to take my stuff?" She snatched the tiara from her head and cradled it against her chest. "Is that it? You think you can come here and help yourself to my precious jewels? Get out of here! I can't stand you, Grace. I never could. Always whining, whining, whining. Why are you here? What do you want from me? You always want so much from me, you always make me crazy. Get out." Her voice rose to a shout. "Go on, you stupid bitch! Get out of here!"

Grace stood, stumbling for words that might appease her mother, but there weren't any, or if there were, she didn't know them. She left the room, went back downstairs and rounded the corner, almost walking straight into Margaret, barely seeing her, her eyes misty with tears.

"Oh dear." Margaret took her by the arm and led her back into the room they were in before. "Sit down, love. Do you want a cup of tea?"

"No. I just . . . I didn't expect her to be so hostile."

"That's the illness, my dear. You never know what you're going to get. She may not be registering happiness today, but she will be happy you came. She talks about you a lot, you know. My daughter, Grace, in America!"

Grace attempted a smile. "Isn't there something I can do? Can't I pay to put her in a treatment program? Or send her somewhere to get help? Hire a nurse? I don't know . . . something!"

"You could do all of those things," said Margaret, "and none of them would help. She has to get to a point where she wants to help herself. Until then throwing money or programs or pills at her won't do anything. She'll leave, flush the pills down the toilet, end up back on the streets. There isn't anything you can do, except maybe visit her. It doesn't look like it makes a difference, but I believe it does."

Grace nodded, unsurprised by what Margaret had said. Margaret left, and although Grace knew Patrick was outside in the car, waiting, she didn't go out straightaway. She thought of her mother, her volatility; the glitter in her eye that could lead to fun or anger or any other emotion that was stretched to its limit.

I can't change her, Grace thought again, only this time the thought floated through her body and settled in her bones. I am powerless over her, she thought, walking out of the hostel and heading for the car.

"Well?" Seeing Patrick was comforting, safe, and it was only when she sat in the passenger seat, closed the door, and turned to Patrick to try and talk that she found she couldn't.

Shaking her head to dislodge the lump, instead tears leaked out her eyes and Patrick leaned over and took her in his arms, as she sobbed.

"I'm okay," she said, attempting to smile when the sobs had calmed down. "I should know by now that I can't ever expect anything. I should know by now that nothing has ever changed, nothing will ever change. I can't help her. I've spent my life trying to help her, but I can't."

Six months later, Sally was dead. A heart attack. Shocking in someone so young, but the alcohol abuse had aged her and worn her body down to the point where it couldn't tolerate life.

Relief. That was what Grace felt when she got the news. Swiftly followed by guilt. She never told anyone about her mother. Not even Ted. It is, she supposed, her guilty secret. The shame of having a mother who was mentally ill, and the fear that this too may happen to her.

Nine

Where have you been?" Ted is thundering up the path from his barn, his face a mask of frustration, as Grace gets out the car. Immediately, she feels her body start to tighten. Tingling starting in her arms and legs.

It is exactly what used to happen to her when she was a child, in the face of her mother's rages. Grace is well aware that each time this happens she regresses to that same, scared child, but there doesn't seem to be anything she can do to change it.

Ted's anger, his dissatisfaction, his rage, even when it has nothing to do with her, even though she should be used to it after all these years, still causes her to tighten, her breath to shorten as her throat constricts, as her mind searches for the perfect words that will calm him down.

"Is everything all right?" she calls, her arms filled with groceries she picked up after Harmont House.

"Does everything look like it's all right?" he says, disdain and derision in his voice as Grace concentrates on keeping her breathing steady, on staying calm, for one of them has to remain the adult here and it is never, ever Ted.

"What can I do to help?"

"You can buy some goddamned ink for the goddamned printer," he says. "I needed to print my first draft today and it ran out after twenty-eight pages."

"Did you look in the office supply closet?" Grace says. "Ellen usually kept spares in there."

"Of course I looked in the office supply closet. What do you think I am, *stupid*? There's nothing there. No one has replaced the cartridges since last time." He fixes a glare on Grace, as if it is her fault, for Grace is quick to shoulder the blame if it will appease him.

"Did you order new cartridges?"

"No, I did not order new cartridges." His voice is like ice. "I don't know the passwords to any of the Web sites."

"Aren't they in the family book?"

"What family book? What the hell's a 'family book'? And where am I supposed to find it?"

He is a child, Grace thinks. This is a child's tantrum and this has nothing to do with me. She keeps the focus on her breathing, noting that her heartbeat is coming slowly back to normal, the tingling in her arms and legs almost gone.

Thank God, she breathes, closing her eyes for a few seconds. When Ted gets into one of his rages, often set off by something as small and insignificant as the ink in the printer running out, there is no telling where it will go.

There are times when it escalates, growing and pulling in anything and everything in its path, other times when, like today, he will lose steam and slowly go off the boil.

His face is now a sulk as Grace expresses sympathy for his confusion and hardship. "That must have been so frustrating," she says, watching him nod, grateful that she understands. "Why don't I go and order the cartridges, and if you put your draft on a disc, or key, I can take it into Nyack and get it printed for you. You'll have it in an hour. How does that sound?"

"That sounds fine." The anger has gone, replaced by an apologetic smile. "I didn't mean to shout. Sorry. Perhaps you can bring me in a scotch. It is, after all . . ."

". . . Five o'clock somewhere." She finishes his sentence for him, waiting for him to turn and make his way back to the barn before her body sags with relief.

In the kitchen she pours him a scotch, realizes she has to call the handyman as the closet door in which the liquor is kept almost comes off its hinges, and buries her face in her hands.

Ellen kept him under control. Ellen made him the kind of man she could be married to. Ellen mothered him, and looked after him, and made sure his every need was taken care of so when he was delivered back to Grace at the end of every working day he was happy and loved, like the happiest of children.

Without Ellen, he is almost unbearable. This isn't what she signed up for. This isn't something she can live with. It is evening time, the time when she should be able to relax, to lie on a sofa and read a book, or watch a television show, or enjoy dinner with a glass of wine.

Instead she is quickly pulling dates from the grocery bag. They are supposed to be for Harmont House, but instead she will give them to Ted, slicing the dates in half to add a fresh sage leaf, wrapping them in prosciutto and popping them in the oven for ten minutes. These are his favorite, and his hunger will not be helping his mood. She will head back out to the barn with the nibbles, and the glass of scotch, before running into town, at rush hour, to wait as a printer laboriously churns out the five hundred or so pages of his manuscript.

She won't be back for ages. She has been in service to other people all day long and is not about to stop now.

Ted, engrossed in his computer, looks up briefly and thanks her for the scotch, eyes lighting up at the dates, flashing her his most charming smile, unaware of the impact his fury has had. Always has.

Grace loves him, but she is tired.

She loves him, but she cannot manage him by herself.

It is only when she goes back to the house, Ted's disc in her hand, to gather her things, that she remembers Beth. Beth! The sweet young woman who was a friend of Clemmie's. Wait. She isn't a friend of Clemmie's, but perhaps of Luke's? A friend of *someone's*, at any rate. Why else would she have been at their table? And Ted liked her! Why hadn't she called? Grace pauses by the phone, excited suddenly, unable to process why on earth she hadn't set up an interview as soon as she got home from the event.

Dialing the number, she is part relieved, part disappointed when the call goes to a machine.

"Beth? It's Grace Chapman here. We met at the gala the other night and chatted a bit about possibly helping us out as Ted's assistant. I'm so sorry I didn't call earlier, but if you're still available, I'd love to set something up. Maybe you could even come in and do a trial. I always think that's the best way to see if someone's a good fit . . . I'm sorry. I'm babbling. Give me a call back, and let's have a chat and see if we can figure something out. Thank you. Have a good evening."

Feeling the weight of a thousand problems leave her shoulders, she heads out to the car.

PROSCIUTTO- AND SAGE-WRAPPED DATES

(Serves 6)

INGREDIENTS

24 fresh sage leaves

12 dates, halved, pits removed

1 pack prosciutto, each slice sliced lengthways down the middle

2 Tablespoons maple syrup

Preheat oven to 350 degrees.

Place a sage leaf on each date half, wrap with prosciutto, place flat side down on a baking sheet.

Bake 10 minutes.

Brush with maple syrup and serve.

Ten

At quarter to eleven Grace looks out the window and frowns. She is so immersed in measuring out the ingredients for the marinade for the chicken she is making today, she has totally forgotten she had anything else planned.

An old burgundy Subaru pulls into the driveway, surely Beth. She isn't supposed to be here until eleven; Grace was planning to use these fifteen minutes to finish off writing checks.

The stack of bills have been piling up for weeks. Last night, when the phone rang and it was an automated message saying their cable was about to be disconnected due to nonpayment of bills, Grace realized how disorganized things had become.

Ellen had paid the bills. When her mother first got sick and Ellen grew more distracted at work, Grace found a bookkeeper, thinking if the bills were taken care of, Grace might perhaps be able to take care of everything else, but it didn't work out, and the responsibility fell back to Grace, who was fantastically disorganized. She was able to pretend to be organized. For about two weeks. Then bills would get opened in the kitchen instead of the office, put down on the countertop, where they would stay until the cleaning lady swept them into a neat pile, stacked the catalogs on top, where they would be promptly forgotten about for weeks. Sometimes months.

Grace's irritation at Beth arriving fifteen minutes early for the interview quickly dissipates when she realizes bill paying need never be this disorganized again.

The doorbell doesn't ring. No knocks on the door. Grace goes again to the window and sees that Beth is not getting out of the car yet. Grace will walk out and welcome her in. Suddenly, she wants Beth to like her. To like them. She wants Beth to fall in love and take the job.

I'm so sorry I'm early." Beth climbs out of the car as soon as she sees Grace walking over. "I was so worried about being late I thought, Better to be early, but I didn't want to disturb you."

"It's fine. Come in. Did you find it okay?"

"I follow wherever my iPhone tells me to go," says Beth. "I don't even bother looking at the road anymore. I just follow the blue line."

I like her, thinks Grace, as she laughs. "Why don't I show you around?"

Grace chats away to Beth, not really sure whether this is how she is supposed to interview. She suspects she ought to be sitting down and firing questions at Beth, but isn't sure what to ask; she figures it will work just as well to show her around and explain what needs to be done as they go, as she remembers.

"This is my little office." Grace leads her into the tiny room, not much more than a closet, off the kitchen, embarrassed suddenly at the piles of papers, at the utter mess.

"Oh God," she winces. "Now you can see what a disaster I am."

Beth smiles gently. "It's all fixable," she says. "I'm an expert at getting filing systems going. I'll have this whipped into shape in a day."

"If you do, I may have to steal you for myself."

"That does lead me to something I've been thinking about ever since you phoned," says Beth. "Is the job your husband's assistant? Or is it more of a family, household thing? I adore the idea of working for your husband, particularly as I'm such a big reader and I've followed his work for years, but I'm not very good at just doing one thing. I know it sounds odd, but I'm much happier when I'm multitasking, and happier still when I'm so busy I barely have time to think. I know when we met at the gala you said it was for your husband, but I could really help you in here. And don't take this the wrong way, but your pantry is in desperate need of some organization."

Grace squints at her. "Are you absolutely sure you're not heaven-sent?"

Beth laughs. "That's what my old boss said! Did you get the references I sent?"

"I did," says Grace. "I just haven't had a chance to call them yet."

"Whenever you're ready," Beth says. "But I realize that cell number is really old and I have a feeling they may have changed it. If there are any problems, just email her. She's much easier to get a hold of by email anyway. Is there another office in the house where your husband works?"

"He's in the barn. Let's take him out some iced tea."

Ted is in the wing chair by the fireplace, notebook balancing on his knee as he makes notes for his next novel. He has always made notes the old-fashioned way, scribbling on a legal pad with a particular Pilot pen. Any other pen, any other kind of notebook and it just doesn't work. For many years he wrote his novels in longhand, and for a while dictated them to Ellen before she brought him into the twentieth century by teaching him to use the computer.

He looks up as Grace knocks, opening the huge doors that line one wall of the barn, the dachshunds running in between her legs, Beth behind her, putting the notebook aside as he notices the tray.

"Darling, you remember Beth from the gala? We've been having a long chat and she's fantastically organized and full of energy, not to mention experience!" Grace hears herself selling Beth, tailing off only when she sees Ted is merely gazing at Beth, assessing her, not really listening to Grace.

"Are you a reader?" Ted peers at her.

"Oh, yes! A huge reader. I just finished the new Richard Beattie."

Ted cocks his head. "And? What did you think?"

"Honestly? I thought it was overwritten. And smug. I loved *The Longest Journey*, but since then I think his writing has become worse and worse. This felt like an MFA student desperately trying to please his professor."

There is a pause before Ted barks with laughter. "Good God!" He chuckles, looking at Grace. "She's right! She's absolutely right!"

Even Grace is impressed. Ted has had a long-running feud with Richard Beattie, which has been hinted at occasionally in some of the more literary magazines, including a piece over ten years ago in *The New Yorker*, but most people wouldn't know that. Most people would have no idea of how much Ted despises Richard Beattie, that the perfect way to Ted Chapman's heart is to stick a knife through Richard Beattie's.

Ted shakes his head. "So who *do* you like?"

"Other than you?"

Ted nods a gracious assent as Beth reels off a list of Ted's peers, including what she thought of their most recent books. Her appraisals are honest and fair, and seemingly completely in line with Ted's views, his face lighting up with delight as she continues talking.

Grace sits back, studying her. She still has no idea how old Beth is, but is guessing early thirties; perhaps thirty-five at the most. She is pretty, in a completely unassuming way. No one could pull Grace aside and whisper, did she really think it was a good idea having Beth as an assistant for Ted? Wasn't she worried?

Beth is not someone who inspires that kind of worry.

And yet, there is something entirely unexpected about her. She looks as if she might bury herself in light women's reads, the kinds of books that sell by the shedload, are in every airport bookstore but are rarely reviewed by the publications that fall over themselves to review Ted Chapman.

Grace would never have expected her to have not only read every one of the serious literary tomes to have been published over the last three years, but to be able to discourse so cleverly about them.

Truly, she wonders. Is there anything this girl can't do?

Ted is, as indeed is she, charmed and disarmed. Her organizational skills have yet to be put to the test, but thus far she is passing the personality and intelligence test with flying colors.

"So?" Ted turns to Beth, obvious delight in his eyes. "When can you start?"

"Now?" Beth laughs, before turning serious. "I just moved here from Fairfield, Connecticut. Literally, last week. I've just finished unpacking in the new house in Northvale, and I really don't have anything left to do today other than a few errands." She turns to Grace. "I could help organize your office, if you'd like."

"Really?" Grace doesn't know what to think. "I'd love it, but we still need to talk about salary and things like that. Vacation time. How we pay you."

"Why don't we figure all of that stuff out on Monday? I can see that you need help and I'm here to help. At the very least, let me do your pantry. How about that?"

"You're sure?"

"Absolutely."

"And while you're here," Ted chimes in, "I've got a pile of signed books that need to be sent out to various charities."

"Perfect. I can stop at the post office on the way home."

Grace has made ginger and honey chicken, braised endive, and sticky rice tonight, with a hazelnut peach meringue. She doesn't make rice very often these days, particularly as they are both attempting a low-carb diet, but every now and then she needs to treat herself, needs to treat Ted. Meringue is his favorite, and his delight earlier, at walking into the kitchen to find her whipping egg whites, has put a spring in Grace's step.

"Cheers." Ted raises his glass to Grace as she sits down opposite him at the kitchen table. "Why does it look so good in here?" He looks around, frowning. "Were the cleaners in today?"

Grace shakes her head. "It was your new assistant, Beth! She said she'd just help with the pantry, but she hit the entire kitchen like a whirlwind. You have to see the pantry! She threw away everything out of date and organized everything beautifully. Then she tidied up the entire kitchen and wanted to stay to do all the bill paying, but I sent her home."

"You didn't want her paying the bills?"

"I do want her paying the bills, but I wasn't sure I wanted to hand our checkbook over to someone on their first day. She actually offered to take it home with her and do it from home, but I just couldn't."

"Why?" Ted cocks his head. "*Do* you think there's something untrustworthy about her?"

"Not in the slightest!" Grace quickly says. "She seems like Mary Poppins. And her references were great."

"How many?"

"Two. They emailed me back right away. Beth really does seem perfect. I'm quite sure she'll take over the bill paying next week, probably on Monday, but I am aware we don't really know anything about her . . . I really didn't want her taking our checkbook home."

"I think that's very wise. So your instincts are good? You, Grace, have always had tremendous instincts about people."

Grace pauses. "Yes," she says. "I have nothing bad flaring up, but . . . well. She's unexpected, isn't she?"

"In what way?"

"In that she isn't who she appears to be. She looks so . . . uncomplicated. Given her plainness and . . . simplicity, I would have presumed her to be married, to live in a house with lots of fluffy white things—pillows and lacy sheets, to treat herself to chocolates on the weekend, and read romantic novels. But she clearly proved me wrong on that count. I wonder how else I'm wrong?" Grace laughs. "I'll say this for her, she seems to be unexpected in entirely wonderful ways."

"Hear hear," Ted says, raising his glass. "Even the way she came in to collect the books was quiet and confident. She seems to know exactly what she's doing. I like that. There was no hesitation. She strikes me as a girl who has a lot of common sense."

"I think so too," Grace says. "Thank God! Thank God we've finally found someone who may make our lives easier. I feel a bit like this is the first day I have actually been able to breathe." Grace raises a glass in a toast. "To easier lives," she says, feeling a levity that has been missing since the day Ellen left.

GINGER AND HONEY CHICKEN WITH SOY

(Serves 4)

INGREDIENTS

4 boneless, skinless chicken breasts
2 Tablespoons runny honey
2 Tablespoons soy sauce
1 Tablespoon olive oil
1 Tablespoon Dijon mustard
1 Tablespoon fresh grated ginger, or 1 teaspoon ground ginger
3 garlic cloves, chopped
Salt and pepper to taste
1 large onion, sliced
3 scallions, chopped
1 cup rice, cooked

Mix honey, soy sauce, mustard, oil, garlic, and ginger together and pour over chicken. Turn chicken over until well coated, season, and place in fridge at least 1 hour.

Heat tablespoon of olive oil in a skillet, and when very hot, add the chicken breasts. Leave to brown for a couple of minutes, then turn over to brown other side. Remove chicken and set aside.

Add onions, and more oil if necessary, and fry them gently until they start to brown. Turn heat down, add chicken back to pan with sauce, and allow to simmer for around 30 minutes. Add 2/3 tablespoons of water if there is not enough liquid. Serve with white rice, and sprinkle with chopped scallions.

Eleven

Ellen spent almost all of her time with Ted, whereas Beth, even in the two weeks she has been here, manages to split her time fairly evenly. She is with Ted in the mornings and tends to spend the afternoon in the house, stocking up household supplies, sorting through the mail, even walking the dogs, with whom she instantly fell in love.

She is, Grace realizes, the sort of girl who is entirely self-sufficient. She rarely comes to her asking what she wants her to do, instead dealing with most things by herself, leaving Grace a list of what she has done.

In two weeks she has made herself invaluable. From the first day, Grace has felt as if she were on vacation. The house is running more smoothly than it has ever done before. Grace would never say this out loud, but as much as she loved Ellen, as much as she always thought they would never find anyone nearly as good as Ellen, Beth is making their lives easier in ways they never would have dreamed possible.

And more than that, she is such a pleasure to have around. She is never intrusive and seems to have a sixth sense, knowing when Grace isn't in the mood to have someone in her kitchen, isn't in the mood to chat; she will make herself scarce, while ensuring everything in the house that needs to be done is done.

Grace's only concern is that Beth may be overworking herself to the point where she realizes she can't take it anymore, or starts to hate the job. She is aware that Beth is young and trying hard to please. She doesn't want her to throw herself into this job with such abandon, do so much of everything, that she will end up resenting Grace and Ted and feel taken advantage of. Grace has seen this happen with other people and is trying to stop Beth from overdoing it, fearful of resentment being the inevitable outcome.

But it is hard to stop Beth. Even when she grudgingly says that if Grace absolutely insists on her not doing it, she won't tidy the living room, or sort out the pantry, or organize the closets, but Grace will come home later to find her house looking more immaculate than she has ever seen it.

Her two references were strong, both emailing nothing but wonderful things about Beth. "She is the best assistant we have ever had," wrote one. "She doesn't know how to sit still," wrote the other. "She is happiest when she is busy and she will take care of everything in your life."

How lucky they are to have found her. The Mrs. Doubtfire of the assistant world; a girl who doesn't take no for an answer; a girl who lives to make other people's lives easier.

It is lunchtime and Grace is first to arrive at the Sidewalk Bistro. She is aware, as she so often is when she goes out, that there are times when she is recognized. A glance that is a little too long, a head bent toward a friend, two sets of eyes appraising her, wondering if that is Ted Chapman's wife, watching her to report back to their friends.

Grace has never welcomed this attention, has done nothing to deserve it. The three women at the corner table have clearly noticed her, clearly know who she is, and Grace just shoots them a warm, friendly smile as they awkwardly smile back, unable to continue criticizing in the face of such honest warmth.

Sybil is always late, but Grace does not mind. She sits comfortably, nursing a glass of wine, quite happy to sit and people-watch, knowing that Sybil will burst in shortly, a flurry of activity and apology.

She has known Sybil since they first moved here. It is the kind of friendship that can only be formed when your children are terribly young, when you complain all the time of having no time, but in fact you have more time than you know what to do with: you are able to organize playdates every day with other mothers, meet friends for coffee, socialize constantly, desperate for your kids to have something to do, desperate for you to have some adult conversation.

Grace remembers the first time she saw Sybil. The playdate was held at someone else's house and it was a beautiful day, early summer. Everyone had been there for a while, when there was a hustle and bustle at the garden gate. In came Sybil, barely five feet, almost as wide as she was tall, in a paisley Earth Mother dress, her long curly hair pulled back in a clip, her face beaming as she alternately covered her children with kisses, before composing her features into a smile for the other mothers as she apologized for her lateness.

She was carrying a plastic bag filled with chocolate chip cookies she had made that morning, but the chocolate chips, she said, had melted in the car, so they were a bit messy, but delicious.

She didn't seem aware that some of the mothers recoiled when she dumped the bag on the grass, all the children descending like starving vultures. None of them had been remotely tempted by the carrot sticks and sliced apples the host had offered, and all were covered in melted chocolate within seconds.

Sybil shrieked with apologetic laughter, but clearly didn't care in the least. She either didn't notice, or chose not to notice, the mothers desperately reaching into their bags for Wet-Naps, shaking their heads as they caught one another's eyes, filled with disapproval.

Grace knew, instantly, she had to be friends with this woman.

"Come over and have tea," she said to Sybil when they were leaving, scribbling down her address. "Tomorrow? After preschool?"

Sybil had come, late, with three small children in tow, each of them dirtier than the last. There was also a large shaggy dog in the car that Sybil had rescued two weeks prior. She let him out the car, grasping onto a leash as the dog gratefully pulled in every direction.

"Sorry," Sybil said. "He's a bit of a terror."

"He looks like he'd love a run around. Perhaps you should let him off the leash," Grace had said doubtfully. "It's very hot."

Muttley had been let out and had proceeded to tear around the property, diving into the Hudson, attempting to catch the ducks. When he came out he shook himself out as Sybil bellowed his name, proffering handfuls of treats, before ignoring her completely to go tearing off in the other direction.

"He'll come back eventually," said Sybil.

"Grace!" Ted's voice came bellowing through the garden as Grace jumped up, leaving Clemmie with Sybil.

"What the hell is this?" Ted was standing, holding on to the collar of a wet but happy Muttley.

"It belongs to a friend."

"Get the damned thing out of here," Ted said through gritted teeth. "It just barged into the barn and shook itself all over my damn manuscript pages."

"I'm so sorry," Grace said, turning away so he wouldn't see her smile, for there was something so funny about this large, shaggy dog with the ever-present smile on its face. It was so clearly the canine version of Sybil.

"I did warn you," Sybil said. "Sorry. Shall I put him back in the car?"

"Can't we just hold him here on the leash?"

"We can try," she said. Muttley got away five minutes later, heading straight back to the barn, which brought their playdate to an abrupt end, but they tried again two days later, this time without dogs, and their friendship was forged. It helped that Sybil found Ted's rage over her dog funny. Most people were intimidated by Ted; it was refreshing to see someone who not only wasn't frightened of his rage, but didn't give a damn. Grace hoped she could learn how Sybil did it, how she was able to find Ted amusing rather than terrifying.

Years later, when Ted was raging about something and Grace was confiding in Sybil, Sybil had shaken her head. "He's just a big little boy in a bad mood," she said. "They're all overgrown little boys who need a mother figure around to tell them to stop."

It's all right for you, thought Grace. Your husband isn't an internationally known bestselling author used to having the world bend over backward for him. And yet, she saw the way Sybil was with Ted—fun, funny, natural, never sycophantic in the slightest. If Ted ever started talking about books, or writing, Sybil would start yawning and tell him she wasn't the slightest bit interested. Which she wasn't. And Ted, instead of being greatly offended, thought Sybil a riot. He adored her. She was the only one of Grace's friends that he truly had time for. She made him laugh and was guaranteed to put him in a good mood.

Sybil had a husband, Michael, who decided he didn't really want to be married or, at least, not to Sybil, and had left her a few years ago. Sybil had been fueled by hatred and a vicious, spitting fury for a little while, but then she came to realize that actually Michael was probably not a very good husband and, much to her surprise, she was much happier by herself, until she met Fred, who does seem to be her perfect match.

Always an avid gardener, she now runs courses on organic gardening and is the one person Grace can always count on. She is warm, and safe, and the one person Grace thinks of as more sister than friend.

Even if she is, still, always late.

. . .

The door bursts open as Sybil bustles in, clutching a purse that is so oversized it is more of a suitcase. She has to maneuver her way through the tables, apologizing constantly for knocking into people with her bag, until she finally reaches Grace, leaning in to kiss her cheek before setting her bag down with a sigh and sitting down.

"What the hell is in your bag?" Grace starts to laugh. "The kitchen sink?"

"Almost." Sybil hoists the bag to her lap and starts rummaging through. "Magazine on gardening, couple of tools that probably shouldn't be in there, wallet . . . God, what's this?" She pulls out a hairbrush, frowning before putting it back. "Flip-flops! There they are! I was wondering what on earth I'd done with them. And . . ." She draws out a plastic container with flourish. "These are for you."

"I can't eat those," Grace feigns unhappiness. "You know once I start I'll never stop."

"Exactly! Not that it ever shows. You're the one who's always telling me as long as it's natural you can eat it. This is pure sugar, pure butter, and pure flour. I made them on a baking binge, but I can't eat them."

"Uh-oh. What diet are you on now?"

"No gluten, no sugar. Which thankfully doesn't mean I don't get to eat good stuff. I just don't get to eat the good stuff I know how to cook, which is why I'm giving it to you."

"Not that I approve of any of your crazy diets, but why don't you just cook things you're able to eat?"

"Thanks to Sandra, I don't have to."

"Sandra?"

"Sandra! You know! Blonde? Short hair? Married to the Greek guy?"

"Of course."

"She's started a business. Organic, all-natural sweet treats, sugar free and gluten-free. She's giving them to various people to sample to get feedback before she's taking it to the stores."

"Lucky for you. And meanwhile, I get yummy cookies. These do look delicious." Grace pops the lid up, frowning as she reaches in and pulls out half a cookie. She raises an eyebrow at Sybil.

"I only had half!" says Sybil. "I couldn't help it. I was starving. I'm back on the wagon tomorrow."

Grace starts to laugh, feeling a wave of love for her friend, who is always late, always disorganized, and always, always, starving.

Grace orders the niçoise salad and an extra baguette for the table, i.e. Sybil; while Sybil has the warm goat cheese on toast, followed by mussels. And a side of fries to share—she looks at Grace for agreement and Grace smiles. Sybil will likely inhale the fries before Grace has a chance to touch them.

"Make that two orders of fries." She smiles at the waiter. "With extra mayonnaise."

"It's been ages!" Sybil says when the waiter has gone. "I've missed you. Have you been busy being glamorous and important? I did read something in the *Times* about a magazine gala where you were honored."

"That was ages ago!" Grace says. "Honestly, we've been trying to get our lives back together since Ellen left. I've been a little overwhelmed. That's why I've barely seen anyone. Between running my house and Harmont House, and looking after my husband . . ."

". . . Which is a full-time job if ever there was one."

"Exactly. I don't need to tell you what that's like, but it's all been a little much."

"Last time I spoke to you, there was someone you were trying out."

"We are now at the beginning of week three with Beth."

"And?"

"And so far she may be the greatest thing since Mary Poppins."

"Really? Does Ted think so too?"

"That's the truly extraordinary thing. My husband, possibly the most difficult man in the whole world . . ."

". . . Unless you know how to handle him."

"Well, that's just it. The only person I've seen able to handle him, apart from Ellen, is you."

"And you, my dear."

Grace sighs. "I'm really not sure I handle him all that well. But this young girl, Beth, really does. He actually seems to respect her. He's been completely calm and happy since she started. In fact, I don't think I've heard him shout once in the last two weeks."

"My God! Is that a record?"

"I think it might be. But there's nothing she's not able to do. I was nervous about giving her the bills to pay—you just never quite know and I do hate giving new people that kind of access, but I just couldn't do it myself. She not only took the bills and paid them, she also redid the whole filing system. Now you can actually see where everything is. And it's logical! Beautifully labeled and alphabetized! I hate to say this, but it's much more efficient than it ever was before."

"She sounds unbelievable."

"She is! She's unbelievably efficient and organized—the house has never looked more spotless."

"She cleans too?"

"No. She doesn't clean, but wherever she goes she organizes. I came home last week and all the chair covers were missing. She said she noticed they all looked a bit grubby, so without asking she'd just removed them all and taken them to the dry cleaners. And she hauled all the pool furniture out from the back barn and cleaned it with teak cleaner. It's ridiculous. I feel like I've died and woken up in some version of heaven."

Sybil fixes her gaze on Grace. "Is she married? How old is she? She's not a big, busty blonde who's going to steal your husband, is she?"

Grace shakes her head. "I'm reticent to ask too much, I don't want her to think I'm prying, but she's thirty-eight, although honestly, she looks thirty-two, and she's newly divorced. She didn't say much about the ex-husband, just that it didn't work out, and I quite like that. I would have felt so uncomfortable if she'd said awful things about him. It shows discretion, which is, as you know, so important to us. And her references were amazing."

"Have you had her sign a nondisclosure?"

"A what?"

"A confidentiality agreement. You must. At this point I am going to say awful things about my ex-husband, who is, as you know, a complete ass. However, I can also say something good about him, which is that he was a damned good lawyer, and he was big on the NDAs. If you're in the public eye, anyone coming into your home has the potential to make money selling a story about what your life is really like. You've been remarkably blessed with Ellen, who would rather die than talk about you, but you have to get anyone new to sign one. Get on to your lawyer and have him send one over, then get her to sign it."

"You're right. You're right. It just feels a little uncomfortable."

"A whole lot more comfortable than opening the *Enquirer* and discovering your husband beats the dogs every night and has sex with the chickens."

"Ha! We really don't have any secrets. There's nothing about our lives that would be interesting for anyone, let alone the *Enquirer*."

"That may be true, but people can and do make things up all the time. Lord, Grace. For someone who's married to such a well-known author, you can be shockingly naïve at times."

Grace extends a leg clad in old, worn-thin leggings, a pair of muddy Bogs on her feet. "Do I look like a famous writer's wife to you?" She grins, pushing aside the thought that she may not be a famous writer's wife for too much longer. The fame part continuing is questionable, given Ted's terrible recent sales, a subject she cannot discuss with anyone, preferring to keep the illusion that Ted is still one of the biggest writers in the world.

"Compared to this?" Sybil extends her own stubbly leg, a Birkenstock on the end. "Yes."

"I wanted to ask you something," Grace says, changing the subject. "I've been thinking of doing something to widen the circle at Harmont House."

"What do you mean, 'widen the circle'? Fund-raising?"

"Ultimately, yes, but I hate bringing new people in and instantly hitting them up for money. I thought of doing something a little different. You know they have an abandoned yard in the back? I thought perhaps we could do an event. You could give a talk on vegetable gardens, maybe create a small garden, and show them how to be self-sufficient. I can cook, and maybe even get one of the local chefs to come in to do a cooking demonstration—that always seems to be a big hit. We could sell tickets, have an auction. Don't you think it's a good idea?"

"Where do the new people come from?"

"That's the point. Everyone I know is already involved. I was thinking if you gave a talk, perhaps your clients would come, plus people who don't know you but would want to hear you speak."

"I'm not that well known!" Sybil says.

"Around here you are."

"I think it would need something else. How about we get one of the big local chefs to do a cooking demo with you? Something using ingredients pulled straight from your garden?"

"That's why you needed to get involved." Grace smiles. "See how clever that idea is? I would never have thought of that. Excuse me?" She signals to the waiter, who comes straight over. "Is the chef in today?" He nods. "Would you mind telling him Grace Chapman would love to say hello?" He walks off to the kitchen as Grace winks at Sybil.

"No time like the present." Sybil raises her glass in a toast.

GLUTEN-FREE COCONUT AND CHOCOLATE MACAROONS

(Serves 8)

INGREDIENTS

2 Tablespoons coconut oil or unsalted butter, melted
¼ cup almond flour
1 teaspoon vanilla extract
1 teaspoon almond extract
2 cups shredded coconut
¼ cup coconut milk
¼ cup agave nectar
1 teaspoon stevia
⅛ teaspoon sea salt
3 eggs
½ teaspoon baking powder
¼ cup dark chocolate chips

Preheat oven to 325 degrees.

Mix together coconut, almond flour, sea salt, stevia, and baking powder.

Mix coconut oil/butter with beaten eggs, vanilla and almond extract, agave, and coconut milk.

Mix wet and dry ingredients together. Fold in chocolate chips.

Mound in small pyramid-shaped heaps on an oiled baking sheet, and bake for 18-20 minutes until golden.

Cool on a wire rack.

Twelve

What are you doing with Beth?" Ted comes into the kitchen just as Grace places the pitcher of iced tea on the table, straightening up the glasses.

"She's helping me with this meeting," Grace says. "Where are my napkins?" She turns in a frenzy. "Good God. Why can't I ever find anything?" She pulls open drawers, whirling around the kitchen. "Where are the damned things?"

"Are these what you're looking for?" Ted points to the kitchen counter, where the napkins are neatly folded.

Grace's face falls. "Oh God. I did them earlier." She looks at Ted, embarrassed. This isn't what she used to be like, she thinks, unable to believe how disorganized she has become, how much she has been forgetting.

"It's our age." Ted interrupts her thoughts, as Grace wonders whether or not to point out how very much older Ted is than Grace. "You remember folding the napkins?"

"Well, yes. Now I do." She shakes her head. "You must be right. It's age. Is it okay for me to borrow Beth? Do you need her? She's just been so incredibly helpful with putting this Harmont House thing together, but if you need her, I understand."

Please don't need her, she thinks. Please be able to look after yourself just this one morning.

"Of course you can have her!" says Ted, reaching out for a mini carrot cake muffin that Grace had made earlier this morning, filling the inside with extra cream cheese frosting and topping them with a maple glaze.

"She is amazing," Grace says. "Honestly. I have no idea how we managed without her."

"Nor I," he says. "She seems to read my mind and have everything done before I've even had a chance to think about it."

"You know, she got the lumber yard to donate the wood to create the raised beds for the garden at Harmont? And she got them to send two men to build it. For free! I have no idea how she's doing it, but she seems to make friends wherever she goes, and people end up doing stuff for her."

"It must be those big brown eyes," says Ted. "She bats her eyelashes and men sink like stones."

"As long as you're not sinking like a stone."

"Darling wife." Ted steps toward Grace, grabbing her around the waist and pulling her tight. "The only woman in the world who has the capacity to make me sink like a stone is you. I sink only for you, repeatedly, and pleasurably."

Grace allows herself to rest against him for a second. If only it were like this more often. If only Ted were always this kind, this loving, this calm; how much happier everyone would be.

"Now, get out of my hair." she kisses him gently on the cheek. "People will be arriving soon."

Sybil is there, Jennifer from Harmont House, Theresa—a friend of Sybil's who begged to be involved in putting this event together, who has thus far sold more tickets than the rest of them put together—and Beth.

The garden has gone in—six raised beds, seedlings taken from Sybil's greenhouse—and they are discussing the food. Grace is planning individual fig and Camembert tarts with a hazelnut dressing to start, poached salmon with a sweet pepper compote, cucumber dill salad, and fresh new potatoes from the garden, followed by a selection of desserts.

Grace is donating not only her time, but the ingredients, the biggest expenditure going to rentals—tables, chairs, tablecloths, plates, glasses, etcetera.

"Where are we on the rentals?" Sybil looks over to her.

"All booked. I spoke to them last week and got the quote. I put the order in yesterday. Very simple, crisp white tablecloths and pretty bamboo chairs. It will look lovely, and we're all in agreement, yes? That it's now a sit-down lunch?"

"It's a bit late now!" laughs Sybil. "The event's right around the corner, but yes, everyone's expecting a sit-down. That's why we were able to increase the ticket price, but you're fine with all the cooking? Can any of us help you?"

"The chef is going to demo the fig and Camembert tart, right? You're using his recipe?" Jennifer asks.

Grace nods. "Beth's going to help me. And the chef is going to demo the food for the audience before we sit down. It's perfect. It's going to be perfect."

"I'm just worried we're overwhelming you, Grace. You're doing the cooking, the renting, and the flowers."

"I'm not really doing the flowers," says Grace. "You're just clipping them from my garden. Frankly I'm delighted. The peonies will be fantastic and you'll get them before they start drooping. It's always such a waste when the heavy rain comes and washes off their petals. I'm having nothing to do with the floral arrangements other than giving you full access to my gardens." She laughs. "Nothing for me to do."

"Are you sure there's nothing we can take off your hands? I've sent all the invitations and I've nearly filled the goodie bags with donated items. I have time."

"Absolutely not," says Grace. "I am fine."

Later, after the meeting, Beth types up the notes and emails them to everyone, clearly defining what jobs are left and who is doing what.

"Can I do something to help?" she says, taking the notes in to Grace in the kitchen. "How can I make myself busy?"

Grace pauses. "You could help with the grocery shopping," she says eventually. "That would be wonderful. And maybe just chase the party rental place. I never received the confirmation."

"No problem," says Beth with a smile. "And nothing else?"

"Can they clone you?" Grace turns to her. "You are amazing. Honestly, Beth, you've come in and in a matter of weeks you've turned our lives upside down, in the very best possible way."

"I'm so happy," says Beth, her face lighting up with that disarming smile. "There was one other thing . . . completely changing the subject, I noticed you have a pile of clothes in the closet. Is that the dry-cleaning because I'm going out now to do some errands."

"Thank you for the reminder! It's actually all for charity. Clemmie will occasionally steal my clothes, but she says these are all too grown up for her. I'm having a much-needed spring clean."

"Oh, but those clothes are beautiful! Couldn't you sell them instead? I'm happy to put them on eBay."

"Thank you, but I don't think that's a good use of anyone's time, and honestly, I'm not sure it's worth it for the hassle. You know." She peers at Beth. "If there's anything at all in there you want, please help yourself. I'd be thrilled for you to take whatever you want."

"Really?" That smile again. "You wouldn't mind?"

"No! As long as they go to a good home, that's all I care about."

Beth flings her arms around Grace and hugs her tight. When she steps back, Grace sees, much to her amazement, there are tears in Beth's eyes.

"I'm sorry," she says, wiping them away. "I know this seems like a bit of an overreaction, but I've been desperately paying off the debt of school, and I've had no money to spend on myself for ages. I don't even remember the last time I bought myself new clothes. You have no idea what an incredible gift you're giving me."

Grace feels her own eyes prick with tears. This poor woman. How hard she has worked, and how conscientious she is. She is swept at once with a wave of almost maternal love as she reaches for Beth's hand and squeezes it.

"You're part of our family now," she says. "You don't have to worry about anything anymore. We'll make sure you're looked after."

Beth's eyes fill with tears again. "I'm sorry," she says, as, this time, Grace takes her in her arms, soothes her just as she has done so many times with Clemmie. "I just didn't expect you and Ted to be so wonderful. I didn't expect to feel like I've come home. My childhood was just so awful, I never knew what it was like to have a proper family."

Grace nods, but says nothing. She knows what it is like to have an awful childhood. Her entire life has been filled with shame about her mother, fear that people may find out, and guilt at never having been able to do anything to save her.

In many ways, her mother dying when Grace had just turned twenty-four should have been a relief. Certainly, relief was the first emotion she felt. But that relief quickly gave way to guilt. A guilt that continues to inform her life today; a guilt that has been behind almost every decision she has ever made.

What kind of difficulties Beth comes from, Grace understands, and knowing this, sees her heart soften even further for this young woman who has so unexpectedly entered their lives. Grace couldn't help her mother, but she can help the women at Harmont. And she can also help Beth.

At 3:26 a.m., Grace is wide awake. Again. She hasn't slept most nights over the past couple of weeks. It could be that she is worried about the event at Harmont House, or could simply be, as she suspects, middle age. Tonight she realizes she has been dreaming about Patrick. How odd, after all this time, to find her unconscious mind going to her childhood friend.

Lydia was not in the dream, but perhaps this is a sign that she needs to call her. It has been a couple of months since they spoke. Might it mean, she wonders briefly, that she should call Patrick? But they have only seen each other less than a handful of times in years—Patrick's career taking him all over the world. The last time she had seen him it had been strained.

Eton mess! That's why she is thinking of Patrick. He was the first person to talk about a dessert she had never heard of—a froth of whipped cream, strawberries, and meringue—that she came to love. That must be why he was hovering in her subconscious.

Either way, it is time to call Lydia. She will. In the morning she will. In the meantime, how to go back to sleep when she is so very wide awake?

She doesn't like taking pills, but has resorted to sneaking Ted's Ambien, so desperate is she to break the pattern of waking up at 3 a.m. to go to the bathroom and finding that by the time she climbs back into bed, her mind is fully awake and sleep is no longer an option.

Perhaps the lack of sleep helps explain her moodiness. Or perhaps that too is middle age. Life is running smoothly again, thanks to Beth, in a way it hasn't for ages. Grace has nothing to worry about, yet frequently she finds herself irritated.

It must just be lack of sleep, she tells herself, climbing out of bed and walking into the bathroom, reaching for the medicine cabinet above Ted's sink. I will surely be back to myself soon.

ETON MESS

(Serves 8–10)

INGREDIENTS

4 cups strawberries

4 teaspoons sugar

2 teaspoons water

2 cups heavy whipping cream

1 packet of individual meringue nests (Or, follow the pavlova recipe on page 30 to make your own meringues, but it's much easier to buy premade meringues.)

Hull and chop all strawberries quite roughly. Place half in bowl with 2 teaspoons of sugar to macerate, and leave for around 1 hour in the fridge.

Take remaining chopped strawberries, place in pan with 2 teaspoons of sugar and 2 teaspoons of water. Cook gently uncovered for around 10 minutes until strawberries have softened. Remove from heat and blend into a puree. Set aside.

Whip cream in a large, cold bowl until thick peaks form. Roughly crumble 8 meringue nests, fold meringue and strawberries into cream. Drizzle with strawberry puree and fold lightly, but make sure you can still see threads of the puree running through.

Reserve a handful of fresh strawberries and a teaspoon of juice on each to serve.

Thirteen

No one would have believed it was possible to create a garden out of a wasteland in just under a week. Between Grace, Sybil, Jennifer, and Beth, not only have beds been built and planted, but sod has been donated and laid to create a perfect green lawn, boxwood balls edge the grass, and hydrangeas, given to them by Linda McLellan, one of their most important patrons, spill their blue flowers over the edges. Inside, the dining room table is crammed with vases stuffed full of peonies, waiting to be moved onto the rental tables as soon as they arrive.

The garden at Harmont House looks beautiful. The chef is busy setting up his demo area outside, Sybil putting the finishing touches to the garden. Inside, the kitchen is covered with aluminum trays and baking sheets, carefully Saran Wrapped, filled with delicious food created by Grace.

"Where is Wondergirl now?" Sybil calls. "Shouldn't all the rentals be here by now? I thought they normally drop off the day before. We've only got two hours to go and I'm in a panic. How are we going to set the tables?"

Grace admits this is pushing it, but Beth has assured her everything will be fine. "They'll be here any second," she says. "We can manage it."

"We have to plate all these tarts, and right now we have no plates," grumbles Sybil. "I've heard of cutting it fine, but this is ridiculous."

"Calm down, Sybil," Grace says, mostly to stop herself from panicking. "Why don't you come with me and help brief the ladies on waitressing. They want me to go over what they have to do one more time. Don't worry." Grace forces a smile as she walks into the kitchen, forgetting about the stress when she catches sight of the residents of Harmont House done up in all their finery, including, in some cases, extravagant hats that are usually reserved for church. Their excitement is contagious and Grace cannot help but give each of the women a tight hug. Some of the women have been here almost a year, others as new as three weeks, but Grace loves each and every one as if they were her sisters.

"This is for you," she says, beaming at them as she wipes away a tear. "This is all to help each of you get back on your feet and reclaim your lives."

"Wow!" Grace turns to hear Sybil whistle as Beth walks into the kitchen, as Sybil claps her hands together. "Look how beautiful you look!"

Beth gestures to Grace. "I have Grace to thank. She gave me these clothes! I feel like a princess!" She twirls, taking a bow at the end as the ladies in the kitchen applaud. "I love them all," she says to Grace, hand on her heart, as Grace smiles, agreeing how lovely the clothes look on Beth.

When she had offered the clothes to Beth, she hadn't thought there would be much that Beth would choose, plus there was no doubt Beth was bigger than her and that many of the clothes—the tight, fitted jackets in particular—would not fit her.

But here Beth is, in the Lanvin jacket and gray silk skirt. Grace had never thought to put those two items together—she always wore that particular jacket buttoned up, with camel pants, but it does indeed look wonderful on Beth, who is wearing it loose, casual, and has teamed it with a chunky shark's tooth necklace. It looks better than Grace could ever have expected, not least of all because up until very recently this jacket, surely, would not have fit Beth, would have been, surely, at least two sizes too small.

"You're so tiny!" Grace exclaims. "I never realized we were exactly the same size. In fact, I think you're smaller than me."

"I wasn't," Beth reassures her, her face serious. "I've been on a huge diet."

"You look incredible. Not that you needed to lose any weight."

"I did to fit into your clothes!" Beth laughs. "And I'm so glad I did. I feel like a new person. Actually, I feel like you, only the ugly version."

"Beth!" Grace instantly reprimands her. "Are you kidding? You're beautiful."

"I'm okay," Beth says. "But I'm not you. I'll never be you."

"And nor should you be." Grace is gentle. "You're perfect as you are."

As Grace tries the party rental place yet again, having already left a number of messages, she realizes there is something bothering her. She cannot quite figure it out. It is a feeling of being unsettled and she knows it has something to do with Beth, with Beth in her clothes, but still, she cannot put her finger on it.

The phone is answered! Finally! A human voice!

"This is Grace Chapman. I'm wondering what time our rentals will be arriving. The event starts in two hours and there's nothing here. We're all starting to get a bit panicky." Grace forces a laugh.

"Hold on a minute, Mrs. Chapman. Let me see what's going on." There is a pause. "Mrs. Chapman? Are you there? We have the event down for next Thursday, the twenty-eighth."

"What?" Grace's voice is a shriek. "No! I filled out the form myself. It's the twenty-first. It's *today*! It's in two hours!"

"I'm so sorry, Mrs. Chapman, but we definitely have it as the twenty-eighth. Twelve round tables of ten, one hundred twenty bamboo chairs, white linen tablecloths, one hundred twenty white dinner plates, salad plates, dessert bo—"

"Yes! I know what I ordered! But it's today! It's now! What am I supposed to do? You have to send it over now. We can start the event later, but we have to have it now."

"I'm so sorry, Mrs. Chapman, but that's impossible. Our warehouse is in New Jersey and there's no way we can get you anything today. I'm sorry."

"But . . . how did this happen? I filled out the form myself. This isn't my mistake."

Deeply apologetic, the woman at the party rental company taps a few buttons on the computer. "It looks like the date was changed on the fourteenth. By phone."

"No!" Grace insists, on the verge of tears. "I didn't call. The date was never changed. Oh God. What the hell am I supposed to do?"

"What?" Sybil just stares at her as the horror dawns. "How did this happen?"

"I have no idea." Grace is almost babbling. "But what the hell are we supposed to do? We have a hundred and twenty people who have paid a fortune for a sit-down lunch and there's nowhere to sit down, no tables, no plates, no cutlery."

"Oh Jesus." Sybil moans, burying her face in her hands. "Maybe we can bring the dining table into the garden and use it as a buffet and people can stand."

"What about plates?" Grace says. "Napkins?"

"Paper and plastic. Not very elegant, but what else can you do? Maybe we can get hold of those nice square plastic plates. At least those are a bit nicer. Where's Beth. Let's send her. She's resourceful."

"Beth!" Beth turns at the sound of her name and walks over as Grace watches her, frowning.

"Beth? There's been a major screw-up with the party rental. They have the wrong date. They thought it was next week." Grace's voice is quivering with shock.

"What?" Beth looks shocked. "But I confirmed the date by email on the thirteenth."

"You never telephoned?"

"No! Why would I telephone? I can forward you the original email if you'd like to see it."

"Never mind. What matters now is trying to salvage this mess. We'll stay here and move what tables we can outside, but you need to find plates, flatware, and glasses. If we have to do paper we will, but please try and find something more elegant. I can't believe how much we charged for the tickets and we're having people stand around eating with plastic knives and forks . . ." Grace groans at the thought.

"Don't worry." Beth lays a hand on her arm. "I'll go now and see what I can find."

The event was not the elegant affair Grace had imagined. The few guests who decided to stay were left standing in the burning hot sun, their heels sinking into the grass, for three hours. They ate their fig and Camembert tarts and poached salmon with sweet pepper confit off X-Men paper plates, with Pinkalicious napkins, drank their Prosecco and peach nectar drinks out of oversize red plastic cups.

There were, according to Beth, no white paper plates or napkins. The only things available given the time constraints were these children's plates. Grace has no idea how this is possible—did everyone in the entire Palisades/New Jersey area suddenly decide to have a party today and buy all the white paper goods? But she has no time to question.

It was a disaster in her eyes the minute she knew the rentals weren't going to turn up. The fact that they are eating off Wolverine's face doesn't make it any worse, only more ridiculous.

Grace Chapman, known for her elegant, stylish parties, her gatherings always the most sought after in town, is today a laughingstock. The *New York Times* is here, covering the event, which had thrilled Grace—the more attention for Harmont House the better—but she knows full well the story will now focus on the terrible aspects of the event, rather than the importance of the cause.

There was a mass exodus after the cooking demonstration. Standing on grass in heels was just too uncomfortable, and that they were expected to eat standing too? Well. It was far more comfortable to run to one of the little restaurants nearby. They had already paid, had done their bit, and anyway, who would ever notice?

Had one or two left, no one would have known, but almost half the people snuck out of the event, leaving sixty-seven good sports who happily bid on the silent auction, but still didn't manage to raise anything near the amount they all anticipated.

Grace has been fighting tears all day. Throughout the event she has forced a smile, despite the mortification threatening to undo her. She cannot believe how disastrous an event it is; cannot believe how badly it has gone wrong, how humiliated she is.

Her reputation as a hostess is now something of a joke. Not that it should matter. At the end of the party, she walked past two women she knows vaguely from town and overheard them whispering about how awful it was, how Grace should be ashamed of herself, charging a hundred and fifty dollars a ticket to stand in the sun and eat oily salmon off children's paper plates.

As the event finishes, Grace takes some chairs back into the living room, hoping she might be able to stay there, won't have to go out and face anyone any longer, for her pretense at laughing it off is now almost impossible to maintain and she is on the brink of tears.

"Grace? Are you all right?" She looks up to see Clarissa Moore, a tall, elegant blonde in the doorway, concern etched on her face.

"Clarissa! So good to see you!" Grace forces a smile as she turns to a woman she had become friendly with after meeting her on vacation. Ted approved of "the Moores," which was rare, and they had driven over to Westport a few times to have dinner or brunch at the Aspetuck Country Club. "How lovely to see you! It's been far too long. How's Mike? And that delicious little Maggie?"

"They're all great," Clarissa says. "And I'm so pleased I came, although sorry so many people left. They missed out. The food was delicious and I loved the cooking demonstration."

Grace sighs, knowing Clarissa is trying to make her feel better. "You didn't mind eating off X-Men plates?"

"I think mine was actually Despicable Me." Clarissa laughs. "Minions. It was sweet—I wish Maggie was here, she would have loved it! In the grand scheme of things, this really wasn't so bad. So we didn't get to sit down and we ate off children's plates. So what? The point of it all is that it's for a good cause. The rest is just details." She takes Grace's hands. "Trust me, when you've battled breast cancer, these are the last things you worry about."

"You're right." Grace is shocked into putting it into the right perspective, if only temporarily. "Of course you're right. This is totally irrelevant. I'm going to just forget all about it."

"Good girl. And let's get together soon. We're back to Sandy Lane this year, and it would be so great if we were there at the same time again."

"Let's definitely talk!" Grace says, and the smile remains on her face until Clarissa has left the room, after which Grace buries her head in her hands.

She can't speak to anyone. She doesn't find Sybil and tell her she's leaving, just slips out and drives home, pulling onto the side of the road on the way in order for her tears of shame and mortification to fall.

• • •

Sybil phones the next day. And the next. Grace doesn't talk to anyone. Her mortification threatens to overwhelm her. She doesn't want to see anyone, knows how her neighbors love a touch of schadenfreude—who doesn't?—knows that she will be the talk of the town.

For a week she sees no one, speaks to no one, returns no calls. She can barely speak, the weight of depression forcing her shoulders down. Is this how my mother felt? she wonders, as she so often does during times in her life when things are not going so well. Am I going to end up like her? Is this how it starts? Not sleeping. Depression. Obsession. For all she can think about is the disaster of the party.

When Sybil shows up, a week later, Grace is in her pajamas at two o'clock in the afternoon.

"Enough," Sybil says, putting the kettle on. "It wasn't what we hoped for, but you need to pull yourself together. It's done. So, big deal, it's giving everyone something to talk about today, but trust me, it will be replaced by something else soon . . . Tell me again, Grace," Sybil continues, her voice flat, clearly as upset as Grace. "How did this happen? How did they get the date wrong?"

"I don't know," Grace says. "It's clearly their mistake. Both Beth and I confirmed in writing. The woman said someone phoned to change the date, but that's just not possible."

What Grace doesn't say is that the woman at the party rental business said that Grace herself had phoned to announce the changing of the date. The day after the last email confirmation of the original date. She was definite. *Grace* had phoned and changed the date.

But I can't have done, thinks Grace. There have been many times recently when she has worried she is going mad—things she forgets, confusion, showing up to things on the wrong day—but this is not something she would have forgotten and, more to the point, this isn't something she would have done. It makes no sense. Why on earth would she do that? This is absolutely the rental company's mistake. Not that it matters now. The mistake was made and they have paid the price.

Yet seeds of doubt creep in. Her memory has been suffering as of late. Even though she knows she would not have made this call—there would have been no reason ever to make this call—there are plenty of recent examples of how her memory has failed her.

"It doesn't make sense to me either. But we have to move on, Grace. I promise you people have started forgetting about it already. You need to pull yourself together and get dressed. Did you have lunch?"

Grace, who has barely eaten anything for the past week, shakes her head.

"Get dressed. Let's go into town and grab something to eat."

"I can't," Grace says. "Please, Sybil. I just don't feel ready to see anyone."

"Because they had to stand for a couple of hours and eat off paper plates? Please! Everyone understands that these things happen. It really isn't nearly as big a deal as you think, and my God, Grace, it isn't even your fault. I have no idea why they think someone phoned, but clearly they are mistaken. Let's just put it behind us. I've seen a ton of people this week and everyone has been incredibly sympathetic. Hiding away at home just makes this whole thing bigger than it has to be. The quicker you get out and about, the better."

"I'm just so tired." Grace slumps at the kitchen table. "I haven't been sleeping, and I really don't feel up to going out."

Sybil stares at her friend, worried. "Grace? Is there something more going on? Because one bad party should not floor you in this way. Is everything okay? Everything with you and Ted okay?"

"It's fine," Grace says, although her voice is flat.

"You just seem depressed. Is it possible that this is unrelated to the event? That you may be suffering from a slight depression?"

"I'm fine," Grace snaps, a little too shrilly. "Just a little down. Not depressed. That's too extreme. I just have . . . the blues. It will pass. I get this from time to time. Nothing to worry about. Usually I just cloister myself away for a bit until it passes. It doesn't last long."

"I'm just worried about you." Sybil reaches out a hand and squeezes Grace's. "This isn't like you."

"There is something else that's bothering me." Grace frowns, looking up at Sybil. "Something about Beth. I know this may sound silly, but I gave her a load of clothes the other day, the ones she was wearing at the party."

"They looked great on her."

"I know. But this has been bothering me ever since then. I don't remember getting rid of the scarf she was wearing."

"It was definitely yours?"

"Oh, yes. Ted bought it for me for my birthday four years ago and it's my favorite scarf. My memory may be bad, but there's no way I would have got rid of that scarf. That scarf would have been hanging on the rack at the other end of the closet. What was Beth doing with the scarf around her neck?"

"So what's the big deal?" says Sybil. "Ask her."

"I know. I just don't want to rock the boat, but the more I think about it, the more certain I am that there is something amiss. I love that scarf. And I don't want to even consider the possibility that Beth may have . . . well. You know." She can't even bring herself to use the word "stole." "But I can't think of another explanation."

"Is she here now?"

"In the barn."

"Get dressed, then go out and ask her. I'm going to make a move anyway, I have some errands in town I need to do and if you're not going to join me for lunch, I'll leave and get started. Good luck. Let me know what happens."

Beth? Can I have a word?" Grace pushes open the door to Beth's office, grateful that she can hear Ted tapping on his computer, Bach emanating from his room at the other end of the barn. This is a private conversation; she is glad he won't be able to hear.

"Beth, there's something that I need to talk to you about. The clothes I gave you, the outfit you wore the other day to the event . . ."

"Thank you again!" Beth's face is so open and grateful, Grace hesitates, reconsidering, wondering if she is going mad. "I love everything!"

Surely, if Beth was guilty, something in her face would have given it away, thinks Grace, but she cannot stop now.

"You had a scarf around your neck that Ted gave me for my birthday four years ago. That scarf wasn't on the pile of things I was giving away." Grace keeps her voice even. "That's one of my favorite scarves. I would not get rid of that scarf."

Beth's eyes widen in shock. "Oh my God! Grace! I'm so sorry! It wasn't on the pile, but it was on the floor and I thought . . . Oh God. This is completely my mistake. I thought it had dropped out of the pile. Grace, I am so sorry. This was all my fault. I just presumed . . ." She shakes her head, quietly berating herself.

"I know better," she mutters as if to herself. "I know I always get into trouble when I presume. I'm so sorry." She looks at Grace. "I almost asked you. I almost asked you if you were sure about the scarf, but I didn't, and now you must think I stole it . . ."

"No," Grace says, flooded with relief. "I just knew there was some kind of mix-up, and I figured it must have somehow got into the pile by mistake. I thought maybe the cleaners put it there."

"No," Beth says. "It was entirely my fault. I promise you from now on I will not make presumptions. I will check with you before doing anything."

"Don't be silly." Grace smiles. "It was an honest mistake. I'm glad I said something. I just couldn't remember what I'd done, but I love the scarf, and I just couldn't figure out why I'd give it away."

"You didn't! I'll bring it back tomorrow!" Beth says as they both laugh, that unsettling feeling now a mere shadow of what it was. Not gone, not entirely, but Grace knows that has everything to do with feeling low, which is probably everything to do with her hormones and nothing to do with Beth.

But mostly she is grateful she isn't going crazy. She has been forgetting so many things recently, has been so absentminded, it was entirely possible that she had given away her favorite scarf. Thank God I'm not going crazy, is the only thing that keeps running through her mind.

FIG AND CAMEMBERT TARTS

(Serves 8)

INGREDIENTS

For the pastry

1 cup all-purpose flour

1 stick butter

1 teaspoon salt

½ cup ice water

For the filling

1 cup heavy cream

2 sprigs thyme

1 Tablespoon Dijon mustard

2 whole Camembert cheeses, broken into pieces

4 egg yolks

1 egg
4 ripe figs, halved
Salt and pepper for seasoning

For the dressing
½ cup extra virgin olive oil
1 Tablespoon red wine vinegar
Juice of ½ lemon
1 teaspoon Dijon mustard
¼ cup chopped hazelnuts
Large bunch of chopped, flat-leaf parsley
Salt and pepper for seasoning

Preheat oven to 350 degrees.

Dice butter and add to a Cuisinart with flour and salt. Pulse gently until it is like damp sand. Very slowly pour the ice water in. You probably won't use the entire amount—you want just enough to bring the dough together. Remove dough, cover in clingfilm, and place in fridge for half an hour.

Grease a 9-inch tart pan with removable base. Lay pastry on top gently, press into all corners, trim off excess. Prick base all over with a fork. Chill in fridge while making filling.

Gently heat the cream on the stove with the thyme, Dijon mustard, salt, and pepper. Drop Camembert pieces into cream. Remove from heat while cheese melts.

Blind bake the pastry crust by lining it with greaseproof paper, pouring in either dry beans or rice, and cooking in oven for 8-10 minutes.

While the tart is blind baking, crack 4 egg yolks and 1 whole egg into a bowl and slowly pour the cream mixture over them, stirring all the time so as not to cook the eggs with the hot liquid. Season well with salt and plenty of black pepper.

Turn the oven down to 320 degrees. Pour the mixture into the pastry case and place the 8 fig halves cut side up. Make sure this is done in a way that when the tart is sliced, each portion has its own fig.

Place the pastry case back into the oven and cook for 20-25 minutes, or until the mixture has set.

Once cooked, leave to cool for about half an hour before slicing and serving with the dressing.

Prepare the dressing while the tart is cooking. Combine the hazelnuts and parsley in a bowl with the Dijon mustard, lemon juice, and red wine vinegar. Season with salt and pepper before slowly adding in the olive oil, mixing all the time until smooth, then drizzle over tart.

Fourteen

"Clemmie! What are you doing here?" Grace is putting together the ingredients for her pork and lemon patties—as Clemmie bursts into the kitchen. She sets them down on the stove and gathers her daughter in her arms. "Especially," she steps back and frowns, "at four o'clock in the afternoon on a Thursday. Shouldn't you be at work?"

"I should," Clemmie says. "But I needed a mental health afternoon."

"And you didn't tell me?"

"Dad told me you'd been a bit low since the event at Harmont House. He's worried about you. I wanted to surprise you, hoped it might cheer you up."

"It has." Grace smiles, once again squeezing her daughter in her arms, wondering why her joy at this unexpected visit could bring her so close to tears.

The kitchen door opens as Beth walks in, her arms laden with files.

"Clemmie? You remember Beth?"

"Of course! Hey, Beth! Nice to see you. I hope my parents are treating you well."

"Are you kidding?" Beth smiles as she slips the files into Grace's office. "I've never been happier in my life."

Grace beams. "Really? You didn't tell me that."

"It's true. This really is my dream job. I love that every day is different, and I love that it almost feels like two completely separate jobs. I have the work with Ted, which is really studious and intense and quiet, and that kind of focus calms me down, which is always what I need, but then there's the household stuff, and helping you, and Harmont House, which is frenetic and busy, and so much fun, and that's the work that keeps me happy. I need both and I never thought I'd find it all in one job."

"That just about sums up my parents," laughs Clemmie. "One's intense, the other's crazy."

"Clemmie!" Grace knows she is joking, that Clemmie has no idea that Grace has spent her whole life terrified she may turn into her mother. That when "the blues" hit, they are always made so much worse by Grace's secret fear that this is when she's going crazy, this is the beginning of the end.

"Your mom's not crazy," Beth says, placing a protective arm around a grateful Grace. "I adore her. She's one of the kindest, warmest, most generous people I've ever met."

Grace turns to meet her eyes, to see tears welling in them. "Oh, Beth," she says softly. "What a lovely, lovely thing to say. And what a treasure you are."

"We're both lucky." Beth swallows the tears away and busies herself putting the food away. "Did you want to have any of this for dinner tonight?" she asks.

"I think that would be lovely. What are you doing for dinner later?" she asks Beth suddenly. She knows so little about Beth's personal life, she now realizes. The bare minimum. Divorced. Childless, although she seems, in so many ways, so much younger than her years, Grace wouldn't expect her to have a husband, the responsibilities of children.

She lives alone in a small house with a garden she loves, and may or may not cook for herself. She has all these incredible skills and no one to share them with. Grace is struck by a sudden sense of Beth's loneliness. This lonely young woman, who has done so much for them, who has, in so many ways, almost entirely transformed their lives, who has virtually no life of her own.

Not even a cat to keep her company.

"Join us," she says to Beth. "Please. I'm insisting. Stay for dinner. Unless you have other plans, but if not, stay. I know Clemmie would love it too."

"I . . ." Beth looks unsure.

"Please," Grace says. "Ted and I would love it. And it's not like it's even a proper thank you. For heaven's sake, it's only supper in the kitchen. Just stay. Family dinner."

Beth smiles, pleasure all over her face. "I'd love to," she says as Grace smiles. It is the very least they can do.

"I'm just going to see Dad," says Clemmie as Grace smiles again. She adores her daughter, but there is a special link between Clemmie and Ted that Grace cannot compete with. Perhaps it is because they are both writers—introverts who also need to be around people, but only on their own terms; perhaps it is merely the incontrovertible daddy-daughter link, but either way, when Ted and Clemmie get together, Grace always feels slightly like the odd man out.

They have the same humor, find the same things ridiculous. Ted would never shout at Clemmie or talk to her with the disdain he sometimes has when he talks to Grace.

Watching Clemmie snake her way down the garden path, Grace sighs and turns back to Beth. "Will you take them down some of these?" she says, pulling some patties from the fridge. "I'll just take a moment to heat them up."

• • •

Beth grins as she looks around the table. "You have an amazing family. I never had anything like this. I would have given anything for this."

"Thank you," says Grace. "That's a sweet thing to say." Grace puts down her glass of wine and waits for Beth to say more.

"You really are lucky, you know. My family was nothing like this," says Beth. "My father was an alcoholic and my mother was the classic enabler. She spent her life trying to keep my father out of trouble—dragging him out of bars and making excuses for him when he was too hungover to go to work. It didn't make for much of a childhood."

"How did you cope?" Clemmie, always fascinated by other people's stories, leans forward.

"Mostly by having to become a mother myself. I was cooking well before most other children are even allowed anywhere near knives and stoves. I had to, or my little brother and sister wouldn't eat."

"But that's awful," says Grace, who feels a sharp stab of pain, knowing exactly what it is like to grow up in a household like that, to take on the responsibility of a parent long before it is time. "You never had a childhood."

"I didn't, but it never seemed awful at the time—it was just my life; all that I knew. And in some ways, today I'm grateful for it. However odd that may sound, I definitely wouldn't be who I am had my childhood been different. It's also why I love reading so much—the only place I felt safe was buried in the pages of a book, preferably one with a happy family. Other kids I knew wanted to be writers, or doctors, or change the world in some way when they grew up, but I knew I loved helping people. That's what I'm best at. And now, here, I get to do it."

"And," Grace reaches over the table and lays a hand on top of hers, "you get to be part of our family."

"I hope so," says Beth. "I am so incredibly grateful to be here."

"As are we to have you," says Ted gruffly. "Who wants some more of this delicious food?"

It is these moments, thinks Grace, later, when she and Clemmie are standing side by side in the kitchen, washing up the last of the dishes, these mundane, ordinary moments that contain the real magic of life.

Beth has gone home, Ted is walking the dogs, and she is here with her daughter, awash with gratitude and love for all that is good in her life, the humiliation of what happened at Harmont House now eased, although every time she thinks of it she feels her body physically clench in horror.

It doesn't matter, she tells herself. None of it matters. All that matters is my family.

Clemmie lays the dish towel down and looks at her mother. "I love Beth," she says. "What a treasure! You and Dad must be thrilled!"

"We are. She's . . . extraordinary. I think of her as Superwoman because there seems to be little she can't do. She's making my life so very much easier, and your father? He thinks the sun shines out of her behind."

"What?"

Grace smiles. "An old expression from home. But he adores her. So far there hasn't been a single complaint." Grace sighs, unsure whether to say anything before taking a deep breath. "You do think she is wonderful, then?"

Clemmie peers at her mother. "I do. But there's something on your mind, isn't there? Something you're not sure about?"

"I don't know. I have no reason to be unsure about anything, but there is something I can't quite put my finger on."

"I actually think you're wrong," says Clemmie. "Usually I think you're the most perceptive woman in the world, but I don't get any weird feeling about Beth. I think she's pretty damn perfect."

"You're right, you're right," says Grace, pushing that ever-so-slight feeling of unease away. Trying not to think about whether there was any possibility that Beth might have deliberately sabotaged the event the other week, might have deliberately slipped the scarf off the rack at the end of the closet and added it to her pile.

But no. That is ridiculous. Almost as ridiculous as Grace phoning and changing the date.

PORK AND LEMON PATTIES

(Serves 4)

INGREDIENTS

½ cup Panko breadcrumbs, divided in half
1 pound minced pork
1 lemon
Large bunch of flat-leafed parsley, roughly chopped
6 sprigs thyme
2 heaped Tablespoons Parmesan
10 anchovy filets, finely chopped
2 Tablespoons butter
2 Tablespoons olive oil
1 cup chicken stock
Salt and pepper for seasoning

For dipping sauce

½ cup plain Greek yogurt
½ cup mayonnaise
2 cloves garlic, minced
Handful of grated parsley
Salt and pepper

Grate zest of lemon into pork and ¼ cup of breadcrumbs. Add lemon juice, parsley, thyme, Parmesan, and anchovies. Season generously and mix.

Make about 18 balls, roughly a heaped tablespoon, and flatten slightly.

Roll in remaining breadcrumbs, melt oil and butter together, and fry in small batches for around 4-5 minutes on each side. Do NOT crowd the pan. When all are browned, pour in stock, bring to boil, and simmer for 20 minutes.

Can be served with a dipping sauce made by mixing together yogurt, mayonnaise, garlic, parsley, salt, and pepper.

Fifteen

Sybil clatters through the kitchen door, dumping her oversized bag in the middle of the floor as she always does, turning as someone walks into the room.

"I'm sorry I'm la—" She stops, laughs. "Good Lord! Beth? You look completely different! You've changed your hair!"

"Do you like it?" Beth smiles and twirls, tilting her head to the side.

"I do," says Sybil. "It actually looks fantastic. You look . . . older. Which should be an insult, but it's a compliment. It's very sophisticated. It really frames your face."

"I'm so glad," says Beth. "I was hoping for a bit more sophistication. It's hard being around Grace all the time, she's just so elegant."

"I'd say you're catching up," Sybil says with a laugh. "Especially in that outfit. Very Grace Chapman."

Beth blushes and smiles shyly. "Thank you. I'm hoping it's the start of a whole new me. Grace is in the garden. Shall I get her for you?"

"No, don't worry." Sybil heads for the back door. "I'll go out there myself."

"Grace!" she calls, spotting Grace just emerging from the chicken coop. "Any eggs for me?"

"Help yourself," Grace calls back, and as she draws closer, Sybil looks at her with concern. Grace looks drawn, tired. And ineffably sad.

"Grace?" Sybil's voice is gentle as she lays a hand on her friend's arm. "Is everything okay?"

Everything is not okay. At 2:12 a.m., Grace woke with a start, her heart pounding, her body flooded with anxiety. Did she have a bad dream? She didn't remember, but that was the only reason she could come up with.

The Ambien was all finished. A few nights previously she tried Tylenol PM, then felt groggy and drugged almost all the next day. She lay in bed for a while, attempting to take slow, calming breaths, focusing only on the breath leaving her body, then coming back in, but every few seconds her mind started clenching in agitation. Eventually she threw back the covers and climbed out of bed.

Throwing on a robe, she went downstairs and put the kettle on for tea. Caffeine in tea has never kept her awake, not that it matters now. There was no chance of her going to sleep for at least a couple of hours, if her recent pattern is anything to go by, although this night she wasn't just awake; she felt agitated, tense, with no reason why.

Sitting at the kitchen table and attempting to read the *New York Times* didn't help. She couldn't focus on the articles, ended up flicking through the magazine, quickly turning the pages, her eyes scanning each one, pausing only briefly if a photograph spoke to her.

She needed something to do, something to focus her mind . . . she looked up, a light in her eyes.

The mudroom closet!

She had been meaning to sort through it for months, never finding the right time. Beth has been begging her to do it, but Grace kept saying no, knowing there were too many personal things she would have to go through herself. Now was surely the right time, the perfect time! She had hours to sort through shoes that belonged to Clemmie, that should have been discarded years ago; cardboard boxes stacked on the shelves containing God knows what; yards of hangers and coats tightly squished together, no one remembering which coat belongs to whom, or whether it was still needed.

Grace opened the door and took a deep breath. It was overwhelming, but once she got started, she knew it would be easy. Armed with a pile of trash bags and two large boxes—one for charity, one for Harmont House—she started with the shoes. Her natural inclination had always been to keep everything, *just in case*. What if Clemmie came home next week desperate for her old hiking boots that she hadn't worn since she was fifteen? What then?

Grace contemplated the hiking boots in her hand, then shrugged and put them in the Harmont House box. If Clemmie should show up wanting hiking boots, Grace would have to buy her another pair, and insist she take them to her own apartment. No more clutter allowed.

The shoes led to the coats—my *God*! Where did all these coats come from? Acres upon acres of rain jackets in various states of distress, some so old and ragged they were rain jackets in name alone.

Piles of umbrellas pushed to the back of the closet, buried under old boots and heavy boxes, their spokes crooked and bent.

At the back, the piles of boxes. Shoeboxes stuffed with photographs when photographs were three-by-five prints, Clemmie when she was tiny, family vacations Grace hadn't thought about for years, Ted gazing at Clemmie with sheer adoration and joy on his face, a disbelief that he could create a child so perfect.

She paused, took time to go through these photographs, each one bringing back a vivid memory. She and Ted on the Ponte Vecchio, she in his arms, both looking so young, so beautiful; so carefree.

She frowned. Life did feel carefree back then. In fact, life, her adult life, had always felt carefree to some extent, until recently. Why had life become so . . . difficult. How had one event the ability to send her spiraling down to a place that felt very different from where she had been only a few months ago?

Grace had always felt unending gratitude for all the good things in her life, but suddenly there seemed to be problems, hiccups, even though Grace couldn't name them. On the surface, nothing had changed, or nothing that should be causing her this vague but omnipresent anxiety.

It was almost, she realized, a sense of foreboding. She felt as if life was getting ready to throw something at them, only she didn't know what. She also knew, intellectually, that this was probably a load of rubbish. Grace had never been one for prescience. Her dreams never came true, she had not yet had the ability to predict the future. She did have good intuition, it was true. She was good with reading people, had a sixth sense about who people were, but she was not used to not being able to place the source of the anxiety.

She only knew that looking back through these photographs, to when they first got married, she had no idea how difficult life would turn out to be. I had no idea, she thinks sadly, exactly who I had married.

Ted came down at 7:30 to find Grace noisily pulling pots and pans out of all the kitchen cupboards.

"Grace!" he barked. "For God's sakes! What's all this racket? And why in God's name is the mudroom filled with trash bags and boxes. What's going on?"

"I'm having a sort-out." Grace picked up an old skillet, encrusted with years of burned oil, shook her head, then tossed it in a box. "I'm feeling rather good about it, actually. I went through the closet in the mudroom and found things I haven't thought about for years. Look!" She got up and brought back a pair of baby shoes. "Remember these?"

Ted's face softened as he puts his hand out to take the shoes, a smile playing on Grace's face as she remembered Clemmie toddling around the garden, wobbly on her chubby little legs. Ted smiled too before turning serious again.

"Grace," he said sternly. "What the hell is the matter with you?"

She turned to him with a start. "Me? Why? What are you talking about?"

"I . . . this being up all night, night after night. Clearing closets in the middle of the night. You're behaving like a crazy woman."

Grace pales. That word. The word she has always dreaded.

"Don't call me crazy." She grits her teeth. "I'm fine. It's just hormonal."

"I can't believe all these changes are just hormonal. I think you need to get yourself to a doctor."

"I'm fine," she said quickly. Too quickly.

"You're clearly not," he responded. "And I'm not the only one who has noticed it."

Grace's head whipped around. "What? Who have you discussed it with?"

"I haven't discussed it with anyone. But Beth has asked me a few times if you're okay. I haven't talked about this with Beth, but I'm aware that you seem to be a little . . . paranoid about her. I know you accused her of stealing your scarf, and—"

"How do you know about that?" Grace's voice was icy cold.

"Grace, she came to me because she was so upset. I didn't know what to say. And that whole fiasco with the rentals not showing for your event . . . well. I can't help but feel you seem to be accusing her of something then too."

"Did she tell you that?"

"She didn't have to. I see it for myself. The point is, she's worried about you. *I'm* worried about you. I'm wondering if there's something else going on."

"For God's sake!" Grace snapped. "How dare you and your assistant sit there talking about me! I can't believe she came to you telling you I'd accused her. I feel like there's some kind of bloody conspiracy going on—"

"Look at you!" Ted said, interrupting her. "Look at how angry you're getting! This isn't like you, Grace. You're not angry. Where is this coming from? What the hell is going on that is making you act like this, because you're definitely not acting like yourself, you're acting like some kind of crazy woman. It's nuts. Completely irrational. I have no idea what to do about it other than suggest you ought to see someone."

Here it is, she thought. The moment of reckoning. I have spent my whole life terrified of becoming my mother, creating the perfect persona, hoping, praying that her mother's illness would not pass down to me.

The prospect, hearing her husband describe her as crazy, filled Grace with instant fear.

"What do you mean, 'see someone'?" Grace snapped, jumping on the defensive. "A doctor?"

"Maybe. Or a psychiatrist."

"I don't need a psychiatrist," said Grace. Crazy people see psychiatrists. Her mother should have seen a psychiatrist. She has never seen a therapist, is one of the few women she knows who is not taking Paxil or Wellbutrin or Celexa, does not believe in burdening other people with her problems. I'm English, for God's sake, she always used to joke. We don't *do* doctors. Unless we're on death's doorstep, and even then we have to apologize for disturbing them.

"Grace." Ted's voice drips with disdain. "I can't stand the way you've been acting. Do you have any idea how difficult this is for me? Jesus Christ. I'm spending so much time worrying about you, my work is suffering. I'm tiptoeing around this goddamned house, terrified of saying or doing anything at all to upset you. Get yourself to a doctor and get yourself better."

Grace just stared at him. Welcome to my world, running over and over in her mind.

. . .

Grace stirs the polenta and looks over at Sybil, weariness exuding out of every pore.

"I think I'm just exhausted," she says. "I couldn't sleep last night and ended up having a massive sort-out. And . . . well. I haven't been feeling too good recently."

"Let me help," Sybil says, leading Grace over to the garden bench. "In what way?"

"I don't know. Nothing I can put my finger on. I definitely feel low." She attempts a laugh. "I'm sure it's just the regular old blues. They'll pass soon."

Sybil peers at her. "Are you sure that's all it is? I've seen you with the blues before, but . . . I'm just worried."

"I know. Thank you. I'll be fine. I suppose I have to admit I do feel a bit . . . unsettled. Almost as if I have a sense of foreboding, and I know this is crazy, but there's something about Beth that is making me feel uneasy."

"Beth?" Sybil's eyes widen. "Really? I thought she was Wondergirl."

"She is. Which is why I feel so nuts thinking that there's something not quite right. I keep trying to remember whether there is any way I could have made that call to the rental company to change the date, and I couldn't have done; I wouldn't have done. And I cannot stop feeling that Beth has something to do with this." She shakes her head. "I feel like I'm going mad. Ted wants me to go and talk to someone. Get therapy. I don't know. What do you think?"

"Therapy changed my life. I know you don't believe in it, but I think Ted has a good point. If nothing else, it may help you sort through the jumble of thoughts in your head, make sense of everything."

"You're right," says Grace. "It probably is a good idea. Maybe I will go and see someone after all."

WILD MUSHROOM POLENTA

(Serves 8)

INGREDIENTS

For the polenta

3 cups chicken stock
½ cup cream
2 cups polenta
¼ cup mascarpone
4 Tablespoons butter
½ cup grated Parmesan
Salt and pepper for seasoning

For the mushroom sauce

1 cup assorted gourmet mushrooms
Olive oil
1 garlic clove, minced
1 onion, finely chopped
1 sprig thyme
4 Tablespoons chicken stock
Salt and pepper for seasoning
Handful of chopped parsley

Combine stock, cream, and seasoning in a pan, bring to a boil, then turn quickly down to simmer. Add polenta in a slow, steady stream and bring mixture back to simmer. Stir frequently with a wooden spoon as you cook over a low heat for 1 hour. If the mixture becomes too thick, add more simmering stock. Finish with marscarpone and butter, then season and add the Parmesan cheese. It should be like loose mashed potato.

For the sauce, rinse mushrooms, slice them, and sauté them with garlic and onion in oil for around 10 minutes. Add thyme, salt and pepper, and stock. Turn heat to high to reduce and thicken the sauce.

When ready to serve, spoon the sauce over the top of the polenta and sprinkle with the parsley.

Sixteen

Ted and Beth thread their way through the restaurant, stopping every few feet to greet someone he knows: a writer, a journalist, an editor, a publisher. The Great and the Good are gathered at Michael's for lunch, as the pair work their way to the table just next to the window in the front, the best table in the house for the great Ted Chapman to have lunch with his publicist.

Beth is resplendent with her new chic haircut, in a dark green silk blouse that is not one of Grace's handoffs, but looks very much like it could have been. Tailored black pants, high-heeled black pumps with a distinctive red sole, and one chunky, gold necklace.

Gone is the shy, demure, mousy girl of old. This Beth smiles as she moves fluidly through the restaurant, aware of the radiance of her smile, aware she is being assessed.

"This is Beth, my sparkly assistant." Ted brings her forward, again and again, as she confidently extends a hand.

"Good Lord," they hear, over and over again. "We thought it was Grace's younger sister!" Beth laughs with a good-natured shake of her head, flattered and delighted at the comparison.

This is not the first time this has happened. Ted brought Beth to an event the week before and frowned the first time someone said they thought Beth was Grace. He had turned his head, taking Beth in, truly looking at her, as if for the first time. Physically, she is not Grace, although when she smiles as she is smiling now, as she has, in fact, been so often of late, she has a luminous beauty that you do not see, do not expect when her face is in repose. Physically, there is little resemblance, but her confidence and poise, the way she places a hand on Ted's arm, are what causes the confusion, causes people to do a double take.

He looks at her now. How little he sees her face in repose these days, he realizes. The hesitant, serious woman who joined their lives a few short months ago now beams each time he looks at her. It is as if she has modified her natural expression from one of gravity to levity. Her face in repose now has a small but permanent smile playing on her lips. Her new haircut has imbued her with a confidence that was missing before.

Could he really be so shallow as to admit he only found her interesting once she cut her hair? It is true he found himself watching her more once she had changed, fascinated by her transformation, but it was more than the hair.

As she grew more comfortable in the job, more comfortable in the house, more comfortable with them, she relaxed into her skin, and the ease with which she now carried herself was really quite lovely to see.

And inspiring.

He had introduced a character into his new book who was largely based on Beth. A young, insecure girl, product of an abusive background, abandoned by her family, invisible to all, blossoms into a great beauty under the care of an older man. Of course, he turns out to be controlling and abusive in much the ways of her family, and it comes full circle. He now finds himself watching Beth each day before he starts writing, taking breaks to take note of how she sits, what her body language says, guess at what she might be thinking.

Naturally he has changed the details, is quite certain there is nothing recognizable in the book. She is his muse, perhaps; not his heroine. No one would know the character was inspired by Beth, he tells himself, not when he is so famous for his characterizations.

"I draw from my life," he says at book readings, signings, events where hundreds of people turn up to hang on to his every word, "without ever writing *about* my life. People I come across may serve as a snapshot, but they quickly become their own characters."

Despite this, there have been many who have recognized themselves within the pages of his books. They have different names, different hair colors, different backgrounds, yet there is something so achingly familiar to them as they read, there is no question that Ted held them in his mind as they were writing.

He denies it. Of course he denies it. He is the first to explain that the character within the pages of the book takes on a character of its own within a few pages anyway—usually nothing like the person who you originally had in mind.

So Beth is his inspiration for the book he is currently writing, and, like all muses, he is increasingly fascinated by her. You would have to be blind not to see how she is attempting to emulate Grace's style. Grace is flattered, as she should be, and he has to admit, Beth does pull it off rather well. If anything though, the look is a little old for her. She is, after all, only thirty-eight. A young woman, divorced, no children. She should perhaps be dressing more provocatively, perhaps in a way designed to entice men her own age.

Although, he flushes slightly at the memory, she had said in passing she had never been interested in men her own age. She had been flipping through the pages of a magazine at the time, looking for an article he had vaguely remembered reading and hadn't looked up. From someone else, those words might have seemed provocative, but there was nothing flirtatious, nothing that would lead him to think anything more.

Except he had. He had found himself thinking about it all afternoon.

Mostly for his character. Initially the husband hadn't been older, until Beth had mentioned that. Of course! It made much more sense! A father figure. A man, he wryly thought, much like himself.

He had been so excited at the change, he had done something he hadn't done in years. Climbed out of bed, at ten o'clock at night, and gone out to his barn, spending the next three hours writing, the words flowing from his fingertips with swiftness and ease.

Looking at her now, in this restaurant, entirely at ease with everyone in here, he smiles to himself, feeling almost like her Svengali. He may not have issued the instructions for her to change, but how delighted he is that she has. Look how self-possessed she is! The very fact that he is bringing her to lunch with his agent proves how invaluable she has become.

Ellen, his old assistant, sometimes came to lunch with his agent, but not to the glamorous lunches in New York: she wasn't that kind of assistant. The thought of Ellen in her dusty sweatpants and comfortable sandals in the elegant environs of Michael's is unthinkable. Beth, on the other hand, looks like she belongs. One would never think she was an assistant. An editor, perhaps, or an agent. His publicist.

Indeed, she is proving to be an entirely different kind of assistant from Ellen in almost every way imaginable. She has given him ideas, suggestions, even advice. Instead of being appalled, he has found her astute and usually correct. She has an excellent mind, he has realized. Quick and clever, with an extraordinary ability to retain information.

He subscribes to all the literary magazines, reading them at night when he is back in the main house with Grace, or over the breakfast table, delighted to find Beth reads them too, has read every article he brings up; has a unique and fascinating viewpoint on all.

It has become almost a game between them.

"I was just reading in *The New Yorker* . . ." he will start

"About Julian Assange?" she will say, and they will both laugh. The stories that most fascinate him are invariably the stories that most fascinate her. He has no idea how she is doing that, only that he is glad she is; that *someone* is. Grace, love of his life, the woman who has always walked beside him, has never been able to share that particular part of his life.

Grace loves her magazines, but not the literary ones. Of course she will read an article if he passes it to her, if he thinks it is something of particular interest to her, but her magazines of choice tend to be *Town and Country*, *Harper's*, *Vogue*.

What a delight to have a woman around who shares his curiosity and is sharp enough to form her own opinions. While Grace will read what he gives her, she rarely enters into a spirited debate, in the way he and Beth have been doing.

"Nice assistant." The journalist Ted had been chatting with en route to the table raises an eyebrow as they both watch Beth sashaying through the room to their table.

With a tilt of his head and a small smile, Ted bids him a good lunch, congratulating himself on what a good assistant he has. At times like these it is hard to remember how he ever got through the day without her.

Steven!" He pumps hands vigorously with Steven Marsh, the head of press at his publishing house. Ted is one of the few authors Steven is still directly involved with, usually assigning young, glamorous girls in their twenties to do the day-to-day work of attempting to gain publicity for their myriad authors.

For Ted, Steven will phone the editors of the largest papers and magazines himself. He will come up with the story ideas and map them out with the editors over lunch, usually here, at Michael's, and they, delighted at the opportunity for something large and exclusive with Ted Chapman, will leave the restaurant in a state of near exhilaration.

Steven is one of the old guard. He and Ted have been together twenty years. A professional relationship has morphed into a friendship and they all sit down as Steven gestures to Beth.

"You must be Beth! I finally get to meet the wonderful assistant! Ted," he clucks gently. "How on earth do you do it? Two beautiful women! If we didn't have years of friendship behind us, I'd hate you."

Ted chuckles.

Beth blushes. "Thank you. This is truly a dream job, and I'm learning so much."

"About what an irascible bastard Ted Chapman can be?" Steven leans forward with a laugh.

"He's not irascible." Beth laughs. "He's charming. And brilliant. And a wonderful mentor."

"You're obviously paying her well." Steven looks at Ted approvingly.

"Will you excuse me?" Beth says, pushing her chair back. "I just have to go to the ladies' room."

The two of them watch in silence as Beth makes her way through the tables, past the bar, and into the ladies' room. As soon as she has disappeared, Steven looks at Ted, no longer bothering to conceal the look of alarm on his face.

"God, Ted! Why didn't you tell me you were bringing her to lunch? I would have booked somewhere discreet. Of all places to bring her, Michael's? Really? The whole town's going to know about it within about two hours."

Ted starts to laugh. "Relax, Steven! You have it all wrong. I know she's quite lovely, but she really is my assistant."

"Oh, I know that, I've been emailing with her for months, but you're . . . well. It's obvious. The two of you are . . ."

"Screwing?" Ted barks with laughter as Steven looks confused. "Are you out of your fucking mind? First of all, I would not do that to Grace."

Steven leans forward. "Ted, you know and I know that's not true. I remember plenty of young publishing assistants at—"

"And how many years ago was that?" Ted says, now serious. "Steven, I was a young man then. I haven't had any . . . dalliances . . . for years. I wouldn't do that to Grace. Not now. I was too young to know any better. Plus, I certainly wouldn't shit on my own doorstep. Good Lord, Ted. She's the best goddamned assistant I've ever had. She's truly gifted, at everything, and I'm hardly going to mess that up. Not to mention, she's twenty years younger than me. And finally, even if I were, which I am not, nor would I ever, the very last place I would bring her would be Michael's. I may be charmed by her, but I am not completely stupid."

They both turn with fixed smiles on their faces as Beth heads back to the table.

"Thank God," whispers Steven quickly. "Sorry, Ted. I read the situation all wrong. Fortunately."

"Or unfortunately," Ted murmurs back as they both survey Beth's endless legs, for she has continued losing weight and has emerged with legs like a gazelle. Shooting Steven a quick, wicked smile to show he was joking, Ted leaps up and holds the chair, waiting for Beth to sit down.

What about a podcast?" Beth says when Steven has finished outlining his plans for the paperback release of Ted's last book.

"Podcast? About what?"

"About writing. Editing. The craft. It could be a book too, but I think you could start with a podcast. If you think about it, the well-known books on the craft of writing are from literary authors. Except Stephen King. No one else crosses the two, literary and commercial, in the way that Ted does, and I think he'd pull in a huge audience. I also think the bloggers would love the fact that Ted Chapman is doing a series of podcasts on writing. It could generate a whole other line of publicity."

Steven nods thoughtfully. "It is actually a rather wonderful idea, if, Ted, you have time to do it."

"It wouldn't take too much time," Beth says, taking a bite of her salmon in pastry. "I could put together a list of topics and even make notes for you, what you would have to say. All you'd have to do is 'Ted Chapman it up,' and we can record it anywhere."

There is a silence as Ted considers her suggestion. He has never been a writer who has relied on anyone else to put words into his mouth. Years ago he was commissioned to write a short nonfiction book on the presidential race, to come out in time for the next election.

The publishers paid him a vast amount of money, the sort of money it would be impossible to turn down for what would, essentially, be about two weeks of work. The reason it was only going to take two weeks was firstly, because they had an incredibly tight deadline and secondly, because they had a team of researchers already putting together all the information for the book.

In fact, they said, they had sample chapters; it had already been written. They wanted his name on the cover and they wanted him to read through and do exactly what Beth had just suggested: "Ted Chapman it up."

It was a coffee table book, resplendent with large, glossy never-before-seen photographs of various former presidents. Ted received the sample manuscript, sat on the old Chesterfield in the barn, and, after three pages, roared with fury.

It was the most horrifyingly written piece of drivel he had ever read. There was no way in hell that could go to print with his name on it. It didn't need Ted Chapmaning up, it needed an entire goddamned rewrite.

Which he did. By basically not sleeping for the next two weeks. It became the worst two weeks of his life, and gave him a headache that no amount of aspirin could solve.

It was the last time he accepted an assignment like that, and now, sitting here, hearing that Beth would put this together—would, essentially, write the basics—he remembers that project.

And he remembers the conversations he and Beth have on a daily basis. The suggestions she makes. The way she has taken over his fan mail, responding to each of his readers individually, personalizing the letters and, magically, effortlessly, managing to sound exactly like him.

She has caught the essence of his voice. From time to time, when Beth has gone home, he scrolls through her computer and reads the letters she has written. Although he signs them all himself, he never has time to do anything but scan them, if that, at the time of signature.

Reading them on Beth's computer, he has a delighted smile on his face, occasionally barking with laughter at how she sounds exactly, but *exactly*, like him. If he didn't know better, he would think he had written these letters himself.

He could do a podcast and Beth could do the work. Finally, he has someone he can trust.

"Do you know what?" he says. "I think that might be a rather good idea. Beth, why don't you draft something and let me have a look. Let's see whether we can make something work."

The text comes in just as Ted is about to climb into the car, Beth already in the backseat.

You're right, Steven texts. *She is gold! You win the prize for most charming, clever assistant. Lovely to be with you both.*

Ted smiles to himself as he slips the phone into his pocket and climbs in next to Beth, ready to be driven back home, to Palisades, to Grace.

While I remember," he says absentmindedly to Beth, who is reading her Kindle on the backseat as he scrolls through his emails and lists of things to do. "Can you phone Dr. Frank Ellery and make an appointment for Grace? Actually, make one for me first, to talk to him about Grace. I'll send you the number."

"Is everything okay? Is Grace sick?"

Ted sighs. "She's . . . fine. She's not sick, but she's not herself. Remember? We talked about this a couple of weeks ago? I've been thinking about your suggestion that she see someone. I didn't think so at the time, but she is definitely erratic. She has a . . . volatility I'm not used to, and I know you've had a number of experiences with her lately that have been . . . difficult."

Beth's face falls. "I shouldn't have said anything. Now I feel terrible."

"Please don't. I know you've been concerned. Now, hopefully, we can help her."

"I really do hope she's all right," Beth says. "But I do understand about the volatility. She seems calm and fine one minute, then the next she is in bed, or crying, or angry. I try not to take it personally, but I do think you're doing the right thing, seeing someone. Didn't you say she hadn't been sleeping recently too? That she was up cleaning all night?"

Ted nods.

"That kind of behavior must be very frightening for you. I have an aunt who seemed to be completely normal until her midforties, and suddenly she changed completely. At first they thought it was hormonal, but her behavior was so erratic, so . . . manic, it didn't seem possible that it was just menopause."

"When you say manic . . ."

"She'd be up all night for nights at a time, making things. Tidying the house, but it was frenzied. And she got angry in a way she hadn't ever before."

"It was depression?"

"Yes. Manic depression though. Bipolar disorder. She started medication and it changed her life. We all got her back. They say it runs in families, and my cousin seems to have it too."

This time Ted says nothing as the thoughts whirl around his head.

Seventeen

The days of Grace being an early riser seem long gone. Lately she is finding it more and more difficult to get out of bed. She has never before used an alarm, or at least, not since the children were living at home and she had to make sure she never overslept, but even then, she was usually awake by 5:30, making lists and tea well before anyone else in the house had roused themselves.

These past few weeks of waking up in the middle of the night, and staying wide awake for hours, is proving disastrous. If she is lucky, she will get back to sleep at around 5:00 a.m., but then has to set an alarm, which invariably jars her out of a deep sleep. Lately, instead of turning the alarm off and hopping out of bed, as would normally be her wont, she has turned it off, to sink straight back into a deep sleep.

Three times over the past ten days she has done the unthinkable, discovering it's around two o'clock in the afternoon, and despite how busy her schedule, how much she has to do, she has been unable to keep her eyes open and has slipped upstairs and into bed, planning on a twenty-minute nap, only to awaken, groggy and feeling infinitely worse, at 4:30. And once, at 6:00.

"You've been asleep? That's not like you. Are you coming down with something? Is everything all right?" Grace walks into the kitchen to find Ted at the kitchen table, reading the papers. She has no idea why her husband is in the kitchen and not in the barn at 4:30 in the afternoon, is irritated he has caught her sleeping in the middle of the day.

"I think it may be the exhaustion of organizing that event at Harmont House," Grace says, lying. This exhaustion could not possibly have come from the stress of organizing that event. It was entirely possible she was reaching the time of life when menopause was fast approaching. All she heard from friends was how awful menopause was, and it may be the most logical of explanations for how she has been feeling.

"You look terrible, Grace. When are you going to see a doctor?"

Grace's mouth is set in a sharp line. "Thank you, Ted. There's nothing like having your husband tell you how awful you look to make you feel better." She turns to go back upstairs, her shoulders hunched and tense.

"Grace! I wasn't saying anything of the kind. Don't be so silly . . ."

"Don't tell me I'm being silly," she says, recognizing she is being unreasonable even as she is being unreasonable, not knowing how to change it, how to get out of this mood that has just descended.

There is a long, awkward silence as Ted just looks at her. "I'm going out," she says, grabbing her purse. "I'm going to town. I'll be back later."

She walks out the door, stopping suddenly as she realizes her car is gone. They have a number of cars—Ted drives a newish Volvo Estate, she has a small Mercedes that she loves; there is a very old Volvo they carted all the kids and their friends around in when they were small that they have never gotten rid of, and a pickup truck that has always been surprisingly useful.

All the other cars are parked where they always are, except for her Mercedes.

"Ted? Where's my car? I need to go out."

"I think Beth took it." Ted seems nervous, halting. "I think she may have taken it to the car wash."

"It didn't need a wash," Grace says. "It's *my* car. No one drives my car without asking me. Oh, for God's sake." Her voice rises with irritation.

"Grace, it's fine. Text her and see when she'll be back, or take my car. Take the Suburban. It's a car, and it's not like we don't have alternatives for you to drive. Please, Grace. Calm down."

"Don't tell me to calm down." Grace is steely cold. "I don't want to drive the Suburban and I hate your car. You know I hate driving your car. Who gave her permission to drive my car?"

Ted looks at her, aghast, just as the Mercedes pulls back down the driveway.

"See!" Ted's whole body sinks in relief. "I told you she wouldn't be long."

Grace says nothing, just marches out of the house and toward the car as Beth climbs out of the car, dry-cleaning in hand.

"Beth." Grace attempts to hide her sudden anger, realizing now how inappropriate it is. "Please do not take my car without checking with me first."

Beth's face falls. "I'm so sorry!" She is clearly mortified. "I just noticed you had spilled some dirt from the plants you've been carting over to Harmont House, and I took it up to the car wash to have them clean it. But you're right. I should never have done it without your permission. I'm so sorry."

"Thank you for doing that." Grace attempts to modify her tone. "It was very thoughtful. I'm just asking that you don't take my car without checking I'm not using it."

"Of course," says Beth. "It won't happen again."

Grace nods, not trusting herself to speak. As she drives off to Harmont House, she starts to feel increasingly stupid. Embarrassed. Beth was only trying to help; why did she feel so . . . violated? How did she reach a point when something so insignificant sent her not only into a temper, but almost to tears?

It must be hormonal. It has to be hormonal, for it is so unlike her. There are other things that have started happening. Night sweats. Her period, still there, but erratic. Sometimes missing for months at a time, sometimes every two weeks.

She hasn't yet been to see a doctor, for she is so averse to taking medicine unless it is absolutely necessary. At various times in her life, it has been absolutely necessary, but only antibiotics for a cold that develops into a sinus infection or an ear infection that wouldn't get better by itself.

One of the first signs that something is a little wrong is when Grace stops cooking. She can't stop altogether, not anymore, not when she has obligations to fulfill, but there isn't the same pleasure there usually is; it is more of a chore that she tries to get done as quickly and painlessly as possible.

Here today, at Harmont House, she brings with her the ingredients for a "paleo" carrot cake. No wheat flour, for two of the women now have an intolerance, and while usually she would be excited at trying a new recipe, today she just wants to be in and out, back to the safety of her house.

There have been times when she has been prescribed an antidepressant. She has hated taking it, hating having to admit there may be something wrong, terrified that she has somehow inherited her mother's illness, and has only ever used them as a temporary panacea.

These mood swings, however much she hates to admit it, remind her of her mother. She used to be certain she had not inherited her mother's illness. She has never experienced mania, nor anything like it, and her depressions are not like her mother's—not enough to send her to bed for months at a time. Hers feel like the excitement and joy have been pulled out of life, leaving it flat, colorless, dull. During those times, she is sad, yes, but she takes the pills, they make her feel better, and soon she *is* better. Her mother would be flattened for months, and mania? Grace has never, *thank God*, had it.

But this anger is new or, at least, the regularity of this anger is. Despite her certainty about the approaching menopause, she is nervous about taking hormones, even the ones her body may need to help regulate her moods.

Grace has changed her diet completely, hoping, believing, that she can change their health—both she and Ted—by changing their nutrition. He is on Lipitor, but she is convinced she can lower his cholesterol naturally, eventually hoping to take him off. She now has two pill boxes in the kitchen, labeled for each day of the week, filled to the brim with supplements to keep them in optimum health, help stave off the inevitable.

Vitamin D, omega-3s, Vitamin E, B-12, choline and inositol, SAMe, zinc, DHEA. Every day she pops handfuls of these pills, but right now, driving to Harmont House, foggy-headed after her lengthy afternoon sleep and embarrassed at being so ridiculous about Beth trying to do something nice for her, Grace starts to wonder if any of it is working.

Grace starts to wonder if Ted may be right. Maybe she is going crazy after all.

PALEO (FLOURLESS, GLUTEN-FREE) CARROT CAKE

INGREDIENTS

6 eggs, whites and yolks separated

½ cup honey

1½ cups carrots, cooked and pureed

1 Tablespoon orange zest

1 Tablespoon orange juice

3 cups almond flour

Preheat oven to 325 degrees.

Beat the egg yolks and honey together. Mix in carrot puree, orange zest, orange juice, and almond flour.

Beat the egg whites until stiff peaks form and fold into egg and carrot mixture.

Spoon into a greased, loose-bottomed 9-inch springform pan and bake for about 50 minutes, or until a skewer pushed into the center comes out clean.

Eighteen

When she first moved to the United States, Grace would sit, mesmerized, in front of the television screen, watching commercials for drugs, desperate patients encouraged to beg their doctors for pills, despite the side effects that may include, it seemed, certain death.

She remembers telling Lydia, on one of her trips home, how hilarious she found them. Patrick had just returned from a trip to Los Angeles, and he immediately adopted the voiceover, warning them all of certain death should they take that aspirin. Patrick and Grace had laughed more than the others, but as hilarious as she found them then, she now finds them frightening.

She has never been on anything for any period of time, and has never, ever countenanced seeing a therapist. Therapists seem so . . . *American*. What good could it possibly do to sit in someone's office week after week and pour out your woes? How self-indulgent! What an unwanted luxury! And if you didn't have woes, what then? Who wants to sit in a therapist's office and talk about the good stuff. If you didn't have woes, you would surely have to create them.

Grace's life has always been pretty good, thank you very much. She will admit there have certainly been times when she has been depressed—Clemmie leaving home was one of the lowest—but her remedy has always worked: stay home for a while, sleep a bit more, drink more cups of tea, and wait for it to pass.

Which is why she is currently sitting in the waiting room of esteemed psychiatrist, Dr. Frank Ellery, wondering what the hell she is doing here.

Ted just wouldn't let the subject drop. It wasn't like her to lose her temper, he said. It wasn't like her to be up all night, then in bed for hours during the day. He was worried about her. *Beth* was worried about her. *Clemmie* was worried about her.

This last part made her sit up and take notice. If Clemmie were worried about her, Clemmie who was troubled by nothing, then perhaps there *was* something to worry about. Perhaps it wouldn't be a bad thing to talk to someone. Just talk. Just see if that might help.

She would get her hormones checked too. Would make an appointment with the endocrinologist this afternoon, when she finished with Dr. Frank Ellery. It was also time for her colonoscopy. And soon, a mammogram.

This was when she missed living in England. For all she knew, it had changed entirely, but growing up she never remembered her parents going to the doctor, and certainly never for checkups.

Over here, the older she gets, the more tests there are. None of them show anything, ever. She doesn't believe they ever will, believes it to be a precious waste of everyone's time.

And yet . . . and yet . . . so many friends have been diagnosed with breast cancer, caught at a routine annual mammogram. Ten years ago Sybil had come back from Mexico with what she presumed was a stomach bug, or parasite, picked up while there. Her doctor insisted on a colonoscopy, discovering that it was indeed giardia, and while he was there, he removed two large polyps. Both of which turned out to be precancerous. At thirty-seven. Long before Sybil was expected or due to even start thinking about her colon.

It wasn't that Grace didn't expect the bad stuff to happen, it was that she didn't expect it to happen to *her*.

She only agreed to this, this therapy, because she doesn't want Clemmie to worry about her, and because Ted had suggested Dr. Frank Ellery, and they had met him at a dinner party last year. Surprisingly, she had felt instantly comfortable with him, had thought that if she were to ever wish to see a psychiatrist, he would be exactly the sort of psychiatrist she would choose.

And now here she is. Nervously flicking through a very old copy of *Town and Country* that she read months ago, trying to still her beating heart, as the internal door opens and there he is. The good doctor, offering her an outstretched hand and a warm smile as he tells her how delighted he is to see her again.

I know you talked to my husband," Grace says nervously. "Thank you for asking my permission to do that. I'm sure he's told you a little of what's going on."

"He did," says Frank—he asked her to call him Frank—saying nothing further, examining her with limpid eyes.

Grace wants to ask exactly what Ted said, but knows it is unlikely he will divulge much. She probably shouldn't ask. It would be pointless.

"What did he tell you?"

An empathic expression as Frank looks at her, pools of understanding and compassion in his eyes. "He said he's very worried about you. That you haven't seemed like yourself. I was hoping we could talk more about that."

Grace takes a deep breath, thinking she has nothing to say. All morning she has walked around the house wondering what it is she should be talking about in the psychiatrist's office, constantly coming up blank. They would sit in awkward silence, she thought. She would perhaps tell him a little about her life, but not much, for how could she reveal her self, her true self, to a stranger? How could she allow herself that vulnerability with someone she doesn't know.

And here she is. Talking, suddenly. Her words tripping over themselves in relief at finally having someone to talk to.

"I feel like I'm going crazy," she says. "I've always been so calm, so happy, and right now the tiniest thing sets me off in tears. I've always loved my life, but all I want to do is go to bed and crawl under the covers. And I know I've been flying off the handle at the slightest provocation. I know how horrible I'm being, but even when I'm in it, I just don't know how to stop myself and I can't stand feeling this way."

Each time she finishes, or thinks she finishes, Frank looks at her, nodding, as if he understands exactly, but *exactly* what she is going through, as if he has felt the precise pain she feels. As if, were professional boundaries not in place, he would gather her in his arms and cradle her like a baby, rocking her to safety and warmth. As if the only thing he cares about, the only thing he wants in the world, is to make Grace better.

She talks, and cries, and laughs. She cries, and laughs, and talks. He has set aside two hours for this first session, and it flies by, Grace barely stopping for breath, aware only that she is in the presence of a warmth and compassion so strong, it feels as if she has come home.

"I'm sorry," Frank says when the two hours are up. "We have to bring it to a close. How do you feel now?"

"Oh God!" Grace sits back with an embarrassed laugh, running her hands through her hair. "I feel . . . stunned. I can't believe how much I had to say. I had no idea. How do I feel? I feel good. Really good! Talking to someone who understands! I never realized how powerful that could be. And I feel . . ." Tears spring into her eyes. "Relieved. I feel relieved. I guess I never realized how alone I've been. Just being here and talking to you makes me feel I don't have to do it all alone."

"That's right. You don't. Would you like to make another appointment, or perhaps think about it?"

"Definitely another appointment. Tomorrow?" Grace says, only partly joking, before they agree to a twice-weekly schedule.

Outside, it is as if she is noticing the sky for the first time. There is a chill in the air and the leaves are starting to turn. She stands in the parking lot for a while, her head thrown back, seeing, really seeing, the trees, and the sky, and the beauty of where they live.

She climbs in the car to go home, smiling all the way.

Nineteen

"Grace really does seem much better." Ted puts down the pages he is editing and looks over at Beth, who has just walked in with a box of books she has collected from the post office.

"I just saw her," Beth says. "She seems . . . exhilarated."

Ted looks at her. "Exhilarated in a good way, though, yes? Considering how down in the dumps she's been, ever since she has started seeing that Frank Ellery, she has seemed like a different person. She has had six sessions, and already she seems . . . better."

"You're right." Beth puts down the boxes, then comes to sit in the chair by Frank's desk. "She definitely seems happier. I guess I'm just worried it's a little *too* happy."

"Is there such a thing as too happy?"

"I don't know. I just worry. I always think the goal in life is to be peaceful, rather than any of the extremes, in either direction."

"Hmm. Peaceful. I don't even know whether that's attainable for the average person, although it's certainly an admirable goal. If peaceful is the goal, then no, Grace definitely doesn't seem peaceful. Do you think I ought to have another chat with her doctor?"

"I don't know. Why do you think that?"

"I suppose because I always see the fatal flaw in any kind of therapy is that you are presenting yourself to the therapist not as the world sees you, but as you see yourself. We build very careful constructs, creating who we wish to be. Asking us to strip those constructs away and present who we really are, when most of the time we rarely have any idea who we really are, seems impossible. How is a therapist supposed to decipher what is real and what is not, when they only have evidence coming from you? Frank did say to keep him advised of any concerns, or any behavior I might find odd. 'Exhilaration.' Interesting." He is now staring into space, talking to himself. "Not peaceful. I'll have to give him a call."

My mother was . . . difficult." Grace has been reluctant to talk about her mother. She has spent hours and hours talking about herself, her marriage, her husband. Anything to avoid the great big elephant in the room.

"You have mentioned that before," says Frank. "A number of times, but you haven't elaborated. Are you able to tell me a little more?"

Grace takes a deep breath, not knowing how to start. "Someone was talking recently about not having had a childhood because of their parents' alcoholism, and I related. My mother was an alcoholic, which I think I've told you, but . . ." She closes her eyes briefly, not having said the words out loud for years. The last time she talked about it was with Patrick, when her mother died. When she made a pact never to talk about it again.

"She also had manic depression." Grace winces as she looks at Frank, expecting a look of sympathy, concern, but his expression is blank. "She had long periods of depression, when she was in bed and basically completely absent, and then suddenly one day she'd be up and out, and come home having spent thousands of dollars. Or she'd put me in the car for an adventure and take me to a casino. She would have these explosive rages that were completely and utterly terrifying to me. I spent much of my childhood trying to hide from her. And," Grace almost chokes out these next words, "I have spent my entire life terrified that I would turn into her." She exhales, stunned at the relief she feels, finally saying those words out loud.

Frank nods, watching Grace, waiting for her to say more, but she is done.

"Thank you for telling me that. I can see that it was hard for you to put into words. Is this the first time you have ever admitted that to someone?"

"That I'm frightened I'll turn into her? Yes."

"I'm proud of you for doing that. Secrets are sickness, and once we voice our worst fears, it diffuses the power, the hold those secrets have had on you. I imagine you already feel better for having said it out loud."

"I do!" Grace almost laughs.

"I'm glad you told me. I won't lie. From the little you had said about your childhood, I had already suspected that that was your mother's diagnosis. I don't, generally, like labels," he says. "I find them mostly unhelpful and often irrelevant. We tend to put someone in a box and treat the label rather than the person, and there is so much we miss when that happens."

"Yes!" says Grace, who is aghast at how she is suddenly surrounded by people whose children have any variety of mental disorder she had never heard of ten years ago. ADHD at every turn, personality disorders—oppositional, defiant, disruptive disorders.

"But sometimes," he says, "it is very obvious to me what is going on, and in these instances a label can actually be more of a help than a hindrance, can help the sufferer really understand why they are behaving the way they are, and what they can do to make it better. Particularly when there is a genetic component."

"Yes?" Grace is cautious, unsure of what she is about to hear, wishing she hadn't voiced her fears, wishing she could just stand up and leave.

"We have spent several sessions talking about what you have been going through, particularly the mood swings and the anger. We have also talked a lot about the lack of sleeping and the bursts of energy you get. You've talked about your mother and I know how difficult it has been for you to admit your own fear of turning out to be like her. The first thing I want to say is that today, bipolar disorder is entirely manageable. If your mother were alive now, the chances are she would be on medications that would make her very normal. Unfortunately, these illnesses do have a genetic component. Even though you clearly do not have the illness to the extent of your mother, I am pretty clear that everything you've been going through is indicative that you are on the spectrum."

"What?" Grace's voice is a shocked whisper. "You're telling me I'm crazy like my mother?"

"No. That's not what I'm saying. I think your mother had a very severe form of what we call bipolar one, periods of depression interspersed with classic mania. I'm pretty certain that yours is far less severe, what we call bipolar two, which is a far less dramatic version, but can still, nevertheless, be very difficult if it isn't managed properly."

"I don't think that's a correct diagnosis." Grace shakes her head. "If bipolar is the modern name for manic depression, where's the depression? And more to the point, where's the mania?"

"Grace," he says. "You're sleeping your days away. What is that if not depression?"

"It's being up all night, that's what that is. It isn't depression. I don't *feel* depressed. And the being up all night isn't mania, it's just . . . a phase. It's more likely to be perimenopause than mania, for God's sake."

"Being up all night is very common. Mania usually isn't what people think, nor depression. This illness, it can manifest itself in a myriad of ways, sleeping being one of the most common. As for the up all night, that is a typical example of hypomania, and what we call rapid cycling . . ."

He continues talking, Grace continues looking at him, pretending to listen, while everything in her mind is fighting what he is saying. There's no way she has bipolar disorder, one or two. Is there? There's no way her worst fears have come true.

She has always dreaded confessing her worst fears, saying them out loud for fear of them coming true, but now that she has, she realizes Frank's proclamation that she does, in fact, have her mother's disease, doesn't *feel* right. There is no *Aha!* Moment, no moment when she feels intense relief at someone having finally diagnosed what is wrong with her, someone finally seeing a way to help.

There is nothing other than confusion and disbelief as she tunes back into Frank.

"I'm sorry," she says when he has finished explaining why he is so sure. "But I disagree with you. It just doesn't resonate with me."

"Why would it?" he says gently. "It doesn't resonate with anyone. This, unfortunately, is something we see in almost all patients who have bipolar disorder—and, by the way, it's important to point out the difference between *being* bipolar, and *having* bipolar—this is not who you are, it is something you have. But this initial resistance? It can take people months to come to terms with something so huge, and most struggle with acceptance until they realize the difference medication can make in their lives."

Grace sits up. "Medication?"

His eyes liquid pools, Frank nods. "Grace, you have been struggling to deal with this very difficult disorder by yourself. Medication will make your life so much easier. Medication," he pauses, "will give you back your life. It will give you back yourself."

"But . . . but . . . are you sure? Are you absolutely sure?"

"Grace." He smiles an indulgent smile. "I've been doing this a very long time and I'm very good at what I do. I'm not saying I've never been wrong, but in this instance there is no hesitation in my mind whatsoever. What I'd like to do is start you on a medication called Depakote.

We'll start at a low dose and gradually increase to the therapeutic level, and I think you'll see very quickly how much better you feel, how much calmer you are."

"Depakote?" Grace is numb.

"Yes. It's often used as an antiseizure medication, but has proven to be remarkably effective as a treatment for bipolar two. But Grace, this is important. I don't want you to go online and read about it. Don't read up about the side effects, because there is so much false information online. I advise all my patients to come to me if they have side effects, and we can deal with them together. In honesty, I think you will be fine on this drug. The only thing you might notice is a little more tiredness, but that should wear off after a week or two."

"I'm really . . . not comfortable with this." Grace feels as if she is about to cry.

"I know. But I want you to think of it another way. Now you have an explanation for the way you've been feeling. The lack of sleep, the sleeping during the day, the anger, the flare-ups. You not only know that it isn't your fault, but that it's treatable. That's the beauty of these medications, and in fact of having this kind of disorder. It's entirely manageable, and very soon you will feel exactly like your old self."

Grace, unfamiliar with doctors at every level, finds herself regressing back to a child, where doctors were akin to God, where when they told you they knew better than you, you believed them. Who is she, wife, mother, friend, who is she to tell the psychiatrist he might be wrong?

He does, after all, do this for a living.

If he says this is so, then what else can she do but let it be so.

It doesn't feel right when Grace climbs into the car and heads to the pharmacy, prescription tucked into her purse. It doesn't feel right when she goes in, forcing a chat with the pharmacist she has known for years, handing over the small green and white slip of paper, watching his facial expression carefully as he reads the prescription, waiting for him to look at her with surprise, but his face is blank.

It takes fifteen minutes. Fifteen minutes, during which time Grace walks around the drugstore, weighed down with shame.

Bipolar disorder. How can this be? How can she have spent all these years being perfectly normal, only to have suddenly developed a mental illness at this age.

Her session, the conversation with Frank, plays over and over in her mind. Her resistance, her arguments, his persistence, his explanations. And above all, his overriding, omniscient, and absolute declaration that in this instance he was right, *and there was no doubt whatsoever in his mind.*

The exhilaration she had been feeling at having found someone to talk to, at no longer feeling she had to shoulder this burden of life on her own, dissipated earlier today in his office, and there is little sign of it returning.

Back home, about to make fish cakes for dinner, Grace pulls the mayonnaise and mustard out of the fridge, then pauses, pulled by the bag from the pharmacy sitting in the middle of the kitchen counter.

Depakote. Grace Chapman. She examines the bottle, turning it over and over, preparing herself to set foot on a journey she does not want to start.

But think, she tells herself, of what you have been feeling of late. Think of the anger, the tears, the way you sometimes feel as if your head will explode with all the chaos it contains. What if he is right, and my resistance, my lack of willingness to believe in the diagnosis, is part of the disease?

What if these pills do indeed turn out to be magic, and I am restored back to my old self?

Then it would be worth it. She doesn't have to stay on them for long. Right now she doesn't have much fight left in her. The easiest thing to do is to take them to make everyone happy. And if they don't work, she'll simply stop.

FISH CAKES WITH TOMATO SAUCE

(Serves 4)

INGREDIENTS

For the cakes

1 pound cod, or similar white fish
1 egg
4 Tablespoons mayonnaise
1 Tablespoon Dijon mustard
1 Tablespoon dill
Zest of 1 lemon
½ cup, or slightly more or less, Panko breadcrumbs
½ cup all-purpose flour
Salt and pepper for seasoning

For the sauce

½ white onion, chopped
1 clove garlic, minced
1 medium can chopped tomatoes
1 Tablespoon olive oil
Cayenne pepper
Salt

Flake the fish and mix together first 6 ingredients. Season. Add Panko breadcrumbs until mixture is firm enough to form into patties. Shape into patties and refrigerate at least 1 hour.

For sauce, soften onions in olive oil around five minutes. Add garlic, cook further 5 minutes. Add canned tomatoes, heat on low heat around 15 minutes. Season well, puree into smooth sauce.

When ready to cook the fish cakes, dip in flour, sauté in butter and olive oil until golden brown.

Twenty

Never in her life has Grace slept as much as she has been sleeping these past three months since starting the bipolar medication, and never in her life has she felt so utterly, completely depleted.

I feel as if I have been drugged, she keeps thinking, remembering with irony that she has been. Frank has assured her this exhaustion is temporary, that it will wear off, but she can barely crawl out of bed. He has prescribed more pills to try and help—Nuvigil to try and reduce the tiredness, try and keep her awake, and Metformin, which has, she vaguely recalls, something to do with blood sugar. It isn't used as a diet pill exactly, said Frank, but it would stop her cravings.

For Grace has been hungrier than she ever would have dreamed possible while taking these pills. Starving. Her stomach a bottomless pit, never full, thinking only about what she can eat next, even before she has finished eating whatever it is she is currently eating.

Grace has always loved food. She loves lemon and almond cake and chocolate mousse and apple pie, and roast beef and sizzling pork sausages, and melting fondues. She has always indulged, never overindulging, which is perhaps the secret to her remaining svelte. Everything in moderation, she has always said, and by everything she meant real butter, real sugar, real food, lovingly prepared.

Now, all she can think about is junk food. The very foods she has spent her life avoiding. She is filled with blind cravings that are all-consuming, that are all she can think about. She has made furtive trips to Northvale, to grocery stores where she can indulge her cravings. She orders six doughnuts, figuring she will eat one, giving the others to Ted and Beth. She finishes the first, barely tasting it, then sits in the car, unable to think of anything but the remaining doughnuts. Whatever willpower she might have had for the past twenty years has disappeared. The doughnuts do not have a chance against her insatiable hunger, and sure enough, they do not last five minutes, let alone the ride home.

Bread. Cheese. Cookies. Anything salty, crunchy, or sweet. She is terrified about putting on weight, has spent her entire life ensuring her weight never changes, her dress size exactly the same as when she first married Ted, but nothing seems to matter in the face of her starvation.

Tonight they are going to Sybil's for dinner. Sighing, Grace thinks about canceling it, as she has canceled just about everything they were supposed to do during the last few weeks.

The thought of getting out of bed, getting dressed in anything other than a robe, doing her hair and makeup, is too exhausting to even contemplate, but it is just Sybil and Fred, and she won't have to make too much of an effort.

Downstairs she makes herself strong black coffee, looking outside the window to see the dogs scampering around Beth's feet as she walks up the path that leads to the barn.

Good. She doesn't have to see Beth. She doesn't have to see anyone. She doesn't want to see anyone, wants just to climb back into bed, pull the covers up, and sleep.

The coffee gives her something of a boost, enough to get her back up the stairs and into her closet, where she pulls out a loose sweater and linen drawstring pants.

She doesn't have a hope in hell of getting into her tight clothes, that much she knows, hanging the pants and sweater on a hook while she goes in to shower.

Grace can't look at herself in the mirror naked anymore and dares not step on the scale. She suddenly has breasts—breasts!—and a stomach that no amount of sucking in can hide. She is terrified of how much she has put on, even though Frank keeps saying this too, along with the tiredness, shall pass.

I must have put on forty pounds, she thinks. Too much to think about. Certainly a reason to stay far away from the scales, terrified of what they would say. She had hoped the Metformin would make a difference in her appetite, a difference in her weight, but so far there has been no difference at all. Frank had mentioned another pill, Topamax, which Grace wanted to try immediately, desperate for anything to stop this ravenous hunger, but Frank doesn't do anything quickly.

"I'm putting you on Lexapro as well," he says. "And we'll see how that goes. You have to give these medications a chance to work," he says.

"How long?" Grace pleads.

"Let's try it for a month."

He cannot hear the wail of anguish inside her body and chooses to ignore the look of horror in her eyes.

"Grace," he has said more than once, his voice gentle. "I want you to focus on the good that the Depakote is doing. Look at how calm you've been. Look at how stable your moods have been. You've been sleeping all night, and all in all I'd say you're in a much better place. I want you to acknowledge that, Grace. It's very easy for you to slip into binary thinking, for you to focus only on the bad, but it's really important for you to see the good that it's doing."

"But I'm not just sleeping at night," Grace said. "I'm sleeping all the time. I can't get out of bed."

"The Nuvigil should change that. And if it doesn't, we'll give Provigil a try."

For someone who has resisted taking medication her entire life, Grace has succumbed to the will of Frank Ellery surprisingly quickly. He is a wonderful listener. He is, she can tell, quite brilliant. And clearly wise.

As he said himself: Who is she to question *him*?

Showered, her hair blown out, Grace slips the sweater over her head, aghast at how this loose, flowing Eskandar sweater has now become—oh God, please say this is a dry-cleaning mistake, or a washing mistake, or some kind, *any* kind, of mistake—tight.

It is tight. There is no mistaking it. Not skintight, but tight enough to show her curves, and since when did she have curves? It looks terrible. There's no way she can wear it tonight.

She pulls her pants on—the biggest pants she owns, cinching in the waist with the drawstring every time she has worn them in the past, liking how baggy they are, how they flatter her.

They pull up, but they no longer cinch in. Her legs still seem . . . normal, but this excess weight she has suddenly gained has all gone, she now realizes, to her stomach. Her taut, flat, hard stomach is now extended to the point where Grace actually realizes she could almost pull off being pregnant.

She looks tubby. Grace, who has never been anything other than reed thin, looks tubby, as, from the corner of the bathroom, the scales begin to taunt her.

No, she thinks. I will not weigh myself. I cannot weigh myself. From now on I'm just not going to give in to the cravings. I'm going to stop eating flour and sugar once again, and this weight will go.

I can do it. I've always done it. I am stronger than the cravings and I'm going to start now.

LEMON AND ALMOND CAKE

INGREDIENTS

2 lemons

1 cup butter

¾ cup sugar

4 large eggs, beaten

⅓ cup all-purpose flour

1⅓ cup ground almonds or almond flour

1 teaspoon almond extract

2 Tablespoons confectioners' sugar

Preheat oven to 350 degrees.

Put the whole lemons in a pan, cover with water, bring to boil, and simmer for an hour, or nuke in water in the microwave for around 25 minutes, until soft. Cut lemons in half, remove pips, and puree in food processor with skin, pith, and all. This gives the cake an intense, lemony flavor.

Cream butter and sugar together until almost white. Beat in eggs, one at a time, adding flour, 1 tablespoon at a time.

Gently stir in almonds, almond extract, and lemon mixture.

Pour into a greased 9-inch springform pan, bottom lined with parchment paper.

Bake for ½ hour, then cover with foil and bake for further ½ hour.

Cool on a wire rack, and when cool, sprinkle with confectioners' sugar through a sieve to decorate, with some additional lemon zest.

Twenty-one

"Grace! Ted!" Sybil flings her arms around Grace, then Ted, welcoming them into her house, taking them straight into the kitchen where she immediately starts pouring a glass of Ted's favorite red wine.

"I miss you!" Sybil links her arm through Grace's as they walk, Ted in front of them. "I feel like I haven't seen you in weeks. What's going on?"

Grace hasn't shared her diagnosis with anyone. She feels, most of the time, locked down with shame at having bipolar disorder. When she isn't feeling humiliated and ashamed at being crazy—for it is hard to think of this in any way other than being crazy—she is skeptical.

I don't have a mental illness, she tells herself.

"I don't have a mental illness," she tells Frank Ellery, who tells her not to think of it as a mental illness, but as a way to explain some of her mood swings.

The thought of telling anyone other than her family that she is bipolar—and whatever her shrink said, she thinks of it as something she *is*, not something she *has*—fills her with horror, and yet she isn't sure this is something she can do alone. Sybil is her closest friend and Sybil knows there is something going on. Their cozy last-minute lunches have come to a grinding halt, Grace having no energy to go out to lunch, no desire to go out in the world and be seen, particularly feeling as awful as she now does, having gained the weight she now has.

"Look at me." She unlinks her arm from Sybil and steps back, gesturing at her body with a frown. "The reason you haven't seen me is because I seem to have crawled into my fridge and stayed there for the past six weeks."

Sybil hoots. "About damned time there was some flesh on those bones." She peers at Grace closely. "So you're no longer a size four. So what? The question is, why have you crawled into the fridge these past few weeks, and why have you disappeared from life? I keep showing up to Harmont House and finding Beth there dropping off food and you're not in the kitchen, and everyone's missing your lessons, and Beth won't tell me anything other than you're busy."

Grace breathes an inward sigh of relief. Whatever reservations she may have had about Beth, hearing this, her discretion, her loyalty, soothes her soul.

"Shall we go into the living room?" Grace says. "I have to tell you privately."

"Is this really bad?" The color has drained from Sybil's face.

"No! No! I'm not ill. Well, not cancer or anything like that."

"Oh, thank God!" Sybil breathes. "Let me just grab a couple of glasses of wine and we'll go and sit down. I'll tell the boys to leave us alone for a few."

Minutes later, Grace takes a deep breath, unsure of how to tell her best friend, terrified it will change things, push Sybil away, frighten her. Terrified that she, Grace, has spent her entire life striving for perfection, has built her life on presenting an image of being able to do everything, and yet all the time there has been this glaring flaw, a flaw that, once people discover it, will make everything else a sham.

Perfection. Grace isn't even sure when she decided she had to be perfect in the eyes of the world, only that the thought of being seen as imperfect, flawed, broken, makes her instantly ashamed.

Her childhood was chaos. When Beth spoke of her own childhood, the alcoholism, the drama, Grace said nothing, unwilling to reveal secrets she has spent her whole life trying to bury.

It was her mother who was the cause of all the chaos. Her mother, who could be the warmest, sweetest, most loving woman in the world, who would then turn, in the blink of an eye, into a vicious, punitive, shrieking wreck.

Her mother who made Grace's home unsafe, who created an environment in which walking on eggshells became the norm; where Grace learned to walk into a room and instantly take the temperature, judge who she was supposed to be, how she was supposed to be in order to try and keep the peace, try and allay her mother's rages.

She has been talking about this a lot with Frank Ellery. Grace has spent her whole life believing her mother's mood swings, her bipolar disorder, was due to her drinking, but Frank has begged to differ. This is the missing genetic component, he says. This is where her mother's drinking came from, and indeed where Grace's own bipolar disorder comes from; just as he is not wrong about Grace, nor is he wrong about her mother.

They have talked endlessly about her childhood. Grace tried so hard to be perfect, convinced that if she was, if she cleaned up after her mother, if she took the place of the grown-up in the family, then everything would be fine.

If she was perfect, no one would judge her, or blame her, or shame her.

She couldn't wait to leave home, moved across the Atlantic to get away from her family of origin, convinced that as soon as she got away everything would be fine and she could leave all her problems behind. The curse of perfectionism followed her to this country and has stayed with her all these years.

Which is why it is so hard to sit here as she does now, ashamed of the weight she has gained, feeling she is no longer good enough, humiliated at not being able to manage her life in the way that has always come so easily to her.

The Grace that sits here today is vulnerable, and being vulnerable, Grace knows from her childhood, means she will get hurt. Being vulnerable means she will be screamed at, diminished, told she is stupid, ugly, incapable of doing anything right.

Being vulnerable, in Grace's eyes, means weakness, and she has spent her whole life pretending to be strong. Building this perfect life with the bestselling author Ted Chapman, telling the world their great love story, hosting elaborate parties that are frequently featured in magazines. She has spent her whole life doing this so no one sees that underneath the veneer, the persona, Grace is still the scared little girl she was back in London all those years ago, sinking into the floor as her mother screamed at her, wanting, wishing, to be anywhere other than there.

Grace takes a deep breath and looks at Sybil. "You know I've been having a hard time lately? I started seeing a doctor, a psychiatrist, a few months ago, and after a while he told me that there's a reason for all the . . . mood swings, and lack of sleeping, and losing my temper. Well, you know. All the stuff I'd been going through."

Sybil nods. "Hormones?"

"Well, no. He's pretty clear that I have bipolar disorder."

There is a shocked silence as Sybil just stares at her.

"What did you just say?" says Sybil eventually.

"I have bipolar disorder."

Sybil just stares at her. "I'm sorry," Sybil says. "Did you just say you have bipolar disorder?"

"Apparently," Grace says. "I know. I didn't believe it either."

"Grace!" Sybil barks. "Bipolar? Are you nuts? I'm sorry, I didn't mean that. I meant . . . I know someone who's bipolar and they are cuckoo. You are not cuckoo. In any way, shape, or form. There is no way in hell you're bipolar. That's just not true."

"Syb, there are apparently two kinds of bipolar. I should know. It . . . it runs in my family." For a second, Grace thinks about telling Sybil, what a relief it would be to let someone else in on her secret, let someone other than Lydia and Patrick, so far away in England, know the one secret that has always defined her.

But no. Even with Sybil, who she trusts implicitly, she is only able to be vague, to talk around it.

"You never told me."

"I never told anyone. I don't talk about it because it's just too damned painful. But I grew up with it and it's . . . genetic. But I don't have exactly the same thing, the kind of bipolar we immediately think of when we hear the term: celebrities going off their meds and suddenly getting caught with prostitutes, or going on mad spending binges, or just being completely manic in every way. That, sadly, was my experience growing up, but apparently there's another kind, which is what I have. Bipolar two. Which is when you don't have mania, you have something called hypomania, which is less dramatic, but still bad."

"I don't care!" Sybil is getting in a rage. "Hypo, hyper. You don't have mania. Grace? This is wrong. There's no way you're bipolar. I've known you for years and this just doesn't fit. It doesn't feel right in any part of my body, and you know I would tell you if I thought it did."

Grace gives a sad smile. "I know. I feel the same way much of the time, but he's very sure, and I trust him. He's a psychology professor at Columbia, and up to date on everything that's happening in the psychiatric world. He was involved in the new *DSM* . . ."

"*DSM*?"

"The *Diagnostic and Statistic Manual of Mental Disorders*. He knows his stuff, Syb. Really. I feel much the same way as you do about this, but I have to trust him."

"Oh, Grace." Sybil's face starts to crumple. "Really? You really think he's right? He could be head of psychology at Harvard for all I care, but you really think this is a correct diagnosis?"

"Yes. No." Grace sighs. "Most of the time I don't, but he says that's incredibly common. Apparently all newly diagnosed people question it; we all feel that this is wrong, and that's when people get into trouble."

"So . . . what are you doing about it?"

"Other than getting fat? Taking medication. That's been part of the problem—the weight gain and then this utter exhaustion. Honestly, that's why you haven't seen me these past few weeks. No one has seen me. I've barely got out of bed."

"Grace! That's terrible. You? Not get out of bed? You have more energy than anyone I know!"

"That's the hypomania, apparently. I certainly don't have much energy anymore, but he keeps reassuring me that will pass. Everything apparently will settle down, but it's really difficult. He's given me different pills to try and help with the tiredness, and more to try and cut my appetite, because I am starving. Literally, all the time I am hollow with hunger."

"Do you want some cheese and crackers?" Concerned, Sybil leans over the coffee table and pulls the tray of cheese closer.

"No, I'm fine," Grace says. "I'm trying really hard to get back on track. Nothing fits. Honestly, if I wasn't depressed before, I'm definitely bloody depressed now."

"Tell me about it," says Sybil, slicing a thick chunk of cheese, laying it on a Triscuit, and slathering it with fig jam. "At least you know you can borrow anything of mine, and you've got pounds and pounds left before my dresses will fit you. Are you sure you won't have some cheese?"

"Maybe just a small bit," says Grace, reaching for the knife and making herself a cracker of her own.

Good Lord!" Ted walks into the living room. "Where's all the cheese?"

"We were hungry," says Sybil. "Sorry. There's more in the fridge. Let me go and get it."

"Don't worry," says Ted. "We're probably better off without it." He catches Grace's eye, as Grace wants the floor to open her up and swallow her whole.

So much for turning over a new leaf.

Later that evening, when food has been eaten, bottles of wine consumed, conversation and laughter bouncing off the corners of the dining room, Sybil whisks Grace into the kitchen, ostensibly to help her wash up, wanting to talk to her privately.

"I don't like it," Sybil says. "I don't feel good about this whole bipolar thing, and I don't feel good about you."

"I don't like it either," says Grace. "But not liking it doesn't make it go away. And what do you mean, you don't feel good about me?"

"You're just not yourself. You've been here all evening, but I feel like you're a shadow of your former self."

"Hardly a shadow when I'm twice the size."

"That's not what I meant. You're here physically, but I don't feel like you're really here. I have this really weird sense that you're completely disconnected from everything. You're talking a bit, and smiling in the right places, but you seem so unhappy. If this bipolar disorder thing is correct, then these pills surely aren't the right pills, no? Isn't any medication of this kind meant to bring you back to yourself? Make you *more* of yourself? It's not supposed to eradicate you."

Grace feels her eyes well with tears as Sybil puts the plate down and wraps her arms around her.

"I'm sorry," Grace says. "It's just . . . you put it so well. I know it has only been a couple of months but I feel eradicated. That's exactly right. I feel like a facsimile of myself, and I hate it. I keep telling Frank, my doctor, that I feel awful, but he says this is calm, this is normal. He says I'm so used to being in a state of hypomania, that what other people consider normal feels flat to me."

"Grace!" Sybil steps back, holding Grace by the arms, staring intently into her eyes. "I have known you for many, many years, and I have never known you to be manic, in any way, shape, or form. Yes, you have more energy than anyone I know, and that is part of your charm. It is why we all love you. What does Ted say about all this? Surely he doesn't agree with it? Surely he's concerned?"

Grace doesn't want to admit that she has barely seen Ted these past few weeks. He seems happier than he has for years, is entrenched in his new novel, is finding the writing process more fluid than it has ever been. Beth is there and able to attend to his needs, so Grace doesn't have to worry. In many ways, having Beth there has been a huge relief through this, it has meant she is able to disappear for hours at a time in her bedroom, knowing Ted will not be making demands of her.

They still have dinner together, at the kitchen table, but not every night. Grace just doesn't have the will. She can't think of anything to talk about anymore, and frankly, it's much easier to stay in bed, or have—gasp—the unthinkable: TV dinners in front of one of the news shows he loves to watch.

Last week they discovered *House of Cards* on Netflix, and both spent four evenings in a row watching as many hours of Kevin Spacey as they could physically manage. It was a relief to Grace to be able to curl up on a sofa with her husband, yet not have to talk. They could delight together in the brilliance of the show, bond affectionately in the soft blue light of the television screen, barely needing to say a word to each other.

And when the show was over, they could softly pad upstairs to bed. They have only made love once. Ted has reached for her many times, but Grace is mortified at how she looks naked. The one time they did make love, she kept her nightgown on, refusing to pull it up farther than her hips, terrified he would see the rolls on her stomach, her cushiony breasts flattened to either side of her body as she lay down.

She loves her husband, but she is ashamed. She loves her husband, but is convinced that if he sees her like this, he will no longer want to make love to her. May, in fact, start looking for a younger, trimmer model.

How is he supposed to keep loving her when she can barely get out of bed and looks so terrible?

And the worst thing of all? She doesn't even care.

Twenty-two

Many months ago, when Grace was still leading an active life, going to dinner parties, charity luncheons, accepting speaking engagements, she had agreed to introduce a charity lunch that helps dress underprivileged women in business clothes—usually designer cast-offs—in order to help them at job interviews.

Grace is on the board. This is one of her pet charities, and she is there every year. She is a pro at this, has done these speeches many times before, knows how to sit at a table with a group of women she does not know and be gracious, and interested, and kind.

She is able to do this because Grace has always carried a quiet confidence. Until today. All week she has been desperately trying to think of ways to get out of today's luncheon, knowing all the while that it would be absolutely the wrong thing to do. However much she hates the prospect, it is something she has to do, an obligation she has to fulfil.

Today's luncheon is at the Cosmopolitan Club in New York. It will only be an hour, an hour and a half at the most, because all the women who have bought tickets to the event are ambitious, driven New York women who are only able to leave their high-powered jobs for an hour and a half at the max, and only then, for "lunch."

Grace is used to walking into this luncheon with her head held high. The room is filled with people she knows—not friends exactly, but many people she enjoys hugely, from the world of media and magazines—and everyone knows Grace.

None of the confidence she usually feels is with her today. Walking up the stairs, Grace avoids looking in the mirror. She is dressed today in a cashmere poncho, newly acquired at Bergdorf's just the other week, for she is spending her days in stretchy yoga pants and oversized sweaters and had nothing dressy that would fit. The shopping trip was compulsory rather than fun. Grace bought two good outfits to see her through, determined these would be the last clothes of this size she would ever buy.

Her hair has been blown out and she is wearing far more makeup than usual, in a bid to disguise how much weight she has put on, how badly she feels about herself. The skirt she wears is floor-length, pleated silk and the poncho the softest cashmere, and beautiful.

Standing before the mirror in her closet was the first time she felt, if not beautiful, then passable. These days she avoids mirrors, avoids seeing people as much as possible, but given she has to be seen in public today, she made enough of an effort that perhaps people will be fooled.

"Grace!" Ingrid, the publisher of one of Grace's favorite magazines, swoops upon her and kisses her on either cheek. "You look magnificent! I love this!" Grace smiles as Ingrid fingers the poncho. "It suits you! You look statuesque and strong, like the Statue of Liberty."

Grace laughs nervously, not at all sure whether to take this as a compliment or not.

"Beautiful," Ingrid murmurs, fingering the Fortuny-style pleats on the skirt. "Just lovely," and Grace relaxes.

"You must meet Annette," she says, gesturing to a tiny, impish woman in one of those black dresses that is so deceptively simple, it must have cost a fortune. She is carrying a power bag—alligator, oversized, shockingly expensive—that elevates her outfit to a level where everyone who looks at her will know, beyond a shadow of a doubt, that she is superior to them.

"Annette is the new editor-in-chief. Annette? Do you know Grace?"

"Grace?" Annette looks surprised.

"Grace Chapman? Our wonderful speaker," Ingrid persists as Grace watches the shock flit through Annette's eyes.

"Oh God!" Annette forces a recovery. "I'm so sorry. I have only ever seen pictures of you. You look so . . . different from your pictures. I'm so sorry. I just . . . I would never have thought it was the same person. I would never have recognized you."

Grace stands there uncomfortably, knowing what this woman is saying, able to hear the message loud and clear. *In your pictures you are slim and beautiful, but look at you! Look how fat you are! You are unrecognizable.* Shame fills her from head to toe as she struggles to find a response.

"Oh?" is all she can manage, desperate to get away, wishing she could hide, wishing she were anyplace right now other than here.

Annette just looks at her, clearly struggling to get out of this mess, to make it right, as Ingrid glares at her.

"You're much more beautiful in real life," Annette stammers eventually. Lamely. Grace forces a laugh and, much to her relief, is steered away by Ingrid.

"Are you okay?" Ingrid does not take her into the room that is already filled to bursting with excited, chattering women, but instead to a quiet corridor.

Grace takes a few deep breaths. "I know I look different. I haven't been . . . well. One of the unfortunate side effects of the medication I've been on is this tremendous weight gain I haven't been able to do anything about. I'm sure Annette is lovely, but I can see what she is thinking, what everyone is thinking: God, doesn't she look awful! What's happened to Grace Chapman? Look at how much weight she gained!"

"Fuck 'em," Ingrid says sternly. "You're still you on the inside and frankly, half the women in that room have no idea whatsoever what it's like to be middle-aged and have your hormones go crazy on you, and find your waistline went AWOL with your memory."

Graces laughs, this time genuinely.

"Truly, Grace. I am not kidding. You are still beautiful, and you will always be beautiful. A few extra pounds does not change that. Quite apart from your exquisite features, your beauty shines from the inside. Your beauty is from all the people you help, and the service you give, and your wide-open heart. . . ." She looks at Grace, steadying her, making sure Grace hears. "And the problem with open-hearted people is that they are liable to get hurt, but that doesn't mean they must close themselves off. You touch too many people, Grace. You have made too much of a difference in too many people's lives to shut yourself away, however you feel about your physical self. I promise you, you are still beautiful. Annette? We adore her, but please," Ingrid leans forward to whisper, "you don't get to be her size without a serious eating disorder. She didn't mean to be cruel, but I had to resist the temptation to squash her minus-zero body with my size-ten shoe."

Grace laughs.

"Better?" She links an arm through Grace's, instructing her to take a deep breath before turning to go into the main room. "You're beautiful, and brave and strong," she whispers. "Keep telling yourself that. That's your mantra, and it doesn't matter what anyone else thinks."

Grace tells herself that, over and over, but when her name is called, and she threads her way through the tables, making her way to the podium to a round of applause, she is aware of the shocked looks, the furtive whispers. She knows what people are thinking, knows exactly what they are whispering.

When she reaches the stage, she scans the room until her eyes settle on Ingrid, who blows her a kiss and lays her hands over her heart. Grace starts to speak, realizing after her first laugh from the crowd that Ingrid was right: It really doesn't matter much at all.

Twenty-three

It is six o'clock by the time Grace gets home. She spent the afternoon with Ingrid, and although she didn't feel anything like her old self, getting out of bed, getting out of the prison her house has become, made her feel almost human again. Valued. Worthwhile.

The house is quiet. Grace does what she always does now, a Pavlovian response to entering her kitchen: she puts her purse down on the table and immediately opens the fridge, reaching a hand in before she even decides what she is going to eat, before she even thinks that they will shortly be eating dinner, that given the amount she has already eaten today, she cannot possibly be hungry. She reaches for the cheese and slices off a wedge, then another and another, before closing the door and going upstairs to change—her skirt cutting into her waist.

The day in the city has exhausted her. Climbing onto her bed, she clicks on the television and turns to the news, giving her iPhone a cursory check. Three missed calls from Sybil. The last thing Grace wants to do is speak to anyone, but what if this is an emergency? Why else would Sybil have tried her three times?

"Thank God!" Sybil bursts out as soon as she answers the phone. "I've been trying you all day!"

"I'm sorry. I was in the city. Is everything okay?"

"No! It's not. Oh, Grace. I don't even know how to tell you this, but they called an emergency board meeting today at Harmont House."

"What? Why didn't anyone let me know?"

Sybil takes a deep breath. "Because it was about you. Grace, I'm telling you this because I am appalled, and I said so, but I wanted to prepare you, I wanted you to hear this from me. Beth was invited along to the meeting."

"What?" Grace's voice is an anguished shout.

"She was asked to describe your mental state, which she said was extremely unstable, and it was decided that it was no longer healthy for you to be on the board."

"I don't understand. How can they even make this kind of decision without me?"

"Beth talked about you as if you were going mad. And they believed her."

"Didn't you say anything? Didn't you tell them she was lying?"

"I tried, Grace. I kept saying this wasn't true, that I saw you almost every day and you were fine, just a little depressed, but nothing that would get in the way of your work at Harmont House. But they voted. And they voted that Beth would replace you on the board."

And Grace, in a moment of anger she later regrets, throws her phone against the marble fireplace in their bedroom, where it shatters as it falls to the floor.

Ted?" No answer. Running downstairs in bare feet, the kitchen lights are still off, the house deserted. Her mind is whirling, it is taking all the energy she has not to burst into floods of tears.

Forcing herself to slow down, she thinks for a moment, but doesn't recall anything in the diary for tonight. As far as she knows, Ted is supposed to be home, although she is the first to concede the unreliability of her memory, which has grown even worse of late.

Through the window she sees the barn lights are on. Please let him be there. Please let him make this better, let him explain to the board that she hasn't changed, this is a huge mistake; she isn't crazy; they cannot take this away from her.

She can't just go down there with no excuse. Throwing a cheese platter together, she puts a bottle of wine on it, two glasses, pretending everything is as normal.

The glasses shake as she makes her way down the path, attempting to take deep breaths to calm herself. Through the door of the barn, Grace stands, frowning at the empty room.

Music is playing, which is not unusual, but then, unexpectedly, a moan.

Or is it a groan? Her heart stops.

Oh, *God*.

Visions of Ted lying on the floor fill her head—a heart attack, a stroke. Three more steps and she is no longer staring at the high back of the sofa, but at her husband and Beth, wrapped around each other on the other side, Beth's shirt undone, her husband's hair tousled, neither of them hearing her as Debussy sweeps through the speakers.

Frozen, she watches as if she is watching a movie. She watches Beth's tongue dart into her husband's mouth as he attempts to swallow her whole, moaning in pleasure. The way he used to moan with her.

Beth's eyes open and look at him, before moving to take in Grace, standing there, eyes wide with shock, as she drops the tray, glasses smashing, her hands flying up to her mouth.

Twenty-four

"What's going on?" Clemmie bursts through the doors of the hospital, into the waiting room where Ted sits, leaning forward, elbows planted on his knees, wringing his hands.

"Clemmie!" He stands, putting his arms around his daughter, attempting to reassure her, attempting to reassure himself for his life is spinning out of control and he has no idea what to do.

"Where's Mom? What's going on? Is she okay?" Clemmie turns at the sound of entering footsteps to see Beth walking into the room, two cups of coffee from the machine in each hand. "Beth? What are you doing here? What happened?" She notices Beth's face is swollen, a faint bruise forming on her cheek.

"Beth was with me when it happened," says Ted. "She's the reason your mother had to be brought here. Oh, Clemmie, I didn't want you to know anything, but your mother's been unwell for a while. Tonight was some sort of psychotic break, but she's been heading this way for a few months."

"What do you mean, 'unwell'?" Clemmie says, her voice catching in her throat, the word "cancer" lingering on the outskirts of her mind. "What kind of unwell? What do you mean?"

"She has bipolar disorder," Ted says softly. "She is medicated, but something snapped tonight."

"What? Whoa. What are you *talking* about? Mom is bipolar? That's *impossible*. There's no way. Bipolar means crazy. That's not Mom. What the hell?" Clemmie runs her fingers through her hair. "What are you talking about?"

"Clemm, I know it's difficult, but it's true. I know this is hard for you, but your mother has had her struggles with depression."

"But depression isn't bipolar," blurts Clemmie. "She isn't manic. She isn't crazy."

Ted and Beth exchange a look. "She hasn't been," says Ted. "Until recently. Her mania has been in the form of anger. She has struggled with these rages to the point where we all decided she had to go and see someone, and he was the one who diagnosed her with the disorder."

"But why is she here? What happened?"

This time, Ted avoids looking at Beth. "I was working late and Beth was helping me. We were sitting on the sofa and your mother walked in. She immediately jumped to the conclusion that something was going on and . . ."

"Why would she jump to that conclusion?" Clemmie says. "That's insane."

"That's the point," says Ted. "It is insane. But she started screaming at us, ranting and raving, then she slapped Beth."

"What?"

"She did," Beth says softly, pointing to the swollen cheek. "That's when we had no choice but to call the police."

"Mom actually *slapped* her?" Clemmie says in disbelief.

"I was on my hands and knees trying to clear up the mess—your mother had dropped a full tray of glass and china—and I heard it. Beth screamed in pain and I immediately restrained your mother while Beth called the police. Honestly, Clemmie, we had no choice. I was terrified she was going to hurt us, or worse, hurt herself. She was a complete mess. I knew this was really bad. I'm sorry, darling, but your mother is really ill."

"I'm so sorry." Beth's eyes are limpid, soft, completely empathic as she holds her arms out to Clemmie, who allows herself to be held, numb at what is happening, still attempting to digest it all. "I'm so sorry," whispers Beth, rubbing her back. "I know how hard this must be for you."

"But why is she in the hospital?" Clemmie murmurs into her shoulder. "Did she hurt herself? I want to see her. Where is she?"

Ted takes a deep breath. "She's waiting outside the psychiatric ward," he says. "We're waiting for her psychiatrist to arrive, Frank Ellery. Beth phoned him while I tried to restrain your mother and he immediately said he would admit her. They don't want her seeing anyone until she's been evaluated. I'm sorry, darling, but you wouldn't want to see her now. She's in no state to see you, and it wouldn't be good for you. She's babbling all kinds of things that just aren't true."

Clemmie sinks down on a chair as tears fill her eyes. "How can this be true?" she whispers, but the only thought going through her head is, I want my mom.

I need my mom to make this all go away.

Grace has been hysterical since the moment she screamed. She was hysterical all the way over here, as they bundled her into an ambulance, so upset she was hyperventilating. They gave her a shot of something, which has made her feel stoned.

Now she is trying to be calm. If she can explain to someone what just happened, they will let her out of here. No one seems to be interested in listening to her; everyone keeps telling her that Dr. Ellery will be here soon and she can explain to him.

Her bare feet are cold on the hospital's linoleum floor. As the hours tick by, as the medication they injected into her starts to wear off, Grace becomes increasingly terrified. Things like this don't happen to people like her. This is like being stuck in a horrific movie, one so dramatic, so terrible, you are sitting on the edge of your seat dreading the next awful thing you know is coming. Or, at least, you would be if it were happening to someone else.

Jack Nicholson in *One Flew Over the Cuckoo's Nest* flashes into her mind. But that wouldn't happen to *her*. Dr. Ellery *knows* her. He *knows* that while she may be many things, a fantasist she is not.

Even when she explains what happened this evening, what made her snap, she realizes her life will never be the same. How can it be when she now knows what has been going on?

Her husband is obsessed with Beth—that much is obvious—and now they are having an affair.

But worse than that was seeing Beth—as Ted was on his hands and knees on the floor, picking up the pieces of glass from the crystal inkwell Grace hadn't been aware of throwing, before she struck Beth—seeing the look of *conquest* on Beth's face.

Grace isn't a violent person. She cannot begin to explain what came over her, a rage, a fury so huge it had to come out somehow. She never thought she was capable of hitting someone, but without realizing what was happening, Grace had brought her hand back and had put all her weight behind it as she slapped Beth on the cheek.

The worst thing of all? How good it felt.

"Oh my God!" Beth had moaned, her hands flying to her eye. "She just hit me. Oh my God! Get away from me! Ted! She *slapped* me!"

"Grace!" Ted came toward her and took her arms, almost shook her in disgust. "Grace! I know you're upset and I'm sorry, but control yourself. For God's sake."

"I'm calling the police." Beth moved to the phone. "She assaulted me."

"Grace." Ted's voice was soothing, conciliatory. "I know you're not well, but you need help, that much is clear. More help than you've been getting. We're going to get you the help you need."

"I don't need help, you bastard," Grace hissed as Beth murmured into the phone at the other end of the room. "*She's* the one who needs help. I walk in here and find my husband entwined with his assistant, and *I'm* the one who needs help?"

Ted ignored her, didn't see Beth look at Grace with a look so cold, so detached from everything that was going on, Grace knew this was exactly what she wanted.

She looked triumphant.

I have won, it said. And Grace knew suddenly that Beth did steal her scarf. God knows what else besides. She knew suddenly that Beth had intentionally called the rental company before the event at Harmont House and canceled everything. She knew that Beth came into their lives very deliberately to ruin them, or at least, to ruin her.

It all became shockingly clear. Beth had been systematically stealing Grace's life for months. Finally she got what Grace realizes, with shocking clarity, she came for: her husband. With a howl of rage, Grace broke free of Ted and ran toward Beth. Beth, younger, lighter, quicker than Grace, darted into the bathroom, locked the door, as Grace pounded on the door, yelling for her to come out.

This was how the police found her when they arrived. Beth locked in the bathroom with Grace banging on the door, howling her frustration as she collapsed, finally, in a puddle of tears.

"Why?" Grace calmed herself enough to turn to Beth, just as she was bundled into the back of the ambulance that accompanied the police car. She was looking directly into Beth's eyes as she said it; only Beth had the answer.

"Why?"

Beth said nothing. Ted couldn't look Grace in the eye, standing next to Beth as his wife was taken away, but Beth looked at her. She stared her in the eyes until the ambulance door closed and Grace was driven off, with no idea why her life was suddenly going so completely, and utterly, wrong.

When Frank Ellery appears at the end of the corridor, Grace leaps to her feet, almost weeping in gratitude at her savior finally having arrived.

"Frank!" She blinks back the tears as she stands. "Thank God you're here! They wouldn't let me talk to anyone, wouldn't let me explain anything until you got here. I'm so sorry to pull you away from home so late."

"That's all right, Grace," Frank says, in a tone similar to the one he uses when talking to very small children. "Why don't we go somewhere and talk, and you can tell me all about it."

"Yes!" Grace lights up. "Thank you!" He excuses himself to have a short conversation with the nurses behind the desk, which Grace can't hear, although she strains her ears in an attempt.

"Let's go in here." He shows her into a doctor's office, where she sits in a wing chair, aware of her bare feet, her yoga pants and sleeping T-shirt; aware she is in clothes she only wears to bed; of how inappropriately she is dressed.

Grace takes a deep breath and explains to Frank what happened tonight. That she caught Ted and Beth in a clinch, that she admitted to dropping the tray and feeling rage, that she had done the unthinkable and lost control, shocked at herself for having lashed out at Beth.

Grace was mindful of keeping her voice calm, level, knowing her only chance of lending this incredible story credibility was to make *herself* credible. She explained that it all became clear to her tonight, how Beth had planned this, had orchestrated a deliberate series of moves to undermine Grace; in all probability to steal her husband. In fact, Grace added, Beth had probably orchestrated that Grace be brought here tonight.

"Having me committed is probably the icing on her cake," she says wryly. "Thank God you're here and you believe me. You know me, and you know I'm not a liar."

There is a pause as Grace waits for Frank to say something, but he is silent, just watches her with that familiar empathic expression in his eyes, as Grace feels a jolt of disquiet.

"Frank? I know it sounds absurd, but there is no reason for me to make this up. You do believe me, Frank?"

Another silence. "I believe that you believe it to be true," he says softly. "Which is really the only thing that matters."

"No it isn't," snaps Grace. "That's psychobabble claptrap. If you don't believe me, then you think I'm crazy. And if I'm crazy, you're here to have me committed, which is exactly what she wants."

"Grace, no one's talking about having you committed. I do think, however, that a stay here for a few days would be valuable. It will help stabilize you and get you to a better place. I think that whatever you think happened tonight, you will agree that you lost control, yes?"

"Yes, I lost control, but anyone would have lost control. I caught my husband about to fuck his bloody assistant. How would you feel if you walked in on your wife about to fuck . . . I don't know, your colleague? Pretty bloody angry, that's how."

"We're not talking about me, Grace. We're talking about you. I think a few days here is a very good idea. We can always reevaluate when things are a little calmer."

"And if I refuse?"

"I think you'll find it's in your best interests to agree."

Grace stares at him, Jack Nicholson back in her mind. Oh *shit*, she thinks. It *can* happen to someone like me.

What the hell am I supposed to do now?

. . .

She is supposed to do exactly what she does. Reluctantly agree to Frank's wishes, telling him she is agreeing because she trusts him, appearing to wait in the hallway, calmly, while he goes off to speak to her husband and have him fill in the necessary paperwork.

As soon as he is gone, she walks casually down the corridor, her heart pounding, as she rounds the corner, smashing open the emergency doors at the back of the building and tearing through the parking lot on bare feet, adrenaline keeping her running until she reaches the end of the road.

Once outside, Grace crouches behind a car, her heart pounding. She has to get away from here, far away, and none of the places she considers safe—at Sybil's, at Clemmie's—are safe anymore.

Escape is the only thing she can think of. If she stays here, they will come to get her—Beth will make sure of it and there is no safety in her family anymore.

A couple walk out, chatting away.

"Excuse me?" Grace attempts to sound as refined as possible. "I'm so sorry, but my phone isn't working. Would you mind if I made a call?" The man is about to say no, but the woman hands over her cell phone, ignoring the reprimanding look she gets.

Grace phones Sybil then, instructs her to go to Sneden's, grab her passport from the dresser in her bedroom, some shoes, her pills, her purse, and meet her by the bank. Don't, for God's sake, tell anyone. No one. Swear on your life.

Sybil swears on her life.

While waiting for Sybil to arrive, Grace is supposed to do exactly what she does: curl herself into a small ball in the corner of the parking lot and rock back and forth, her whole body shaking with tears.

Twenty-five

On the plane, Grace sits, shaking uncontrollably, unable to touch the food, unable to focus on the movies, unable to do anything other than sit and shake, accepting the wine on offer, in utter disbelief about the events of the past two days.

Her life, as she knows it, is over. That much is clear. This sense of Beth being out to get her, Ted being drawn in, is no longer, she realizes, in her imagination. England is the only place that feels safe to her, and even then, she has no idea where to go once there.

Lydia is safe, but how can she turn up to Lydia like this? She will spend a few days in London, in a hotel, a few days in which she will be able to get on her feet, calm down, get herself together enough to be able to be seen by people who know her.

She will go to Belgraves, the hotel she and Ted occasionally used to stay in when they were in London. She doesn't need a suite, not on her own, but will take a small room, a bath, will go down to Knightsbridge tomorrow and get some basic clothes—they're bound to have a Gap or somewhere inexpensive for some clean leggings and tops.

No luggage, she thinks, as the pilot instructs everyone to get ready for landing. A purse. That's it. When has she ever taken a plane without, at least, a carry-on bag. Everything she owns is back at Sneden's Landing and, with tremendous shock, she realizes she may never see any of it again.

No, she tells herself. I will not dwell in that kind of fear. If I need to send someone to collect my jewelry, the few things that have meaning to me, I will do so. This will blow over. In some shape or form, I must recognize this is a crisis, and as such it will resolve itself, and life will get back to some kind of normal.

At the airport she waits in line for a cab, forcing herself to make small talk with the chatty Cockney driver, almost weeping at the familiarity of it all.

She and Ted used to come to London regularly. He would come every year for a book tour, then fly home, leaving Grace to go down to Dorset to stay with Lydia a few days.

They stayed at the best hotels. First Claridge's, then, as Ted's fame grew and he wanted something smaller, Belgraves. They were treated like royalty, hotel staff falling over themselves to help, baskets of fruit and champagne inevitably waiting for them in their suite.

Things have changed over the past couple of years. Grace is careful not to say anything, careful to continue giving the impression that her husband is still at the top of his game, one of the most successful authors in the world, but the sales of his last two books were terrible.

His publishers have tightened their belts. Everyone is doing it, they said. Publishing is down over thirty percent, they said, explaining why they were no longer sending him on extended book tours. We are all suffering, they said, as they booked him into a Hilton, a world away from the Four Seasons or St. Regises of old.

To an outsider, their lifestyle hasn't changed in any real, noticeable way. Grace laughingly explains they are no longer going on vacation after Christmas this year because Ted is ensconced in a new book, or they will not be joining friends on a boat off the coast of Capri this summer because Ted will be on book tour, but it has been a long time since they have stayed in a hotel as lovely as the ones they used to stay in as a matter of course.

I don't have a room booked," she explains to the young girl behind the desk at Belgraves. "This was a last-minute decision." She smiles, hoping to charm, hoping she doesn't look quite as much of a mess as she fears. "I'm in your system. Well, my husband is. Grace and Ted Chapman?"

The woman taps on the screen for several minutes before extending a smile. "Of course," she says. "Here you are. Are you interested in the suite you used to stay in?"

"Not this time." Grace smiles. "It's just me. A room is fine."

"May I have your credit card," says the girl, as Grace pulls out her American Express.

Minutes go by. The girl frowns. "I'll try that again," she says. "I'm so sorry." She hands the card back. "I'm afraid it's being declined."

Grace flushes a deep red. "I'm so sorry," she blusters. "Try this." She hands over her Visa card, then her MasterCard. All are declined. The young girl is embarrassed for her, but not nearly as embarrassed as Grace is herself.

"I don't understand it," she says.

"We could take a check, I think," the girl says. "I'd have to check with my manager."

"I have no checks," says Grace. "Never mind. Thank you." And she walks out of the hotel, knowing Beth has stopped her credit cards, pausing on the corner to check how much cash she has left after the taxi ride.

Seventeen pounds.

Oh, God. Why didn't she take out money when she got to JFK yesterday? She feels sick with panic. What is she supposed to do?

Take deep breaths, she tells herself. This is going to work out. I'm close to Victoria Station, she thinks. I'll go and find a fleabag hotel there, somewhere cheap, and I'll phone the bank tomorrow, get money transferred. Something. I will figure this out as soon as I find a warm place to sleep.

The Bellagio Victoria Hotel on Hugh Street is about as far from its Las Vegas namesake as it is possible to get. What might once have been an impressive white-stucco terraced house now has most of the white stucco peeled off, leaving it dirty and unkempt. The dirty glass of the door is covered in stickers advertising it as a budget hotel for the traveler on the go, as Grace hesitates outside, knowing how awful it will be, knowing she doesn't have a choice.

It smells of old, dirty carpet and smoke, despite the NO SMOKING signs everywhere. The middle-aged woman who comes out from the back room when she hears Grace's "hello?" walks out scowling at Grace.

"I'm so sorry to trouble you," Grace says in her most charming of ways. "I just arrived here from America and there seems to be a problem with my credit cards. I only have seventeen pounds, but I was hoping you might have somewhere for me to sleep tonight, just until I can sort this out." Grace, so used to people saying yes to her, looks at her expectantly, knowing she will help, for this is what people do for the Chapmans: they go out of their way to help.

"Out!" the woman commands. "I'm not a bloody charity. Out."

I'm no one anymore. These words ticker tape through Grace's head as she stands, mutely, staring at the woman, unable to comprehend the world she has landed in, a dull buzzing in her ears as she turns on her heel and walks out the hotel.

Grace walks and walks. The hours tick by as she wanders through the streets of a town she used to know so well, no idea where she is going or what she is going to do.

Of course she must phone Lydia, must find a pay phone, if indeed they even still exist in this digital age. They must, she thinks. There has to be a way.

In Victoria Station, Grace sighs with relief at the sight of pay phones. *Thank God.* And when she approaches and discovers they take credit cards only, she howls in fury and bangs the receiver down, sinking her head in her hands.

Walking. More walking. Sneaking into the garden at St. George's Square, late, late at night, ignoring the couple of locals walking their dogs and looking at her suspiciously, she lies on a park bench, her bag under her head as a pillow and, shivering with tiredness and cold, she eventually falls asleep.

Excuse me? Excuse me?" Shaken awake, Grace blearily opens her eyes, feeling pain throughout her entire body, her neck stiff and sore. She looks up into the eyes of an older man with a toy poodle on the end of a leash. "You can't sleep here. This park is for residents only."

Grace sits up, pushing her hair back, clutching her bag on her lap.

"I'm sorry," she automatically apologizes. "I didn't mean to fall asleep," she lies.

His face softens. "There's a shelter around the corner," he says. "Not far to walk. I think you'll find it's much more comfortable."

"Shelter?" Grace frowns, still half-asleep.

"For the homeless." He nods encouragingly. *Like you*, are the words he doesn't say, but nevertheless, they hang in the air between them.

Grace just stares at him, blinking back tears. I'm not homeless, she wants to shout. I'm Grace Chapman! I live in a beautiful house on the water in New York!

But she says nothing. Merely nods, stands up, and walks away.

Her cashmere scarf has pulled on the bench and it is now crumpled and dirty. She washes her face in the bathroom of a McDonald's, where she buys a meal and finds herself unable to eat it, able only to drink the coffee.

Her breath is bad, her skin now dry and stretched with no moisturizer after washing with the harsh soap, not meant for the face of a middle-aged woman.

She has absolutely no idea what to do. Her phone is probably still in pieces in the barn back at Sneden's Landing; she has no access to contacts, to phone numbers. She could walk to the Soho offices of Ted's London literary agents, but she barely knows them, and it is such a very long walk.

Heading back to St. George's Square—it is quiet, away from the hustle and bustle—she sits on the same bench she slept on last night and cries silently, tears dripping down her cheeks.

Is this what it has come to, she thinks? All these months of not believing the diagnosis, not believing I am anything like my mother, and here I am, sleeping on a bench, nothing to my name and no home to go to.

I am homeless, she realizes, with shock. I have become the thing I have feared my entire life. I am my mother. This was her life, and I have spent my life terrified it would happen to me, and here I am.

"Excuse me? Excuse me?" It is the same older man with the same poodle.

"I know, I know. This is for residents only," Grace says wearily. "Please leave me alone," she says. "I'm not hurting anyone here. I haven't got anywhere else to go and I don't know what to do." Her voice breaks on the last word as she starts to cry.

"The shelter was full?" he says.

"No! I didn't go to the shelter. I'm not homeless. I'm just . . . stuck."

He looks at her for a while, examining her. "Is there someone you can call?" he says. "Someone who can help?"

"I could," Grace says, "but I don't have a phone. And I haven't got credit cards for the pay phones."

"Use mine." He hands her his cell phone. "Make a call."

"Really?" Grace wipes the tears away, a small ray of hope lighting up her eyes. "You're sure?"

"Go on," he says as Grace calls Information, then taps Lydia's number into the phone, almost collapsing with relief when Lydia picks up.

Twenty-six

Grace may not have had much of a mother in Sally, but she had a wonderful mother figure in Lydia.

On that very first day at university Grace had fallen in love with Catherine when she welcomed her with a huge smile and an offer of the best side of the room. As soon as Grace met her family, she understood what was so appealing to her about Catherine.

Catherine came from a loving family. She had older twin brothers who teased her with gentleness, but never cruelty. She had a father who was quiet and kind and a mother who seemed more like a wonderful best friend than a mother. At least, that was how it seemed to Grace at the time.

The first time she had gone back with Catherine to her home in Dorset, Grace had peppered Catherine with questions about her family all the way there. She had seen pictures of the brothers—open faces, large smiles, sporty—and had an image of Catherine's mother as a svelte, elegant woman in slacks and ballet pumps.

They turned off the main road just outside Sherborne, onto a pretty country lane, twisting around until they reached the thatched farmhouse at the end.

"This is your home?" breathed Grace, gazing at the picture-perfect Dorset stone house, roses climbing up the walls and over the arbor in the front garden. "It's gorgeous!"

"Only on the outside." Catherine parked her Mini next to a battered Saab and an old MG Midget in the driveway. "Inside it will be upside down, guaranteed. The boys are home, which means total chaos for the next week. Are you absolutely sure you're prepared for this?"

"Absolutely sure," Grace said, because she had spent much time gazing at the photograph of Catherine's brothers and was particularly interested in Robert, who Catherine described as the broodier of the two. He was also, at least in this photograph, infinitely more handsome. Patrick, or Twin B, as Catherine often called him, had a cheeky charm, but not the smouldering looks of the more serious brother.

"Moonface!" The back door burst open as a boy in football shorts and an unbuttoned plaid shirt came barreling toward the car.

"Moonface?" Grace turned to Catherine, an eyebrow raised.

"A childhood nickname. Obviously one I adore." She opened the car door and tumbled out, grabbed by her brother, who danced her around the gravel driveway as she laughed and pretended to try and push him away.

"God, Patrick. You're still a huge pain in the ass."

"Why? Because I'm showing my baby sister the love? Don't be so ungrateful. Where's this gorgeous redhead you told Robert about? And why did you tell Robert and not me?"

Grace stepped out of the car, clearing her throat, although she realized as she did so she was meant to hear that. She was already smiling in secret delight—Catherine had talked to Robert about her? She had no idea!

"Seriously, Catherine." Patrick stood still, looking at Grace. "Why did you tell Robert and not me?"

"Mostly because Grace would never be interested in a little squirt like you."

"Bollocks," he said, regaining his composure as he walked over to Grace, arm extended. "I'm Patrick," he said. "I'm the very funny one. Entertaining. And far more brilliant than Robert. He is good looking, but no personality. Shame. You're much better off with me."

Grace burst out laughing. "I rather suspect I'm much better off without either of you."

Patrick placed a hand on his heart, hurt. "Ouch," he said. "You can't take away all my hope already."

"Yes she can," said Catherine, pulling their suitcases out from the backseat. "And she did. She's my friend and not interested in either of you. Now be a gentleman and grab these cases."

"Your wish is my command." Patrick swept low to the ground in a mock bow before grabbing the cases and disappearing inside.

"Sorry," Catherine said. "Very annoying. Let's go and find Mum." Grace followed her in the back door, old worn hearth stones on the floor, dog beds pushed to the corner, and piles of boots that probably should have been, might even once have been, lined up neatly in pairs, but were now scattered haphazardly around the hall.

In the corner was the culprit—a large, hairy lurcher holding down a hiking boot with its paws as it gnawed on the tongue.

"Boscoe!" Catherine crooned in delight as the dog looked up, dropped the boot, and leaped toward her in paroxysms of joy, standing on its hind legs and licking her all over the face as Catherine giggled. "No!" she said weakly. "You're not supposed to be standing."

"Oh, Boscoe." An older woman's voice drifted in from the kitchen. "Tell him to get down, darling. The dog trainer was here last week and she said we have to stop him jumping on everyone. She was very stern."

"Did she tell him to stop eating boots?" Catherine and Grace both looked down at the boots piled everywhere, noting how many of them had distinct teeth marks in them.

"She came because he's been eating Jim's chickens. He keeps escaping and heads straight for the farm. I swear, he knows exactly which days Jim lets those poor little things free range. He never tries to go over there on the days the chicken are kept in the run. We've turned it into a verb. The poor chickens have been Boscoed. I told Jim we'd pay for a new flock."

"New flock? How many has Boscoe eaten?"

"I think it was eight at the last count. Oh, *hello*!" The voice manifested itself in the doorway, in the form of a large woman, tall, voluptuous, her hair a mix of dark and grey, gathered up in a loose clip at the nape of her neck. She was in a long flowery skirt, a T-shirt, Birkenstocks, and a white apron tied tightly around her waist. Tiny gold flowers in her ears, a matching pendant on a fine gold chain, she had Catherine's huge smile and was quite the most beautiful woman Grace had ever seen.

"You must be Grace! Look at that stunning hair! Good Lord. We'll have to keep Robert away from you."

Grace blushed, her skin turning a hot red as she busied herself pretending to look for something in her backpack. "Nice to meet you Mrs. Propper," she said, praying her skin calmed down so she could actually look up again.

"Don't call me 'Mrs. Propper,' " said Catherine's mother. "It makes me feel desperately old. Call me Lydia."

"Mum, you look desperately old with that grey hair. Since when did you stop dyeing it?"

"Don't you say anything about my grey hair!" Lydia said sternly. "I'll have you know I am enormously proud of my grey hair. I've decided there are far too many chemicals in hair dye. The only thing I'm comfortable using is henna, but every time I've tried it my hair turned orange. I'm growing everything out. Your father and I both quite love it."

"I don't think you look old at all," Grace said honestly. "I think you're absolutely beautiful. You have such a young face, and your grey makes it all the more striking."

"Bless you!" Lydia put an arm around Grace and squeezed her close. "I like this one," she said to Catherine. "She can come again. Flattery will get you everywhere," she said to Grace, who looked stricken.

"I wasn't saying it to flatter . . ."

"I know. I was joking. It was a lovely thing to say and what's more, I know you meant it. Come on in and my apologies for the mayhem. It's the twins. When they're not here, it's bliss. Next time I'll make sure it's just us girls."

Grace felt a surge of joy at the possibility of there being a next time. Here five minutes, already she wanted to be part of this family. She wanted her boots chewed up next to theirs, her coat hanging on the coat pegs along the wall. She wanted Boscoe jumping all over her, older brothers who teased her mercilessly, a mother who was so comfortable in her skin, in her beauty, she could let her hair go grey, safe in the knowledge it didn't reduce her charm, or grace, or power.

Grace wanted to live just like this.

The kitchen was exactly what she would have expected, exactly what she would have chosen for her own kitchen, only messier, but even that was perfect. An old scrubbed pine table in the middle, a basket in the middle overflowing with newspapers and bills that had yet to be opened.

A huge red Aga tucked into a brick opening, copper pots and pans hanging from a pot rack above. A wood dresser that took up one entire wall, its shelves crammed with plates and bowls, and a sofa tucked into the bay window, two cats contentedly curled into balls on the cushions.

"Would you like some tea?" Grace nodded as Catherine darted out to the hallway.

"I'm just going up to my room. Back in a sec," she said as Lydia handed a tin to Grace.

"Grab some biscuits and put them on a plate would you, Grace?

Make sure there are lots. The boys wolf them down like they're going out of fashion."

Grace laughed, getting a plate and thinking how it is so often the simplest of pleasures that had the ability to make you happy. The thought of her own mother making tea, or keeping a biscuit tin, was almost laughable, let alone lifting the lid of a big orange Le Creuset to check that whatever delicious meat within was braising the way it should be.

"So tell me all about yourself, Grace," said Lydia, pulling up a chair. "Do you love university? I know Catherine adores it, and largely because the two of you are as thick as thieves. Where are your people from? Brothers? Sisters? Please tell me your home is tidier than this one."

Before Grace had a chance to answer, the garden door opened, as Robert walked in. Grace caught her breath.

He was one hundred times better looking than his photograph, in tennis whites that showed off the tan of his arms and legs. He was, quite simply, the best-looking boy Grace had ever seen. She felt her skin start to flush again as he looked at her before walking across the kitchen without a word and dumping his tennis racquet in the back passage.

Thank you, God, Grace prayed silently. For sending me a roommate with a godlike brother, and for having his intervention mean I don't have to talk about my family. *Thank you. Thank you. Thank you.*

"Robert!" Lydia said. "That was rude. Come and say hello to Grace."

"Hello, Grace," called Robert from the other room.

"I'm sorry." Lydia shook her head in despair at Grace. "You think you raise your children well and teach them good manners and they become thugs anyway."

"I'm not a thug, Ma." Robert came back in the room. "I'm just distracted. Hello, Grace." He looked at her, but without a smile. In fact, if Grace didn't know better, she would have decided he was almost glaring at her, but why on earth would he dislike her? He didn't even know her.

"Thank you," Lydia said. "Where's your brother? The kettle's almost boiling. Can you call him in for tea?"

"Patrick!" bellowed Robert, not moving, making Grace jump. "Teatime!"

"Oh, Robert." Lydia shook her head again. "That wasn't what I meant and you know it. Please just go and find him."

"I can't. I'm not talking to him. He got bored playing tennis and just walked off, leaving me on my own. Bastard."

"I give up." Lydia threw her hands in the air and walked to the bottom of the stairs. "Catherine?" she called up. "Go find Patrick and both of you come in for tea."

Later that afternoon Catherine was sent off to see her grandmother.

"You can't possibly inflict that terrible old woman on the lovely Grace," said Lydia. "I'm keeping her here with me. She's going to help me cook."

"I'm not that good a cook," said Grace nervously. "I love it, but it's always a bit hit or miss."

"Good. That means I can teach you. Anything to save you from Evil Granny."

"That's what she calls Dad's mother," Catherine explained. "Mum thinks she hates her because Dad was supposed to marry the doctor's daughter in town, but he ran off with Mum instead and Granny has never got over it."

"It's true." Lydia shrugged. "I am that childish. But I do have her over for tea every other Sunday and frankly, I think that's pretty good going, all things considered. And what's more, I serve her gorgeous homemade cakes and scones."

Catherine started to laugh. "Granny only ever has these disgusting fish paste sandwiches when we go for tea. I think she still thinks we're living in 1941. We have to pretend to eat them, then shove them in handbags and pockets when she's not looking. Patrick used to shove them down the side of the sofa and no one could figure out why her house smelled so disgusting for years."

"At least you've filled up on Hob Nobs," said her mother approvingly. "You can tell Granny you're full."

"I think the boys should come too," said Catherine, as Patrick walked into the kitchen.

"I'm not coming!" he said. "I went yesterday, which is my good deed for the month. Anyway, someone has to stay here and look after the lovely Grace."

"I think that Mum has that under control," said Catherine witheringly.

"She could teach her how to cook, and yes, I was in the next room earwigging, but I would be much more fun. How about I take you over to Jim's farm? He's just got some baby lambs in."

"Oh!" breathed Catherine. "Baby lambs!"

"Patrick!" Lydia turned, attempting not to smile, but not doing a very good job. "You are incorrigible."

"I know," he said. "But I am devilishly good," and he winked at Grace as he threw a sweater at her. "Take this," he said. "It's getting chilly out."

"Be back in an hour," said Lydia. "If you do want to help me with cooking, that is."

"Yes!" said Grace. "I definitely want you to teach me to cook. Promise we'll be back," and feeling as if she was already part of the furniture, she ran outside with Patrick and over to his Beetle.

Robert appeared as she was climbing in. "Where are you two off to?" he said with a scowl.

"Hot date," Patrick called, gunning the engine before Grace could think of anything to say, and they took off, Grace turning around to see Robert standing in the driveway, his face dark with scorn.

"Is your brother always this horrible?" Grace said. "Or is it just me?"

"It's just you," Patrick said lightly. "He fancies you."

Grace started laughing. "That's *fancying* me? How does he behave with people he hates, then? Seriously, what is his problem?"

"Seriously, he fancies you, and he's embarrassed at fancying his little sister's friend, so he's pretending to hate you so you couldn't possibly ever tell because the mortification would be huge. Also, he's always had a thing about redheads, so there's a double whammy with you. I, on the other hand, not only fancy you, I am perfectly happy to admit it. A relationship with me would be infinitely preferable to one with him, because A, I am completely straightforward, and B, I am, as I think you're beginning to see, much nicer in every way."

"Would you be offended if I told you I didn't fancy you?"

"No. I'd only be offended if you told me you fancied Robert." He cast a sideways glance at Grace, who looked away. "Fuck. Well. It won't last. He falls madly in love with girls until they fall madly in love with him, which they always do, at which point he becomes utterly disdainful and cruel. I'm not joking, Grace. You would be much better off with me. I'm an excellent long-term prospect, and sweet too." He batted his eyelashes at Grace, who laughed.

"How about we become best friends instead?"

"Bugger," said Patrick morosely. "That's what they all say."

By the end of that week, Grace had forgotten she hadn't ever been part of this family. Patrick with his teasing felt like the naughty brother she had always wanted, Catherine was Catherine, and Lydia was the kind of mother Grace thought only existed in books. David—Catherine's father—was away on business, as he seemed to be most of the time, and Robert continued to be darkly elusive. Grace would look up from the kitchen table to find Robert staring at her from the doorway, but if she tried to engage him in conversation, he would mostly stalk off, or roll his eyes as if he found her very presence disdainful.

Her favorite moments were in the kitchen with Lydia, poring over recipe books as Lydia instructed her to choose something, which Lydia would then teach her to cook. They started, that first week, with meat. It was winter, so Lydia showed her the basics for rich casseroles and creamy mashed potatoes.

Grace learned never to add salt to the water when cooking potatoes until the very end, so as not to break down the starch. She learned to sear roast meats on the stove first, to caramelize the proteins and turn the meat a rich golden brown before placing it in the oven; she learned to keep a pan of water in the oven when roasting meat to keep the meat moist; she learned the importance of marinating, and of adding an acid—lemon juice or vinegar—to the marinade to break down the proteins in the meat and allow it to fully absorb the flavor and moisture of the marinade.

She surprised the family with salmon parcels wrapped in puff pastry, Lydia delighting in what a good student she was as they all polished off the food.

Slowly, over the week, as Grace grew more and more comfortable with Lydia, she revealed little bits and pieces about her family. Never enough to give Lydia the full picture, but enough to confirm what Lydia sensed about Grace the minute she walked in—here was a child with an aching need for a family, an aching need to be loved, and nurtured, and *seen*.

Patrick spent the week following her around like a lovesick puppy and when she eventually left, Lydia made Catherine swear to bring Grace home again at Christmas. Not that Grace needed any persuading.

Every holiday was spent with the Proppers. Every holiday saw Robert being darkly broody, although their mutual crush went unrequited, largely thanks to Robert suddenly showing up with his girlfriend, Emily. Emily was willing to put up with his moods and in fact seemed to ease them somewhat.

By the time Robert and Emily split up, just after Grace and Catherine graduated, Grace was making plans to go over to America, and it was clear her years of daydreaming about Robert would come to nothing.

The very last time she stayed there, with the whole family, before she moved to the States, met Ted, and became someone entirely different from the unhappy, insecure girl she had been back in England, Robert was not supposed to be there, but had turned up unexpectedly.

"Probably because someone," Patrick had glared at Lydia, "told him you were here." He looked at Grace, who shoved him playfully.

"Patrick!" Lydia looked at her son with love. "I do think it's time you moved on from this big crush on Grace. Stop blushing, Grace. It's not as if you don't know. Good Lord. All of us know. Patrick, you are a wonderful boy . . . man . . . boy-man. And you will make some lucky woman inexplicably happy one day, but it is not going to be Grace. Do you hear me? Mooning after Grace is not going to bring you happiness."

"Yeah," echoed Catherine. "Moonface."

So Robert had come, and Catherine had gone into London for a job interview, and Patrick was at his summer job, teaching football at a boys' summer camp. Lydia said she was taking a nap and left a picnic hamper on the kitchen table with a note for Robert.

Darling boy.
Take whoever's around for a picnic. I'll be down later.
Love you.
Mum xxx

"I think she means you," Robert said, looking at Grace as she lounged on the sofa in the bay window, a cat on her lap, one leg on the floor, reading Jeffrey Archer, which is all she found in the library that she hadn't already read.

"What?"

"A picnic. Do you want to go for a picnic?"

"Is there a catch?" Grace still thought Robert the most glorious man in the world, but was, after all these years, resigned to his moodiness, which had become irritating, and also resigned to the fact that despite everyone thinking his unpleasantness toward her was actually because he fancied her, in actual fact she was pretty damn certain it was just because he hated her.

"What do you mean?"

"I mean, do you actually want me to come on a picnic with you? Because I'm quite happy reading if you don't."

"This isn't a puzzle," Robert said. "If you want to come, come. If you want to read, read."

Grace thought about saying, "What do *you* want me to do?" but had a sense this might push him into a rage. Instead she removed the cat from her lap, brushed off the cat hairs, slipped her feet into espadrilles, and walked toward the door.

"All yours," she said with a grin, as Robert picked up the picnic basket and followed her out.

Across the street there was a stile over the fence where the cows grazed. You could follow the field down to a hiking trail, which is what they did, not speaking, Grace walking in front, Robert following with the basket and a blanket he had grabbed on the way out.

Grace shook out the blanket, then sat back as Robert unpacked the hamper. Closing her eyes, she felt the warmth of the sun on her face, opening them again to find Robert's face inches from her own, his eyes gazing into hers, searching, before leaning forward and kissing her.

Grace's heart almost leapt into her mouth. She was kissing Robert! Robert was kissing her! He groaned and pulled her closer, tangling his fingers in her hair, pulling away only to kiss her all over her face, back to her lips, insatiable, a moment she instantly knew he had been waiting for for years.

Grace felt herself float out of her body, delirious with years of anticipation. She couldn't believe this was happening. Robert had only split up with Emily last week, and they had been together so long Grace had stopped thinking about any possibility of anything ever happening between them, whether it was a daydream or anything else. She just hadn't bothered; clearly it wasn't ever going to happen.

Except now it was, and when they eventually stopped kissing, Robert took a deep breath as he leaned his forehead on hers.

"Do you have any idea how long I have wanted to do that?" he whispered, opening his eyes and looking into hers.

"Maybe as long as I've *wanted* you to do that?" Grace said, and this time, he smiled. A genuine smile. One that contained warmth, lust, and—dare Grace even think it—a little bit of love?

They spent the afternoon lying on the blanket, Grace in Robert's arms, both of them giggling, teasing, kissing, Grace unable to believe she could be this happy, unable to believe this was really happening.

As she lay, quietly this time, cradled in his arms as he kissed the top of her head and ran strands of her hair through his fingers, she imagined their future, for of course they would have a future. She would still go to America, but only for the summer, for camp, and when she got back Robert would have missed her so much, he would suggest living together.

He would move out of the flat he shared with friends in West Hampstead, and they would get a tiny flat of their own. There was no question of today's encounter being anything less than a relationship, anything less than permanent. Grace was already part of Robert's family; this was fate. This was meant to be.

She saw herself cooking for him when he came home from work every day. He was a lawyer—young, hotshot, and almost breathtakingly gorgeous in his navy suits—going out with a circle of friends they would undoubtedly quickly develop, sitting in trendy cafes, drinking wine and laughing.

Lydia and David would be her in-laws! Of course! This was exactly what was going to happen, and the more Grace thought about it, the bigger her heart grew. This is what it is like to be happy, she thought. This is what it is like to be loved. I never knew it growing up, but I don't have to yearn for something I worry I'll never have anymore. Now I have Robert. Now I'm going to be fine.

They walked home hand in hand, stopping every few feet to kiss, tease each other. Robert was the gentle, loving, sweet man she had always hoped he might be, the man she occasionally thought she saw glimpses of behind the scowl.

They wandered down the road home, weaving, drunk with love, pulling up as they looked at an unfamiliar car in the driveway.

"Who's that?" Grace had a sense of foreboding as she looked at the car.

"Emily." Robert let go of her hand and Grace knew it was all over.

Years went by, Robert avoided her. Enough years that when they did see each other, after Grace was married, on one of her trips home to see Lydia, he was able to kiss her on the cheek and lightly enquire how she was, and she was able to respond politely, after which time the two of them had a gracious conversation and Grace wondered what had happened to all the pent-up emotion they both had carried with them for years.

"Why don't you just fuck each other and get it over with," Patrick had said after watching their exchange with amusement.

"How about, because I'm married?" Grace said.

"Oh, yes. Sorry. Forgot. Jesus, Grace. How did you turn into an old married woman? You do realize to me you'll always be a gorgeous eighteen-year-old."

"Rather than a gorgeous twenty-nine-year-old?" Grace said.

"Exactly. If you did ever split up from the great Ted Chapman, which obviously is unlikely because you'd have to be out of your mind, but if you ever did, then you really should fuck me rather than Robert."

"If I ever did, which I never would, because I love my husband very much, thank you all the same, fucking anyone would be the last thing on my mind. And really, Patrick. Do you have to say 'fuck'? It's so . . . crass."

"Oh, I'm sorry. Would you prefer 'making lerrrve'?"

"Yes, actually. I think I would."

"Well, you can make lerrrve with Robert, but if you were with me, it would be a fantastic dirty fuck."

"You're still impossible."

"And still loveable."

Then, for many years, Grace would fly over to stay with Lydia and David, sometimes with Clemmie, sometimes without, and wouldn't even see Catherine, Robert, or Patrick.

Catherine was living in Australia with her husband. Robert was in Scotland with Emily and five children, and Patrick was becoming a rather well-known film director. He had made most of his films in the UK, but had moved out to L.A. for a while to see how it went.

David died suddenly of a heart attack ten years ago. Grace went to the funeral and tiptoed around the house, bringing Lydia cups of tea and glasses of scotch when the tea didn't do the trick.

She barely spoke to Robert—he seemed too immersed in chasing his children around the house to try and keep them from destroying everything in sight—and Patrick seemed distracted and a bit full of himself.

Grace had only been back three times since then. The last ten years went so quickly. She emailed Lydia, of course, all the time, and they spoke every couple of weeks, but life had raced along and suddenly it had been six years since she was last in Dorset, six years since she felt Lydia's arms around her in a reassuring hug.

SALMON PARCELS WITH WATERCRESS, ROCKET, AND CREAM CHEESE

(Serves 4)

INGREDIENTS

1 bunch watercress
1 bunch rocket, aka arugula
1 bunch spinach, all equal amounts
1 cup cream cheese
Zest of 1 lemon
1 pack puff pastry
4 salmon filets
1 egg, beaten
1 Tablespoon milk
Salt and pepper for seasoning

Preheat oven to 350 degrees.

Blend watercress, rocket, and spinach in a food processor until finely chopped. Add the cream cheese, lemon, and salt and pepper and pulse until blended. Put half to one side to serve alongside the salmon parcels.

Roll out pastry and cut into 4 squares. For each parcel, place one salmon filet in the middle of the square, season, spread ¼ of the cream cheese mixture over the top. Pull the corners of the parcel over the fish and seal at the top with beaten egg. Mix rest of egg with the milk and brush the parcels.

Cook for around 25 minutes, or until the pastry is golden.

Serve with the rest of the cream cheese mixture and a green salad.

Twenty-seven

Grace wakes up in her old bedroom, unchanged since she was last here, unchanged since she was a student: the Laura Ashley sprigged wallpaper, the pretty yellow and white quilt, the mahogany dressing table and little stool. On the bed, where he has always been, is Buff—the knitted teddy bear Patrick gave her for Christmas one year, his knitted paw clutching a knitted red rose.

Grace slept clutching Buff, too exhausted by all that had happened to even talk about it with Lydia. She fell into Lydia's arms, allowed herself to be guided to the car, where Lydia switched on Radio 4 as Grace was lulled into a state of calm.

Straight to bed, where she slept the sleep of the dead, waking up to see the view she has always loved—through the many-paned windows straight out to the fields opposite, the cows gently grazing next to the pretty old brick farm.

Waking up, shuddering with horror at the previous night spent on a park bench. Unwashed. Unfed. No longer living with the fear of turning into her mother, but the realization that—thank God, now temporarily—her fears had been fulfilled.

It is deathly quiet. She had forgotten how quiet it was here. Sneden's Landing was never noisy, but the birds sang, the water rushed, their house built of wood allowing all the noises of nature to pass through the walls.

Here the stone mutes everything. It is still. Peaceful. It is the sound of *safety*, Grace thinks, throwing her legs over the edge of the bed and examining herself in the mirror.

Tall but now round. She turns to the side to look at her stomach, her breasts that were always so tiny, now pillowy and large. She wishes she could accept what she now looks like, wants to feel beautiful, regardless of her size. Her shame is just as much at how unaccepting she is of her new shape, how harsh her judgment is of herself.

She turns and pulls her pills out of her bag. Sybil hadn't grabbed the pillbox in which Grace diligently empties every day's worth of pills, but instead had grabbed every pill bottle in the medicine cabinet and had swept them into a bag.

Thank God I wasn't stopped by customs, thinks Grace. They might have arrested her for being a walking pharmacy.

Automatically she empties out the pills she is supposed to take today: Lexapro, Lamictal, Provigil, Phentermine. She looks at them, then back to her reflection in the mirror. There is no doubt that her exhaustion, her weight gain, the dullness of her life is connected to these pills. The pills she never wanted to take in the first place, took only because she had no other choice.

She cradles the pills in her hand, considering. She has spent her life terrified she might have the same disease as her mother, which is perhaps why, when Frank Ellery made the diagnosis, some part of her accepted it, even though she didn't believe it; even though she read copious amounts about it and struggled to make it fit.

Surely, Sybil said, taking medication is supposed to make you more yourself? Make you better? Bring you back to your best self? What is the point of taking medication that makes you feel nothing? That has turned you into twice the woman you once were? That, if anything, has stolen your life?

She honestly doesn't know what to do, so does the easiest thing. Taking a gulp of the glass of water next to her bed, she swallows the pills. Sometimes not thinking too hard is the easiest thing of all.

Lydia is feeding the cat when Grace comes downstairs, dressed now in the clothes she was wearing yesterday, the clothes she had flown in.

Lydia looks up, beaming. "Did you sleep well? Oh, Gracie. I'm so horrified you weren't able to reach me. I still can't believe you slept on a bench. I'm just mortified I wasn't there."

"I can't believe it myself," says Grace. "The whole thing feels completely surreal. Had that kind gentleman not offered me his phone, I'd still be there. I had no idea what to do."

Lydia gazes at her. "You must have been thinking about your mother."

"Oh, Lydia." Grace wells up. "It was all I was thinking about. This all-consuming shame at my mother being homeless, this fear that anyone would find out, that I might somehow end up in the same boat, and there I was. It has been months and months of hell, of me dreading I was like her . . . and then the culmination on a park bench."

"It was one night," Lydia says. "Maybe there's a lesson in there somewhere. They usually say that we are mostly frightened of the fear itself. The worst thing imaginable happened to you, and you survived it. You are, I suspect, much stronger than you know."

"I survived it because it was only one night, and because of you."

Lydia shakes her head. "No. You survived it because you are a survivor, Grace. You always have been. You don't get to come from a background like yours and get to where you have got, carve out the life you have carved out for yourself, without a reserve of enormous resilience and strength."

Grace says nothing for a few moments. "Thank you," she says eventually, her voice quiet. "It has been a very long time since I have felt resilient and strong."

"But you are."

"I was," Grace says. "And I will be again."

"Here. I have croissants for you. And delicious yogurt my friend Judy makes. Can I do a pot for you? With honey?"

"That sounds gorgeous," Grace says, settling down at the table, ravenous suddenly.

"Tea?"

"Actually, do you have any coffee?"

"Ah! I always forget you Americans drink coffee in the mornings. I think I have some ancient, horrible old instant somewhere in the back of the pantry. Will that do?"

"It's perfect. I'll get it." Grace rustles around in the cupboard that is Lydia's pantry, amused at how little food is there. When Grace used to visit, during university, Lydia's pantry was always stuffed.

"Where's all the food?" she calls out to Lydia, easily locating the jar of Gold Blend. "It looks like the pantry was burgled."

"It's only me now," says Lydia. "It's only ever full these days when the family comes to visit."

Grace flicks the kettle on before sitting down at the table again, where Lydia has placed the croissant and yogurt.

"Are you ready to talk?" Lydia sits opposite her, cradling a large mug of tea. "I completely understand if not, and I know a little, but . . . there's so much more, isn't there, Grace? Months and months of hell? What has been going on?"

Grace pauses. Lydia knows about her mother. Would she judge Grace when Grace reveals her own story? Would she sympathize?

Would she question the diagnosis, as Sybil had done, leading Grace to try and convince her that the doctor knew best, even though she wasn't convinced of that herself.

"I'm not sure I even know where to begin," says Grace.

"How about at the beginning? I find that's usually best."

So Grace does.

Lydia has not spoken until she has heard the whole story. When Grace grinds to a halt, Lydia takes a deep breath as her eyes fill with tears.

"Oh God, Grace. I'm sorry. I had no idea. Why didn't you tell me? Why didn't I know you have been feeling so awful for so long?"

"Because it started to feel normal. This became . . . the new normal. I'd forgotten that I felt anything other than depressed, dull, fat."

"You're not fat. You're cuddly."

Grace lets out a bark of laughter. "Thanks. I think."

"You are still beautiful." Lydia lays a hand on hers. "And this is medication weight. You will lose it as soon as you stop. Can we talk about that? The drugs? The diagnosis? Can I give you my opinion?"

Grace nods.

"I have known you since you were eighteen years old, and there is absolutely no way on earth you have bipolar disorder. And just in case you think I don't understand what the diagnosis is, and what it means, I have an aunt who has it, and I am very well aware of what it is like, which means I am also absolutely qualified to know, deep down in the core of my being, that you do not have it." Lydia shakes her head in disgust. "We all hear about American doctors and how they overmedicate and how huge the pharmaceutical industry is, but darling girl, I never thought you would be victim. I think this doctor . . . what was his name? Ellery? He should be bloody well struck off for what he's done to you. Lithium! Are they insane? You certainly aren't, and you should never, ever have been put on these drugs, not least because you do not have, nor have ever had, bipolar disorder."

Grace sits mutely, unable to speak. Lydia is voicing everything Grace has been trying to suppress. Everything she has thought for months, refusing to acknowledge because Frank Ellery is a doctor at Columbia! Frank Ellery has never been wrong! Frank Ellery must surely know her better than she knows herself!

"I want you to go and see Dr. Harry, my doctor. He's in Sherborne, and he's known all of us forever and, most importantly, he's a big believer in alternative remedies. I know he'll be horrified by your story, but most importantly, he'll help get you off."

"Couldn't I just stop?" Grace says, wishing she hadn't taken her pills this morning.

"Lord, no!" Lydia says vehemently. "You have to be terribly careful coming off medication, particularly, I would think, ones as strong as you've been taking. Let's get an appointment with Harry and see what he prescribes. It's worth looking up on the computer too. Have you done any research on the drugs?"

Grace feels stupid saying no, but she hadn't done much. Frank had told her not to look up the side effects, had warned her that there was much misinformation that would scare her, and said if she had any side effects or issues, to come straight to him. Of course, Grace had gone straight to him every time another side effect raised its head and his solution was to prescribe more pills, which was the very last thing she wanted, although she would have done pretty much anything in a bid to try and feel better.

"When do you think we can go and see Dr. Harry?" Grace asks with urgency. Suddenly, she wants to be off the pills as soon as possible. "Today?"

"I'll try." Lydia smiles. "I do think that if we take this one step at a time, the first step has to be getting you better, and the only way to do that is to get you off these drugs."

"What's the next step?" Grace reaches for a Danish pastry.

"I think perhaps getting your life back. Finding out what the hell your husband is thinking and figuring out what it is you want." She leans forward, peering closely at Grace. "Do you know what it is you want?"

"Yes." Grace nods resolutely. "I want what I had before. I want the life I used to have. I want to feel like me again, to have energy. I want to be cooking again. Of late I can't be bothered to do anything except lie in bed and read. I want," her eyes fill with tears, "my house back. I want to be believed. I want to be respected again."

There is a pause. "And Ted?" Lydia says.

"Of course!" Grace says. "That goes without saying, doesn't it? I want my life back and Ted is the center of it. I want everything to be exactly the way it was."

Twenty-eight

On her fifth day at Lydia's, Grace wakes up at three in the morning with a band of pain around her head unlike anything she has ever experienced. Gasping, she staggers to the bathroom and reaches for a bottle of ibuprofen in the medicine cabinet, tipping three into her hand and swigging them down.

It feels as if someone has a vice around her head that is gradually tightening and the painkillers have no effect. An hour later, she staggers to the bathroom where she throws up, retching until there is nothing left to come up.

"Grace?" The noise has awoken Lydia. "What's the matter? You look terrible."

"I think it's a migraine," Grace manages through gritted teeth. "The pain is terrible."

"Have you had migraines before?"

"No," Grace grunts as she crawls back into bed, moaning with pain, while Lydia runs downstairs to fill a bag with ice.

"This is so odd," Lydia murmurs, almost to herself, as she sits on the bed next to Grace, holding the bag of ice on her head as Grace continues to moan. "Why would you suddenly get a migraine now?"

"The pills," Grace groans.

"What pills?"

"I stopped."

"What? I thought you were going to wait until after we saw Harry."

"Too long. I needed to stop immediately."

"Tell me you didn't just stop cold turkey."

"Yes."

"Oh Lord, Grace. Let me go and look it up. This might be part of the withdrawal." Taking Grace's pill bottles from her bedside table, Lydia goes downstairs to her computer, where she reads up about the side effects of withdrawal. She sits for an hour, scribbling notes, before going back upstairs where Grace is still groaning.

"Any better?"

"Nuh," Grace grunts.

"Take one of these." Lydia hands her a pill, which Grace obediently swallows, desperate to do anything to stop the pain.

"What is it?"

"Lexapro."

Grace frowns. "Why? I don't want to take anything anymore."

"But that's why you feel like your head is going to explode. It's one of the delightful symptoms of withdrawing from Lexapro too quickly. Along with, if you're interested, something called brain zaps, which apparently feels like you're getting small electric shocks every few minutes. The way to do it, they say, is very, very slowly. You reduce your dose every week by two and a half milligrams, and take supplements—fish oil and B-12, which I'll get for you tomorrow. I know Harry couldn't see you until Friday, but I'll call in the morning and say it's an emergency. You can't carry on like this. I'm sure there must be something he can give you."

"I don't think I'll ever be able to get out of bed again," manages

Grace, wincing with the pain, but an hour later, the Lexapro has indeed taken the edge off the headache and she is able to go back to sleep, the bag of ice slowly melting into the pillow behind her head.

Dr. Harry is appalled by Grace's story.

"Do you know," he says, shaking his head with disgust, "ninety-five percent of these types of medications are prescribed in America, and America only makes up five percent of the world's population! What does that tell you about your diagnosis? Not to mention, and forgive me for getting worked up about this, but I just read that in 1996 the rate of diagnosis for bipolar disorder was one in twenty thousand. And do you know what it is today in America? Do you know?"

Grace shakes her head.

"*One in twenty!* And they think it's going up to one in *ten*! It's the drug companies pushing these terrible drugs, and I'm sorry you're going through it, but happy you came to see me." He looks down at his notes, shaking his head in disgust. "Perphenazine!" he mutters. "I'm sorry. You've been put on a cocktail of some of the heaviest antipsychotic drugs available to man. And you weren't just taking one! You were taking a cocktail! These are drugs used to treat severe mania; schizophrenia. I'm appalled. I'm sorry, but I'm just appalled." He takes a deep breath, composing himself. "Lydia is right about a slow weaning off and, as you said earlier, reducing by two and a half milligrams every couple of weeks should be fine. The supplements are going to help, but take double the dose of fish oil and take more if you get headaches. I'm going to give you a couple of things that will help. The first is a migraine medication, Imigran, in case the headaches are as bad as they sounded last night, and Prozac."

"Prozac?" Grace is horrified.

"Prozac is only in the short term and has no withdrawal symptoms, but it will help with the brain zaps and help you transition off the Lexapro.

I also want you to have some acupuncture and physical therapy, which will help tremendously with the headaches."

"I'll do anything," says Grace. "Anything not to go through what I went through last night. That was the worst pain I think I have ever felt, including childbirth. I honestly thought about throwing myself out the window at one point, anything to stop the pain."

"Do you have a headache now?"

"Yes," admits Grace. "But it's bearable, although I'm terrified it's going to escalate."

"And you took the Lexapro last night? The full ten milligrams?"

Grace nods.

"Tomorrow try seven-point-five. If the headaches come back, try and alternate days—one day ten, one day seven-point-five until you're able to do seven-point-five every day. It's going to take a little while to get you off, but it will be worth it. In my opinion you should never have been on any of this medication in the first place."

"So, why do you think they thought I had it? I definitely wasn't . . . myself. I was getting angry in a way I never had before."

"Of course you were," Dr. Harry says. "Unfortunately it happens to all women your age as they approach the menopause. Do you know at what age your mother went through the menopause?"

"No," says Grace. "She died a long time ago and we weren't . . . close."

"Ah. Well, I'd hazard a guess it's around the age you are now. We'll run the tests, but I already know everything you described is entirely down to your hormones."

"Thank you, Doctor," says Grace, finally feeling as if she has found someone who will be able to bring her back to herself.

That afternoon, as Grace's eyes are watering from slicing dozens of onions for a French onion soup, the phone rings.

"It's Clemmie," says Lydia, as Grace slowly takes the phone. Grace had emailed Clemmie as soon as she arrived in Dorset, telling her not to worry about her, that nothing was as it seemed, and that she would be in touch in a few days. She had asked Clemmie to give her just a little space, that they would speak very soon.

Clemmie had clearly spoken to Sybil, knew Grace had her passport, and deduced she was staying at Lydia's. Where else could she possibly be?

"Mom?" Clemmie's voice, so achingly familiar, brings tears springing instantly to Grace's eyes.

"Darling!" Grace says, then finds she cannot say anything else.

"Mom? What's happening? Why are you in England? Why did you run away?" Clemmie sounds like a little girl, frightened and alone, as Grace's heart aches for her.

"I didn't know where else to go," Grace says. "I'm sorry. You know this isn't that I left you. I was just overwhelmed by the direction my life was taking and I knew I wasn't going to get better in that hospital."

"Are you sick then? Is it true? Are you bipolar?"

Grace takes a deep breath. "Clemmie, it's true that that's what your father thinks, but it isn't true. There's no question that I've been depressed, and that I haven't felt right for a long time, but I truly know most of that is because of the medication I've been on. The doctor I'm seeing here seems pretty sure I'm coming up to the menopause, which is why I was so . . . moody, I guess. Angry. But he's very clear that there is no way I'm bipolar, and the drugs I have been on for the past six months are the ones that have made me ill, not the other way round."

Grace hears Clemmie take a deep breath. "Did the drugs make you assault Beth?"

"Oh, Clemmie. I know that's the story she's telling you, but I'm beginning to realize all kinds of things about Beth. I slapped her, yes, but I was at the end of my tether. She isn't what she appears. I know you may think that I'm telling you this, imagining all kinds of things because I am crazy, bipolar, whatever, but I assure you, she is not what she appears and there is no doubt in my mind whatsoever that she is behind much of what has happened."

Clemmie is skeptical. "Mom, how could she have made the diagnosis? She couldn't have been behind it."

"No, but I believe she planted the seed in your father's mind. I believe she decided, very early on, that she needed to discredit me in order to make the moves on your father."

"I . . . I don't know," says Clemmie. "It all sounds a bit far-fetched. I like Beth, Mom. You liked her, no, loved her before all this."

"I did. But if I'm honest, I have to say there has always been something I'm not sure about. Clemmie, darling, I'm not even asking you to believe me, but watch what happens next. You think she is innocent and just your father's assistant, but I guarantee she will have moved in within the month and will be sleeping in my bed."

"There's no way, Mom!" Clemmie actually laughed. "First of all, she's young enough to be Dad's daughter, and secondly, you're his wife. There's no way any of this would happen."

"If it did, would you believe me?"

"It's not going to so it's irrelevant."

"But if it did, wouldn't you then say I wasn't out of my mind?"

"Yes. If it did, I would then have to concede that the world had gone crazy, rather than my mother. But Mom, seriously, what are you going to do? Beth says she's pressing assault charges, although Dad's trying to persuade her not to. He says it will instantly become a news story and that will be terrible publicity for him."

"Christ," says Grace, realizing there is little Beth won't do to stake her claim. "Do you think he will persuade her not to?"

"Yeah. I think he's going to give her some fabulous bonus to convince her not to say anything."

"What a mess." She sighs. "Clemmie, you do know I love you?"

"Yes, but I still don't understand why you went to England."

"I'm safe here," Grace says. "This is home."

"I thought home was Sneden's."

It *was*, thinks Grace, but doesn't say it out loud. "They've had me on a lot of medications which have done a tremendous amount of damage. I need to get better and I can do that here." She doesn't tell Clemmie that the thought of returning to America, to the mayhem that is surely waiting, makes her feel nauseous at the very thought.

"I love you," says Grace again. "I love you so much." When she puts down the phone, she bursts into tears.

I am in England," she writes to Ted, later that night. "I spoke to Clemmie earlier, to reassure her that I love her and that I'm fine. I have no idea if you are worried about me, but I needed to write and let you know that there is no need. I can't quite believe how things spiraled out of control in the way that they did, but I do know I need to stay away for a while. Whatever you might think, I am not bipolar. I have found a doctor here who agrees and who is horrified at all the medication I have been on. At some point I will be ready to sit down with you face-to-face and sort out our future, but I am not ready yet. If our marriage has meant anything at all to you, I would hope that you will let me heal in peace. Grace."

She is still in tears an hour later when Lydia walks in, with tea.

Lydia says nothing, plants the tea softly on the table, then sits next to Grace, slowly rubbing her back until Grace's sobs become hiccups, then exhausted shuddering inhales, before finally ceasing.

"I just miss him," Grace says, her voice breaking as the sobs threaten to return. "I miss Ted. He's my husband and I can't believe what's happening to my life. I can't believe it's all gone so horribly wrong. He's obsessed with this Beth, this evil, Machiavellian girl. He even based the character in his new book on her, or at least on who he imagines her to be. This is obsession, and when Ted is obsessed, there's no room for anything, or anyone, else. She has her claws firmly into him and she isn't going to let go, even if he wanted to get out, which I can tell quite clearly he doesn't."

"You still love him?"

"Of course I still love him! He's my husband!"

How, she thinks, could everything go so wrong?

FRENCH ONION SOUP

(Serves 4)

INGREDIENTS

½ stick butter (8 Tablespoons)
4 onions, thinly sliced
4 cups beef stock
1 Tablespoon of brown sugar
1 cup red wine (or brandy, cognac, sherry, or white wine)
Salt and pepper for seasoning
Dash of Worcestershire sauce
Thyme
Grated Gruyere cheese
Grated Parmesan cheese
One baguette
Olive oil

Melt the butter in a large heavy pan (I use a Le Creuset, which is perfect) and add the onions, stirring constantly on a low heat until they are soft and caramelizing, around 20 minutes.

Add brown sugar. Stir. Add stock, wine, and seasoning. Bring to boil, cover and simmer for half an hour to 1 hour. Add Worcestershire sauce.

When ready to serve, slice baguette, toast, ladle soup into bowls, and cover each with thick handful of Gruyere. Top with slice of toast, drizzle with olive oil, sprinkle with Parmesan, then run under broiler to melt and brown.

Twenty-nine

It has been three months since Grace landed in a safe place, three months since she came home to Lydia. She is settling into the quiet rhythm of Lydia's life, hours spent reading, recovering, cooking, and finally, now that she is clean of all medications, she is beginning to feel like herself.

Lydia walks into the kitchen where Grace is sitting at the kitchen table, sipping coffee and reading the *Times*. "Grace? I spoke to Patrick yesterday. He's coming to London next week and I told him you were here. He'd love to see you."

Grace looks up and groans. "I'm not sure I want anyone to see me looking like this."

"What are you talking about? You're gorgeous, and didn't you tell me yesterday you'd already lost twelve pounds."

"Yes, but I think that was all bloat. I have to go shopping though. I love that you're lending me all your clothes, but Lydia, if I have to wear another floral maxiskirt I think I might scream."

Lydia barks with laughter. "And here I was thinking how beautifully everything suited you. Why on earth didn't you say earlier that you didn't like my clothes?"

"I didn't want to buy anything new in this size. I was hoping your clothes would tide me over until I got back to my normal size, or if not a small, at least a medium, but I give up. Three months of floral skirts and I'm about ready to slit my wrists."

"Fine. Let's go into Sherborne today. Do you need money?"

Grace nods. "Only temporarily. I'll be able to pay you back in a couple of days. Sybil is wiring me money, thank God, so I'm going to be fine."

"And Patrick?" says Lydia. "What do you think? He wants to come down for lunch on Sunday. He begged me to do a lunch like I used to do."

"Roast beef and Yorkshire pudding!" Grace smiles at the memory. "I don't know, Lydia. The last time I saw him was admittedly years ago, at David's funeral, but Patrick seemed a little . . . smug. I'm sorry. I know you love him and he's wonderful, but he had an arrogance about him I'd never seen before, and frankly, I didn't really enjoy his company. I don't know that I'm up to Patrick just yet."

Lydia nods. "I remember that well. It's what I came to call first film syndrome. He'd just made his first film and it was a huge success and all these offers from America came flooding in, which all went straight to his head. You're quite right, he was utterly unbearable. His head grew so big I'm still astonished he managed to make it through these doorways. You'll be happy to hear, he has gone back to his normal self. His second film was big, but the third was a disaster. The most viciously terrible reviews I'd ever read. One called him single-handedly responsible for the death of the British film industry. Thankfully, as hard as it was to hear, it brought him crashing back to earth where he has remained ever since."

"Well, that's a relief to hear, however hard it must have been. And how are things with the lovely Alicia?"

"She left him. I can't say I was ever terribly impressed with her. She always struck me as a crazy actress type and, it seems, I was right. She had a passionate affair with . . ." Lydia whispers the name of a very famous, very married movie star, furtively looking around as if the kitchen walls might be listening, going back to normal tones as Grace hoots with laughter. "So Patrick is busy playing the field."

"And he lives in L.A. permanently?"

"He seems to divide his time fairly evenly between L.A. and London. It would be lovely to see the two of you together again—the two of you always had such a lovely, teasing friendship."

Grace smiles at the memory. "He really was the annoying brother I never had. Okay." She nods. "Let's do it. Roast beef and Yorkshire pudding on Sunday. And I'll make the trifle, although," she pats her stomach, "I won't be eating any of it myself. Speaking of which, how much weight do you think it's possible to lose in four days?"

"Is there any reason why you care so much?" says Lydia, a small smile playing on her lips.

"Just that I don't particularly want Patrick to look at me and think I'm a fat blob," says Grace ruefully.

"He won't, because you're not," says Lydia. "And please, Grace. Please stop being so hard on yourself. I understand you are carrying this . . . shame, about your body, but this is the size you are meant to be right now, and you have to have some measure of acceptance or you won't ever be happy. It will help, you're right, to have clothes that fit that are clothes you have chosen. How about shopping this afternoon?"

"You're on," says Grace, thinking how lovely it is to have something in life to look forward to once again.

Grace's shopping trip is extravagant. After months and months in yoga pants, she is deliberate in her choices—they must be comfortable and flattering, but they must be proper clothes. No more stretchy Lycra and oversized sweaters for her.

She buys jeans—jeans!—in a size her mind refuses to compute, yet when she puts them on, tight, stretchy, with a tunic top that hides the worst of her thighs, she has to admit she looks good. In fact, she turns around in the mirror, admiring the newly acquired curve of her ample rear, and thinks she looks pretty damn sexy.

Boots with a heel low enough to walk comfortably in, high enough to further enhance this new feeling of sexiness are bought, with a selection of tops and the thinnest of alpaca scarves in assorted colors.

A lightweight jacket, sneakers, and by the time they hit Boots for makeup, Grace is feeling more like herself than she has in months.

"Rimmel!" She plucks a brown eyeliner from the shelf, laughing in delight. "I feel sixteen again!"

"You seem sixteen again." Lydia smiles. "Or at least young. You seem like Grace again. This is the Grace I've always known and loved. You're alive again, not the husk that arrived after a night sleeping rough three months ago."

"Was I really that bad?" Grace turns to Lydia, no longer smiling.

"Yes. And I was really terribly worried. You seemed like an empty shell. I was terrified we had lost you completely. It was almost impossible to reconcile this depressed, flat creature with my bubbly Grace. That first night you arrived, after you went to bed, I almost wept for you."

Grace reaches out a hand and squeezes Lydia's.

"But you're back," says Lydia.

"Yes. Only more so." Grace gestures to her now-shrinking, stomach.

"Stop, Grace. Enough with the berating yourself for putting on weight. You're off the drugs and healthy again. Your body will go back to its natural weight, but it will take time."

"And in the meantime"—Grace turns and grabs a No. 7 lip gloss, examining the color, which is remarkably similar to the Chanel she always wore—"Boots can help me cover up a multitude of sins."

Thirty

Getting ready for Patrick's visit has to be one of Grace's most nerve-racking days of recent times. The last time Patrick saw her, at his father's funeral, she was, she remembers, in a tiny black jersey dress that showed off her small waist and long legs. In those days, she never gave her body a second thought, took it completely for granted that she could go into any shop and try on anything she liked and buy it if she loved it, rather than because it flattered, or fit.

She chooses not to wear the jeans she has barely taken off since she brought them home a few days ago. Instead, she opts for a long navy skirt, the tan boots, a thin navy sweater with one of Lydia's belts loosely around her hips.

I don't look too bad, she thinks, looking at her reflection, not believing it, but hoping if she says it enough times out loud it will start to be true.

Why am I so nervous? she wonders. It is only Patrick, after all. If Robert were to suddenly show up, that would be a different thing entirely. They had paid little attention to each other at the funeral, but why would they? Robert may have been grief-stricken, but he had put it aside to focus on his wild children, used to running amok in their grand house near the Firth of Forth.

Robert was just as handsome, she had thought, while feeling nothing at all. He seemed stuffy. Uptight. Exactly as, she realized, he had always been. How much nicer he would be, she thought, if he were able to let loose a little, to be the boy she had only once had a glimpse of, the afternoon of the picnic and kiss.

If Robert were coming she would need to look good, would need him to look at her with some regret over what he never pursued after the day they arrived home to find Emily's car in the driveway.

As for Patrick? Could it be as self-serving as Grace needing him to still like her, needing to feel admired by the one man she had always been able to rely on? She is loathe to admit to having such a shallow, self-absorbed thought, at the same time as knowing it is true.

She applies all her new makeup, thinking of her makeup drawer, in the vanity in her bathroom at Sneden's. All the labels she uses—Chanel, Laura Mercier, Bobbi Brown, Trish McEvoy—and how she is making do with good old Boots. When finished, she looks approvingly at her reflection before going to the sink and washing it off. She never wears much makeup, and why should today be any exception?

In the end, she sweeps a luminescent blusher over her cheekbones, a tiny bit of eyeshadow, mascara, and the lip gloss that is almost, almost as good as her Chanel, jumping when she hears the familiar crunch of the gravel downstairs, instantly wishing she didn't have to come downstairs.

Patrick has never been quiet, she thinks, smiling now as she hears him barrel into the house, whooping as he greets his mother.

"Where is she?" he says. "Is she hiding from me?"

"Yes!" Grace calls, taking a deep breath and emerging from her bedroom. "I am hiding from you because the last time I saw you your arrogance was terrifying."

"Oh. That." He grins up at her from below. "Everyone told me I had become a little shit. Luckily I got humbled pretty shortly afterward and now," he extends his hands innocently, "I am just the sweet, handsome boy you have always known and loved."

"Hi." Grace stands in front of him, looking into his eyes as he smiles, and her own fill with tears.

"Hi, you," he says and holds out his arms as Grace falls into them, her throat choking up.

She can't explain why she is choked up. She isn't entirely sure, other than the sweetness of Patrick's familiarity, an aching nostalgia for her youth, a reminder of all that is good, and solid, and stable. All that she once had. All that she has lost.

Patrick has grown into a big man. Solid. Imposing. His embrace is all-enveloping, tight, stable. Like being held by a bear.

Safe, she thinks.

I am safe.

And almost immediately after: I have come home.

You can't not have trifle." Patrick gets up from the table, grabs a plate from the dresser, and brings it back to the table. "It's against the law. Sunday lunch means trifle. If there's no trifle, it isn't Sunday lunch, and I've come all the bloody way from L.A. to have Sunday lunch, so if you ruin it, I'm blaming you."

"Patrick, I can't. Look at me! I have to lose this weight and trifle, delicious as it is, is not the way to do it."

"Why do you have to lose the weight? I think you look fantastically sexy. Plus, if you lost weight, you'd lose those magnificent boobs, and that would be a terrible shame."

"Patrick!" admonishes Grace, instantly turning scarlet.

"Look!" Patrick's eyes widen in delight. "Grace is blushing! Grace! I had forgotten how red you go! Look, Mum! Grace is burning up!"

"Oh, stop," Lydia says. "Leave the poor girl alone. And do you really have to be so crude?"

"They're boobs, Mum. Nothing to be embarrassed about. Particularly when they are so spectacular. Terrible thing about L.A.," he muses, almost to himself, "is that everyone has giant boobs, but they're all as hard as melons. All fake. It's the single most disappointing thing about being single. I dream of sinking my head into soft pillows and instead it's like being hit with a matching pair of footballs. Dreadful."

"So, are you a huge man about town?" Grace asks, her face now back to its usual color.

"I am." Patrick nods enthusiastically. "I will say that I did rather love being married, although I didn't much love who I was married to. No, let me say that again. If Alicia had been who she'd pretended to be during our courtship, after we were married, I would have been very happy indeed. Sadly, I fell for the perfect cliché—the actress who seduced her director intending to get the leading role in all his films."

"And now you're the perfect cliché of the single movie producer in Hollywood."

"It's a tough job," he sighs, "but someone has to do it. So many women . . ."

"So little time," Grace finishes off for him, as Patrick hands her a spoon and, unable to resist, she digs in.

"We should go for a walk after lunch." Patrick sizes Grace up a little while later. "Particularly after you ate all that trifle. Jesus, woman. Anyone would think you'd been in the desert for a year."

"Oh, go away." Grace smacks him on the arm. "You can't win with you."

"No," he agrees. "No one ever can. Shall we go and see if we can find some baby lambs?"

Grace grins in delight at the memory. "I bet you say that to all the girls," she says.

"No. Only the ones I really, really like."

"You really haven't changed."

"Neither have you," he says, and this time, instead of pointing out that she is twice the woman she once was, Grace keeps her mouth firmly shut.

So, I do sort of have the skinny from Mum," he says when they have climbed over the stile and into the field, the very field she once walked in with Robert, all those years ago. "She did tell me all about your adventures in the world of psychopharmaceuticals, and how you were now off everything. And obviously, she told me about your marriage and stuff. You seem like you've really been through the mill."

"That's the funny thing about going through the mill," says Grace. "Even when you're in it, it doesn't really feel like anything other than just your life. An outsider looks at it and is horrified, but you just keep plodding along, putting one foot in front of the other because that's all you know how to do. Hell becomes normal. Hell definitely became my new normal.

"So how are things with Ted? Are you in contact with him?"

"Barely," says Grace. "And only then by email. Usually logistics. Where are the keys to the barn. That sort of thing."

"Are you going to try and patch things up?"

"I want to. But I can't do anything until he's got this woman out of his system. I tried to call twice and both times she answered the phone, so I just put it down. I don't even want to email him because she'll answer it. I did write to him, care of his agent, and asked him to give the letter to Ted directly, not to Beth, but I have no idea whether he got it."

"God, Grace. What a horrible story. And you're definitely sure he's with her?"

"Oh, yes. I know my husband, and he can never resist flattery, particularly from a younger woman. I am quite certain this was all premeditated, that she has had a plan, from the very beginning, to replace me." Grace sighs. "We know so little about her. I just took her on because I was desperate."

"But you got references on her?"

"I couldn't get hold of anyone by phone, the numbers were out of service, but she gave me their email and the references were glowing. Of course, now I have to wonder if she was behind it."

"A Gmail account?"

"Hotmail, I think." Grace is stunned she hadn't remembered this until now. "Same difference. I never thought . . . God, how utterly stupid am I? It never occurred to me to question it at the time. Anyway. It's too late now."

"Is it, though? Don't you think of exposing her? Surely if Ted were to realize she had machinated all of this, he'd see the error of his ways?"

"I don't think it's as simple as that. I think he's completely obsessed and won't listen to any kind of reason. The only one I really want to believe me now is Clemmie."

"How much does she know?"

"She's confused. About whether to believe me or whether to believe what her father says is the true diagnosis; she doesn't know if Beth is this sweet woman who has befriended her and is looking after her dad, and appears to be deeply concerned about her mother, or if she's actually someone whose motives are, as I believe, far more sinister. Poor girl. I hate that she is being dragged in, but she's a smart girl. Time will show the truth. At least that's what I'm praying for."

"I hope so," says Patrick, holding out his hand to help her over the next fence. "And if not, we could always turn it into a film."

"Don't be so blasé about it," says Grace, turning serious. "She's my daughter and I love her. God only knows whether I'm able to repair our relationship. God only knows whether she'll ever be able to see the whole truth."

PUMPKIN GINGERBREAD TRIFLE

(Serves 8–10)

INGREDIENTS

For the gingerbread

3 cups all-purpose flour
1 Tablespoon ground cinnamon
2 teaspoons baking soda
1½ teaspoons ground cloves
1 teaspoon ground ginger
¾ teaspoon salt
1½ cups white sugar
1 cup vegetable oil
1 cup dark molasses
½ cup apple juice
2 eggs
1 Tablespoon grated fresh ginger
½ cup chopped crystalized ginger

Preheat oven to 350 degrees.

Butter and flour a 10-inch springform pan.

Stir together flour, cinnamon, cloves, ground ginger, baking soda, and salt in a container.

Mix sugar with oil, juice, molasses, eggs, and fresh ginger in a large bowl. Mix in crystalized ginger. Stir in flour mixture. Pour into prepared pan, then bake for 1 hour. Cool this for 15 minutes, then remove from the pan and cool completely.

For the pumpkin custard

3 cups half and half
6 large eggs
½ cup granulated sugar
½ cup brown sugar, packed
⅓ cup molasses
1½ teaspoons ground cinnamon
1 teaspoon ground ginger
1 teaspoon ground nutmeg
⅛ teaspoon ground cloves
¼ teaspoon salt
3 cups pureed pumpkin, or about 1½ cans

For the assembly

1 quart heavy cream, whipped until stiff
½ teaspoon vanilla extract
¼ cup crystalized ginger
8–10 gingersnap cookies

Scald the half and half in a heavy saucepan ("scald" means, take it to the edge of boiling, then remove from heat).

Beat eggs, two types of sugar, molasses, cinnamon, ginger, nutmeg, cloves, and salt. Mix in pumpkin and half and half. When it is smooth, put it in buttered baking dish, which you then put into a bain-marie: put dish into larger baking dish and fill larger dish with hot water to about 1 inch below the rim of the custard dish. Bake this at 325 degrees for 50 minutes and start to check it. You want a set, firm custard—when a knife is inserted into the center, it should come out clean. Cool and refrigerate overnight.

To assemble your trifle, get your trifle bowl out.

Whip one quart heavy cream with half a teaspoon vanilla extract, then fold in ¼ cup crystalized ginger, and set aside.

Spoon half the pumpkin custard into the bowl and layer half the gingerbread over that and half the whipped cream over that. Do it again. Top the final layer of whipped cream with gingersnaps, or gingersnap crumbs, and, if you like, drizzle with Calvados.

Thirty-one

Well, don't you look lovely?" Patrick stands up from the table and holds his arms out to kiss Grace, holding her at arm's length to examine her from head to toe. "Fantastic dress," he says approvingly, Grace smiling, loving how Patrick has the unnerving ability to make her feel sexy, even now.

"I can't believe you dragged me up to London," Grace said. "All this way for a dinner. It had better be good."

"It will be magnificent." He gestures around the restaurant. "You have my word. Did you book a room at my hotel? I would have offered mine for you to bunk up in, but I didn't want you to get the right idea."

"You mean the wrong idea."

"No," says Patrick deliberately. "I meant the right idea."

"Patrick Propper! Are you still flirting with me? After all these years?" Grace shakes the napkin into her lap as she shoots him a schoolmarmish look of disapproval.

"Absolutely!" he says. "My crush on you is still as strong as ever.

Maybe even stronger." He glances down at her breasts as she crosses her arms with a scowl. "Sorry. What will you have to drink? Martini?"

"Perfect!" she says, looking around the restaurant at the other tables, many of whom appear to be on romantic dates. I wonder, she thinks, if they will think that we are on a romantic date. How odd, and how funny, and how enormously flattering.

She turns back to find Patrick smiling at her as the waiter delivers their drinks and they toast one another.

"To old friends!" Patrick's eyes sparkle warmly across the table at her. "And new loves."

"Hang on!" She bursts out laughing. "That's a bit presumptuous of you, isn't it?"

"I just meant generally. Not you and me specifically. Although obviously, if you're offering, I'm hardly going to turn you down. Are you?"

"Offering? No!" She takes a sip of her drink. "Although I'm not sure I'm ready for the 'new loves' bit. I'm still trying to figure out how I feel about the old. There has been a development, in case your mum didn't already tell you."

"Beth has, in fact, taken over your life and moved in on everything you care about."

Grace shakes her head. "God, Patrick. Your mother is impossible. You'd think at her age she would have learned the art of discretion. She tells you lot everything."

"Of course she does. She considers you to be one of her children and there's nothing better than family gossip when you're on the phone to Mum. How do you think I know that Robert had a secret vasectomy after Emily threatened to have more sprogs."

"No!" Grace's eyes open wide. "Does Emily know?"

"Absolutely not! She'd murder him in his sleep. Poor old Robert. He never did have any balls, just a great big bloody scowl. But enough about him, let's talk about the evil Beth and her dastardly plan of world domination."

"I don't think it's world domination," says Grace. "I think it's just Ted domination."

Patrick shudders. "I just had a vision of handcuffs. Thanks for that."

Grace is smiling. "How is it that we are talking about my husband's betrayal, maybe my soon-to-be-ex-husband, and you have me smiling? In fact, worse than that, I'm having fun."

"You always did have the most fun with me," says Patrick. "I can't think how you didn't run off with me when you had the chance."

"When I had the chance? What chance was that?"

"Any chance. Every chance. Any time. But back to the point, what are you going to do about Beth?"

"What can we do? Other than hope it all plays itself out."

"Grace. There is more you can do. Surely. I think maybe you start with the reference. You said it was by email, so you could start by tracking the actual woman down and seeing what she says. Or Google her, find out about her. There must be something."

"I already Googled her." Grace sighs. "I've Googled her a million times and there's nothing."

"How about Intelius?"

"What?"

"It's a site where you pay for an online background check. I use it for all my employees. I almost took on a show runner once who had a rap sheet as long as my arm."

"Really?" Grace stares at him.

"Well, not quite. But he had been to jail for tax evasion, which is much the same thing. The point is, we have to find out about Beth. We have to find out whether she's ever done this before."

"Stolen another woman's husband?"

"Yes. Ruined other people's lives. I have no idea why I feel this, but I'm certain you're not the first."

Grace is astonished at the flutter of excitement in her stomach. She does want to find out more about Beth, if for nothing else than to satisfy her own curiosity, to try and find out why Beth has done what she has done.

Not that it will change anything, but suddenly knowing more about Beth feels like the most important thing in the world.

Patrick insists on paying for dinner before they share a cab back to the Charlotte Street hotel.

Charlotte Street is packed with people standing outside pubs, restaurants, racing down the street to try and catch up with friends.

"God, I'd forgotten this," says Grace, turning as a drunken woman staggers down the road, trying to pull her skirt down. "All the people! Everyone out on the streets having fun after a long day's work!"

"I know." Patrick looks at the girl staggering down the street. "I do miss drunken women out on the piss. Somehow, however wonderful L.A. is, without a drunken secretary roaring to her friends, it misses a certain charm."

"I never miss it when I'm in the States," says Grace, linking her arm through his as they step into the hotel. "At least, I don't miss London. I miss Dorset terribly, but London was never much of a home."

"Shall we have a nightcap in the living room?" says Patrick, waiting while Grace checks in. "They have an honesty bar. What can I get you?"

"Vodka on the rocks, please." Grace sinks into a squishy sofa as Patrick prepares the drinks. She watches him, astonished suddenly at the man he has become. More astonished that a judder of something she vaguely remembers as lust jolts through her body.

It's Patrick, she thinks. Surely not. It must be the vodka, she decides, crossing her legs and smiling over at him in as benign a way as possible, hoping to give nothing away.

"Let me run upstairs," he says. "I'm going to grab my computer. Let's get to work. It's Intelius time."

...

Background check or criminal record check?" muses Patrick, both of them hunched over his tiny screen.

"We don't know if she has a criminal record," says Grace. "Let's start with background check. Here. Let me fill it in." She grabs the computer off his lap and swiftly types in Beth's name, then Northvale as the town, before deleting it. "I just remembered she moved to Northvale right before working for us. Before that she said she was living somewhere else. Bugger. Where was it? Somewhere in Connecticut. *Fairfield!* That's where she lived! Let's try Fairfield."

She hits enter, and they both watch the words on the screen: Intelius is searching billions of records for Beth McCarthy in Fairfield, Connecticut.

Moments later, it says they have found six people that match Beth McCarthy in Fairfield.

"That's the one," says Grace, moving the cursor to one name.

"Here goes nothing. Let's get the report."

Patrick gets his credit card, fills in the form. As they wait, the air is heavy with anticipation for the computer to pull up the records, the results of which, it says, will then be emailed to them.

"I feel weirdly excited," says Grace. "If nothing comes up I may actually cry."

"I know!" Patrick cannot tear his eyes off the computer. "I'm praying she's a serial killer." Grace shoots him a look. "Okay, not a serial killer, then, but I'm dying to find out whether there really is a backstory there."

"Here goes." Grace logs in to her Gmail account and clicks the email, both of them craning forward to read.

"Well," he says after a while. "That's interesting. We haven't been able to find anything on Beth McCarthy, but we haven't thought to look for Liz McCarthy. Or Betsy McCarthy. I presume her given name is Elizabeth?"

"It never occurred to me she might go by other names." Grace is wide-eyed as she looks at Patrick, turning straight back to the screen to search the other names.

And there she is. Betsy McCarthy. Smiling widely in a photograph taken at the Near and Far Aid gala in Westport in 2010. She looked entirely different. Blonde, coiffed, elegant, she was as far away from the dumpy girl Grace met as you can imagine.

"Now what?" asks Grace, stumped at where they take it from here.

"Near and Far Aid gala. What is that? Presumably a charity with a committee."

"Aha!" Grace's eyes light up. "You're brilliant. Who was the chair that year?" A few taps and they come up with a name: Anne Lindstrom; a few more taps and her home details are there on the screen. An address in Greenfield Hill and, more importantly, a phone number.

Grace looks at her watch. "It's only five in the afternoon in Connecticut," she says.

"Let's be honest," says Patrick. "Now that we know, it would be rude not to call."

Thirty-two

Is that Anne Lindstrom?"

"Yes?" The voice on the end of the phone is cautious, cool. Before Grace moved to America she had the deep misconception that all Americans were superfriendly, would instantly go out of their way to help. She hadn't met the New England Yankees, but swiftly grew to recognize the Mayflower WASPs, the ones with stiff, gracious smiles, who were polite, but never warm, unless you were one of their own.

"Mrs. Lindstrom, you don't know me, but my name is Grace Chapman. I am trying—"

"Grace Chapman?" The voice is now warm, intrigued. "*The* Grace Chapman? Ted Chapman's wife?"

Grace is embarrassed. "Yes."

"I was just reading about you in *Country Flair*! What an honor! What on earth can I do for you? And please, call me Anne."

"Anne. I'm trying to find someone who was in a photograph taken at the Near and Far Aid gala back in 2010, when you were the chair. I don't know if you know her, but I was hoping you might be able to point me in the right direction. Her name is Betsy McCarthy."

There is a sharp intake of breath, then silence.

"Anne? Are you there?"

The voice is now cold again. "What do you want with her?" There is almost a sneering quality. Grace knows, instantly, that the story isn't good, but that she won't get anything more out of Anne unless she explains, at least a little.

"Anne, I don't know you, but I have to ask you to keep this to yourself, at least for now."

"Okay."

"My husband has an assistant who goes by the name of *Beth* McCarthy. Without going into too much detail, she has fairly successfully ruined—or maybe I should say, stolen—my life. Today I found out she goes by a series of other names, 'Betsy' being one of them. I'm trying to find out more about her. I'm trying to stop any further damage being done."

Anne's voice is quiet. "I'm so sorry," she says. "This isn't the first time she has ruined people's lives. You need to talk to Emily Tallman. Let me get her number for you. Can you give me five minutes just so I can let her know you're going to be calling?"

"Of course. Thank you so much."

"I won't discuss this with anyone. If you went through anything like what Emily went through, I know just how devastating this woman is. I'm sorry. Good luck. If there's anything at all I can do, please let me know."

"Thank you." Grace is overwhelmed by the kindness of this stranger. "Thank you."

Emily Tallman's number goes straight to the machine. Grace doesn't leave a message, fearful of being misunderstood, of not being called back. Instead, she and Patrick sit on the sofa, drinking more and more vodka, trying to figure out what happened to Emily Tallman. There were photographs of her with her husband, Campbell Tallman, and then there weren't.

There were records of a house being sold to Emily and Campbell Tallman, a big, rambling house on the harbor in Southport, and then, less than two years later, selling it for less than they bought.

Emily Tallman's address comes up now, in Southport. There are no names associated with her. What happened to her children, Grace asks, for the former address lists children—Daisy and Ben. The view of her home is one of a pretty little cottage on a quiet side street, not big enough, Grace thinks, for two children.

A quick search shows Campbell Tallman living in Norwalk, the children listed at that address.

"I'm intrigued." Grace turns to Patrick. "Why are the children living with him? And what does this have to do with Beth?"

"You know what I think? I think it's time to go home. America home. I think the only way to get to the bottom of this is to go and see her. And anyone else you might find. I wish I could come with you, but I'm always here for you. You can phone me anytime. You aren't alone anymore, Grace."

"You're an amazing friend, do you know that?"

Patrick smiles. "I'm also an amazing lover. Just in case you were wondering . . ."

Grace doesn't smile this time. She just stares at him, knowing she ought to look away, but there is that jolt again, so unexpected, so discombobulating.

"I'm sorry," she says. "Excuse me. I'm just going to the bathroom."

In the bathroom, she is stunned at what she sees in the mirror. Her eyes are glittering, her lips full. This is not the sylphlike Grace that she was before, nor is it the bloated, unhappy Grace of a few months back. Although bigger, tonight she is beautiful.

Perhaps, she tilts her head as a smile of delight plays on her lips, perhaps it has nothing to do with my size and everything to do with how I feel.

I am drunk, she thinks. It has been years since I have been drunk, and what fun it is. I am drunk, and I am beautiful.

These past few days are the first time that she has felt beautiful in a very long time. Today might even be, she thinks, the first day in her whole life that she has felt beautiful on the inside, where it counts.

And there is a man waiting for her outside, a man who has, she knows, always desired her. She has always treated it as something of a joke, something to be trifled with and teased, until tonight. When all of a sudden it doesn't seem funny at all.

You seem . . . jittery," Patrick says, raising an eyebrow at Grace, who is concentrating very hard on making it back to the sofa in a straight line. She sounds sober, she knows, but she has had enough to drink that her inhibitions are now below what they would normally be.

Patrick brushes her hand with his own as Grace stills, looking at their hands together on the sofa. Without thinking, without realizing what she is doing, she strokes his hand, turning his palm over and tracing it with her fingers.

Looking up at him, Patrick's smile has disappeared. They stare at each other.

"I think I need some fresh air," she says. "Do you want a walk?"

They stand just outside the entrance of the hotel, saying nothing, as people weave their way around them. They do not look at each other, the air between them thick with all that has not been said.

A girl shouts down the street after her friends and falls into Grace, pushing her up against Patrick, who steadies Grace but doesn't let her go. They both smile at the girl's loud apologies as she disappears off down the street, turning back to each other as the smiles on each of their faces slide off.

"Do you not think . . . ?" Grace whispers, Patrick's face now inches from her own. "Do you not think that now might be a very good time to kiss me?"

"Are you serious?" he whispers back, even as his face moves imperceptibly closer to hers. "Are you drunk?"

"Yes," she says as her lips brush his. "And yes. But not so much so that I don't know what I'm doing, or that I'll regret it in the morning."

His mouth opens to meet hers as Grace melts into his arms.

Waiting for the elevator, they kiss again, ignoring anyone who might be passing, Grace feeling a passion and excitement she's not sure she has ever felt before.

"Get a room," leer a crowd of young men leaving the restaurant, and it is to Patrick's room they go, Patrick fumbling to get the door open, pulling Grace back into his arms as he kicks the door shut.

"Oh God," he groans, slipping the dress over her shoulders, Grace embarrassed, for a moment, at how ample her bosom has become, then sinks into lust as Patrick slips off her bra straps with reverence, moving from one breast to another, his lips, his tongue, hungrily suckling, nipping, licking as Grace sighs with an otherworldly pleasure.

She reaches down to undo the zipper on his pants, pulls him out, no longer aware that this is Patrick, taken into another realm with the feelings sweeping through her body. Her turn to lift his shirt over his head, marvel at his body, the strength, the firmness.

What bliss is this, this body, this man, she thinks, stroking her hands up and down his body, pulling down his pants, his underwear, sinking to her knees to help him get them off, then taking him in her mouth as he gasps.

Then she is pushed back on the bed, Patrick moving down her body, his head between her legs, expertly going down on her until she clasps his hair between her fingers, her back arching as the waves take her over.

And then, he is on top of her, inside her, kissing her eyes, her cheeks, her lips. It is only then that she realizes he is crying, tears welling in his eyes and dripping onto her chest.

"What is it?" she gasps, placing a hand on his chest to stop him. "Do you want to stop? I'm so sorry."

"No," he says, smiling through the tears. "It's just . . . I've waited so long."

"Oh, Patrick." She pulls his head down to hers and kisses him, tasting the saltiness of the tears on his lips.

Thirty-three

Patrick is right: she isn't alone anymore. Grace, who, despite husband, daughter, friends, has felt alone all of her life, seems to not be alone now that Patrick has reentered the picture, the irritating elder "brother" she inherited somewhere in her eighteenth year.

Her childhood truly was spent largely on her own and when she now thinks of her marriage to Ted, which she hasn't done nearly as much the last few weeks, she sees herself as alone in that marriage too.

Not that she doesn't want it back. They had found a way to make it work, Ted with his writing, with Ellen taking care of him; Grace with Harmont House, her cooking, her lunching and socializing in New York.

But how empty it now seems, looking back. Of course she was going to be on her own much of the time, married to a writer, and more, one so much older than her. She hadn't ever felt, all those years, lonely. She hadn't felt in need of a partner, someone who was more on her wavelength, someone who made her laugh.

Ted hadn't ever made her laugh. That hadn't been their dynamic.

He made her think, made her happy, she had always thought, but laughter? Fun? That had never been a big factor in their relationship.

She turns, examining Patrick's profile in the car as he pulls onto the motorway on their way back to Dorset. It is a profile she knows almost as well as her own. He has always been my brother, she thinks, startled that she is not looking at him in the way she ought to be looking at a true sibling. She is looking at the curve of his chin, the softness of his lips. She is looking at his strong hands expertly steering the car, his hair, longer than she had ever seen it, gently curling over his collar.

"I know you're staring," Patrick says, never taking his eyes from the road. "Didn't anyone ever tell you that was rude?"

"I was just thinking how grown-up you are."

He shoots her a confused glance. "You're always accusing me of never having grown up. Make up your mind."

"No, I meant physically. You're really a man."

"Please tell me that this moment, today, in this car is not really the first time you have noticed that."

Grace flushes. "Oh God." She drops her head in her hands with a sheepish grin. "I think it actually is."

Patrick shakes his head as he reaches over to take her hand. "Better late than never."

That night, Grace cooks dinner. With an affectionate nod to her adopted home, she makes chicken and dumplings, followed by apple pie, which sends Patrick off in rapturous praise.

Lydia watches them, saying nothing. They are careful not to touch each other, not to give anything away, unaware that the chemistry between them is electric; that even a blind man could tell there is something going on.

"I'm off to bed, you two," says Lydia when the table has been cleared and Grace and Patrick are standing by the sink, finishing off the dishes. "Make sure you turn off all the lights."

"Yes, Mum," they both say in unison, and laugh, giddy in the first spell of lust, Patrick sidling up to Grace as Lydia disappears up the stairs, pulling her in and lowering his lips to meet hers as her arms snake up around his neck.

"God, you are gorgeous." He nuzzles into her neck. "You'd better be sneaking into my room tonight."

"I haven't got the nerve." Grace laughs. "What if your mother catches me? You come sneak into mine."

"Done." He smiles, taking her by the hand and starting to lead her up the stairs as Grace hesitates.

"Emily Tallman," she says. "Let me just try again. One more time, then we'll go up."

Upstairs, Grace emerges from the bathroom, wrapped in a towel, to find Patrick lying on her bed.

"You really do have to go home," Patrick says. "I know you don't want to, and I certainly don't want you to, but Emily Tallman isn't picking up the phone and she isn't responding to your messages. The only way you're going to get an answer is to go. You haven't seen Clemmie in over six months. Grace, you know it's time."

Grace nods. She is strong enough now to deal with whatever might be waiting for her.

She misses Clemmie. Desperately. Their regular phone calls do nothing to assuage her guilt at leaving, even though she has always known it was the only thing she could do.

As for Ted, now might be the right time to see him. He is with Beth, it is true, but Grace knows him better than anyone. He falls hard for his obsessions, but they do not last long. When they are over, when he has moved through, he comes out on the other side loving Grace more; needing her more.

And then there is Beth.

Grace shudders as Patrick looks at her with concern. "What?"

"The thought of seeing her. All these months away I've built her up into this terrible, evil creature. The thought of seeing her now completely terrifies me."

"It terrified you before because you were so vulnerable. You're not anymore, Grace. And you're not alone. I do see how you've demonized her, and I see that you don't have to do it anymore. I promise you, you don't have to be frightened anymore. I may not be there physically, but I'll be with you every step of the way."

Grace nods.

"I love you," he says, standing up to hold her.

"I know." She smiles, allowing herself to be held, as Patrick gently unwinds the towel and lets it drop to the floor.

Grace immediately covers herself as Patrick gently takes her hands. "Stop," he says, gazing at her naked body with such love and such acceptance that Grace, so awkward in her nakedness now, starts to relax.

"Please don't lose any more weight," he says, tracing the roundness of her stomach, cupping her full breasts in each hand and leaning forward to kiss them. "I have never seen anyone more beautiful, more womanly than you."

"You're biased," says Grace, who has not had anyone worship her body, be she fat or thin, *ever.*

"Maybe. But I have known you at both sizes, and to me this is truly the most perfect you have ever been." His hand slips between her legs, and soon she is sighing with pleasure, as both of them sink back on the bed.

Grace awakens early. It is 5:34 a.m., but the possibility of sleep has gone. Patrick hasn't bothered sneaking back to his own room so

Lydia doesn't find out. It wouldn't have mattered, thinks Grace, for Lydia almost certainly already knows.

She turns to examine Patrick, fast asleep on his back, his strong profile reassuringly familiar, his body less so. She pulls the sheet down slightly, shivering with lust as she looks at his hands, remembers what they were doing to her just last night.

He has awoken her sexuality, something she had long ago put to bed in her marriage to Ted. It had been years since she had thought of herself as a sexual being, years since she has felt what it is to desire someone, to look at them and itch with longing.

I am home, she thinks, marveling at the familiarity and safety of being with someone she has known, and loved, for so very many years.

She has loved him like a brother, but will never think of him in that light again. She studies his chest, watching it rise and fall, wanting to reach out and touch his skin, not wanting to wake him up.

I don't want to leave, she thinks. Never have I felt more myself than these days with Patrick. I don't want to leave him, but this is not my life. This is not where I belong. This may feel like home, but it isn't home. Home is where my family is, home is where my house is, my life.

Whether I want to or not, she thinks, Patrick is right: It's time for me to go back to America.

She reaches out then, gently traces the profile of his face as he stirs, opens his eyes, rolls toward her.

"What time is it?" he mumbles.

"Too early to get up," she says. "Go back to sleep."

"Why are you awake?" His eyes are still closed, his voice thick with sleep, sluggish.

"Too much on my mind. I've been thinking about what you said last night, about going home."

Patrick opens his eyes then, sits up in bed, looks at Grace.

"You're right. I can't hide forever, and I can't move forward unless I go back. I'm going to see if there's a flight tomorrow. It's time."

Patrick nods, but doesn't speak, just looks down at the sheets.

"Patrick? This was your idea," Grace says gently. "This . . . us . . . has been lovely. It has been the most gorgeous thing to have happened to me in years. But it can't last. You know that, yes? You have your life in Los Angeles, and I'm married. Even if everything's over, I can't dive into something else. There are too many moving parts."

"I know," Patrick says quietly, still not looking at her.

"I will always love you," Grace says. "And we will always be friends."

"Yes," says Patrick, reaching out to put his arms around her in a hug, blinking the tears that have sprung so unexpectedly into his eyes.

Thirty-four

In New York, in their Manhattan apartment, Luke stretches his long legs out on the sofa and pulls Clemmie toward him as she walks past, saying, "I like this," pulling her down for a kiss as she shrieks and playfully tries to disengage.

"I have to go," she says, pausing for a few minutes to sink into his arms. "What do you like?"

"This. Us. Living together," says Luke, gesturing around the tiny apartment they had just rented together. "I even really like going to the bathroom and having girl things around."

"Girl things?" She barks with laughter. "Like bras drying on the radiator?"

"Yes. And makeup on the sink. It's weird, but in a good way. It makes me feel all responsible and mature."

"Careful," says Clemmie. "Next thing you know, you'll be asking me to marry you."

"You should be so lucky," grins Luke as they both smile into each other's eyes, knowing they are both far too young, that marriage is something only to be joked about, that if it were to happen for the two of them it wouldn't be for years, something that stretches out into the future, allowing them to treat it lightly now.

"Are you sure you don't want to come with me to my dad's?" Clemmie's voice catches itself. For years it was "to my parents," and it has only been recently that she has started saying, "to my dad's." It doesn't feel good. It doesn't feel right. It lends a permanent air to a situation Clemmie prays is temporary.

She has spoken to her mom, but the conversations have been light, neither of them daring to speak about anything too deep, anything that may cause a wider rift. What she wants to say is, When are you coming home? When are you and Dad going to talk? Why is any of this happening? And most of all, Are you really okay?

Clemmie thinks her mother is. She sounds okay. She sounds like herself, and it has been a very long time since her mother has sounded like herself. Clemmie hadn't even realized how bad things had got, but now she is hopeful it is over.

And if it is, couldn't they all carry on with their lives as they were before? For a while Clemmie hoped she might be able to orchestrate them getting back together or, at the very least, her mother coming back home to America, where she belongs. At least if she were here, Clemmie might have a chance, but her mother is adamant that she has to be in England to get better.

Clemmie tried talking to her father, which felt awkward, and wrong, as much for him as it was for her.

"This isn't something that's appropriate for you and I to discuss," he said gruffly, turning away. "I'm sorry this is difficult for you, but it will resolve itself in the way it is supposed to."

But how? thought Clemmie. How can this messy, awful situation ever resolve itself?

Perhaps by Clemmie being around more, she thought, aware always of the seed planted by her mother, that Beth would move in. But Clemmie has taken to turning up unexpectedly, walking into the house, her heart in her throat, expecting to find her father and Beth in flagrante, but there is never anything going on other than what you would expect between a writer and his assistant.

Admittedly, he seems to rely on Beth more. But why wouldn't he? He says she is his savior. The one woman who has got him through the most insane period of his life.

"If it weren't for Beth," he has said, numerous times, to Clemmie and to anyone else who will listen, "I don't know how I would have survived."

Word has gotten out now that Grace has bipolar disorder, has deserted her family after refusing the help she so desperately needed. Luckily, word hasn't reached the press, but the village is buzzing with gossip, with people wanting to know, indulging in a spot of schadenfreude, for who does not enjoy seeing the mighty fall from grace, or indeed, Grace fall from the mighty.

Clemmie doesn't call before driving out to Sneden's. She wants to collect her warmer coat, which hangs in the closet of her bedroom, with the rest of the clothes she doesn't have room to store in their tiny apartment.

"Hello?" she calls into the kitchen, out of habit, jolted always that her mother's voice doesn't sing down the stairs to her. The house feels dead, as if the life has been sucked out of it, which, Clemmie thinks, it has, despite the fresh flowers on the table and new curtains in the window. Odd, she thinks. Her father would surely never have bothered with new curtains.

Out to the barn to see her father, she stomps along the garden path, watching her breath mist in the air. Perfect timing for her coat, she thinks, pushing the door of the barn open.

"Clemmie? What are you doing here?" Beth walks out of the office at the end, holding a file. "We weren't expecting you."

"No. Sorry. I just came by to pick up a coat and say hi to my dad. Is he here?"

"He's very busy," Beth says. "He's working on deadline for an article to coincide with the launch of the new book. You know how he is when he's working, he hates to be disturbed."

Clemmie laughs in disbelief. "Right." Then peers at Beth, who does not smile. "Are you actually serious? Are you telling me my own father won't see me because he's busy writing?"

Beth smiles this time. "I know. Crazy, right? But you know how he is."

"Yes. I know how he is," Clemmie says slowly. "And he loves when I visit. Is he in the house?"

"He's in the city today," Beth says smoothly. "I think he's working at the New York Public Library. He says every now and then it helps for him to change it up."

"Really?" Clemmie doesn't recall him ever saying anything like that before. "How odd. Beth? Is he okay? That doesn't sound like him at all."

Beth flashes a bright smile. "Everything's great!" she says. "You know, you can always give me a call before you come up. That way we know if he's here or not. I know he'll be sorry he missed you, and if you call next time we can make sure he's here."

Clemmie blinks at her. There is something . . . proprietary about Beth suddenly. Her mother's words echo in her ears. Could she possibly be right?

"Great idea," Clemmie says. "I'll just quickly go and grab my coat."

"Want me to come?" Beth says.

"I'll only be a second," lies Clemmie. "I have to dash straight back home. Luke has a concert tonight and the traffic's hell."

"Luke has a concert? Why didn't you tell us? We would have loved to come!"

"Us?" Clemmie raises an eyebrow.

"Your dad." Beth laughs. "He hates going anywhere alone, so he tries to force me to go with him to lots of the events these days."

Clemmie just nods, walking out of the barn, knowing that something is definitely not right.

Of course she can't just grab her coat and leave. Of course she goes straight upstairs to her parents' room and opens the door, feeling sick and scared as she pushes it open, her eyes scanning the room for evidence.

It looks much as it always has. The same clock on her father's side, the same pile of manuscripts and books. On her mother's side a pile of books, but that is no proof that Beth is there—the books could have been left from when her mother was here.

She pulls open the drawer. Nothing that is recognizably anyone's, and it isn't until she reaches the bathroom that she knows her mother is right. Makeup is dotted on the vanity, a lipstick, Beth's lipstick, still with its cap off. Her mother's brushes lie haphazardly on the table, having just been used, her robe thrown over the back of the chair, still damp from this morning's shower.

"Fuck," Clemmie whistles, turning as she hears footsteps.

"I thought you were just going to get your coat and leave," says Beth from the doorway.

"I thought you were just my father's assistant, not his lover," says Clemmie. "I thought you'd have the decency to leave my mother's things alone."

"If your mother were well," says Beth, evenly, "I wouldn't be here. You should be grateful someone is looking after your father."

"Grateful? Are you fucking kidding me?" snorts Clemmie, pushing past Beth and pausing at the top of the stairs. "You have just proved my mother entirely sane and absolutely right about you. She said you had orchestrated everything, including making her appear crazy. She said you would do anything to get her out so you could get your hands on my father."

"Really?" Beth's voice is light, as if they are making polite small talk, a smile on her face. "I wouldn't trust anything that comes out of your mother's mouth. Poor thing," she says, turning and going back into the bedroom, closing the door with a sharp, but firm, click.

Clemmie reverses out of the driveway blind with rage. Beth's smug face, her voice saying "poor thing" echoing around and around her mind. She drives up the road, then pulls over, digging her cell phone out from her pocket and calling her mother. The phone isn't answered, it goes straight to voicemail.

Over and over, she calls. Over and over, she gets voicemail.

Thirty-five

Grace dozes on and off throughout the flight. Her excitement at seeing Clemmie again is tempered by a pang of loss at leaving Patrick.

She didn't expect to feel this, hadn't expected to be so emotional at having to leave. It was more than that, she told herself, it was that she didn't know when she would see him again.

"We'll phone," he whispered into her ear as they hugged good-bye at the airport. "I'll email you every day. Maybe not every day, but at least once a month."

Grace had laughed into his shoulder, pulling back to look him in the eye.

"I love you," she said, turning away, swallowing the lump in her throat.

"I've always loved you," he said, kissing her one last time before turning and walking away.

Her thoughts on the plane ride have been jumbled between Clemmie and Patrick, excitement and pain, no movie able to distract her from her circular, incessant thinking.

Sybil is standing in arrivals, her face in a wide smile of joy as she spots Grace, leaping forward to fling her arms around her, take her case, babbling at how wonderful Grace looks.

"Look at you! Look at you!" She keeps stopping in her tracks and turning to look at her friend. "Oh, Grace! How I've missed you! Nothing has been the same since you've been gone."

They drive along the Van Wyck, Sybil talking and talking, asking questions, then interrupting Grace's answers to tell her something else she has suddenly thought of.

"So?" Sybil asks finally. "I'll drop you at Clemmie's, go and do the errands in the city I need to do, then we'll go home. How does that sound?"

"Perfect."

There is, finally, a comfortable silence, broken after a few minutes by Sybil looking slyly at Grace: "Don't you want to tell me more about Patrick?"

Grace arranges her features into an expression of nonchalance. "What about Patrick?" Don't blush! thinks Grace. Not now. For God's sake, don't blush. Nobody knows about Patrick, and Grace is convinced that is for the best. She takes a deep breath and wills herself to stay calm. "What about him?"

"Wasn't there something going on between you?"

"What on earth would make you think that?" Grace feigns surprise. "We're very old friends," Grace says lightly. "He's like a brother to me."

"But he's in love with you, isn't he? At least that's what it sounded like from your emails."

"I don't think so," tries Grace, who doesn't sound convincing, even to herself. "He did always have a crush on me when we were young," Grace deflects. "It hadn't occurred to me he still did, but maybe you're right."

"So, nothing happened in England between the two of you?"

Grace thinks back to her time with Patrick, feels a flutter of lust and loss that is instantly discombobulating.

"Nothing happened," she lies smoothly, swiftly changing the subject. "Syb, there is something I want to ask, and I wanted to ask you face-to-face. I need you to tell me what Beth was saying about me. I know you don't want to tell me, but now that I'm here, I really need to know what I'm dealing with."

Sybil turns to look at her friend. "What's the point?" she says. "It's only going to hurt you."

"I need to know, Syb. It won't hurt me, I promise."

"I'm sure you already know most of this. She said you were crazy. That's basically the brunt of it. She told the board at Harmont House, and it seems anyone else who would listen, that you're bipolar and she and Ted tried to have you committed, but you escaped. That you had these unbelievable tantrums and rages, that she and Ted were terrified of you, that never has there been such a discrepancy between a public image and the private person."

"Wow." Grace shakes her head. "She really did a number on me."

"She did. Have you come back to get revenge?"

Grace laughs. "I don't know. I don't think it's revenge that I want, but I do know I need to get things resolved. I just don't have any idea how."

Thirty-six

om!" Clemmie rocks in her mother's arms, hands clasped tightly behind her mother's back, squeezing her mother as the two of them stand wrapped so close, it looks as if they will never let each other go.

"Clemmie," croons Grace, smelling her daughter's hair, feeling it soft on her cheek. "My baby girl. My love."

Clemmie steps back to look deep into Grace's eyes before clasping her again, releasing her only after Luke clears his throat.

"Hello, Mrs. Chapman." He steps forward. "You probably don't remember me, but we met once at a gala."

"Of course I remember you!" Grace laughs, putting her arms out and giving him a loose, easy hug. "Not to mention that I've heard so much about you, I feel as if I know you."

"I'm glad you're home. Clemmie has missed you a lot."

"She knows," Clemmie says, putting her arm through Grace's. "Can I show you the apartment?" Grace moves with her past the foyer.

"I've been desperate to see what it's like. Oh, Clemmie!" Grace takes in the French doors that separate the living room from the bedroom, the breezy white curtains at the window, the white flokati rugs on the floor. "It's so stylish! And cozy! I love it!"

"I know! Right?" Clemmie proudly brings her mother in, showing her the tiny black-and-white–tiled bathroom, the galley kitchen that, Clemmie proudly says, has actually been cooked in!

"A New Yorker who cooks!" Luke says. "Wonders will never cease."

"I am my mother's daughter." Clemmie smiles. "Everything I learned, I learned from her."

"You're a lucky fellow, that's all I can say," says Grace as they go into the living room and sit down in front of a tray of fresh lemonade and chocolate chip cookies Clemmie has prepared.

"You look amazing," Clemmie says, curling up on the sofa next to her mother, taking her mother's hand and playing with her Russian wedding ring, the ring Grace has always worn on the third finger of her right hand. She looks into her mother's eyes. "You look like you again. Only . . . happier."

Grace laughs. "I feel like me again. It was a rough time, having that misdiagnosis, then feeling like I truly was going nuts. I'm glad it's all over. I'm glad I'm back to almost feeling like myself."

"Almost?"

"I don't feel the same as I did before," Grace says. "It might just be timing, that my body still has to adjust to being pounded by those heavy-duty drugs, but I have a feeling I won't ever go back to being exactly who I was before. I can't even explain it. Some of it is probably a good thing."

"I had no idea," says Clemmie.

"I know," says Grace. "Neither did I. I thought my entire life was coming apart, but I think I just realized that sometimes the thing you think is going to ruin your life is the thing that saves you."

"The thing you think is going to ruin your life being Beth?" Clemmie's eyes flash.

"It's not just Beth. It's the whole bipolar thing . . ." Grace takes a deep breath. "Clemmie, I've never told you this, or your father, but part of the reason this was so awful is that my mother was bipolar. She was what was then called a manic depressive, and the one fear I have always had was that I would somehow turn out to be like her." Grace looks down at her hands to see they are shaking. For over twenty years she has been terrified her husband or her daughter might find out, and now that she has just confessed, she realizes it is as if a huge black cloud has finally lifted from her shoulders.

Clemmie just stares at her.

"There are very few people who know. Your father doesn't know. I've always carried such tremendous shame about it, I tried to keep it a secret. And of course, when that diagnosis was given to me, it was as if my greatest fear was coming true—that I would end up like my mother.

"And I think that's why, even though I was so certain he was wrong, but it's why I thought he might be right. My mother never took treatment. She was an alcoholic, and mentally ill, and it killed her. I thought that if it was true—and I know there is a genetic component, which is why I was so scared—but if it was true, I could have a different outcome if I was treated. But I don't have it, Clemmie. You know that, don't you? I never had it." Grace is smiling now, unable to believe the levity of confession. What is it that they say, she thinks, about you being only as sick as your secrets? I should have done this years ago, she thinks. What was I so frightened of?

Clemmie nods. "I didn't know what to believe," she says. "Dad was so clear that you were ill, but nothing I read about bipolar sounded like you. Yes, you were obviously depressed, but there was no mania, no grandiosity, none of the things that signify the duality of it. And now that I've really seen what's going on with Beth, I know she's behind it all. You weren't crazy. You were right all along. About everything. It's a nightmare. She's a nightmare . . ." Clemmie's words rush out of her. "She's completely taken over everything and she's distancing Dad from everyone, even me, and she's spending all your money and I can't believe any of us believed her. We have to stop her, Mom. We have to do something. Dad is totally miserable, but he doesn't know how to get out of it. His book comes out next week, and normally he's doing tons of interviews, but it's been really quiet, and I think he's nervous."

"Have the magazine reviews come out?"

Clemmie winces. "A couple. And they were terrible. 'A shadow of his former self,' they said. Weak, and insubstantial. He's pretty devastated, and now we're dreading the *Times* review. And you heard he fired Molly? Beth is apparently now acting as his agent. It's going from bad to worse."

Grace shakes her head. "There was a lot banking on this book," she says quietly. "Publishing is not what it was. His agent confided that the publisher wouldn't do another deal if this book doesn't do well. I'm sorry. I'm sorry things are going badly." She looks up at Clemmie. "This must be so hard for him."

"What are we going to do?" says Clemmie. "We have to do something."

"Let me call Molly," says Grace, any trace of jet lag disappearing. "Maybe she has some insight. I can tell Sybil to go home and I'll get a car there later. Let's see what we can find out."

Molly Sullivan is, has always been, larger than life. A bleached blonde, always in some variation of a red jacket, dripping with gold jewelry, she has a heart as big as the ocean, is regularly caricatured on the literary blogs, represents some of the biggest names in the business, is both feared and admired, in equal part, by the publishers she deals with on a daily basis, and is unreservedly adored by all her authors.

"No one has ever left me," she is fond of saying, and it is true, her loyalty and love for her authors is unquestionable, her ability as a dealmaker unparalleled. She represents few of the younger authors—they want to be represented by someone sexier, younger, someone with their pulse on social media—but the old guard loves her, know they can rely on her to always have their backs.

Her office is in midtown and Grace nervously enters the office she used to know so well.

"Grace!" Molly flings her arms around Grace, holding her at arm's length before pulling her in to squeeze her so tightly, Grace actually struggles for breath.

"Gracie!" murmurs Molly again, and when she pulls back, Grace can see the genuine emotion in her eyes. Molly may have represented Ted, but she came to know the whole family, came to love everyone as much as she had once loved Ted.

"You look wonderful!" Molly says, clearly surprised.

"You expected me to be a raging crazy mess?" Grace asks, a smile hovering at the edges of her lips.

"Well, yes. I rather did. That's what that *Beth* would have me believe. You do know that, Grace, yes? I'm not telling you something you don't already know, because, dear God, I would never want to hurt you."

"It's okay, Molly. I know. Clemmie told me everything today. Beth is a very smart girl who is incredibly devious. I have this feeling she orchestrated everything from the beginning, but of course I can't know that for sure until I try and figure out why."

"Oh, I'll tell you why," sniffs Molly. "She's an evil golddigger. I knew it the first time I met her. She spent the whole time pretending to be deeply concerned about you, explaining how ill you were, and I just found myself sitting there thinking, Grace? Grace has a mental illness? Surely I would have known that, sometime over the almost twenty years I have known you. Surely there would have been some hint if that were true."

"And Ted said nothing."

Molly purses her lips. "It's very clear to all of us who know Ted that he is completely under her spell. Now we think he's just terrified of her, but he has made his bed and will just have to lie in it. Apparently she's talking to anyone who will listen about how they're planning on self-publishing, with her as the editor. It's all a complete disaster. Do you know, he didn't even have the guts to fire me? She did it! Can you imagine? After all these years together, everything we've been through, I get a phone call from her one afternoon telling me she—this *nothing*—is taking over as his agent. Can you imagine? Not to mention that this book is just not ready. It needs a huge amount of work. The publisher tried to tell him, apparently, but Beth has 'edited' it, and Ted refused to listen. When I told him, I got fired. I don't know if you've seen the early reviews, but they're terrible. Grace, his career is just heading down the tubes with this girl." Tears of rage fill Molly's eyes. "And I . . . I'm so hurt, Grace. So hurt! They're going to be there tonight and honestly, I haven't seen him since all of this happened, and I'm dreading it."

"Tonight?"

"The Library dinner? ALA? Usually I love nothing more than seeing everyone, but tonight I don't want to go."

Grace stares at her. "Tonight? Is there a reception first?"

"Of course!" Molly peers at her. "Grace? Do you want to go? I can get your name on the list if you do."

Grace pauses. "I don't know that I want to go exactly, but I want to see it with my own eyes, however painful it might be. I won't stay for the dinner, but I'd love to be a fly on the wall for the reception."

"A fly on the wall? With that blazing red hair?" Molly lifts an eyebrow. "You know there are some remarkable washout sprays at the drugstore if you really do want to go incognito."

Grace smiles. "I don't know that that's altogether necessary. I'll just do my hair differently, I'm sure that's enough. God, Molly. Thank you." Grace wraps her arms around Molly in a warm hug. "I know there's more to this story. I just have to find out what it is."

"You were the best thing that ever happened to that man. He'll come to his senses, Grace. He has to. You can see he's regretting it already. At least, you'll see for yourself tonight."

BEST CHOCOLATE CHIP COOKIES

INGREDIENTS

1 cup butter
3/4 cup white sugar
3/4 cup brown sugar
2 eggs, beaten
2 teaspoons vanilla extract
2 1/4 cups all-purpose flour
1 teaspoon baking soda
1 teaspoon salt
2 cups chocolate chips

Preheat oven to 350 degrees.

In a large bowl cream together butter and brown and white sugars until pale and fluffy. Add eggs, a little at a time, beating well with each addition. Stir in vanilla.

Combine flour, baking soda, and salt. Gradually stir into the creamed mixture. Finally, fold in chocolate chips.

Drop in rounded spoonfuls on greased baking sheets or Silpat baking mat-lined cookie trays.

Bake for 8-10 minutes until light brown. Place on wire rack to cool.

Thirty-seven

"You really don't think he'll see me?" Grace adjusts her hair in the mirror of her hotel room, turning to look at Clemmie, lounging on the bed.

Clemmie takes in her mother. "I don't think he'll recognize you. You wouldn't normally wear clothes like that, and you definitely wouldn't ever put your hair in a top knot."

"It's the best I can do. I'll stay out of the way, but I do need to see them for myself. I want to see what everyone's talking about. I need to see just how he is with her, whether he loves her . . ." she trails off as Clemmie's face falls. "I'm sorry. I shouldn't talk about this with you. It's completely inappropriate."

"It's fine, Mom. Who else are you going to talk to? I'm just so happy you're back." Clemmie slips her arms around her mother and leans her head on her shoulder as Grace strokes her back.

"Me too, Clemmie. Me too."

. . .

People have already started arriving, filing up the front steps of the hotel. Grace thought being early would mean she could avoid people she might know, but that might not be the case. In a long, almost Gothic black dress for the occasion, her hair swept into a top knot, her face overly made up, with glasses, she does not look like the Grace Chapman people expect. Were you to study her, you might think she bore a resemblance to Ted Chapman's wife, but that would be all.

She waits nervously in the corner of the banqueting hall as the room starts to fill up, half turned toward the room, already beginning to see faces she knows. The editor she worked with years ago in publishing, a publicist who had once worked on one of Ted's books.

There are so many people she knows, but in the corner, hiding behind her new hairdo and glasses, she is there, but removed; an impartial observer.

The room starts to fill, people shouldering their way through the crowd, raising their glasses up high so they don't spill, when there is a palpable buzz, a whisper that runs through the room.

"Apparently," Molly whisks over, whispers in her hair before disappearing into the crowd, "they're here."

Instantly Grace feels nausea rise. She squeezes through the crowds, her eyes instantly catching Beth. How could she *not* see Beth, in a low-cut sparkly evening gown, pale grey chiffon dotted with silver sparkles, a train behind. Her hair is piled up on her head as if she is going to a ball, and huge diamonds—oh God, could those be *real*?—sparkle in her ears.

But it is not the outfit that has Grace open-mouthed. It is Beth's attitude, her confidence, her regal bearing. She is *swanning* in, thinks Grace. What happened to the shy, quiet, rather plain girl she had taken on? Nothing is left of her tonight. Beth has metamorphosed into a butterfly, one with regal bearing who sweeps through the room, laughing as everyone flocks to her, all paying homage to the queen bee.

And she is the queen bee, thinks Grace. Ridiculously overdressed, ridiculously bejeweled, she nevertheless has every eye in the room.

Where once they couldn't wait to gather around Ted, now it is Ted who shuffles in the wake of this radiant creature.

Ted. A sharp stab of pain as Ted appears. Clemmie was right, he looks ancient. Weight has dropped off him, leaving him pale and gaunt, and so very much older than he looked when she left. A handsome, charismatic man, all of it seems to have left him as he ambles behind Beth, shaking hands.

He still has his trademark scowl, thinks Grace, although as she watches, the scowl leaves his face from time to time, during which he looks simply bemused. Grace cannot tear her eyes away from him as suddenly, he turns and looks through the crowds, and straight at her.

She inhales sharply, as his face changes. Confusion, then delight, and bewilderment, as he starts to make his way toward her.

With her head down she moves away from Ted as fast as she can, scooting out an exit door as her heart threatens to pound right out of her chest. And right behind her, having watched it all, is Molly.

"He saw you?" Molly pants, out of breath with unfamiliar exertion.

"I think so. Yes. I didn't mean for that to happen."

"Maybe he just thought you were a familiar face?" Molly says. "Maybe he didn't realize it was you. I have to say, Gracie, you don't look like you."

"Maybe." Grace quickens her step as they round the corner on the way to where their car is parked. "But I didn't want to take a chance."

"She's quite something, isn't she?" Molly says. "Talk about overkill. She looked like she was accepting Best Actress at the Academy Awards."

"But she's beautiful, isn't she? Everyone was staring at her."

"Because they couldn't believe how ridiculous she looked!" says Molly. "All the women were incredulous. She looked like a little girl playing fancy dress—Cinderella, you *will* go to the ball!"

Grace laughs, despite herself. "You're right. She did look like Cinderella."

"Except it wasn't a ball. It's a damned Library Association dinner. It isn't even black tie! What was she thinking? Ridiculous dress. Ridiculous girl."

"Thank you for making me feel better."

"Was it awful? Seeing them?" Molly peers at Grace with concern.

"No. I think perhaps that's the most awful thing about it. I thought I'd be furious with Ted, or devastated, or . . . something. But I just felt sad. I don't know if it's sad for him, or for us, or for everything that's happened. I had always seen Ted as this pillar of strength. He was my rock, the man I thought was capable of anything. And tonight . . ." She pauses, remembering his shuffle, his frailty, the hopeful delight when he caught sight of her. "Tonight he just seemed pathetic. He wasn't the man I was married to. It just made me desperately sad. And I want to make it better for him. I want my husband back."

Thirty-eight

You must stay as long as you want," says Sybil, ushering Grace into the large bedroom of her guest suite, stacks of fluffy white towels on the bed, fresh flowers on the dresser. "You know that, yes? Grace? That you must consider this your home."

"Thank you." Grace's eyes fill with tears as Sybil stands looking at her.

"Oh, Grace!" she says quietly. "I'm so relieved you're still you. I've been so worried. You know that Beth told everyone who would listen that you were crazy."

"I know," says Grace. "She's very credible. I'm not sure how she does it, but I know her story sounded good. It's okay, Sybil. It's okay if you weren't sure."

"I've been feeling so guilty."

"You don't have to. I would have wondered too. Who knows what really goes on behind closed doors, after all."

"But you're my closest friend! How could I have questioned you?"

"Syb. It's okay. I forgive you." She forces a smile from Sybil before hugging her, watching as Sybil quietly exits the room.

Clemmie had offered to have her mother stay, but there was so little room, it would undoubtedly go sour within a few days. Grace could continue staying in a hotel and phoned Sybil largely because she missed her. As soon as Sybil heard Grace was in a hotel, she drove over and collected her, insisting Grace move in to the guest suite. Had it been anyone else, Grace would have declined.

Sybil's guest suite is the entire floor above the garage. Two bedrooms, a living room, a kitchenette, and doors opening to a deck at the back, it is private, luxurious, and isolated. It is the perfect place in which Grace can heal and hide as she figures out her next move.

Back in Sparkill, at Sybil's, so close to Sneden's Landing, Grace has no idea what her next move should be. In England everything felt so far away, and there was Patrick, who proved a godsend in making her feel loved and distracting her from what would be waiting for her when she had to make the inevitable return home.

Now that she is here, the events of London have receded. It is hard to know what she was thinking, allowing herself to be swept up in a romance with Patrick, and yet it is so clear to her that his presence was the determining factor in her recovery.

Back home, she doesn't think of him much. Her thoughts are consumed with Ted. And Beth. And Ted and Beth. She doesn't know where this has come from. It wasn't that long ago that she was able to sit with Ted feeling little other than sadness and pity, but in the weeks since that sadness has turned to anger, and that anger to obsession.

I want my life back, she thinks. I want to get rid of Beth. I want to be waking up in my house, working at Harmont House, carrying on where I left off before my life was stolen from me.

Ted isn't perfect, far from it, but seeing him has opened something up in her heart that she thought was permanently closed.

We are all flawed, she thinks. We make mistakes. It is easy to see how Ted was seduced by someone so young, so manipulative, so charming when she wants to be. Easier still to see how the veneer must be starting to wear off, how he must miss his old life; his old wife.

Sybil had peered at her earlier when they were sitting at her kitchen table, chatting.

"You want him back?" She was frowning. "Are you certain?"

"Yes," said Grace. "I want my life back."

For the last few months Grace has become accustomed to driving small cars through narrow, winding streets. How quickly she had forgotten the size of the cars here, looming, monster SUVs, weaving in and out of the lanes on I-95, as she zips along in Clemmie's Volkswagen Bug.

Her phone vibrates on the seat next to her, and carefully, trying not to take her eyes off the road, she accepts the call, dropping the earpiece twice as she tries to untangle it to place it in her ear.

"Hey, you." It is Patrick, and her heart breaks open into a smile.

"Hey, you," she says, marveling at how safe she feels just hearing his voice.

"I wanted to find out how the event was last night," he says. "Did you see them? Did they see you? Tell me everything."

And she does.

"I think you're incredibly brave," says Patrick. "And enormously clever. I'm glad Molly is there with you and clearly on your side. What a complete mess. I just hope you find out what you need to find out today, and that Ted will actually listen."

"Seeing him yesterday was very hard. I don't recall ever seeing Ted look vulnerable before. I had a sense," Grace says carefully, unsure that she should be saying this to Patrick, "that he misses me. He was clearly discombobulated when he saw me, and he did see me. I am quite certain he knew it was me. But there was also delight. Before he had a chance to check his emotions, I saw delight."

As she speaks, Grace recognizes she still has loyalty; she still cares. This is her husband of over twenty years. Whatever betrayal has happened, whatever infidelities there have been, he is still her husband. She does not want to see him destroyed.

They talk for a long time. About everything. And nothing. Hitting traffic in Stamford, Grace reluctantly says good-bye, turning off the highway and taking the back roads. Through Darien, the pretty water town of Rowayton, through Norwalk, Grace delighting in the gorgeous old homes.

When she couldn't get ahold of her by phone days ago, Grace went back to Anne, who arranged this meeting. Emily didn't want to talk on the phone, she said, but they could meet; she would tell her everything.

Past the churches, under the railway tracks, she turns into the pretty village of Southport and pulls up outside the Driftwood Diner. She knows who Emily must be as soon as she walks in, a pretty woman sitting at a table by herself, her face drawn and tired.

"Emily?" She nods as Grace sits, orders a coffee, makes small talk, hopes they will both be relaxed enough to be honest with each other.

"It's beautiful here," says Grace. "What an amazing place to live."

"To live and work," Emily says, gesturing across the street. "I work in that clothes store over there. And I have a part-time job at the bar next door. It keeps me busy."

"Being busy is a good thing. Too much time on my hands always gets me into trouble," says Grace.

"I'd like to be a bit less busy," Emily says quietly.

"This wasn't always your life, was it?" Grace says gently as Emily's eyes fill. "I'm sorry, it's just . . . I Googled you. I know you had a big, beautiful house and I know things changed for you. I had a beautiful house too," she says, knowing the only way to get Emily's story is to tell some of her own.

"I know all about you," Emily says. "I remember the *Architectural Digest* piece on your house. It's beautiful."

"It is. But I don't live there anymore. Beth does, or, as you know her, Betsy."

Emily snorts. "That sounds familiar."

"Emily, I think you and I might have the same story to tell. Would you mind sharing yours with me? She tried to ruin my life, and now that I know I'm not the first, I'm pretty sure I won't be the last. I want to stop her from doing this to anyone else and I can only do that if I know your story."

"My husband took her on," Emily says wearily. "He was a banker in the city and he had a great job. He was an institutional salesman, but still, he earned a great living and we were happy." She looks up, meeting Grace's eye. "We were really happy. That's the thing I still don't understand. I always thought that people only had affairs if there was something very wrong in the relationship, but there was nothing wrong in our relationship. We were the people everyone looked at and wanted to be." She sighs, shaking her head. "Things started to change when Campbell left his job. He wanted to do private venture capital. He'd found this tech company that needed help, and he decided to raise the money and buy it, which he did on the side while he was still working, and once he bought it he decided this was the thing he really wanted to do. That he could leave his paying job and make a go of it. I was totally supportive of him, I knew he'd always wanted to have his own business and it seemed like a great idea. He took a little office in Fairfield, and put an ad out for an assistant."

"Craigslist?"

"I don't even know. I just know he put ads in a few places and met with a few people, then came home one day saying this girl had been in for an interview who seemed great. Betsy McCarthy." Emily involuntarily sneers as she says her name. "I remember asking him what she looked like, because, I don't know . . . maybe I sensed something, but he said she was totally dumpy and plain and that I was so cute to even ask the question and to be nervous. I came into the office just after she started because Campbell wanted me to meet her, and he was right, she was dumpy and plain, and there was no way I had anything to worry about.

"After a couple of months the guy who owned the building Campbell's office was in decided to sell, so Campbell moved the office into the bonus room above the garage. Betsy came to our house every day and, I have to say, I started really liking having her around."

"She got involved with your life too? Offered to help? Organized your closets?"

"Yes! She did the same to you? That's exactly what she did. She made herself indispensable and I thought she was amazing. And she *was* amazing." Emily's expression clouds. "The children adored her. She was like this incredible nanny, assistant, friend. Everything. But you know," she leans forward, "I never wanted to say it out loud, but there was always something I wasn't sure about. I couldn't have put my finger on it and I told myself I was being ridiculous. She made herself my friend. My best friend. I was flattered by all the attention. I thought it was sweet."

"I know," says Grace. "Trust me, I know."

"We became friends, and then one day she shows up and she's in this brand-new little Mazda Miata and she's almost giddy with delight. Apparently her uncle died and left her one and a half million dollars, and this was the first time she had ever been able to buy herself anything nice. I remember being really happy for her, and then, a couple of months later, she went off to Atlantis in the Bahamas for a week, which just had me green with envy. I mean, Atlantis! It's a fortune.

"She came in one day soon after that and, by the way, everything had changed by then. It was as if the money had bought her this incredible confidence. Suddenly she was in great clothes, she'd lost weight, she started buying up crazy expensive designer handbags, and she didn't look like an assistant anymore, she looked like a partner.

"Which is what she suggested to Campbell. She wanted to be an investor, and she wanted to be a partner. It would have been laughable a few months before when she first started, but suddenly it made sense. She would go to meetings with him and Campbell said she just wowed everyone with her smarts.

"We were still friends, kind of, but I wasn't sure I liked who she was becoming. Suddenly she had this air about her, like she was better than me. She had this idea of doing regular girls' nights out with my friends, and we'd go out drinking. . . ." Emily tails off, shaking her head.

"You'd go out drinking?" Grace prompts gently.

"Obviously it sounds crazy now. But I thought we were friends. I would be drinking—but never very much, I've never been a big drinker—but everyone was drinking, that was the point of these evenings. To let loose and let our hair down. I'd usually have a couple of drinks, which for me is a lot; I've got horrible tolerance for alcohol. The next morning I'd always wake up embarrassed that my tolerance had gotten so bad that two drinks would make me completely drunk, but everyone was drinking. No one cared. That was the point of the night out. So there was Betsy, building up quite a collection of videos from our Thursday night outings. Things started changing between me and Campbell. He suddenly became really stressed. Work had been going fantastically, but suddenly it all started to look bad, and everything I said or did seemed to irritate him. The only person who could get through to him was Betsy. I know this sounds nuts, but by this time I had withdrawn. I felt like Betsy had morphed from being this amazing girl, to this all-powerful creature who had taken over my life. She would march into the kitchen and help herself to coffee, or breakfast, as if she owned the place. She'd even make the kids packed lunches for school, and if I said anything she'd look at me in disbelief, as if I was the crazy one for questioning her packing a healthy lunch.

"I'd feel so stupid, I'd just disappear and hide in my bedroom. That was basically the only place I could get away from her, our bedroom.

"I tried telling Campbell that I didn't like her, that I didn't feel safe around her anymore, but he wouldn't hear it. And then, three months later, he announces he's really unhappy, he's been unhappy for years, and he wanted some time out from the relationship."

Grace reaches over and squeezes her hand. "I'm so sorry."

"I had no idea what happened. I'd had this amazing marriage to the only man I've ever loved and it was all slipping through my fingers and I had no way to stop it. Two weeks later I'm out for dinner with a girlfriend, in a restaurant in town surrounded by people I know, and I'm served with papers. There in the restaurant. Divorce. He's going for sole custody because of my 'alcoholism and sexual addiction.'"

"What!" Grace is shocked.

"She talked about me constantly being drunk on our girls' nights out, and lied, saying I always drove my kids to school drunk, replaced water with vodka in the water bottles I took everywhere with me. And she'd been on my computer at home, had placed two ads from a woman looking for a bit of 'extramarital fun.' She put my email address on it."

"You couldn't prove this in court?"

"It was my word against hers and she had the evidence. She had witnesses. All my friends who were subpoenaed and had to say it was true, they had seen me drunk when we went out on Thursday nights. I lost custody," Emily says quietly as her eyes spring with tears. "They live with their father and I get visitation every other weekend."

Grace says nothing, staring at this poor woman in shock.

"And what happened with Betsy?"

"Her inheritance? It turned out to be Campbell's. She had Campbell sign a contract he hadn't read properly entitling her to a salary, and bonuses, and benefits we knew nothing about. Campbell was so consumed with trying to build it up, he didn't know until it had all gone. I think my house is shabby, but you should see Campbell's. He's been trying to get a job in banking again for the last year but no one wants him. He's been working as a driver, driving former friends of ours to the airport and back. I guess that's his penance. All of us have suffered. All of us had our lives ruined."

"I don't understand why you couldn't do anything," says Grace.

"We tried. But it was, as I said, her word against ours. Campbell had signed the contract. She claimed we had agreed to all of it."

Grace reaches into her purse and brings out a stack of photographs, placing them on the table in front of Emily. "Just to be absolutely sure, this is who we're talking about?" Shots of Beth she'd found online, taken at literary events over the last few months, now lie on the table.

Emily reaches down and picks them up, looking carefully at each one. "She looks different now. Different hair color. Older. But yes. That's her. I'd know that face anywhere." She looks back up at Grace. "I can't believe she's still doing it. Maybe this time you can do something, you can stop her."

"I don't know that my story is quite as bad as yours." Grace thinks of the public humiliation of being called an alcoholic and a sex addict, the humiliation, in a town as small as this, and the unending pain of losing custody of your children. She thinks of Clemmie, grateful she did not have to endure this, grateful to be sitting here today as a whole person, even if one who has no idea what her future holds. "But my story is not dissimilar. I didn't get slapped with alcoholism, I got bipolar disorder, and she also created enough evidence that if you didn't know me, you would have believed it. I even believed it myself or, at least, I didn't know with certainty it wasn't true." They both shake their heads in shared disgust before Grace continues. "I need to ask you to trust me with this, Emily. I imagine you want to phone the police right away, but I'd like to be able to do that myself, if that's okay with you. There's one more thing I need to do before we bring her down."

"Can I help? Is there anything I can do? Please! I want to be there when she falls."

"I promise I'll let you know what happens. If there's a way for you to be there when it happens, I'll make sure of it."

"At least I've discovered I'm a survivor," Emily says, as they pay the bill. "I lost everything. My husband, my children, my home, and most of my friends. And here I am," she gestures around the diner. "In Southport, which is lovely, but in a crappy little cottage, which I pay for all by myself, working two jobs to try and treat the kids to nice stuff when I have them, but able to stand on my own two feet. This isn't the life I ever expected to have."

"Are you happy?" They stand outside, in the parking lot, looking at the cars speeding by.

"No. I'll never be happy until I get my children back, but they're older now. They're reaching a stage where they want to be with me and their father won't be able to stop them. Hopefully one day I'll be able to explain what happened, the lies that were told. So, not happy, but made of strong stuff."

"What is it they say? What doesn't kill you makes you stronger?"

Emily lets out a bark of laughter. "Sadly I never wanted to be this strong, but yes, it's definitely made me stronger. Take care of yourself, Grace. Stay in touch and let me know what I can do to help."

"I will," says Grace, wondering how on earth she's going to get her old life back.

Thirty-nine

"Dad says he thought he saw you at the Library dinner in the city the other night."

Grace turns her head to watch her daughter drive. "Did he tell you that before or after you told him I was back and wanted to see him privately."

"After. He said he knew it was you, but that you disappeared before he had a chance to talk to you. I think he misses you, Mom. He won't ever admit it, but it's clear to just about everyone he knows he's made a terrible mistake. I ran into your housekeeper in the market the other week and she said every time she's there cleaning she overhears them having the most terrible fights."

Grace feels a pang of both shameful pleasure that he is getting what he deserves and sadness. "I just can't imagine your father having anyone scream at him. He was always the one doing the shouting."

"I'm not sure she screams at him. I think she's more subtle than that. Calmly cruel seems to be her thing. Either way, she has him firmly under her thumb. Everyone knows, but no one can do anything about it. He misses you desperately, Mom. You need to make him see. Then you can get back together with him."

"Yes." Grace stares out the window as Clemmie drives along Route 6, looking at all the familiar houses perched on the cliff over the Hudson, remembering all the years she has driven this route, every inch of this road containing a memory, a part of her life.

"Do *you* want to get back with Dad?" Clemmie's voice is fearful as Grace thinks carefully about how to answer.

She sighs. "I didn't. If I'm honest, while I was in England I felt so enormously betrayed, I just couldn't contemplate it. But now . . ." She pauses. "We've been together for so long, we have, in so many ways, such a good life together. I can't imagine a life without him. But . . . it's hard. I honestly don't know. I wish I did, but I really don't. The only thing I know that I really want right now is for Beth to be gone. For all of our sakes. After that, we'll see."

They continue driving, on their way to meet Ted. Grace isn't sure this is the right thing, but Clemmie has insisted and Grace will do anything to keep Clemmie happy.

They pull up in front of the Starbucks, Grace unexpectedly nervous at seeing the man she has been married to for so long.

"I'm really not sure about this," she says to Clemmie.

"That's okay," says Clemmie. "You don't have to be. You and Dad just have to sit down and talk."

Ted is sitting at a table in the corner when they walk in. Clemmie leans down to give him a kiss, but he barely looks at her, unable to take his eyes off Grace.

"Grace." He shakes his head in disbelief. "Grace. You came."

"Well, yes." She pulls out a chair, unexpectedly nervous. "I was the one who asked to see you."

"Of course," he says. "Yes. You look good."

"Thank you," she says as Clemmie goes to order her a cappuccino.

She studies him, the shadows under his eyes, the way his face has fallen, how very much he has aged since she left. She cannot decide whether she wants to slap him or take him in her arms and make it all better. "You look . . . tired."

"I *am* tired," he says.

"Actually," Grace pauses, "you look, as we say in England, bloody awful."

He manages a wry smile. "*I feel* bloody awful," he says as his face crumples. "Everything seems to be a bit of a disaster. Career-wise. I suppose you've seen the reviews?"

Grace nods.

"More today. They are calling me a has-been, saying it is hard to reconcile the flowery, romantic, puerile writing of this book with the formerly great writer that once was Ted Chapman. That's a quote, by the way." He winces.

"I'm sorry, Ted," Grace says. "I haven't read the book. I don't have an opinion. But I know how hard this must be."

"The sales are terrible. It's a disaster. I've never experienced this in my career, feeling like such a failure."

"Beth was involved in this book, wasn't she, Dad?" Clemmie says. "Didn't she edit it?"

"She was involved," he says. "But the publisher would have told me if they were unhappy with it."

Grace and Clemmie both catch each other's eye, knowing full well the publisher kowtows to the terrifying Ted Chapman, no one there daring to tell him this book didn't make the grade.

"Does Beth know how bad the reviews are?"

"She does. She thinks they're all wrong, of course. I don't know anymore. I'm too close to it, I can't tell."

"And she's . . . still there?"

Ted looks at Grace. "What do you mean, she's still there?"

"My impression of Beth is that she's very keen to be close to success and money, but that were things to change, she wouldn't necessarily be quite so keen to stay."

"Grace, I know you've been terribly hurt, and I know you must still be terribly angry, but I resent you saying anything negative about Beth."

Grace, so calm when she walked in, shakes her head in disgust, a wave of anger washing over her. "Would you like to talk about resentment, Ted? Because we can do that. We can start with the big picture of how that woman came in and stole my life from under me and how it is taking everything in my power to get it back. And by the way, that doesn't mean I want to get back together, that means I'm still trying to get my health back after the joke of a diagnosis that I'm quite certain was orchestrated in some way by Beth."

Grace is astonished at the fury in her voice. She hadn't known how livid she was, but it comes out now, in a flood, a brace of words that won't be silenced.

"Clemmie? Wait outside. This needs to be private, between your father and me." She watches until Clemmie reluctantly walks out the door, before turning back to Ted. "Do you have any idea of what you did to me? I know it wasn't you, Ted, I know the idea didn't come from you, but you listened to her, to every suggestion, to every gentle push, didn't you? I know she was behind me going to see the bloody doctor in the first place, and then those pills! Ted! Those pills!" She groans at the memory. "They stole my life, Ted. Remember? You probably don't remember because you were too busy being seduced by Beth, too busy obsessing over her every move with the ridiculous idea that it was because you were basing a character on her, when it was quite clear she was deliberately pushing me out of the marriage to make way for herself.

"You let her edit your book, which seems to be the book that is bringing your career crashing down around your ears, and so blinded by, God, I don't even know. Lust, infatuation, your ego seduced by the attentions of a young woman—you let her move straight in! Oh, I know all about it. Straight into our bed, and into your life. Now, I hear, she's blowing through our savings and, yes, those are *our* savings, Ted, because all these years I have done nothing but support you, and look after you, and accompany you, and be the perfect bloody dutiful wife, and I get repaid with this betrayal."

Grace stops then, tears springing in her eyes, planning on saying so much more. There is so much more left to say, but Ted looks as if he might have a heart attack and she wills herself to calm down, to focus on her breathing, to say what else needs to be said in a reasonable tone.

"You need to know this, Ted. I have done my research. She has done this before. I met with a woman in Connecticut who had her life ruined by Beth. She spent all their money and disappeared when everything was gone. That's why I'm asking if Beth is still around. I know financially we're not in the position we used to be. I know your advances have been cut and I know that everything in publishing is down thirty percent, but does Beth know? Does she understand the impact one bad book can have on a career in these times?"

Ted is white, seeming, suddenly, so very much more frail than he ever has before.

"I have to ask this one thing," Grace says, her anger diffused, softly now. "Our finances. I know about all the spending. Please tell me what's in our accounts. Tell me we still have our savings account, our pension fund. Tell me you know we're still okay."

"I don't know," he says. "I never look at these things. This was always Ellen's domain."

"And now? Who is looking after it now?"

His voice is quiet. "I imagine it is Beth."

"I don't suppose she has been showing up with new clothes, cars, jewelry?"

Ted shakes his head, but there is doubt in his eyes. "I don't notice these things particularly, Grace. You know that." He pauses, seems to gather himself, rising from the table. "This is a witch hunt, Grace. It's not true. I understand that hell hath no fury, but that you would come here and say all these things is just . . . beyond me. You aren't the woman I thought you were. I am so disappointed in you trying to paint Beth in this way."

"You naïve fool," Grace says. "You won't see it. She's using you. She'll drain you dry and when the money, or your career, has gone, whichever comes first, she will leave and you will be left with nothing."

"You have no idea what you are talking about. She loves me, Grace. I'm sorry that's so hard to hear, and I'm sorry that this is hurting you. You and I are very different, Grace. I never felt you understood me, and what I go through, and how hard my life is, but Beth understands; she understands me in a way you never have. I will always be grateful for the life we have had, and for Clemmie, but the rest of my life is with Beth. She is the woman I am supposed to be with now. Whatever you think of her, whatever ridiculous notions you come up with about her having some ulterior motive, you are wrong. She has fallen in love with me, and I with her, and our only regret is that someone had to get hurt in the process."

Grace's mouth drops open in disbelief. "You won't listen, will you? Your ego is so damned huge, you aren't able to hear any of this. After all these years of loyalty, everything I've done, this is how you repay me? You're hurting me more than anyone has ever hurt me before, and you don't care. Who are you? I don't even think I know you anymore."

"I'm sorry," Ted says quietly, turning and walking out the door.

When Clemmie walks back in, Grace is shaking, fighting back the tears.

"I'm sorry," murmurs Grace, over and over. "I didn't expect this to happen. I didn't expect to be so upset." She breaks down, catching her breath as an unexpected sob makes its way into the room.

"It's okay," says Clemmie, putting her arm around her mother and gently rubbing her back. "It's all going to be okay."

"It isn't going to be okay," says Grace when the sobs have subsided and Clemmie has brought her sweet, milky tea. "There's so much more to Beth than meets the eye, so much that your father is refusing to see. I'm quite sure she's blowing through all the money. This is what she does. We're not the first. I have just met with a woman in Connecticut called Emily Tallman who lost everything she had to Beth. She stole her husband, her children, her reputation, and drained them of every penny. And when she left, she reinvented herself as Beth McCarthy, and here she is. Doing it again."

Clemmie just stares at her mother.

"I think she planned this," Grace says. "I have no proof, but the more I think about it, how she came into our lives, how she happened to be at your table at the gala, the more I think she targeted us somehow. She's a clever, clever girl and ruthless, I think."

"You can't be serious," says Clemmie. "She *planned* this? She *targeted* us? I don't see how that's possible, Mom."

Grace nods. "Remember where we met her? The *Country Flair* gala? *Country Flair* had been promoting that event for months. She knew Ted was the guest of honor and she got herself a ticket. I remember at the time thinking how odd that she was there alone."

"But how did she know you were looking for an assistant?" Clemmie is still skeptical.

"I think that was just a lucky break for her. Had we not been, I imagine she would have asked for a job as an intern. She would have offered anything to get to us. I think she started off thinking she could reach us through you, Clem, but then she didn't have to. It was the perfect opportunity."

"Do you really think this is true? If you're right, what could be in it for her? Why would she do this?"

"I think she's a mixture of things. I'm not a doctor, and God knows, given what I've been through, I'm the last person to go around labeling people with mental disorders, but I think she's probably something of a sociopath. She does this because she can, maybe she gets a thrill, maybe she's jealous of people who have a life she perceives as somehow better, but she doesn't show remorse. Or empathy. She deliberately sets out to break up marriages to get what she wants, or at least that's how it seems, without ever worrying about the consequences."

"And why do you think she wants that?"

Grace shakes her head. "I don't know. Narcissism, insecurity, jealousy. I would think some combination of the three. She talked a couple of times about her dysfunctional upbringing. I can't believe that it's as cruel as wanting to break up lives that seem happier than hers, but perhaps there's something in that."

"So, what are you going to do?" Clemmie says. "What are *we* going to do?"

"I think she may be hoist by her own petard," Grace says slowly. "She wants money and power. If your father's book is as bad as the reviews are saying, things will be a disaster. I can't believe she'll stay. She doesn't love him. She loves the cachet of being his consort. And that won't last if there's no cachet."

"And when it's over?" Clemmie says tentatively. "Then you'd go back?"

"I would." The tears spring back. "I can't believe I'm saying it, but I would."

Forty

The longer she is back home, the less she thinks about Dorset, about Patrick. It is painful to think about him, stirs up feelings she is certain would be best laid to rest.

She misses him. Misses his easy humor, how he made her laugh, how she was able to truly be herself, secure in the knowledge that that was enough; that it had always been enough.

But here she is, back in America, so close to the man who is still her husband, with a part of her longing to get her life back. Grace has spent years with Ted. Her life is with him, and even though he is now with Beth, it's impossible to think of a future on her own. At least, a future on this side of the Atlantic.

Grace and Ted. Ted and Grace. If he were to ask, if he were to change his mind, want her to come home, how could she possibly say no?

And yet today, Grace has not been able to stop thinking about Patrick.

In the corner of her room in the guest suite at Sybil's is a large chaise, a cashmere throw draped over one arm. Patrick has been in her thoughts all day, and finally, after dinner, she curls up in the chaise, pulling the throw over her feet, picking up her phone. Her heart jumps a little at the prospect of hearing his voice—it has been a while since they spoke—but it's only Patrick, she tells herself. Nothing to be nervous about.

At the very least, Grace should tell him what has happened, she thinks. At the very least she owes him closure, of the story with Beth, if nothing else. She looks at her watch. Who knows where he is at eight o'clock in the evening in California.

"Grace?" His voice is familiar enough to instantly dissipate her nerves. Nerves? What was she thinking. It's Patrick. *Patrick!*

"Patrick."

She can hear the smile in his voice.

"I was hoping you'd call. I was just sitting on my terrace having a drink and I found myself thinking about you."

"You mean, you're not thinking about me all the time?"

"Almost all the time." She can hear his smile down the phone, pictures him on a sweeping wood terrace lined with glass, looking out over the twinkling lights of Los Angeles. "I just had a break today during a lunch meeting, but don't worry, I went straight back to thinking about you as soon as it was over."

"I hope you were wining and dining some bright young thing."

"If you can call Harvey Weinstein a bright young thing, then absolutely. Oh, Grace. It's good to hear your voice. Are you still at the hotel?"

"No. I'm in the spare room of Sybil's, at Sparkill."

There is a pause. "You're *home*?"

"Depends on how you look at it. A few minutes away, yes."

"And how is it?"

"Weird. In many ways it doesn't feel like my home anymore. I feel like an alien uprooted. I'm not sure I belong anywhere anymore, and it's difficult, obviously, knowing I could bump into Ted or Beth wherever I go."

"Have you?"

"Not bumped into them unexpectedly. I did see Ted, but it didn't go so well. I was so sure he would be able to see that I was telling the truth about Beth . . ."

"That story was extraordinary!" Patrick interrupts. "I couldn't believe it when you emailed me. We were so right, that she had done this before."

"I know! But Ted wouldn't hear it. Any of it. He ended up storming out."

"Ouch."

"He has always been stubborn, but I still thought he'd listen to me. Not that I behaved that well. I didn't expect to be so upset, but I ended up getting terribly angry, which surprised me. I had no idea I was carrying around so much rage, but I was furious. How could Ted be so stupid? And financially! It's a disaster! She's in charge of the money, so God only knows how much she's been spending. And his book. Oh, Patrick. His book. Have you heard?"

"I have. The reviews haven't been very good."

"Not good? They're terrible. He's made himself a laughingstock. God only knows what his next book deal will be, or if he's even able to get a book deal. The truth is he's been struggling with the last few books. No one knows, other than his publisher and agent, of course, but his sales have been plummeting, and everyone's hope was that this book would be the comeback. I think his career might be over. I do. I think this girl has ruined his life too."

"So, what's the solution?"

There is a silence. Grace doesn't say what she has been thinking, which is that if she moves back in, if they get back to normal, Ted will be able to write again. Together they will be able to revive his career, save face, again be the golden couple they have always been.

She doesn't say it, doesn't want Patrick to know this is what she has been thinking. She isn't thinking it now, the mere sound of Patrick's voice enough to wash her with a familiarity and safety that she doesn't feel with Ted, has never felt with Ted.

Home, she thinks to herself, listening to Patrick's breathing down the line. With Patrick I am home.

"I'm sorry," Patrick says eventually. "About the money, about everything. Even though we suspected she was after the money, but still. It must have been a shock to find out that had happened."

We, thinks Grace, melting at the idea of her and Patrick still being a "we," shaking her head to dislodge the thought, because thoughts like that, at this stage, will not lead her anywhere good.

"It was," Grace says. "According to Clemmie, she's been a complete nightmare. By the sounds of it she's ruined Ted's life."

"And other than Ted, how are you?"

"Thinner," laughs Grace, for it is true. Her body is shrinking back to her usual size, and vain as it might be to admit the pleasure this is giving her, it is nevertheless true. "And better, generally. I take no pills now, at all, and I look back at all the crap that doctor had me on and I'm stunned that I ever allowed it to happen."

"You weren't yourself."

"Clearly. So now, drug-free, with a whole new life, all things considered I have to say I'm doing pretty well. It's hard to be home without being 'home,' but I'm trying to be accepting of the fact that this is the start of a new life. Whether I wanted it or not is irrelevant. This is how it is, and the more I can accept that, the easier it seems to be. But how are you, Patrick? How is life back in L.A.?"

"Crazy. And fun. And as surreal as ever. We're going into preproduction of the next movie, which will film in England, so I'll get to see more of Mum. Other than that, same old, same old."

"I miss you," Grace finds herself saying, shocked at the words that hang in the air.

"I know," he says. "I miss you too. You're doing what you need to do. You've found your life again."

"Right," Grace says, wondering suddenly if she has found her life; if, in fact, this is a life she wants at all.

Forty-one

Grace checks her phone to make sure the date is right, then looks again at the poster on the wall. Yes. This is the night Ted is speaking at the Barnes & Noble on the Upper East Side. This is the venue that always attracts the biggest crowds, standing room only, lines and lines of people waiting to have their books signed.

In the event room at the back, there are a handful of men dotted around the room, clutching copies of Ted's new book. Not three hundred, as has been the case in the past. Not even thirty. She counts them. Thirteen.

How the mighty fall.

She wasn't sure she would come, worried that she is close to stalking Ted, but she can't let go, has a burning need to see them together, to see how they are with each other with her own eyes.

Sybil does not know she is here. Grace told Sybil she was having dinner in the city with friends, because Sybil would not approve. She is not a fan of Beth, but sees her multiple times a week, thanks to Beth's taking over Grace's role at Harmont House.

"Is she doing everything I used to do?"

"She's nothing like you, if that's what you're asking," said Sybil. "She doesn't have the relationships with the residents. They don't actually like her very much, so she hasn't bonded with anyone. She's efficient though. She doesn't cook there like you used to, but seems to cook at home and bring it in. I suspect it's because she doesn't want to spend much time with the women. I also suspect they know that too."

"So how is the food?" Grace couldn't help but ask.

"Uninspired, but perfectly edible. Meatloaf, meatballs, teriyaki chicken. The residents say everything tastes the same. They miss your food, and they miss you."

"Have you seen her with Ted?"

"Only by mistake, in town. I haven't socialized with them, Grace. I wouldn't do that to you. How are you feeling now? Are things getting any easier?"

Grace nods. Sybil does not know that Grace cannot go to sleep without obsessively thinking about Ted and Beth, picturing them together, wondering how their life is, unable to imagine how different their relationship must be to Ted's relationship with Grace.

I always thought Ted was a bully, thinks Grace, browsing through the bookshelves downstairs, but perhaps I need to look at my part in it. Surely one can only bully those who allow themselves to be bullied. There's no question of him bullying Beth; she is very definitely the one in charge.

Would our relationship have been different had I not been so passive? she wonders. Could I have been any different than I was? My mother was aggressive, a bully, she thinks. No wonder I cast my husband in that same role, no wonder I lived most of my married life with exactly the same trepidation and fear I lived with as a little girl.

How do you change if you have no awareness? she thinks. There is no doubt she has changed, she is a very different person from the one who ran barefoot from the hospital, crying in pain and fear. The Grace of today has an inner strength the old Grace may have had, but it was buried so deep she certainly had no idea of its existence.

There is a word floating around her consciousness. "Safety." The feeling of safety she had on the phone with Patrick the other day, the feeling of safety she had in England.

I deserve to be safe, she suddenly thinks, startled, unsure as to where this came from.

I deserve to be safe.

The words whisper in her head and settle in her bones. Grace closes her eyes for a few seconds, feeling a strength and serenity she doesn't remember feeling before.

And then, propelled by some invisible force, Grace finds herself turning to watch Ted and Beth walk through the store, Beth unrecognizable, dressed as she is in Grace's elegant clothes, appearing more sophisticated, more grown-up than Grace would ever have believed possible, the dumpy, plain girl she once employed long since disappeared.

The manager comes to greet them, Beth clearly seducing him with that winning smile. Grace inches closer to try and hear the conversation.

"I think it's the weather," the manager says. "We always have a terrible turnout when it's raining."

"That's it?" Beth says sharply as she sees the empty chairs in the room. "Did you not publicize it?"

"Don't worry." Ted lays a hand on her arm, which she brusquely shoves off. "I actually prefer the smaller events, more intimate, gives me a chance to get to know my readers."

Grace knows this is not true, that nothing enrages Ted more than a small turnout at an event. His arrogance hides a deep insecurity, but now that everything he has always feared has actually come to pass, it seems he is dealing with it far better than Grace would ever have thought.

"This is just ridiculous," huffs Beth. "What a waste of time."

She comes across as imperious, grand. Everything that would alienate whoever was left of Ted's readers.

This room will fill up, thinks Grace, standing well out of eyesight. We have twenty minutes to go. This latest book may be bad, but he has long-standing fans, people who adore him.

And even more suddenly, she realizes she doesn't need to be there. She has seen them together and, for the first time in months, a sense of closure settles on her shoulders. The only insight she has gained is that she doesn't need to be there.

It's time for Grace to go home.

She picks up a copy of Ted's book. She has avoided it until now, but suddenly she knows it is time to read it. She will be able to read it without dissolving in pain with every page.

There is one person in front of her in line. She pays, and then Grace is at the front. The salesgirl looks at the book, eyes widening with excitement.

"You know he's here? Ted Chapman! Right now! In the store! You could have the book signed!"

"I know," Grace says. "It's fine. I'm in a hurry."

"The event hasn't started," insists the girl. "I could run over and get it signed for you now."

Grace turns and looks over at the empty room, at a career gone sideways, and shakes her head. "Really. Thank you, but no."

"Grace?"

Grace turns, an expectant smile on her face, to see Beth staring at her in horror.

"Hello, Beth," she says, silently congratulating herself on her calm. "You look well."

"What are you doing here?" Beth's voice is cold. Superior. It makes Grace smile.

"I was just passing," she says. "I saw Ted had a reading and, well, I thought it was high time I read the book everyone's talking about, although I understand the reviews have been . . . mixed."

"It's jealousy," Beth says. "The media can't stand his success."

"Maybe," Grace says. "Although 'success' is a relative term, isn't it? The publishing business is so fickle these days, but I'm sure the next book will be wonderful."

"Why are you here?" Beth says. "Why are you really here?"

"I'm leaving, don't worry." Grace takes a breath. "Do you know, I've been dreading bumping into you. I've spent months and months demonizing you, but actually, I'm looking at you tonight and I now see you as terribly sad. I met Emily Tallman, by the way. She was very open about your influence on their lives. I don't think you can help it. I think you are probably propelled by a desperate need for money, or power, and that destroying people's lives comes very easily to you because you feel no remorse. You came very close to destroying my life, but I got it back. From what I understand, you've spent whatever little money was left, and word on the street is that Ted's going to be lucky if he signs a publishing deal at all. If he does, there won't be any money in it. I'm sure that's the last thing you anticipated."

Beth's face is set in fury, but Grace is no longer frightened.

"You wanted my life?" says Grace quietly as she leans toward Beth. "My dear, you can have it." And, leaving the book on the table, the sales assistant open-mouthed, she walks out of the store.

Forty-two

They don't talk divorce. Not yet. Separation is the first step, putting the house on the market for all that they have left is in the house, which they can no longer afford.

Beth disappears. One morning Ted awakens to find all traces of Beth gone. He phones Clemmie in a panic, who phones Grace as soon as she is off the phone with her father.

"Can you believe it?" says Clemmie. "Can you believe she did that?"

"Yes," says Grace, who has been counting the days.

Ted moves into the barn for Grace to come back home, at least until the house sells. They do not eat together, have little to do with each other, although Ted has started to find excuses to wander up the garden path and ask Grace a question. She ought to feel irritated, she thinks, but instead she feels, mostly, nothing.

"He's trying to win you back," says Sybil one afternoon over tea with Grace, after Ted has just popped his head in the back door.

"I know," says Grace. "He's like a different man. If only this had happened twenty years ago."

Everything about the way Ted treats Grace these days is different than how it was before. He is sweet, solicitous, gentle. When he does come up to the house, he follows her with an adoring gaze, his eyes filled with a gratitude that makes Grace want to scream.

Ted is finally the sort of man who could be a partner, she thinks, wryly. He asks how she is every day and truly seems to care what her answer is. He offers to help, to do the chores that Grace has never enjoyed—mundane things that he never would have lowered himself to do before—putting gas in the car, going to the grocery store for milk.

"I have changed," he said to her just this afternoon as Grace was starting to get ready for Sybil and Fred to come for dinner. She hadn't been ready to entertain, but Sybil is family, and she is making truffled porcini and Gruyère individual tartlets, a tenderloin of beef, and a fig and apple compote with homemade ginger ice cream.

She had chopped the celery, the carrots, the onions, is cooking them slowly in oil, ready to add the seared meat and the aromatics, and is realizing that suddenly, on this chilly day, in her cozy kitchen, she is enjoying cooking again.

It was one of the hardest things about the medication. It had stolen the one thing she had always been passionate about—gathering people in her home, or Harmont House, and feeding them. The food she craved when she was on the drugs were carbohydrates and sugars, the more processed, the better; she lost the energy to cook and even when her energy started to come back, the will hadn't.

But here she is, this afternoon, searing the meat in hot oil, removing it from the pan when it is golden brown, replacing it with the rest of the vegetables, the stock, the wine, with a smile on her face. She wipes her chopping board clean as she has been taught to do, washes her hands, yet again, then takes the eggs from the bowl on the counter and starts cracking them into a bowl, separating the whites from the yolks, measuring out the milk and cream, the sugar, the finest vanilla essence, grating the gingerroot and finely dicing—*brunoise* cutting—the candied ginger to fold into the ice cream. She tips the ginger and sugar in a pan, adding a couple of tablespoons of water, and cooks slowly before adding the milk and cream. Whisking furiously all the while, she holds the pan high and adds the liquid to the whisked egg yolks, stirring constantly, pulling it straight off the heat when the custard perfectly coats the back of a spoon.

Through a sieve, she adds the cream, the vanilla, before putting it straight into the freezer. She should have made this yesterday, the day before, But she has made last-minute ice creams before, and even if it isn't as firm, as chilled as she would like, it will still be the perfect accompaniment to the fig and apple compote she made first thing this morning.

Ted walks in as she is sieving the ice cream, watches her silently, wanting to have her full attention, but she can't give it to him, busy trying not to splash a drop. He clears his throat, waiting for her to turn, moving forward until he is right behind her in order to make her stop what she is doing and look at him.

"I have changed," he says. "And I am sorry. How can I prove it to you, Grace? How can I show you that I am not the same man? That I deserve forgiveness. This whole separation thing is ridiculous. We belong together, Grace. You know that and I know that, and I will do anything, Grace. Anything to have you back."

"You *have* me back," she says when she has finished sieving, squashing the curds and lumps into the sieve with the back of a plastic spatula, up and down, side to side, until every drop has been squeezed out. "I am here, aren't I?"

"Physically, yes, but I want us to be together. As husband and wife."

Grace stops then, looks up at him. "Do you mean back in your bed?" She may have moved back to Sneden's, but cannot go back to the family bed, is sleeping instead in the guest room, filling it with her possessions in a bid to make herself feel more at home.

"No!" he says. "Well, yes! But no, that isn't what I mean. I just . . . want you to forgive me."

Grace looks down at the counter, at her hands, her thin gold wedding band, studded here and there with tiny diamonds, like the tiniest constellation of stars on her finger. "I have," she says. For it is true.

This life had made her so happy, for so many years, she had never wanted anything or anyone else. She had never thought to question her role, to question her happiness. Most of the time she truly felt that somewhere up high, perhaps to make up for the hell of her childhood, the gods, or angels, were smiling upon her.

She had been *charmed*. She led a *charmed* life. At least if you didn't look too closely; at least if you pretended, as she did so well for so long, that if you put on a good enough act, it would make it so. But then the gods and angels had deserted her and she fell to the ground with a crash. And now? This is a decision of necessity. She has nowhere else to go, has to put her new life on hold until the house sells, until she knows where she will go next.

Nothing is the same. Harmont House has reached out via Sybil, letting Grace know they miss her and are thinking about her, but they don't ask her back. It's far too soon for that.

Not that Grace would go back, her hands too full taking care of herself, trying to figure out the next right steps.

Ted goes back to the barn, irritated at having made no headway. Grace finishes making the porcini tartlets, sets the table, then takes the scraps outside for the chickens.

She sits on the bench by the chicken coop, watching her girls cluck gently around her legs, taking carrot peelings from her hand, setting the bowl down to clutch her wrap more tightly around herself to stave off the chill.

Pulling her cell phone from her pocket, and scrolling through the numbers, she finds herself pressing Lydia's, needing suddenly the comfort of Lydia's voice; the comfort of home.

"Grace!" Hearing Lydia on the end of the phone has Grace's shoulders sagging in relief. "What a lovely surprise!"

"It's so good to hear your voice." Grace blinks back the tears. "Where are you? What are you doing?"

Lydia laughs. "Do you want details?"

"Yes! Details and descriptions. I want to feel as if I'm with you in Dorset."

"It's not very interesting, I'm afraid. I'm at the kitchen table sorting through lots of boring old bills, which I will then take out to the post box. I just picked up some eggs from the farm, and I'm going to make an omelette for supper. What else can I tell you? I spoke to Robert earlier today and he's invited me up to Scotland to stay, and as much as I adore those grandchildren of mine, I'm not sure, at this age, I can bear the noise and chaos. I might find an excuse and stay in that nice little bed-and-breakfast down the road from them. Haven't spoken to Catherine, but Patrick has just arrived in the Lake District for the new film, and he suddenly has this fanciful idea of buying a cottage here in Dorset, down the road."

Grace's heart does a small skip. Of course Lydia was going to talk about Patrick. Grace wanted her to talk about Patrick, but still, at the mention of his name she couldn't help but feel that jolt.

"How is he?" Grace keeps her voice light, but of course this isn't what she wants to say.

Does he talk about me? is what she suddenly wants to say. Does he miss me? Does he think about me? Does he do what I have found myself unable to stop doing, waking up in the middle of the night and thinking about him? Replay every second we were together? Think about the way he laughs when he's sitting across the table from me? The way he makes me feel? Does he even think about me at all or has he moved on? I don't want to know, but I have to know . . . does he have someone else? Has he fallen in love? I need to know, at the very least, if he still misses me or whether those were empty words he just said in response to me.

"Patrick? He's . . . Patrick! Happy to be back on these shores, I think. Los Angeles was a tremendous amount of fun for him, but he needed, he said, to get back to reality. What about you, Gracie? What are you up to?" Lydia says. "How is life back at the ranch?"

Grace pauses. At that moment, something falls into place for her. Something, finally, after this awful year, feels completely right.

"Grace? Are you there?"

"Yes. I'm here." She smiles, her heart light. "Lydia? How much are flights to England these days?"

GINGER ICE CREAM

INGREDIENTS

3 cups heavy cream
1 cup whole milk
1/4 cup grated fresh ginger
1/4 cup finely chopped crystalized ginger, more if, like me, you love it!
Pinch of salt
8 egg yolks
3/4 cup sugar

In a large, heavy saucepan, combine the cream, milk, ginger, and salt over medium heat and simmer for 20 minutes.

Whisk the egg yolks and sugar together until pale, pale gold and fluffy. Ladle one ladleful of the hot cream mixture into eggs, combine, then add all eggs into hot cream mixture. Stir constantly for around 5 minutes until the custard mixture is thick enough to coat the back of a spoon.

Strain over a fine-meshed sieve into a large bowl, pressing with the back of the spoon to extract as much liquid as you can. Cover tightly and refrigerate until cold, at least 3 hours.

Add the crystalized ginger to the cold cream mixture, then pour into the bowl of an ice cream maker and make the ice cream according to manufacturer's instructions. Transfer the ice cream to an airtight container and freeze until ready to eat.

Epilogue

The basket of eggs is overflowing today as Grace drops them off to Abbots, telling them to pay her next time, for today she is in a hurry, today she has to get back home and get the spare room ready for Clemmie and Luke's visit, finish baking rhubarb and apple pies for the country market, figure out next week's menu for the food truck she runs, driving all over Dorset and Somerset, feeding those who can't afford to feed themselves.

She climbs into the ancient Deux Chevaux, scowling yet again at the rust on the driver's door that she keeps meaning to take care of but hasn't gotten around to, before pulling out onto Long Street and heading down Piddle Lane, delighting every few yards in how pretty the village of Cerne Abbas is, how lucky she is to live here, and how completely at home she has been made to feel.

Patrick found the house just weeks before Grace arrived. He collected her from Heathrow and drove her straight to Dorset, to the cottage in Cerne Abbas he had fallen in love with. He had exchanged contracts, he said, but had not yet completed, and if Grace absolutely hated it, he could afford to lose the down payment and move on.

There was never any talk of them doing anything other than live together. As soon as Grace phoned him and told him she was leaving Ted, that it was over, that she had been thinking of moving to Dorset *permanently*, they both knew this was the beginning of their future together. It didn't need to be discussed, was an unspoken assumption—now that they had recognized everything Lydia now said she had known her entire life: that they would spend the rest of their lives together.

Patrick drove up Long Street pointing out all the wonderful places they would go—Skittles at the Giant Inn, dinner by roaring log fires at the Royal Oak, Abbots for proper Dorset cream teas—Grace feeling partly terrified, partly excited, no longer settled in the world, no longer sure where to call home, only certain that it is not Sneden's Landing. Not with Ted. Not anymore.

Up Piddle Street, down a tiny cul-de-sac to a thatched storybook cottage backing onto farmland, horses grazing in the distance. Close enough for a brisk walk to the village, the house has been added onto over the years—a conservatory containing a large country kitchen with—joy of joys!—an Aga, a big kitchen table, and a sofa for the lurchers Patrick was determined to get now that he was back and settled in Dorset. Back to settle down with Grace.

Seventeenth-century beams stretched across the living room, a huge stone fireplace taking up one wall. The master bedroom is large and tucked under the eaves, window seats looking out over the fields.

"You know, this isn't *my* house," Patrick said that first day as Grace silently walked through the house, going into every room, breathing in the house's history. "It's *ours*."

And Grace just nodded, knowing then that all these years of searching had, finally, brought her here. Brought her to a place where she no longer felt guilt at being a bad daughter, and then, as an adult, a wife who was never quite good enough.

Those years of searching have finally brought her home.

. . .

Across the pond, Marissa Weiss sits on her living room sofa, apologizing for her nine-year-old constantly darting into the room to show off yet another elastic band bracelet she has made on the rainbow loom.

"I'm so sorry," she says to the woman sitting opposite her. "As you can see, we're in desperate need of a babysitter, not to mention everything else."

The woman laughs, calling the little girl over, complimenting her on the bracelet and asking if she might make one for her.

"I know it's not my job," she looks up at Marissa as the little girl skips out of the room, "but I adore children. I'm really happy to roll up my sleeves and do whatever needs to be done, and if that includes babysitting, that's perfectly fine with me."

Marissa shakes her head. "I'd love that, but my husband would kill me. You're really here to help out with the running of our lives. Bill paying, QuickBooks, organizing events, scheduling—both our schedules and the kids. And then there are really mundane things too: taking the dog to the vet, going to the post office, shopping for office and household supplies. It really is a little bit of everything. You said you were well versed in running this kind of household. Can you perhaps tell me a little more about what you're looking for, Liz?"

She looks at the woman expectantly, although she already knows she will employ her. She is perfect. A little plain, a little frumpy, she has a sweetness and eagerness about her that Marissa finds appealing.

The last assistant had been a glamorpuss and Marissa had never felt comfortable having her in the house. She and Jack would laugh about the outfits—the skirts got shorter and the heels grew higher week after week—but each time she saw Jack and the assistant having a conversation, she grew nervous. It wasn't that she didn't trust Jack, but she didn't trust the assistant.

Since then, she had tried out a number of different women. There was the Brazilian girl who was lovely, but her energy was so frenetic, so nervous, it put everyone on edge; the girl who came with glowing references but had no initiative whatsoever and, Marissa joked, turned stupidity into an art form. Then there was the one who had been efficient and organized, but who had demanded they double her pay after a month as she hadn't realized what the job entailed, and she was "effectively COO of your company."

They had despaired, until placing an ad in *The New York Times*, and receiving Liz's résumé. She had all the right qualifications, seemed to be exceptionally bright and well read, and clearly knew the job inside out. Her references were wonderful, although Marissa liked to think that references were never as important as her gut feeling. Marissa could generally tell what someone was like within the first minute and her instincts about people were never wrong.

Jack teased her about it all the time, particularly after she had got it wrong so many times in recent months. He wanted to be involved in the interview process after the last few disasters, but he was always traveling. His job in wealth management saw him meeting with clients all over the country. He regularly left their San Francisco home to travel across the coast, often for days at a time. That's why they need an assistant—with three children and a traveling husband, there's no way Marissa can handle all the household things on her own.

"The first thing you have to know about me," Liz says sweetly, "is that I love doing this work. I live to help people and nothing gives me more satisfaction than organizing someone's life and keeping everything running smoothly. My job, as far as I see it, is to make your life easy, and I will do whatever it takes to make that happen. That's what gives me pleasure."

Marissa almost sighs in delight. "And you don't think it's too much for you? You think you can handle all the different things? Even the menial tasks?"

"Absolutely," nods Liz. "I am happiest when I'm busy."

Marissa sits back. "Well." She smiles. "I will obviously be checking your references, but I'm wondering whether we shouldn't just dive in and give it a go? I always think the only way to see if it's a fit is to start working together and see if we like each other."

Liz smiles then, as Marissa stares. How odd that such a plain girl could be transformed into such a pretty one when she smiles. "How does that sound?" asks Marissa, beguiled by the smile.

"Perfect," says Liz. "I promise you, you won't be disappointed. If there's anything you need me to do now, I could even help today. I have availability this afternoon."

"No, no," Marissa starts, before realizing she does have to pick up a prescription and she has run out of milk, which she needs for breakfast tomorrow morning, and she hadn't been planning on leaving the house again. "Actually . . . I know this is the most mundane thing in the world, but is there any chance you might be able to pick up a couple of things for me?"

"It would be a pleasure," beams Liz as she hoists her bag over her shoulder. "You don't have to worry about a thing. I'm here to change your life."

Acknowledgments

As always, a team of people have helped, not only with this book, but with the life I had to live in order to write it.

My enormous gratitude, as ever, to my long-term agent in the UK, Anthony Goff, and my newfound agent here in the US, Christy Fletcher, who continues to astound me with her wise and continous presence in my life.

My team at St. Martin's: Jen Enderlin, Sally Richardson, Stephanie Hargadon, Lisa Senz, Nancy Trypuc, Jeff Dodes, Angelique Giammarino, and Laura Wilson at Macmillan Audio.

Julie Chudow, Danielle Burch, and Sarah Hall of Sarah Hall Publicity.

Meg Walker of Tandem Literary.

Carly Sommerstein for the great editing.

Shayla Smith and Sue Redston.

To Rae and Molly at the Squam Lake Inn who provided me with a beautiful place to write, and sweet treats to keep me happy.

Xavier Mayonove and all at the International Culinary Center in New York.

The very many bloggers, book lovers, readers, and people who have supported me for so long, particularly Melissa Amster, Amy Bromberg, and Robin Kall Homonoff.

The doctors who put right the wrongs, and brought me back to myself—to them I do, truly, owe my life: Dr. Frank Lipman, Dr. Michael Doyle, and Dr. Amiram Katz.

Tish Fried and Patrick McCord of Write Yourself Free in Westport, where I write my books and cuddle Bertie.

Michael Ross and Mark Lamos at the Westport Country Playhouse, who have been endlessly supportive.

To my many friends, my tribe, my family of choice. And my husband, Ian. Still beloved, after all these years. I love you.